Apprentice

The Shadow Atlas Book Two

Jenny Sandiford

VELIKOR
PUBLISHING

JENNY SANDIFORD

2

THE SHADOW ATLAS

APPRENTICE

Contact: jennysandiford.com

Cover designer: Miblart

Editor: Mandi Oyster

Proofreader: Amy McKenna

Map creation: Shah_alom1 on Fiverr

ISBN (ebook): 978-0-6454449-6-4

ISBN (paperback): 978-0-6454449-7-1

ISBN (hardcover): 978-0-6454449-8-8

First Edition: April 2023

To my cats, Chinggis and Shimo. The most expensive street cats on the planet, but the best writing buddies I could ask for.

THE TOWER OF LONDON
Ground Level

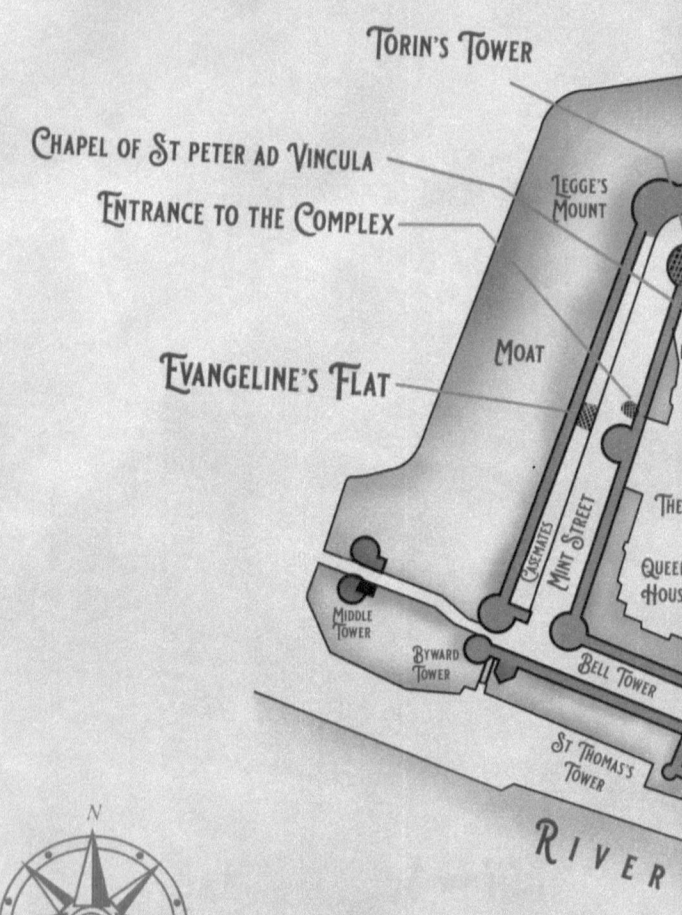

ENTRANCE TO

TORIN'S TOWER

CHAPEL OF ST PETER AD VINCULA

ENTRANCE TO THE COMPLEX

EVANGELINE'S FLAT

LEGGE'S MOUNT

MOAT

CASEMATES

MINT STREET

THE

QUEEN'S HOUSE

MIDDLE TOWER

BYWARD TOWER

BELL TOWER

ST THOMAS'S TOWER

RIVER

N

W   E

S

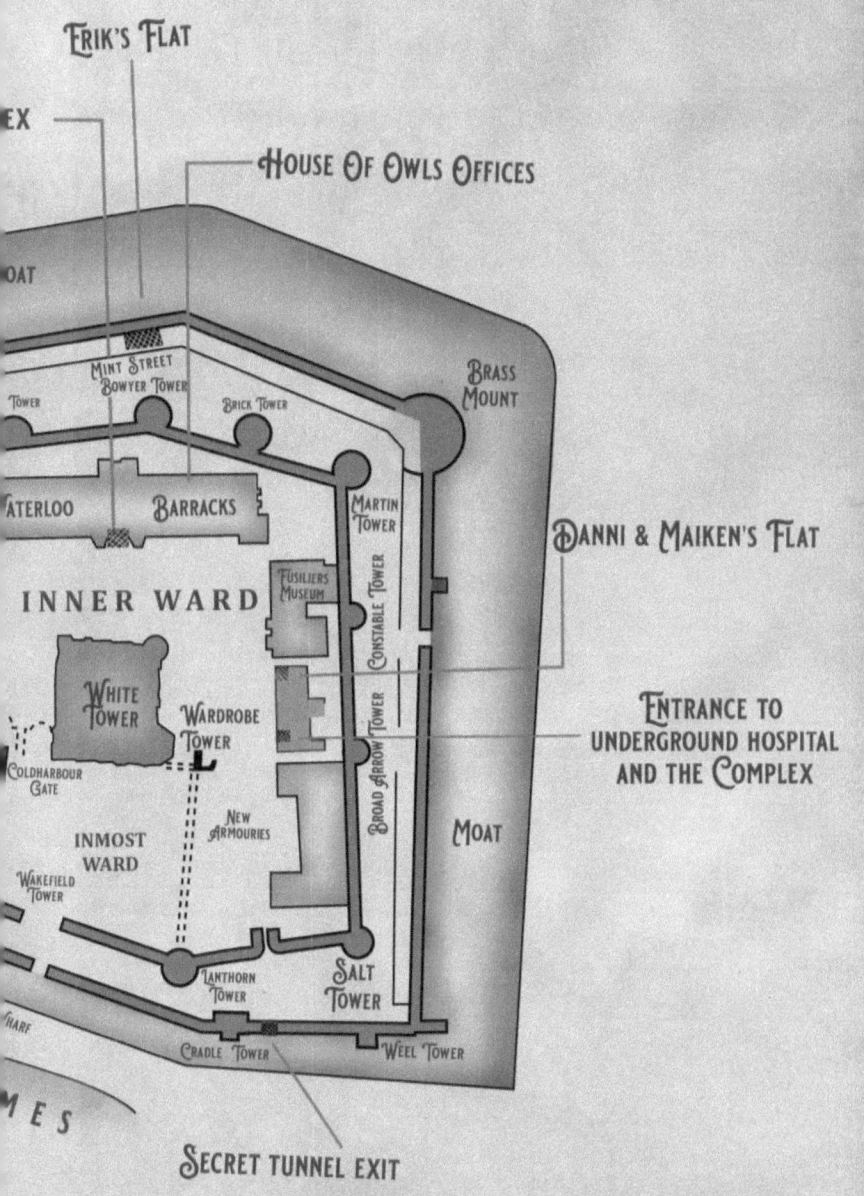

ERIK'S FLAT

EX

HOUSE OF OWLS OFFICES

OAT

MINT STREET
BOWYER TOWER

TOWER

BRICK TOWER

BRASS
MOUNT

WATERLOO

BARRACKS

MARTIN
TOWER

DANNI & MAIKEN'S FLAT

INNER WARD

FUSILIERS
MUSEUM

CONSTABLE TOWER

WHITE
TOWER

WARDROBE
TOWER

ENTRANCE TO
UNDERGROUND HOSPITAL
AND THE COMPLEX

COLDHARBOUR
GATE

BROAD ARROW TOWER

NEW
ARMOURIES

INMOST
WARD

MOAT

WAKEFIELD
TOWER

SALT
TOWER

LANTHORN
TOWER

HARF

CRADLE TOWER

WEEL TOWER

MES

SECRET TUNNEL EXIT

THE TOWER OF LONDON
Underground Complex

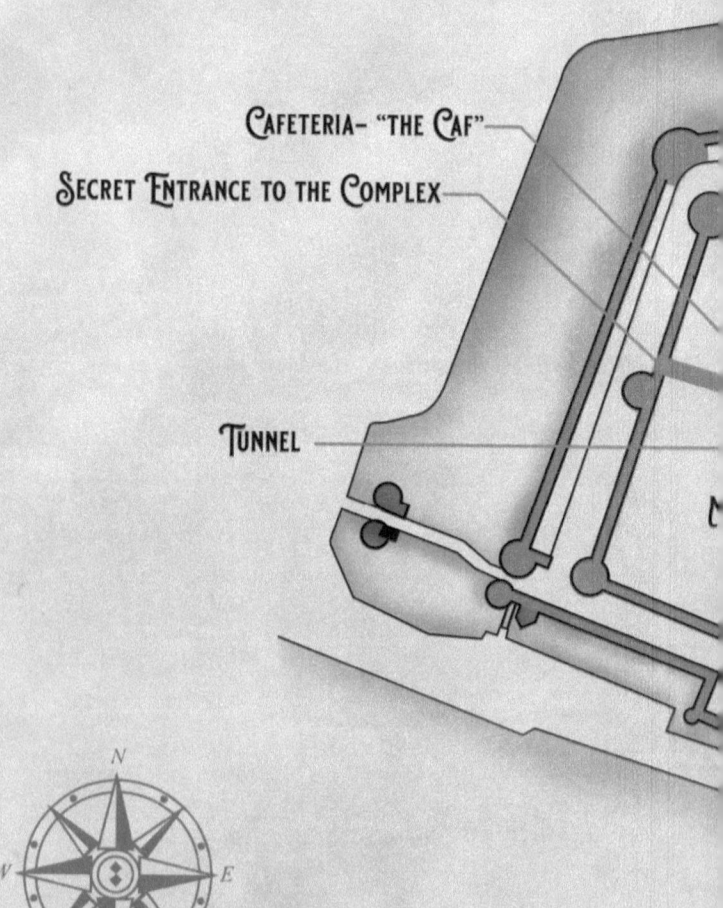

CAFETERIA– "THE CAF"

SECRET ENTRANCE TO THE COMPLEX

TUNNEL

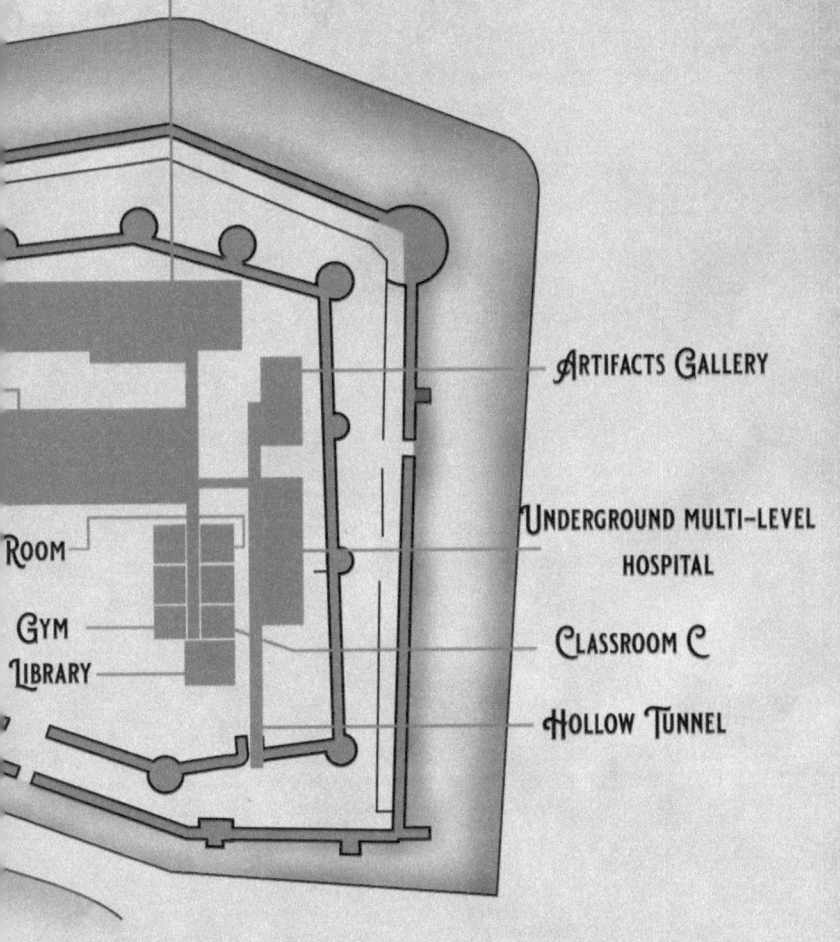

F OWLS OFFICES AND CONFERENCE ROOMS

ARTIFACTS GALLERY

UNDERGROUND MULTI-LEVEL
HOSPITAL

ROOM

GYM

LIBRARY

CLASSROOM C

HOLLOW TUNNEL

Before...

Thousands of years ago, the gods abandoned the mortal world and left behind two gateways: one to the Shadow Dimension, whose location remains unknown, and another to the Echo Dimension, whose secret was entrusted to the keepers of twelve jade animal relics.

As the deities departed, they entrusted a warrior from each House of magic with the protection of one relic.

The Echo Dimension gate was sealed, never to be opened unless all Houses came together in peace and with great need. The warriors dispersed throughout the world, while the Shadow Dimension deities vanished without a word in the darkness of night.

Over time, the memory of the gods and relics faded into myth. The truth was lost to ancient history.

Until now...

SHADOW MAGIC HOUSES

Dark Magic. Source: Shadow Dimension

HOUSE OF SNAKES
The Goddess Ereshkigal
Spirits and Necromancy

HOUSE OF WHITE DEER
The Goddess Gula
Healing Magic

HOUSE OF RAVENS
The God Zakar
Sleep and Dream Magic

HOUSE OF WINGED BULLS
The Goddess Nanna
Divination

ECHO MAGIC HOUSES

Light Magic. Source: Echo Dimension

HOUSE OF OWLS
The God Enki
Mind and Water Magic

HOUSE OF PHOENIX
The God Utu
Fire Magic

HOUSE OF EAGLES
The God Enlil
Air and Weather Magic

HOUSE OF BEES
The Goddess Ninhursag
Plant Magic

CHAPTER 1

Even with several hospital rooms separating them, Azalea could sense Torin was awake. She hated the feeling. Hated knowing that the man who had killed her dad was so close and had been all along. How the hell was she so blind?

Beside her, the slow beep of machines tapped at her brain, and the low drone of voices from the hallway threatened her sanity. She rolled her head on the unfamiliar pillow, trying to get comfortable, but everything felt wrong; the air was thick and hospitally—pungent antiseptic mixed with too much lavender. The sheets were like weights against her tender skin which still tingled from the magic that had blasted through her just hours before, and worst of all, the unsettling fact that she could feel what Torin was feeling. It was all too much. His waves of guilt, confusion, and fear mixed with sharp surges of pure rage had her on edge. She could only hope the anger was aimed at his dad and not her.

The clock on the stark white wall told her it was only 4 am—the longest night in her life, and a nightmare she would never wake up from. *Elam was dead, and Torin had murdered her father*. The words repeated over and over in her mind. How was it possible that Elam had been her classmate just the day before and now he was dead? Nerdy, quiet Elam, the Archmage's grandson, who was supposed to visit the Vatican City with the gallu hunt money, was gone, and it was her fault.

Lying here was the last thing she needed right now. She needed to get home; just a few hours of decent sleep would be enough. Then she could focus on what to do next. She had to be ready for Korbyn Dumont *and* find a way to break the soul bond with Torin so she'd never have to see him again.

She closed her eyes, but Elam's face appeared, his eyes hollow and empty as the life drained out of them. *Nope! This was all too much.* She threw off the stiff hospital sheets and dipped her toes toward the cold white tiles. She didn't deserve to be here in this safe place, not when Livia was suffering her own personal hell.

The floor was freezing against her bare feet as she tiptoed to the chair where someone had left fresh clothes, probably her flatmate Evangeline—Van. She stripped off the hospital gown and slipped on the black tracksuit bottoms, an oversized gray fleece, and wool socks as quietly as possible, hoping no one would come in. She could make it back to the flat in those without looking too much like an escaped patient.

Her backpack rested on a chair; she didn't remember having it on her. Someone must have brought it through the Hollow when they came back. Her elemer sat next to it with her leather jacket draped over the top. Her fingers slid around the bone handle of her elemer, so smooth and right-feeling against her skin. The knife blade and key were both tucked inside the handle as she placed it in her pocket. She turned to the inside of the jacket and thanked the gods; the Shadow Atlas was still in there. That arsehole of a book—she wouldn't be in this mess if she had never found it. But the urge to protect it was real; no one could find it, or she'd be in even deeper shit. She tucked it in her backpack and shrugged it on.

Now to get out. Hopefully, Van was rostered on tonight so she could help Azalea slip out and tell her family she went home. Her mum, her grandmother RoRo, and her Uncle Fabian had been out in the hallway waiting when Maiken, Danni's wife, who was also the head healer, ordered her to get some rest. Hopefully, they'd all gone off to sleep by now. She was surprised they'd even let Fabian stay as long as he had, being banned and all.

Her long brown hair hung loose; it was well down to the middle of her back, and a mass of tangles and knots she didn't want to deal with. She gathered it into a twist and set it over one shoulder, irritated to find she didn't have a hair tie on her wrist. A no-fuss ponytail would be her preference.

The door swung open, and Azalea froze. Her mum stood there with an all too familiar look of disapproval on her face.

"You're in no state to be leaving, Petal," Leda said with forceful kindness. She was still wearing gardening overalls and a denim jacket as if she had left in a rush.

Azalea felt bad for the fright her mum must have gotten when she was called to the Tower of London, specifically to the secret hospital beneath the Tower grounds. Fabian would have been the one to catch her up on what had happened and pick her up. Though she wasn't sure exactly how much of the truth her mum knew. Did she know it was Azalea who released the gallu into the city? Did she know the Archmage's grandson was dead because of her? Did she know Azalea had been learning Shadow Magic from her father's murderer all this time? Azalea wasn't about to bring any of that up.

"It's fine, Mum. I've just got a few cuts and bruises, nothing major." Although nothing major felt like her whole body had been used as a punching bag, and her veins were still humming from the magic, despite feeling completely drained of it now. "I just need a bit of rest, and I'm not going to get that here. I'm going back to my flat. You can walk me over there if you're that worried."

"Back into bed, Missy, now. Go on."

Azalea let her mum steer her back to the edge of the bed, wondering if she had the energy to fight this—turned out she didn't, and she let her mum sit her down.

"Mum, I know you're trying to help. But this stuff that's going on, I need to deal with it on my own. I don't want you involved or getting hurt because of me." Her throat grew thick.

Leda pulled her into a hug. "You're such a big girl now. I know I can't do much to protect you. But I'm always here when you need me. Just ask."

"Thanks, Mum." She relaxed into the warmth of the hug.

Uncle Fabian's and RoRo's voices drew near, and her mum released her. Her grandmother, RoRo, flitted through the door first; a wave of color and brightness dressed in a yellow flowery dress she usually saved for special dinners.

Rage instantly rose in Azalea's chest as Fabian stepped into the room wearing his long black coat with his hair slicked back in a ponytail as if he was purposefully trying to look like a bounty hunter. She refused to be intimidated by him, but he made her feel so small, and she felt like an absolute fool. He had known this whole time who Torin was, knew what he had done, and yet he had said nothing. Well, nothing useful or specific. He'd bloody well set her up.

Azalea reached into her pocket and gripped her elemer for moral support.

She glared at her uncle. "You should have told me who he was."

"I tried to warn you." Fabian walked across the room to stand in front of her, his arms folded across his chest, and held her stare without backing down.

"No, you banned me from studying with him with no real explanation." Her throat tightened. "What the hell did you expect me to do?"

"I expected you to listen." His nostrils flared.

"Are you serious?" Her rage and sorrow mixed together, and if she could feel even a spark of her magic, she would've blasted him like she had the gallu. "You expected me to follow your ridiculous requests blindly with no reason? I'm not one of your servants." *Arsehole.*

RoRo's gaze set on Fabian. "Now, now. Let's not go blaming one another."

"Why did none of you tell me the truth about Dad?" Azalea looked around. "How did I not know he was murdered? You let me walk into this place knowing nothing." She refused to cry. She was done with that. From now on, she would not give in to her emotions and would use every inch of strength to hide them. Especially from Torin, since he could mortifyingly feel everything she was feeling—currently— betrayal from everyone she knew.

Looks shot between her mum and RoRo.

Fabian let out a sigh. "Spit it out already." He waved a hand at RoRo, but she didn't speak, just gave him a look that said, *this is your problem.* "Your mum and grandmother didn't want you turning into me, alright, they didn't want you to use Shadow Magic because they were scared you'd turn into a killer."

Neither woman denied it.

"We didn't want you to sink into the darkness. To get caught up in such hatred for someone you could never let it go." Leda wrapped her arm around Azalea's shoulders and pulled her in.

"We were just looking out for you, dear," RoRo said.

Fabian let out a snort. "They didn't want you obsessed with getting revenge. They don't understand Shadow Magic; they aren't from the House of Snakes."

"Revenge and hatred never helped anyone." RoRo looked down her nose at Fabian.

"I don't give a shit about that! How can I *not* hate Torin?" She wanted to jump up and yell but forced herself to stop and lower her voice. "He killed my father! I studied with him, trusted him, I liked him..." *I'm bound to him.*

What the hell were the gods thinking when they did that? Had they known? She needed to calm down. Deep breaths, rational thinking—that's what she needed.

Fabian crossed his arms and stood at the end of the bed; the edge of his mouth pulled into a teasing sneer. "You've certainly changed your tune. What happened to Torin Dumont changing? To him not being *that* person anymore? Isn't that what you said when you were defending him for his past you knew nothing about?"

"Oh shut it, Fabian. None of this is helping," Leda snapped and rubbed a hand across Azalea's back protectively.

More than anything, she wanted to melt into her mother's arms and forget about everything. But she couldn't afford a breakdown. *I will not cry.* She ordered herself. But Fabian wasn't wrong. She was a bloody hypocrite and was in well over her head.

The door creaked open again, and Danni stepped into the room still dressed in a leather jacket and black jeans. She wasn't her usual bright, confident self. Her freckled face was pale as her eyes darted between Azalea's family members. Another person who had also known about Torin all along, another betrayal. Danni knew all about Torin's past and who he had killed. She had set them both up to fail from the start.

Rage bubbled under Azalea's skin all over again. She took in deep breaths to calm herself and not scream at everyone for keeping her in the dark for so long.

"Azalea, I'm sorry about everything, but we can talk about it later. Right now, the Archmage wants to see you. She requested you come to her office immediately," Danni said with a grim twist of her mouth; she was in Paranormal Justice Unit agent mode. The Archmage seemed to have the PJU under her thumb, as well as everyone at the Tower of London.

"It's four am." Azalea glanced at the clock, a reminder of the weight around her neck from the locket Torin had given her. She wasn't about to take it off in front of everyone and have to explain it.

"Correct. But the Archmage waits for no one." Danni's eyes darted to the clock.

Ice rushed through Azalea's veins. She hadn't expected this straight away. It was too early. But like everyone else, she supposed the Archmage hadn't slept either.

"I guess I better face the music," Azalea said through her dry mouth. This was it. She was definitely being kicked out of the Tower, and hopefully not being arrested if the Archmage had somehow gotten to Torin first and knew about what they had done—shared magic.

"I'll come with you," RoRo and Fabian said at the same time.

Danni shook her head. "She specifically said to come alone."

"Elam is dead because of me." Azalea tried to squash down the growing panic. Worst-case scenarios crashed across her mind of the Archmage, torturing her with mind magic or handing her over to the House of Ravens as revenge for killing her grandson. She didn't know what this woman was capable of.

"She's still protected by the laws of the High Council, right?" Fabian looked to Danni.

Danni gave a weak smile and nodded. But no one appeared convinced. That proved it. Azalea was on her own.

Azalea leaned over and gave her mum a proper hug and a kiss on the cheek. "Don't worry; I'll be okay, Mum."

"Course you will, love. Just be honest; you have nothing to hide, and you have done nothing wrong." Leda squeezed Azalea's shoulder.

If only that was true. Azalea had planted the idea in Erik's head about gallu hunting. She had hidden her Shadow Magic from her classmates and lied to them. She had drawn in the gallu that killed Elam. She had attempted illegal necromancy and somehow formed an unnatural bond with a murderer. A *lot* of this was her fault.

Azalea eased herself off the bed, trying not to show how much pain she was in.

Danni took her by the elbow and led her across the room. Azalea didn't turn back. She didn't want to see the looks of concern on her family's faces.

Something cold slipped into her palm, and her eyes darted to Danni's.

"Drink this before you go in. Torin says to trust him. I know you don't right now, but just do this for me, okay?"

Biting her lip, Azalea was slow to realize what it was. But she glanced at the vial and recognized the smooth curve of the glass bottle with a rounded stopper—Torin's memory protection potion. This, she could use. Before Danni opened the door, Azalea drank the contents of the bottle. The silky-smooth liquid trickled down her throat, sweet like honeysuckle, and the effect was instant, warming her mind like a smokescreen holding in her thoughts. She slipped the bottle back into Danni's palm. Maybe there was hope yet.

CHAPTER 2

Did she have a curse on her, or did the gods just hate her? Azalea couldn't ask for worse luck as she stepped out of the hospital room and found herself face-to-face with Millie, her classmate, and Elam's cousin.

"Millie—" Azalea's voice cracked. Millie's usually perfectly made-up eyes were red and her face blotchy from crying. She was still wearing the same tight jeans and too-short sweater she went gallu hunting in.

"You! Elam's gone because of you. This is all your fault!" Millie lashed out, but Danni darted in front and pulled Azalea aside at the same time Erik appeared and caught Millie's hand in mid-air.

Erik—he'd somehow slipped her mind. Their kiss in the moonlight seemed like years ago rather than hours.

"It isn't Azalea's fault, Millie. Elam chose to leave the circle." Erik held Millie back. His blue eyes were bright but had the same black rings under them as the rest of them.

Millie spun around, thrashing to untangle herself from Erik, but he pulled her in closer, clearly not wanting to hurt her. He was much bigger, looming over her with stocky shoulders and a grip she couldn't escape, though she was giving him a run for his money.

Somehow, Erik managed to look put together. His ash brown hair was swished aside, and his olive skin seemed luminescent in the harsh hospital light, the opposite of Azalea's, which only seemed to glow paler and more sickly looking.

"Trust you to take her side! This whole thing was your bloody idea, you're as bad as she is!" Millie screamed back at Erik, then turned her glare on Azalea. "You're a slut and a filthy shadow witch. It's your fault Elam's dead, and you'll get what you bloody well deserve from our grandmother. I hope she kills you." Millie spat on the floor, her eyes blazing.

Azalea could feel Millie's magic attempting to probe her mind. But it was weak and unrefined. Even without the memory protection potion, she wouldn't have been able to do any damage.

"I'm sorry, Millie. I didn't want any of this to happen." She meant it, but it was clear there was nothing she could say to Millie to make up for the death of her cousin. At least Elam's sister, Livia, wasn't there. That, she couldn't handle right now.

Millie collapsed, sobbing into Erik's chest.

Azalea felt numb as Danni led her through the tunnel out of the hospital and into the corridor that headed into 'the caf,' a wide underground cafeteria. The room was lit by moonlight from the magical skylight above. Ripples in the pond caught shards of blue light, as frogs jumped off the sides, woken by unexpected visitors in the night. Azalea wished she was a frog that could jump into the inky water and disappear.

Danni let go of her arm, and they walked side by side toward the stairs to the Barracks and the House of Owls offices above ground.

Before they went up the stairs, Danni stopped her. "I know you must hate me right now for lying to you about Torin and your dad. But I had my reasons, so trust him, okay? He *is* the good guy here, despite what he did."

Azalea nodded and bit her lip, not wanting to look Danni in the eye. There better be some bloody good reasons, but for now, she needed to focus on the immediate problem: the Archmage.

"What will she do to me?" Azalea swallowed and forced her glare to the stairs, moving one foot in front of the other.

"She could expel you from the initiates program for using Shadow Magic. I'm sure she won't blame you for what happened to Elam. It was the gallu that killed him." Danni's voice held conviction, like she believed it.

"What if she hurts me, or tries to get into my mind?"

Danni gave her a sideways glance. "I don't think she would resort to such extreme measures. Just be honest, and you'll be fine." Danni patted her shoulder as they started up the stairs, but it wasn't reassuring.

Was Danni in denial, or did she really believe that? Maybe she was just trying to make Azalea feel better. All she felt was a pool of dread churning in her stomach.

"Okay." Azalea held her tongue, and they continued up the stairs. She was already out of breath and out of energy.

"Understand the position the Archmage is in. She fought her whole life to get where she is. Not only is she a powerful mage, but she's chairman of the board for the Paranormal Justice Unit, Head of the House of Owls, Grand Master of the Tower of London, *and* a member of the High Council. She has a lot of sway around here."

"How did she get to be so powerful?" What Azalea really wanted to ask was: Why was she so evil? But she didn't want to make Danni worry any more than she was. It wouldn't help the situation.

"She worked extremely hard and earned her place. Even when everyone was against her, she never gave up." Danni glanced around the dark stairwell, and Azalea moved closer to her as they went up another flight of stairs. "Did you know the High Council executed her parents? It was over fifty years ago now, but people still hold it against her, despite her only being a little girl at the time. Her mother and father were manipulating the High Council from within and tried to destroy the entire governance system of the magical world."

"What happened?" Azalea placed a hand on Danni's arm to stop her. She wanted to hear this before they got to her office.

"They died. She was raised in the Tower of London by an old couple. But people never forget something like that. She had a hard life separating herself from her parents' crimes. People don't talk about it around here anymore," she whispered as if the paintings on the landing might hear them. "Come on."

Maybe that explained why she was so controlling, but it was no excuse to be a horrible person or treat people the way she did. If anything, she should relate to Azalea and Torin being outcasts for their magic. But Azalea suspected that was not the case.

They climbed a couple more steps before Danni said, "She's armored herself with a hard exterior to protect herself from the comments and the looks, but underneath it, she really isn't a bad person."

Old-fashioned wall lamps lit the red brick corridor as they reached the third level within the Barracks. Azalea had never been up this far into the offices and had a powerful urge to turn around and run away into the night. Her prospects were bleak. Her family didn't know how bad it was. It wasn't like she could explain how the woman had gouged into her mind with magic and plucked out all her secrets, how the Archmage had the power to destroy her life, and Azalea had now given her a reason to hate her. No one would believe her, anyway. The Archmage was respected and powerful. Azalea was nobody.

Even worse was the idea of facing what was outside the Tower—Korbyn Dumont and his vow to kill her. Another detail she had failed to mention to her family. There wasn't much she could do about it right now, and they would only worry or take her away, and she couldn't leave until she broke this bond and sorted out the spirits using her as a doorway.

Sweat trickled down her back despite the biting cold from the open windows. Danni stopped at a door with a sign that made Azalea's heart plummet to her feet: Archmage Esther Norwich, Head of the House of Owls, Grand Master of the Tower of London.

Azalea swallowed hard and forced the barriers up in her mind, hoping the potion was strong enough to withstand the Archmage.

Danni knocked.

"Enter." A bitter voice echoed from inside.

Danni nodded to Azalea and placed a hand on her shoulder.

Azalea took a breath and forced herself into the room against her better judgment. Her feet were heavy as lead. The Archmage sat rigid at her ostentatious wooden desk, but that wasn't where Azalea's eyes fell.

She felt him before she saw him. Sitting there all calm, his blank face giving away no emotions; his shaven hair, the familiar lines of his cheekbones and jaw, his flawless brown skin, and that tiny scar on his eyebrow—they all looked the same. Yet now Torin seemed like a completely different person, a stranger.

Anger welled in her chest with unexpected force. How could he sit there like that? As if he hadn't murdered her father, as if his father hadn't just asked for her head on a plate, as if they hadn't shared magic in such a spectacular way. Like they weren't cursed by being bound to one another.

Nope. No way she could be in this room. Her breath came in short, shallow gasps as she twisted back toward the door. Her emotions were so strong she couldn't feel Torin's.

"I wouldn't leave if I were you, Miss Sharp. You have some explaining to do." The Archmage's voice was harsh and unforgiving. Its glacial tone shocked her out of her panic.

A thread of compassion projected from Torin, and Azalea did her best not to react to the paradox of shock and relief. A moment of calmness washed over her; it came from him as his brown eyes met hers, pleading silently. She knew she had no choice but to stay.

"Sit." The Archmage pointed to the seat beside Torin, and Azalea slid into the chair without protest.

"I believe congratulations are in order to you both." Her voice was laced with venom, and the curl that lifted the corner of her lips was anything but friendly.

Azalea froze. What the hell was she on about? Did she know about the bond? Was she joking? Azalea's muddled and sleep-deprived brain ordered her mental shields up stronger.

"Thank you, Archmage," Torin said in a low, silky, sleep-deprived voice. "It was merely luck we could track the gallu through the Hollow after the... incident. I'm very sorry about your grandson. He was a good lad."

Oh, so she meant the gallu hunt. Not the other illegal things.

"He was. He would have been a strong mage." Sadness briefly touched her eyes before she covered her face with an emotionless mask. Perhaps it was her way of grieving.

Azalea held her breath, waiting for the brain-crushing spell, for the torture to begin. She wouldn't blame the woman, Azalea deserved it. But the silence hung in the air and more guilt settled on Azalea's shoulders. Her heart hammered in her chest, wishing more than ever that Elam was here, and that she had spent more time with him when he was alive. She hardly knew him, and this woman, despite her evilness, had lost her grandson.

Azalea bit her lip, trying to think of anything else, so she didn't cry. But her thoughts were jumbled being next to Torin.

She hated him more than she'd hated anyone in her life. Yet she could feel him worrying about her and not giving a shit about himself. This idiot would keep sacrificing himself to repent for his sins. She tried to push his feelings aside, to hold on to the hate. She owed her dad that much.

The Archmage turned her cold blue eyes to Azalea. It was the same look Millie gave her, but something worse—like she had a plan.

A chill spiked up Azalea's spine, and her instinct was to reach out for Torin's hand. She forced herself to stop before she actually did it. *It was just the bond. It's not real.*

"It has been a long night for us all, so let's get to business. It has come to my attention that you, Azalea Sharp, have Shadow Magic abilities and have withheld this information from me, the House of Owls, and the Tower of London since you arrived five months ago. Is this true?"

"Yes. But you already knew that," Azalea said without thinking as Torin tensed up next to her. What game were they playing here? The Archmage had dug that information out of Azalea's mind weeks ago and was actively blackmailing her with it. What more did she want?

"I knew of no such thing and will declare ignorance to anyone who suggests otherwise. Tonight, you openly displayed your Shadow Magic abilities and revealed your deception to this institution and, in doing so, demonstrated your lack of respect for our esteemed Echo Magic education program."

"But..." Azalea started.

Torin cleared his throat. "Yes, Azalea has kept her Shadow Magic a secret. But it was for her protection. She is from the House of Snakes who are actively being hunted by my father and the House of Ravens. But she has shown significant improvement in control of her abilities and played a crucial role in the capture of the corporeal gallu and many wraith gallu tonight."

"How noble of you to defend your student, Mage Dumont, but I doubt it is true. You must claim full credit for the gallu capture and be proud. You deserve it." A tight smile tweaked at the edges of her thin lips. "What I believe the truth to be—" The Archmage's gaze fell on Azalea. This was it, the moment she'd been dreading. The steely probe of magic touched the edge of Azalea's mind, and she ground her teeth together to remain still. "—is that Miss Sharp here planned all along to take on the corporeal gallu herself and lured her classmates, my grandchildren, into this scheme of hers and got my grandson killed."

Azalea gasped as the memory shot to the front of her mind. She barely let it go, and the Archmage was gouging into her thoughts. But Azalea was in control. She pushed forward the memory of Elam running from the circle and her calling out, then let the rest of the horrible event play out for the Archmage to see.

Agony ripped through her mind as she relived the moment Elam's lifeless body fell to the ground and his head cracked on the road. She fought back the pain and hid the thoughts of his spirit speaking to her one last time, as well as the horrible moment he passed through her, stealing several heartbeats with him as he went. It was an image emblazoned on her mind; one she could never erase.

Then she saw his body, just lying there, crumpled in the alleyway.

For what seemed like hours, the Archmage rifled through Azalea's memories, and every step of the way Azalea fought to control which images got through until her head felt like it might burst.

Then the Archmage released her. Azalea felt herself fall forward, but a steady hand caught her in time and propped her back up in her chair—Torin. No way she was going to cry or show any weakness; this woman wouldn't win.

"I tried to call him back. You saw it was an accident." Azalea's voice cracked as she moved her dry lips.

"I don't care for excuses. They will not bring back my grandson." Her voice had a slight tremble to it.

Azalea sat there, numb and silent. Nothing she could say would fix this or help her cause. Why was Torin even here if all the Archmage wanted to do was probe her mind and torture her? She probably wanted him to watch, the sick bitch. It was clear she hated anyone with Shadow Magic, despite her obvious need for it to hunt down the relics and use shadow mages to travel through the Hollow.

"No, it won't bring him back, but it also won't help to blame anyone for his death. It was an accident," Torin said, like an idiot. *Did he want himself fired as well?* He'd be better off keeping his mouth shut and running with the fifty thousand in reward money for catching the gallu.

"The truth is of no consequence. Justice must be served, and people will demand action from me."

"I won't let you hurt her anymore," Torin said, cold and calm.

She deserved whatever the Archmage was going to do, and it was better to just get it over with. Her head hurt, her body hurt, and she was too tired to fight. This woman was probably the most powerful mage in London, and neither of them could do anything to stop her.

The Archmage laughed, a chilling, humorless cackle. "I have no intention of harming her, dear boy. Who do you think I am? No. I have come up with an appropriate punishment for Miss Sharp." A pregnant pause hung in the air, and Azalea gripped the base of her seat. "The punishment is expulsion from the Initiate Program. She will no longer be welcome to study Echo Magic at the Tower of London or any House of Owl Institute."

Expelled? That was it?

Azalea sat there, blinking slowly. She didn't know whether to jump for joy at not being murdered or locked up or cry for being expelled from the only stable thing in her life. How would she break the bond with Torin now? How could she stay safe from the House of Ravens and Korbyn Dumont's death threats? How would she survive the spirits without Torin? She needed to stay. Despite hating Torin, there was too much unfinished business.

"You can't do this!" Torin slammed a fist into the desk. "We wouldn't even have this gallu if it wasn't for her. It would still be out there killing and calling more wraith gallu through. You should be thanking her!"

"I appreciate your dedication to your student, but that simply isn't true. I saw the memories myself. She has passable magic, at best."

Azalea let out a shuddery breath. Her memory diversions had worked.

"You can't just send her away." Torin's jaw clenched, and she could feel the determination radiating off him.

He was probably defending her for the same reason she wanted to stay: He wanted to break the bond as much as she did. Either that or he was actually planning to hand her over to his dad to regain his inheritance. Though the latter seemed unlikely. Still, she couldn't trust anyone anymore.

"Oh, no. I won't be sending her away." A sly grin crept across the old woman's face. "As I said before, two shadow mages are always better than one. And you, Mage Dumont, have mentioned that you need help if you're to get the relics within my unreasonable timeframes. That is what you said, isn't it?" She pursed her lips.

Unease crept over Azalea as the Archmage continued. Was she expelled or not? Azalea didn't dare speak. She shuffled in her chair, pressed her fists into the top of her thighs, and prayed this wouldn't get any worse.

The woman made no attempt to hide the spite in her voice. "No. What I am suggesting, or more precisely, ordering, is that Azalea is to be your new apprentice."

Azalea's breath froze like she'd been dropped into frigid water. This woman knew exactly what she was doing. This was punishment for both of them *and* a way to make sure she got what she wanted.

She swallowed as heat flushed through her body. The well of rage and hatred exploded out of Azalea before she could cap it.

"He murdered my father! You can't expect me to work with him after I just found that out. His insane father literally asked him to hand me over to the House of Ravens. You can't put me in this position!"

The Archmage had been waiting for something like this to happen so she could use them and chain Azalea to her just as she had Torin.

"Unfortunate circumstances. I'm sure you will work it out," she said without a hint of sympathy.

Torin sat rigid in his chair, his face blank, but Azalea could feel his stress levels rising, like a second heartbeat thundering alongside her own.

"Why are you doing this?" he spoke through his teeth with forced restraint.

"I would have thought that obvious." She folded her hands together over the desk and leaned forward. Her gaze pierced through them like an owl ready to dive down and clutch its prey in its talons. "Because I need shadow mages to get my relics, and you are both in debt to me now. I will get want I want, and I suggest you both play along. Do we all agree?"

Azalea knew another reason: She wanted someone to spy on Torin. Something Azalea had already agreed to, so there was little choice in the matter. Azalea nodded her head, hoping it would be enough to get her out of this room.

"I can do this on my own. You don't need to do this to her," Torin growled.

Just shut up.

He flashed her a look as if he'd heard her thoughts.

"Oh yes, I do. You are both dismissed. Please vacate your flat this week, Miss Sharp. You will reside in Mage Dumont's tower as his apprentice."

Her stomach plummeted. *Apprentice? Live with him?* This couldn't be happening.

CHAPTER 3

Danni was waiting outside, slumped against the wall, but jumped up when Azalea rounded the corner, dragging her backpack alongside her. "Are you okay?"

"I'm fine," Azalea lied and bit her lip to stop herself from falling apart.

Danni gave her a sympathetic look. "Your mum and grandmother are waiting in the caf if you want to go down."

"Thanks. Can you tell them I'll be down in a sec? I want to get some air first." Azalea took in a shaky breath.

"No worries, love. Take your time. I'll meet you down there."

She rushed past Danni, heading for the stairs and freedom.

"Azalea, wait!" Torin called after her, but she didn't stop. She flew down the stairs and pushed the doors of the Barracks open to the night air, drinking in the chill, willing it to freeze over her pressure-cooked brain.

"Azalea, just talk to me." Footsteps drew close behind her.

"I can't deal with all this right now, Torin. Just give me some space." She stopped at the top of the stone stairs and looked past the massive square structure of the White Tower that stood in the very center of the Tower of London grounds. She focused on the hazy stars dulled by the moonlight filtering through the clouds.

He stopped behind her. "I honestly didn't know the head of the House of Snakes, the man I killed, was your father. You have to believe me." His breath was heavy; he really shouldn't be chasing after her when he was out of magic and had nearly died several times that night.

She twisted around to face him and met his eyes. Immediately regretting doing so. He was in pain; she could both see it and feel it. At first, she hadn't thought the bond was so bad. The way they had shared magic had been spectacular, and it had saved them. But it had also strengthened whatever was between them. She had barely noticed it before—now she could sense him all around her like his magic was calling to her. She turned away; she couldn't feel sorry for him now. She wasn't ready for that.

"Not now." She shook her head and swallowed, forcing herself to answer. "Let's just find a way to break this bond. Then we can go our separate ways. Okay?"

She felt the hidden pain bleeding off him.

A flash of black caught her eye, and Fabian was at her side, like a guard dog she didn't ask for. "Get away from her. She doesn't need you around," Fabian growled.

Torin pulled out his elemer and stepped forward with a wave of defensive anger rolling alongside him.

Fabian angled himself opposite Torin on the top steps, his elemer raised. The glint of the silver blade reflected the white lamp light above them.

Torin glared at Fabian. "What she needs is protection. My father is coming after her. You, of all people, know what that means."

Azalea inched herself forward so she could jump in between them if necessary.

"And you think you're the man for the job? The bloke who murdered her father. You think after finding out what you did, she'd stay here? No, she's coming back with me." Fabian moved up a step.

Azalea's muscles tensed.

"No, she isn't. Put your elemer away. I don't want to fight you." Torin didn't move, but his eyes flicked to Azalea briefly.

Her heart skipped a beat. She could feel how much he wanted to protect her, and despite everything, she didn't want him to get hurt, either.

"Because you know you'll lose. Maybe I should just fix this problem for good and kill you right now." Fabian planted his feet wide as he cut into the Shadow Dimension and hooked the faint purple light with the key end of his elemer, threatening to make a move as shadows streamed from the blade and wove around him. His eyes turned solid black.

"Go on then." Torin flashed a cold smile, and Azalea couldn't help but admire his confidence, however foolish it might be. For his sake, she hoped Fabian was all talk. Torin was in no state to defend himself. He was barely alive after what he went through, and his magic must be close to zero. This wasn't a fair fight, but she knew Fabian, and he wouldn't be the one to back down.

Azalea took a deep breath and stepped in front of Fabian's elemer with her back to Torin.

"Torin's right. I'm not going. I'm staying here." She set her jaw firm and rolled her shoulders back with false confidence.

Fabian immediately lowered his elemer, and the buzz of magic in the air shrunk away. "Why the hell are you taking his side? After everything you found out about him?"

"I'm not taking his side. The Archmage told me to." Azalea gripped her elemer, unsure if she could trust Fabian not to go for Torin.

"What? Why? She didn't kick you out for the Shadow Magic?"

"No. Well, actually yes, she expelled me from the Initiate program. But she wants to use my Shadow Magic."

Fabian's black eyes drilled into her. "Oh no. No. That is much worse. You need to leave. I can get you out of here now."

"I can't. I don't have a choice." Azalea swallowed hard and held Fabian's angry stare.

"There is always a choice. I refuse to let this happen. That witch has something on you. What is it?"

"She knows what I did. She knows I tried to use necromancy and brought the gallu through. She pulled it from my mind weeks ago. She'll have me arrested if I don't stick to her plans."

Fabian ran his hand over his slicked-back hair and swore. "What plans?"

Azalea squared her shoulders once more, hoping this wouldn't send Fabian over the edge. "She ordered me to be Torin's apprentice."

A jolt of disgust surged from Torin at the word *apprentice*, but he remained silent. It was obvious he didn't want to be around her either. He'd made that perfectly clear when he decided it was better to give all his magic to her and risk dying rather than live with whatever this bond was.

"His what?" Fabian moved up a step, and shadows crept from his elemer at his side.

Azalea backed closer to Torin. She could feel him there like static electricity, all charged up and tense. Feeling him in the background was unsettling and something she wanted to get rid of as soon as possible.

A shadow moved out of the corner of her eye. No. Not a shadow, a spirit. A disheveled man, right out of World War II, trudged up the steps. His eyes locked on Azalea with cold determination. Fabian glanced at the spirit but ignored it. Azalea tried to do the same.

"Perhaps I didn't hear you right, *his what*?" Fabian narrowed his eyes.

She knew he had heard perfectly fine.

"No. No *way* you are being this man's apprentice. Out of the question." Fabian pointed his elemer at Torin and held it there, staring him down.

"We weren't given a choice," Torin snapped.

"Shit," Azalea mumbled to herself as the spirit kept coming. She nearly bumped into Torin but sidestepped and edged herself closer to the building, determined not to look to him for help this time.

"You haven't even passed your initiate training. You can't be an apprentice. It's too dangerous. Oi, Azalea, are you even paying attention?" Fabian glanced at the spirit and frowned. "It's just a spirit. No need to give it the gratification of showing you're scared. Just ignore it."

It wasn't *just* a spirit. It was coming for her, and she didn't have the energy for this right now. She attempted to pull her aura back in around her, but she didn't have any strength to control it. What little magic she had right now was seeping out of her like ink in water, and there was nothing she could do.

"You're drawing the spirit in, Azalea. Pull your magic back in or go inside," Torin muttered under his breath.

She could do this; she wasn't going to cower inside; she wasn't going to show she was weak. But it happened too quickly. The spirit darted up the stairs and hit her like a freight train. Stumbling back, she dropped her bag and hit the wall, rough stone biting into her shoulder. The spirit's hand pressed onto her chest, and her breath hitched. Then the spirit disappeared, stealing away several of her heartbeats.

Time stood still. Torin lunged toward her but doubled over. The pain she was feeling mirrored in his own expression.

"Holy shit, that spirit went right through you." Fabian crouched over her, and she caught her breath enough to sit up. He glanced between the two of them. "What the hell was that, and what aren't you telling me?"

Azalea pressed her hand to her chest as the pain dulled. "It's a small problem I've been having with spirits. Nothing to worry about."

"You know what this is. You did something to her!" Fabian got up and shoved Torin's chest. "If you want me to kill you, you're giving me lots of reasons, *mate*."

"This has nothing to do with him, Fabian. Leave him alone." Azalea stumbled up and poked Fabian in the chest.

Torin held his hands up in defense. "Hey *mate*, all I've been doing is trying to help her." Torin gritted his teeth. He was nearing his snapping point. His rage pumped through her heart as if it was her own.

"This is ridiculous. Fabian, please go find my mum and tell her I've gone to bed. There are Phoenix guards all around here watching us, so you can't kill Torin now. If you both want to be idiots, do whatever you like outside the Tower, but I'm out."

She glanced back, just to make sure they were done. Torin marched off and slammed the door to the Barracks, and Fabian stormed off toward the ground-level entrance to the hospital.

Left with only her own emotions, Azalea didn't allow herself to relax as she passed the looming White Tower, turned the corner, and dashed past the green to avoid any lingering spirits.

She hurried by the Bloody Tower, and when she made it to Mint Street, her hand automatically fell to her necklace in relief, but the warmed silver of the locket sent chills of discomfort through her. She didn't want to wear something Torin had given her. She slipped off the chain and shoved it into her pocket.

With legs as heavy as kettlebells, she finally made her way up the street to her red door in the outer wall of the fortress. She just needed a bit of sleep and a chance for her brain to regroup and work out what to do next.

CHAPTER 4

A loud banging drummed inside Azalea's head. Why couldn't she just keep sleeping? She groaned and pulled herself from the super weird dream, where she killed a raven just by touching it with her bare hands. Not surprising after what she'd been through, but she couldn't help but feel sorry for the raven. She covered her face with her pillow. It couldn't have been more than a few hours since she'd fallen into bed.

"Morning sleepyhead." Isaac? Was she still asleep? If it was him, he definitely sounded pissed off.

"Friends don't wake friends up this early," Azalea croaked and removed the pillow, realizing she was awake.

"Friends don't leave their friends hanging and waiting up all night thinking they got killed by monsters."

A weight sunk onto the end of her bed. She felt her cat, Faraday, walk over her side with pointy claws, and she forced herself to sit up.

Reality blurred, but at least her best friend, Isaac, remained a constant friendly face, except at this particular moment.

She blinked and rubbed her eyes as he came into focus. "Sorry, Isaac. Things didn't exactly go as planned."

"No shit. Van messaged me and let me know you were alive. Thank you very much. Then called me this morning and said some very confusing shit."

Confusing shit was an understatement. "I'll explain everything, Isaac. Can I just wake up a bit?" Her thoughts were a jumbled mess, but she was glad Isaac was here.

"Fine. Hurry up with it then," he grumbled.

Azalea pushed the blankets and pulled Isaac into a hug, and his mop of blond hair went all over her face. "I'm so glad you're here." Her throat grew thick.

She sat back, and Isaac gave her a concerned look. "Are you okay?" he asked.

She nodded, not trusting herself to speak. She needed to get moving; she should probably get dressed. Her long t-shirt barely covered her bum and her not-for-human-eyes floral undies. Not that Isaac would care, he had seen her in various disheveled states, and things had always been strictly platonic between them. She was certain he had his eye on Van.

"At least Faraday was kind enough to greet me at the door this morning," Isaac said as Azalea pulled on a pair of black jeans and tied her hair back up where it belonged.

She sat back on the bed and smiled as the little cat head-butted Isaac on the chin. "He saved me last night. Poor little guy. He was like a tiger."

"You invited your cat on the monster hunt and not me. Rude."

"I did not invite him. I don't even know how he got there."

"He's certainly a mystery, this one," Isaac's voice softened.

"Anyone home?" A voice called from the hall. It was Erik. Butterflies jolted in Azalea's stomach, remembering their kiss last night.

Azalea swallowed back her nerves and jumped up. "Coming."

She followed his voice down the short hall to the kitchen-slash-living-room-slash-dining-room—it was all one tiny space crammed in with mismatched furniture, colorful cushions, and plants. She found Erik's black, snow-dusted, winter coat draped across a chair in the hallway and Erik in the kitchen already turning on the jug. He spun around and leaned against the bench with his arms crossed, but unlike his usual cocky posture, his shoulders were slumped, and his eyes were red.

"Are you okay?" Azalea moved toward him, and he opened his arms and folded her into a hug. She closed her eyes and sank into his warmth.

His head buried into her neck. "I'm okay. Are you?"

"I'm good." She breathed in the scent of his clean shirt, and neither of them mentioned Elam. His death was a weight pressing on her heart, so heavy she couldn't block it out.

She pulled away and did her best to smile, but it was a poor effort.

"Should I be concerned about finding you walking out of your bedroom with some bloke?" Erik raised an eyebrow with a hint of a smile and nodded toward Isaac who was standing quietly with his eyes narrowed at Erik.

"Depends how insecure you are. Erik, this is Isaac, Isaac, Erik," Azalea said, trying to sound cheerful.

Erik smiled and shook Isaac's hand. "The famous Isaac."

"And you're the twat from her class, I take it?" Isaac joked.

"Sounds like me." Erik gave a weak smile but didn't even defend himself.

Azalea looked between the two and decided they would be fine. No silly arrogance on Erik's part, and Isaac was always friendly to strangers. "Let's sit down."

"What's wrong? What did I miss?" Isaac studied their faces with a frown.

Her fake cheerful look couldn't have been working. A lump lodged in Azalea's throat, and she couldn't speak. Erik's arm curled around her shoulder, and she stared at a spot on the floor as her eyes misted over.

"Azalea told you what we were up to last night. Right?" Erik asked.

"She told me." Isaac glanced at Azalea.

Azalea nodded.

"Things didn't go as planned. We got the gallu, but our friend Elam got caught by one. He died." Erik squeezed Azalea's shoulder, and the warmth of his arm moved away as he turned back to the kitchen bench.

Isaac's mouth dropped. "He died?"

"How about some coffee?" Erik skirted around Azalea in the tiny kitchen space, and Azalea drifted over to the sofa and sat down.

"What happened?" Isaac sank into a chair at the table and ran a hand through his curly hair. He was wearing a new gray sweater that suited him nicely, and his face was freshly shaved.

"He left our trap. It wasn't anyone's fault." Erik set cups out on the bench.

Azalea stared at the wooden coffee table. Erik was just being kind. It was all her fault, and it felt like her world was falling apart around her.

Van walked in with a wave of humid shower air smelling of coconut shampoo. Her auburn hair was damp and hung in loose waves over her shoulders, naturally pretty. Her face was already made up, and her tan stood out against her form-fitting, white crop top. Her white deer tattoo was a stark contrast to the vibrant roses that cascaded behind it. Isaac couldn't take his eyes off her or her tight jeans. Azalea allowed herself a tiny smile.

"Morning lads, morning Azalea." Van winked at Isaac and turned to Erik, clearly trying to lighten the mood. "I'll take a soy coffee, thanks."

Erik got out another mug. "Yes, ma'am."

"Morning, Van." Azalea tried to sound alive as Van rushed over and fell on her in one intense hug.

"It will be okay." Van gave her a big squeeze, then untangled herself, patted Azalea on the head like a cat, then moved to sit across from Isaac.

Erik placed two coffees in pink cups on the table in front of Van and Isaac; they thanked him, and Van passed Isaac the sugar bowl with a smile.

Azalea took a deep breath. She'd get all the news over with before she had a meltdown.

"While you're all here, I've got something to tell you." Azalea pulled a yellow cushion onto her lap and hugged it.

Erik placed two coffees on the small table and sank in next to Azalea. His arm slid around her, pulling her against his side and Van raised a curious eyebrow at them. Azalea wasn't sure how she felt about Erik or the kiss. But leaning into him felt nice and like she wasn't so alone.

"Tell us then." Erik tapped his foot against the coffee table.

Azalea squeezed the cushion to her chest. "The Archmage expelled me from the initiate program."

"No!" Van exclaimed.

"What? She can't do that. She knows you didn't kill Elam, right?" Erik removed his arm from her shoulder, leaned forward, and took an angry slurp of his coffee.

"I might as well have." Azalea looked down at her hands.

Isaac swiveled in his chair. "Why would she think that?"

Azalea avoided Isaac's eyes. "It's a very long story." She let out a slow breath and knew she had to get this over with. She updated Isaac and the other two on everything that had happened the night before: the gallu hunt, Elam dying, her and Torin taking down the gallu, Torin's crazy dad showing up—she hadn't even told her family or Danni and Maiken about that yet. She carefully left out the parts about her and Torin sharing magic and their weird soul bond—no one could know about that. It all came out in one rambling, rapid explanation, but hopefully, she got the main points covered.

"Zaels, this is mad. Maybe you should just leave this place," Isaac said, chewing on his thumbnail.

Erik slammed his coffee cup down. "Go back to the part about you getting expelled."

"Yes, I'd like to hear more about that. Do you have to leave? Where will you go? Did she really expel you? Can she do that?" Van tapped her fingers on the table until Isaac leaned over and put his hand over hers.

"She can, and she did. And it gets worse. Erik, please hold your I-told-you-so's till the end." She took a shaky breath and picked up her coffee cup, so she had something to hold. "Last night I found out that it was Torin who killed my father. And, before you ask, no, neither of us knew."

The room filled with the appropriate stunned silence. Azalea gripped her cup, waiting for them to react, her heart drumming like crazy.

Van clasped her hands to her mouth, and Isaac just stared. A smirk crept across Erik's face, then he reined it in.

Azalea put the mug down and squeezed the cushion, so she didn't hit Erik. She knew he didn't like Torin, but he didn't have to look so smug.

"What? How did he not know that?" Van's hand went to her breastbone.

Azalea shook her head. "I never told him anything about my family. I didn't even know my father was murdered. I had my suspicions, but it wasn't exactly something I would think to put together."

"Not to be the arsehole here... Buuut, it's hardly surprising, is it?" Erik shrugged. "I probably should have worked it out. I mean, your dad must have been in the House of Snakes, and it's common knowledge who Mage Dumont killed."

"Well, you could have filled me in on this *common knowledge* about my family. No one told me, and I have a different last name than my father, so no one else made the connection. Except Danni and Maiken, and they chose not to tell me for whatever reason."

"Sorry. I didn't think you wanted to talk about any House of Snakes stuff." Erik looked at her as if it wasn't a life-changing thing.

She did her best not to glare at him, just picked up her cup, and took a steadying sip. "It gets worse. The Archmage has ordered me to be Torin's apprentice, and I have to move in with him." She bit her lip and stopped talking, knowing her news kept getting worse, and they didn't even know the worst of it—the soul bond.

"Oh, hell no." Erik slammed his mug onto the coffee table and drew his palms into fists before flattening them out on his thighs.

So that got a reaction.

Isaac cleared his throat. "You have to tell her he was the one who killed your dad."

"She already knows," Azalea said, tasting the bitterness on her tongue. "She knows exactly what she's doing."

"You can't do it Azalea." Van stood up and put her cup in the sink and walked back with her hands on her hips like she didn't know where to stand or sit.

"I don't have a choice." Azalea shook her head. She hadn't even had time to think about this.

Erik lit a fireball in his hand and started bouncing it in his palm. "I don't like this. But at least you'll get to stay at the Tower," he said bluntly, not acknowledging the fireball and clearly not happy with the idea.

"Please don't set fire to the curtains." Van frowned at him.

Isaac's eyes widened. He hadn't seen fire magic up close before. It certainly wasn't Azalea's specialty; after Shadow Magic, water and plant magic were her next go-to. Fire was pretty much her worst. Air was somewhere in the middle.

"We'll think of something," Van said, reassuringly.

"Don't worry about me. I'm not giving up yet. I'll find a way out of it." Azalea set her jaw, determined it was true.

Erik's fireball turned blazing blue before he squeezed it out and pressed both his fists into his knees. Azalea reached out for his hand; he needed to calm down, or their curtains would end up on fire.

"It'll be fine. I'm sure I won't have to actually move in with him." Azalea patted their entwined hands awkwardly. Isaac gave her a questioning look.

"Shit. I'm so sorry Azalea. She really has it out for you, hun." Van's face fell. Probably sad for Azalea but also because she would have to find a new flatmate.

Azalea could feel the heat radiating off Erik. Hopefully, he wouldn't burst into flames or something; she took her hand back, just in case. "Um, Erik. Are you okay? You're not usually this quiet."

"Course I am, love. Just trying to be supportive and not say exactly what I'm thinking about Dumont, as it is highly inappropriate." A new fireball burst into life in his hand.

Azalea angled away. "You've got a funny way of showing it."

He leaned over and kissed her on the cheek. She felt the warmth of the fireball as he leaned in, and her face warmed.

"Um, Erik." The fire got a little too close.

"Sorry, bad habit," he said unapologetically and didn't put the flames out. He was probably trying to intimidate Isaac as well.

Her phone buzzed against the coffee table, and she picked it up.

Mum: *Danni and Fabian filled us in on everything. I hope you are okay and got some sleep. We are staying at Fabian's house. Just give us a bell if you want to come over and he will fetch you if you need some time away from the Tower.*

Azalea: *Thanks mum. I'm good. Just catching up on sleep. Will let u know.*

She put the phone down. *Away from the Tower.* Now that sounded good. But first, she had to get out of this mess of moving into Torin's place.

CHAPTER 5

Fabian stepped out of the Hollow to the familiar wrought-iron gates at Blackbourne Manor, his family home and the residence of the head of the House of Snakes which, by serious bad luck, was him. He had never wanted it. But the house was his, and after ignoring it for as long as he could, he was attempting to put it to good use.

The white stone facade looked pristine against the backdrop of blanketed snow. A driveway of light stone wound its way from the skeletal winter trees at the entrance of the inner estate and led to the grand house with its circular turrets, tall windows, and pompous entranceway complete with a pair of strutting peacocks, though hopefully, they were safe in the barn with this recent snow.

It really was beautiful. It was too bad he hated the place, bloody money pit. They used to hold weddings here before all this nonsense, and he could do with that income again. A shame security was more of a priority now.

Fabian crossed the bridge that curved over a small brook and looked back at the solid iron gates. They were the barrier against entering or exiting the Hollow inside the grounds. No one could get in or out of the inner estate, not without magical clearance. He'd also added a bonus measure of keeping spirits out. More so he didn't have to listen to their whining, though there were still a few harmless ones he'd left milling about the grounds.

"Good morning, Sir. How did your meeting go?" the groundskeeper, Mr. Yates, stood beside the old Land Rover like an obedient dog.

He ran a hand over his ponytail of brown hair, then sighed and pulled his trench coat around him. It was bloody cold. "It was shit, thank you for asking, Yates. They fired me and sent me on my merry way. No more gallu hunting for me. I also need to pay them back for all the gemstones I failed to retrieve, just what I need on top of setting up this bloody refugee camp."

"You're a good man. These people need help, and this is the safest place they can be." Yates slapped him on the shoulder.

At least someone thought he was doing some good. He'd done nothing to help Azalea. His mind kept going back to her and how he'd let her down, wishing he could be more useful to her. But staying away seemed to be for the best. He just hated that she was forced to apprentice to Torin Dumont. His blood boiled at the thought.

"Perhaps we should sell old Betsy here." Fabian rapped the truck bonnet with his knuckles, and Yates cringed. It had been Samael's, his brother's and Azalea's dad's, car. He only kept it because Yates was so fond of it and didn't have the heart to take it away from him.

Fabian slid into the leather passenger's seat, and Yates made the two-minute drive to the house. The icy front lawn, once used for galas and elegant Victorian picnics in bygone days, was now a shanty town of circular Mongolian tents known as gers. More had somehow popped up since he'd seen it last.

He'd originally gotten them as cheap accommodations to charge guests to stay for weddings. Apparently, people paid good money for *glamping,* though he had no idea why. At least they had arranged them in pleasant rows. He had to admit, the bright white tents with patterned orange doors looked rather lovely, all aligned and facing south with lines of smoke trailing into the sky from their central chimneys.

He and Azalea's grandmother, Rowena, had traded stories on the horrors the House of Snakes families were facing at the hands of Korbyn Dumont and the House of Ravens. So she had organized setting up a refugee village for House of Snakes families.

Over the last few weeks, Fabian's front lawn had turned into a camp of people from all over the world hiding from the House of Ravens. He had reluctantly brought Azalea's mother, Leda, there for her own safety. Though she and Azalea's grandmother were the exceptions he allowed to stay in the main house, but it was clear Leda didn't want to be there. Her connection to the forest was a strange one. He suspected she was suffering from being away from it, but she was safe.

Rowena ducked out of the orange door of a ger and waved as Fabian got out of the truck.

"Good, there you are Fabian. There's been another attack," Rowena yelled.

Bloody hell. He strode across the gravel drive and down the path that led to the pop-up village. "That's the third this week," he yelled back. He was getting sick of the House of Ravens and their bullshit, and there were too many people at his house now. He'd preferred it when he could hide there in peace instead of being accosted by relatives and House of Snakes families.

"Why the hell is Korbyn Dumont doing this after all these years? He's tormenting these poor families." Rowena stopped in front of him on the path with snow piled up on either side.

"Other than his grudge against our House you mean?" Fabian rubbed his hands together as his breath misted on the air.

Rowena was a tough old bird, and it was clear she cared deeply for these people despite her being from the House of Bees and being a plant mage, not a shadow mage like most of them here. She just couldn't sit aside while people were suffering.

"There must be more to it than that." Rowena shoved her hands deep into her long red coat, her long brown hair, the same as Azalea's, hung over her shoulders.

"There is one other thing. Korbyn's been looking for an old book for years, and he thinks we have it. Either that, or he's looking for some old relics, take your pick. If I knew what it was he wanted, I'd bloody well hand it over to stop all this." He recalled Kat—his ex-lover, House of Ravens informant to the Paranormal Justice unit, and the woman who attacked him and stabbed him not so long ago—had yelled something about relics at him when she ambushed him in the graveyard.

Rowena frowned. "A book? You've never mentioned it before. Let's get inside. It's freezing."

Fabian trudged after her up the new gravel path toward the mess tent: an old wedding marquee, complete with fairy lights, chandeliers, and warming charms.

"There was no point because it isn't relevant. I'm certain it doesn't exist, and Korbyn is a crazy old bloke chasing fairytales." Fabian pulled his black coat in closer around him.

"How do you know that's what he wants?" Rowena asked.

"I had a friend on the inside years ago. That's what she told me, and she was the one who mentioned the relics too." He pushed the sliding door open and gestured for Rowena to enter first. He spotted a plate of sandwiches right away. "My ex-friend, Kat, works for the House of Ravens, but she used to help me out when I was with the Paranormal Justice Unit. Though she also stabbed me in the back and used information I gave her to help Korbyn murder my brother and half the council, so I can't really take her word for it now, can I? She also literally stabbed me the last time I saw her." He got no sympathy from Rowena. He grabbed a sandwich and bit into it. *Yuck, mustard on ham, he hated mustard.*

"So you admit it was Korbyn who murdered your brother, not his son, Torin?" Rowena raised her eyebrows.

Quick, this Rowena, and just as sharp-tongued as Azalea. She even looked like Azalea, both thin and tall with brown hair and intense gray eyes. Rowena barely looked over forty, despite probably being in her sixties. "You know what I mean, Rowena. Stop putting words in my mouth."

"I saw Torin at the Tower. I honestly believe he had no idea he knew who Azalea was. He cares for her."

"It doesn't matter. She sees him for what he is now." He forced himself to take a bite of the sandwich.

Rowena's features softened. "She's apprenticed to him, Fabian."

"I know. But she made it clear she didn't want my help. I've got Danni and Maiken watching over the both of them like hawks. They'll make sure she's okay."

"I take it you're out of a job now?"

Fabian shoved his sandwich back onto the plate. He didn't need reminders. "Yes. Obviously."

"Good, then you can go find this Kat from the House of Ravens and apologize for whatever it was you did to get her off-side and make amends. We need to know what Korbyn wants. And ask about that book and the relics."

Fabian poked at the sandwich. "Did you not hear me say she stabbed me the last time I saw her?"

"So, you have seen her then? Excellent."

"That's what you took away from that statement. Look." He held up his shirt to show the sliver of his silver scar. "It's barely healed."

"I'm too old for you to be trying to impress me with those abs, Fabian Blackbourne. Now stop crying about a little cut and go find that girl."

That sly woman. Trust her to be checking out his abs when he was trying to show her a serious wound. "Fine. But you keep control of this lot on my lawn. You, Leda, and that shaman fellow who's in charge can come in the House, but no one else. I won't have my family home overrun by hooligans."

"They aren't hooligans, Fabian. They're children."

"Same thing, children and strangers who might steal my stuff. Just keep them away from me, and everyone shall remain happy and well-fed."

She gave him a knowing smile and pinched his cheek. "You've got a kind heart in there, Fabian, but you sure have a funny way of showing it. Not to worry, I've got everything under control."

"Good." He selected another sandwich, this time cucumber, *much better*, and marched back to the House without talking to anyone else. He ignored the stares of people in gers hanging out their orange doorways, hoping for answers he didn't have. What he had was the perfect plan to lure Kat, but first, he needed a decent meal and a swim in his pool without anyone bothering him.

CHAPTER 6

Azalea couldn't stand being in her room any longer. It had only been one day of keeping out of the public eye, but through her tiny gap of a 'not window,' she watched everyone gather in the grass moat for morning training. Light snow fell overhead, but it never made it to the ground thanks to some sort of weather wards that kept the moat just warm enough to train. Fuck it. She was going out there. She would not hide away, scared of everyone. She needed to train.

She rushed to get dressed in black running tights and a gray long-sleeved thermal shirt.

Once she was down there, she immediately regretted her decision. She halted near the edge of the group—Livia was there. Fortunately, Millie wasn't, any excuse to get out of exercise. Azalea chided herself for the mean thoughts. They'd both lost Elam; they had every right to be horrible to her.

But it wasn't just them; stony stares bombarded her from every direction. She scanned the moat, seeking any friendly face. Fucking rumors. They spread like wildfire around here. Of course, the House of Owls had all banded against her. She didn't even know most of them.

But that was the way it would be now, everyone knowing she had the widely hated Shadow Magic from the House of Snakes and blaming her for what happened to Elam.

She spotted Van on the other side and gave a small wave. She darted to Azalea's side immediately.

"I'm saying this as a friend, but you should leave. This isn't the safest place for you right now." Van gripped her arm.

So this is what it felt like to be Torin. At least now, he would be seen in a better light after getting all the credit for the gallu and all. He was never stupid enough to show himself at morning training. He always stuck to his intense gym schedule and worked out alone in the middle of the day when it was quiet.

Whispers hissed all around her. Maybe it was time to go...

"Oi, shadow witch, nobody wants you round here," some random guy yelled, a House of Phoenix guard by the look of his fiery tattoos.

Murmurs grew louder in agreement.

Erik swooped to her side and linked his arm with hers. "I think you were just leaving."

"I suppose I was..." She didn't want to. Didn't want to show defeat. But she also felt like she might crumble from within at any moment.

Erik walked with her out of the moat, into the blasting wind that had picked up, and back into the Tower grounds. They passed the Yeoman warders at the front gates and walked toward Mint Street where she lived. "Maybe you should stay inside another day. Wait for the hype to die down," Erik suggested as they rounded the corner.

"I need to get back to normal." She sighed, hating that everything would be different now. That there was no going back.

"No, you need to lie low and recover from whatever crazy magic you did the other night." His voice held genuine concern.

She still wasn't used to this thoughtful version of Erik. She swallowed and tried not to think about everyone hating her. He was probably right. "Okay, I'll try to go back to sleep. You get back to training."

"I'll make sure you actually get home first." He grinned and nudged her shoulder.

It brought a hint of a smile to her face. He walked her to her flat and through the red door in the casemates, into the hallway out of the wind that was now blasting snow sideways. She brushed the flakes off her head and tried to find the key to her flat in her skintight pocket with numb fingers.

"I know what might cheer you up." Erik's silky voice breathed onto her neck.

She turned around, but before she could answer, Erik's hands were on her waist, guiding her against the wall. She glanced up and took in his hungry look. Before she blinked, his lips were on hers, wild and urgent. She leaned into him, kissing him back and relishing the unexpected thrill.

Wait. What was she doing? She pulled away. She couldn't get distracted by whatever this was. There were so many other things to deal with.

"Hadn't forgotten you kissed me, had you?" Erik said with an overconfident smile.

She couldn't help but grin. "I hadn't forgotten, just didn't want to get your hopes up. I thought I was about to die, re-member?" Part of her wished he *had* forgotten, the other part wanted to invite him in right now and turn this into even more of a distraction. That would be more fun than getting out of moving in with Torin.

"Tell yourself whatever you like if it helps you sleep at night." He pushed off the wall, grinning.

"I haven't had time to think about anything." She spun around and fumbled to find her key. As much as she wanted a bit of fun, she really shouldn't lead Erik on. She may have given him the wrong idea about her feelings. She didn't even know what she wanted anymore.

She slipped the key into the lock. Erik leaned casually on the door frame, watching her, probably trying to psych her out.

"Thanks for walking me back." She opened the door and glanced back at him.

"Thanks for the snog." He winked.

An unwanted flush of heat ran through her, and she couldn't think of anything to say.

"Bye, Azalea." He blew her a kiss and strode out the door.

He sure was confident. Her feelings were all over the place. She knew it would be safer to stay away from him, but then again, it had been a while...

Focus Azalea! Erik might be distracting her with these back-and-forth feelings, but she certainly wasn't going to lie low and wait around for things to happen around her. She needed to know what her future held and needed to get back control. Starting with confronting Torin and sorting out this living situation. She didn't want to go back inside and be all alone while she was hovering on the edge of breaking. She needed to keep moving.

She locked the door, slipped the key back in her pocket, and darted out into the snow. Regretting not grabbing her winter coat, she jogged up Mint Street to stay warm. She headed into the inner ground of the Tower, past the Bloody Tower, and toward the Chapel of St. Peter Ad Vincula.

She spotted a few odd figures in the snow, and a light bulb went off in her head. If what she suspected the other night was true—if Torin could feel the spirits the same as she could—he was in for a shocking morning wake-up right about now.

She jogged toward the chapel, letting her aura seep out around her, imagining it spreading like purple ink diffusing into the air and mingling with the falling snowflakes. Two men turned their heads as soon as she did it.

They were both dressed in old-timey suits, maybe Victorian? She didn't know enough about historical fashions to tell. But they were spirits, she was sure of that.

She took two deep breaths, psyching herself up as she walked straight toward them.

"Morning, gents." She gave a sharp nod.

They stared at her blankly but stepped closer, heads tilted to the side as if they were trying to recognize her from somewhere.

"Good day to you, miss." One man tipped his hat.

She wouldn't let herself back out. "It's your lucky day, kind sirs." She stepped up to one and grasped his shoulder. His eyes went wide and locked with hers as if he was staring into her soul. He didn't seem to know what was happening as his life flashed across Azalea's eyes. He'd been a bachelor, rich, generous, and loved by the tenants of his vast estate. But he made friends with the wrong people, and in the end, it cost him his life at the Tower.

Azalea gasped back a breath and opened her eyes to see the man was gone.

"You're a witch!" the other man exclaimed.

"Actually, I'm about to be an apprentice mage, but witch works if you prefer."

His eyes widened with fear. "What did you do to him? Where did he go?"

"To a happier place." She had no idea where that was. "You'll be going there too, but I would like you to send a message to whoever is on the other side." Perhaps that alien-looking Damu guy or his strange mother from her dream, probably someone in the Shadow Dimension, as Torin had suggested.

The man stared at her, perhaps unsure what to make of an outspoken girl and this whole bizarre situation. He probably didn't even know he was a ghost.

"Tell them I want out. I'm going to break this bloody curse, and I'll be turning off their spirit portal tap very soon."

"I'm afraid you're quite mad, my dear. Should I fetch a doctor?"

She sighed and shook her head. "Yes, please do," she said sarcastically.

The man turned, and she put her hand on his shoulder. His life montage sunk Azalea into darkness. His path had not been a happy one: he was a gambler, abusive to his wife and family, and had died of late-stage syphilis. Great guy... this one deserved to be a lost spirit wandering the world. But it was too late, and he was gone.

Her heart thrummed like a bass in her chest, trying to catch up on the lost beats. She hoped Torin had felt every second as she had. It still sent panicked chills down her body every time, but she was getting more used to it.

Sooo, Torin *should* be awake now if her theory was correct. She pulled her aura back in before any more spirits could be attracted. She took a few off-balance steps, then got her feet in line, and traipsed down the alley behind the chapel to the courtyard in front of Devereux Tower, Torin's private tower in the northwest corner of the inner fortress wall. With her heart going way too fast, she forced herself up the steps to his front door where his office was.

A flood of panic rushed over her as she stood there, threatening to overwhelm her as Torin swung the door. The panic was coming from him.

"You okay?" He wasn't wearing a shirt, just blue-striped pajama bottoms, and looked like he'd rolled right out of bed. His shaven hair was perfectly neat and spikey, but his eyes were red and puffy, and he seemed to have trouble focusing.

Her gaze went straight to the disturbing tattoo on his left pec. It was the same as hers, only reversed. She had been so interested in that crescent moon when she first saw it, in awe even. But now it made her feel ill, that same brand on her chest linking them to some sick game the gods were playing.

She crossed her arms, willing herself to stop shivering. "I'm fine. I just came to tell you I can't move in with you. I'll find somewhere else to stay." Part of her wished she could just escape the Tower altogether and hide away at Fabian's house with her mum and RoRo. She had no idea what they were up to there, but it had to be better than being here.

"Did you let those spirits walk through you on purpose?" His brown eyes narrowed. There was the paranoid Torin she knew.

"No. Of course not," she said sarcastically. It was clear he wanted to tell her off. But she knew he wouldn't dare right now.

"Azalea, I'm so sorry about everything. My father... your father—"

Her chest grew tight. She hadn't expected him to cut to the chase like that and didn't want her fragile glass exterior to shatter in front of him. She did her best to bottle her emotions up and cut him off. "Let's not do this now. I'm not here for apologies or to forgive you. I just want to get on with my life and get this apprenticeship done with and break the bond. I'm sure you want the same."

She didn't have to tell him she had no intention of following through with the apprenticeship. Once they broke the bond and sorted out these spirits, she was *Out* with a capital O. Maybe Fabian could teach her, or anyone else, frankly she didn't care.

"I understand that, but the Archmage won't allow for any deviations from her plan."

"We'll see." Azalea turned her back and walked away, feeling lighter for getting that off her chest.

"I've cleared out the boxes from the spare room. You can move in any time," he called after her with a distinctive wave of guilt.

She knew what he was doing. He was trying to make it all up to her by being agreeable for once. Not going to work, mate.

Now to find out who was going to be taking her room and find somewhere else for her to live.

CHAPTER 7

It was already the afternoon, and Azalea hadn't come up with a solution. She lay on her stomach on her patchwork quilt-covered bed, arms and head dangling off the end, hoping the blood rushing to her brain might help as she frantically brainstormed ideas for her living situation.

The heater in her room was on so high it was too hot to think, but it was better than being cold. Faraday sauntered across her shoulder blades with harder than necessary footsteps, then seated himself in the dip of her lower back to have a bath. His purrs rattled up her spine and made her feel a little better.

She thought about going to Danni and Maiken to see if they could come up with a solution, but she was still mad at them for not telling her about Torin, and deep down, she suspected no one could help her. Not when the Archmage was giving the orders.

Maybe she could stay with Erik for a while? That seemed like a *really* bad idea. He wasn't her boyfriend; she wasn't sure if she wanted him to be. Either way, moving in with him was definitely a bad idea. Living in the library might be nice. There were some pretty cozy chairs in there. She could shower at the gym and eat in the caf...

This was not going well.

A loud knocking sounded at the door, and she jerked up. Faraday flew off and glared at Azalea from the floor as she rolled off the bed.

She instantly regretted not getting dressed properly, still wearing gym clothes, though she never made it to the gym. She opened the door to find the Archmage glowering at her with thin, evil eyes, and her owl-headed cane at her side.

Azalea probably looked exactly how the old woman wanted her to look, defeated and moping. She hardly noticed the girl standing behind her.

"Good afternoon, Miss Sharp. I trust you are recovering well from your ordeal," she said without a hint of caring in her voice.

"I'm doing very well, Archmage, thank you for asking." Azalea flashed a half smile.

The Archmage pursed her thin lips. "I *believe* I ordered you to move out."

She was not about to give this woman the satisfaction of knowing she had wrecked her life. "Yes. I have. I'm just... getting the last of my things."

"Excellent. Perfect timing." She stepped aside. "This is Miss Jade Pike. She will take your room."

Take her room? Oh crap.

Azalea forced a smile as a girl—probably around the same age as Azalea, nineteen—stepped forward to shake her hand.

The words ran through her mind as she shook Jade's hand on autopilot.

"It's so nice to meet you," Jade said with a slightly off accent and a cheerful smile.

Azalea eyed her up. She would find something she didn't like about her. But Jade picked up her bag, and her eyes lit up when she spotted Faraday. Damn her and her good first impression.

She would not let this get to her. "It's very nice to meet you, Jade. Please come in."

"I shall leave you to it, then. Good day, Miss Sharp, Miss Pike." The Archmage gave a nod and marched off before Azalea could think of any decent remarks.

Dropping off the new girl was a job far below the Archmage's station. She had come purely to gloat and make sure Azalea was miserable.

Jade wandered in, and Faraday wound around her legs. She bent down to pat him. She was short, thin, and petite. Her hair was dyed jet black and cut into a perfect short bob, like a cute anime schoolgirl wig. She had dark cat's-eye makeup and wore a black pleated skirt and black leather corset top. Very old-school goth.

"That woman is intense." Jade stood back up. Azalea couldn't place her accent. *Maybe Australian?*

"You noticed?" Azalea joked.

Jade chewed on her lip, not meeting Azalea's eyes. "Sorry to be dropped on you like this. I take it you weren't expecting me?"

"Not exactly, but it's not a problem. I'm not one to go against the Archmage," she said, testing the waters. "Are you one of her grandchildren?" *Please don't be.*

"Gosh no. I'm new here, fresh off the boat."

"Where exactly are you from?"

"New Zealand. You know... Lord of the Rings." Jade sighed as if that wasn't a good thing.

Azalea's curiosity suddenly took over. "Wow, that's a long way. Did you come by the Hollow? Can you travel that far?"

"Yeah, although you have to register for international travel through the Hollow. Some mage guy came and picked me up, and here I am."

That 'mage guy' was most certainly Torin. So he would already know Jade was here and would expect Azalea to turn up. Damn him for being one step ahead of her.

She took a deep breath. She would have to give in, as she was out of options. At least she could go with graceful defeat. It wasn't Jade's fault Azalea's life was fucked up.

"Let me show you to your new room. Although I haven't actually packed yet, so bear with me."

"No worries. I'm just glad I finally made it here. I never thought I'd get out."

Azalea bent down to pick up the bag, and so did Jade. Their hands met on the handle, their heads bumped, and they both giggled.

Suddenly, Jade's eyes went all white. Her hand gripped Azalea's so tight she couldn't get away. She tried to yank her hand free, but Jade remained frozen.

Her voice changed to a whisper. "Your choice will change the course of history for the world. One path will lead you to the destruction of many. The other to the destruction of one. The scales will balance or tip. The choice is yours."

Azalea froze in place, staring at the girl.

Jade suddenly blinked and released her hand. "Shit. I guess I disappeared for a second there. Sorry, that happens sometimes."

"What *was* that?" Azalea clasped her hands against her chest. "What did I say?"

"Um, I have no idea. Something about choices and history?" She wasn't about to repeat it. It was already burned into her mind and exactly what the goddess Ereshkigal had told her when she accepted the Mark of the Gods, *One path will lead you to the destruction of many. The other to the destruction of one.* She had pushed that far to the back of her mind and written it off as nonsense.

Azalea tried not to show her panic. "Are you a seer or something?"

"Not by choice." Jade laughed and picked up Faraday, who held his chin up for a scratch. Knowing her bad luck, Faraday would decide to live here and abandon Azalea altogether.

"You can't control it?"

"No, it's just a thing that happens sometimes. I'm House of the Winged Bull, divination and all that jazz."

"I've never met anyone from your House. When I arrived last year, I didn't even know what houses were. I thought they were actual physical houses, not these massive groups of families all over the world with different magic types." She laughed awkwardly, trying to ease the tension.

"That's okay." Jade smiled. "I'm pretty sheltered. I'm sure there's a lot for me to learn here as well."

Azalea relaxed a little. "So House of Winged Bulls uses Shadow Magic, yeah? How did the Archmage allow you in here?"

"I'm not really into Shadow Magic or divination" She shrugged. "It's just the odd thing that spurts out of my mouth. I can't wield shadows or cut into the Hollow. I'm pretty useless, but I'm half House of Eagles as well. My parents got me in here last minute, and the House of Eagles programs were all full. I'm here to study Echo Magic; water and air magic are more my style. But between you and me, I don't even want to be a mage. I just wanted to come here to go to art school in London and escape my crazy family." She laughed.

Azalea wasn't sure if it was polite to inquire further. Jade must have picked up on it.

"Oh, it's nothing bad. I just grew up in a House of Eagles commune in backcountry New Zealand. But it's not a cool cult or anything. Super boring, in fact, a bunch of hippies farming and living in peace and harmony, that shit. No partying or orgies; they're more into meditation circles and slow living. I just want to live in the real world for a while, you know?"

"I can relate to that. My mum's a forest guardian, and I've had my share of wanting to escape the countryside." Though a hippie cult sounded kind of nice right about now. Peace, love, and not being cursed and chased by a crazy shadow mage sounded downright pleasant.

"So you have plant magic?"

Azalea rubbed her arm with her snake tattoo. "Yup. But I'm House of Snakes as well."

"That's neat. I heard all about the gallu hunt in London. Were you involved in it? It sounded pretty crazy."

"You don't know the half of it," Azalea said, surprised at the lack of reaction to the House of Snakes thing. "Well, I better go pack. Help yourself to chocolate digestive biscuits on the table. My flatmate... your flatmate, Van, Evangeline, will wake up for lunch soon. Just make yourself at home, and I'll be out of your hair in no time."

Better to get this whole thing over with like ripping off a plaster. Putting it off would only make things worse.

"Come on Faraday. We're moving." New plan—keep it together and stay with Torin for now while finding somewhere else to live. She could do this.

CHAPTER 8

Torin paced his office. He hadn't been able to sit down or focus on anything all afternoon, despite the amount of planning he still needed to do for the following day's relic hunt. Azalea would be turning up soon. He knew for a fact she had nowhere else to go, and there was a blizzard outside, though he wouldn't put it past her to sit in the snow rather than move in with him.

Should he call her to find out if she needed help moving? Check that she hadn't chosen to freeze to death outside? He knew how stubborn she was. He'd even put on proper clothes, trousers and a gray cashmere sweater, in case she turned up. But it was back to tracksuit bottoms and a baggy t-shirt if she didn't show.

A pain shot through his heart. He didn't know whether to be happy, relieved, or pissed off. But he knew she was by the chapel, and she had let another spirit pass through her. Was she doing it purposefully? He wouldn't put it past her.

He peered out the window and saw her marching across the courtyard, brown ponytail swishing behind her. She was dressed in a fitted black coat which must be new; it looked good on her. In her hands were a large suitcase and a sports bag, and Faraday was in tow. Most noticeable was the scowl on her face, understandable with this whole situation. He swallowed, suddenly nervous.

Rather than stand there and watch her struggle up the stairs, he marched out and took the suitcase from her without asking.

"Are you doing that on purpose?" he couldn't help but ask as he hauled the ridiculously heavy bag up the icy stairs.

She glared at him. "What?"

"Letting the ghosts pass through you?" He made the mistake of meeting her gaze. Her steely gray eyes drilled into his, and despite the hatred behind them, he couldn't help but be drawn in. He swallowed and looked away.

A flicker of fear bounced off her. "Fewer ghosts there are, the happier I'll be."

"You shouldn't do that. You don't know what it's doing to you." He tried to sound concerned, but it came out forceful.

"So, you *can* feel it, then?" She smirked as they got to the top of the stairs.

He took in a slow breath. He wasn't going to get mad, but he'd suspected correctly; she had done it to hurt him. "Yes. But that's beside the point. It could kill you. So stop it."

She didn't answer, just walked past him inside. They stood near the doorway dusting off snow before either of them spoke again. Faraday ran off up the stairs to the next level where the living area was. At least he felt at home.

"I guess I'm moving in," Azalea stated. The wave of defeat rolling off her was unmistakable, though it didn't show on her face.

She wouldn't even look at him. His guilt hit him hard. It was the guilt that would drive him. Make him do everything in his power to make this easy for her.

"Azalea, I know this is the last place you want to be, but if we work together, we can break this—" he was going to say *curse,* but that seemed like the wrong way to start this out "—bond, and find out what the gods want from you and these spirits. But we need to play along with the Archmage so we have the time to do this." He swallowed, wishing more than anything that they could go back to the way things were before.

"I am well aware of that fact," she snapped.

"We can also get things done faster if you're living here." His short list of highlights didn't seem to improve her mood. "And you don't have to pay rent. It's covered in my contract."

He didn't mention that he had no plans to spend the fifty thousand dollar reward money from the gallu hunt either. She should be the one to have it. It could pay for her university. Call it what it was—guilt money, but it made him feel better.

"That's good," she said, and they stood in uncomfortable silence. Azalea hadn't even removed her coat or shoes, as if she couldn't resign herself to the fact that she had to stay. As much as he felt guilty about everything, his level of patience had not increased in the slightest.

"Take off your coat and shoes, and I'll show you your room." He grabbed her suitcase again, without asking. If she was going to be mad at him forever, he might as well remain productive as she did so.

He didn't look back as he heaved her suitcase up the awkward spiral stairs, past the living room and kitchen level, and up the next flight of stairs to the small landing on the third level with two bedrooms and a bathroom. Fortunately, he had an en-suite off his room so they wouldn't have to share.

He wheeled her suitcase into the room and found that she had followed him up after all. Once he'd cleared out all his crap and put it into storage in the attic above, he'd found a pleasant room and had set it up with the help of Maiken, who knew a hell of a lot more about design than him or Danni. He was still mad at them for not telling him who Azalea was—who her father was. But he wasn't so mad that he wouldn't ask for design help, and they seemed to think they owed him.

Maiken chose simple white linen for the iron-framed queen bed and set one of his blue Turkish rugs under half the bed. There were little side tables, modern lamps, and some sort of rounded, blue, fashionable chairs that made the room look like a hotel. Things he never would have picked but hoped Azalea would like.

She kept a wide berth from him as she entered the room and didn't let slip any impression that she liked it, but he felt her approval as she breezed past. He hated that fact. It was like cheating, invading her privacy without wanting to.

Worse than that was knowing she could feel his insecurities, see past his false confidence, and know he didn't have it all together as he liked to pretend. The sooner he could block the effects, or at least lessen their effect on each other, the better. Distance certainly did the trick most of the time, but sleeping in rooms next to each other could be a whole other problem.

She dropped her sports bag on the bed and, ignoring him, took out several items and set them on the bedside table: a glass cat that he knew Erik had made her, a fluffy dinosaur toy from her friend Isaac, he wasn't sure why he even knew that, and a pocket watch. A chill shot through him—he knew that watch.

Azalea shot up, her elemer in her hand.

"What the hell was that?" Her eyes were wide with panic.

The blood drained from his face. "What?"

"You just freaked out about something. I felt it." She stood frozen, gripping her elemer.

"It's nothing, an overreaction." He brushed it off.

"It wasn't nothing, Torin. I felt it. If we're going to do this, live together and work out all this bullshit, you can't lie to me anymore."

She was right. It wouldn't work.

"Well then. Spit it out."

He really didn't want to let this conversation go any further. "It was your watch. I've seen it before."

"My dad's watch," she said as if she was thinking aloud.

"I know." His mouth went dry. The last time he saw it, he'd been digging through her father's jacket seconds after he was dead. The watch had slipped out. That's how he knew the man had a daughter. He'd been pleased to discover that at the time. That the girl would feel the same pain he had felt losing a parent. It was safe to say he felt the complete opposite now, but that wasn't going to help anyone.

Azalea's hands flew to her mouth in realization. But to his surprise, she didn't start crying or screaming at him. She just turned away and took a deep breath.

"Look, Azalea. You know how sorry I am. I know you can feel it, so I won't beg and try to win you over. I know it won't change how you feel. But I am sorry this all happened. I'm sorry you don't have a dad because of me, and I will continue apologizing for the rest of my life. But right now, we don't have the luxury of time. We can't wait for a day when this doesn't feel so raw. The reality is we need to work together so we can get out of this situation. I don't know how we can do that if you hate me."

"Just get out." Her voice trembled.

He turned to walk out, but a surprising wave of empathy rolled over him. It was so unexpected his eyes closed, and he basked in the warmth of this new feeling, then spun around to check if it was real.

Of course, none of it showed.

"I'll be in my office if you want to get started. I'm going to get another relic tomorrow if you want to hear about it." He got the words out despite his chest feeling like it was being crushed by guilt.

⊃ ⊃ ⊃ ● (((

For two hours, he sat in his office, debating with himself about whether or not she would come down. Waiting, stewing in his dark thoughts as the anxiety built up. It had since gone dark outside, and the fire threw comforting shadows around the room full of books, the only other source of light was the green lamp on his desk.

He had nearly completed his report for the Archmage on his mission tomorrow to Xi'an, China. A mission that had taken over five years in planning, but he was certain he had the right place. It was a complicated one, but one he was the most excited about. And, if he didn't make it back, the Archmage would be happy to know where to get the relic herself, though good luck to her if she tried.

Faraday came down first and sat in his usual chair by the crackling fire. Twenty minutes later, Torin was wrapping up the report when Azalea trailed down.

He felt her presence before he heard the light footsteps of her slippers on the stone stairs. She wore flowery pajama bottoms that didn't seem at all like something she would pick, a gray hoodie that engulfed her slim frame, and her slippers had floppy dog ears. Her hair hung loose over her shoulders, damp from the shower, and he realized he had never seen her hair down before. *Gods, she was pretty.* He yanked his gaze away and stared at the fire. Where had that thought come from?

"I'm not going to forgive you," she said as she curled into the chair opposite Faraday, tucking her slippered feet under her.

He swallowed, not wanting to move in case it upset the balance of their precarious relationship. "I don't expect you to."

"Good. You're right about not lying to each other. We need to be totally honest. I've learned my lesson, and since we have this weird, feeling-each-others-feelings-thing, there doesn't seem to be much point in trying to hide things," she said.

"Agreed. Look, I know this is strange, Azalea. But we just need to push through."

"And how are we going to do that?"

"We remain civil and keep conversation to my work... *our work*, and I will continue your training as before. Our number one goal must be keeping the Archmage off our backs, and we can quietly work on solutions for your spirit problem and the bond in the background."

She frowned, and the light of the fire highlighted the soft angles of her face. "You make it sound very simple."

"We can make it that simple if we stay focused on what's important," he said as if trying to convince himself that was true, or even possible.

"And what about your father?" She pulled her knees up to her chest. "He wants to kill me."

"I will not hand you over to him if that's what you're worried about."

Her shoulders dropped slightly, and he felt a hint of relief wash over him from her. He did his best to rein in his reaction and try not to show how offended he was that she had thought he might actually do that.

"I wasn't worried." She shrugged.

Bloody liar. He held his tongue. "You're safe here for now. He won't come for you at the Tower. I'll deal with him when I need to." Next time, he'd be prepared, rather than thrown off guard completely while being depleted of magic. Next time, he would ask all the questions he had wanted to ask and be prepared for a fight if that was what it came to.

Azalea nodded, appearing to be in a calm state of denial. "Sounds good to me. The sooner we get this done, the better. You have a deal."

He nodded.

Neither of them made a move to get up to shake on it. It was clear she didn't want to touch him, and he was terrified of touching her. They didn't know what sharing magic had done to either of them, and he hadn't used the hand of death on anyone in years, but he didn't trust his magic right now. He couldn't risk stopping her heart with his bare hands.

He vowed never to use it after he killed Azalea's father, and never, ever, wanted to relive the horrific accidents with his best friend, Kira, and his pet raven, Licorice. A heavy pain in his chest grew with the memory.

"There's one more thing you'll need to do."

She shot him a wary look.

"You'll need to pass your initiate's test so you can become my apprentice."

"This whole thing is ridiculous. I didn't even complete the training. How am I supposed to pass a test?"

"I think you'll be okay. Since you're to be my apprentice in Shadow Magic, the test will be different from your Echo Magic training. It will be a practical test, basically a trial to prove you have enough control to be an apprentice."

"And you think I do?"

"Yes. I think you've more than proven yourself in practical Shadow Magic after taking down the gallu."

"But I had your help."

He didn't want to be reminded of that. Nor of the mind-blowing rush in his veins when her magic entwined with his. "Trust me, you're ready."

"What's the test then, and while you're at it, what is the difference between being an apprentice and an initiate anyway?"

"The Archmage requested your test to be in the field. It will be the first relic hunt you accompany me on." He didn't give her time to protest. "Apprentice is more on-the-job training. Since you'll be training in Shadow Magic, a lot of the things you learned in class won't apply to a test. If you were going to be doing a House of Bee apprenticeship, you would need to complete the extra year of theory and practical initiate work to pass. But Shadow Magic has more practical training, so different rules apply."

"But we're from different houses."

"It doesn't matter. I'm an azurite-level shadow mage, so apparently I'm qualified to teach you." Not that he felt qualified at all. His teaching method so far was basically, don't go as far as the House of Raven's training and you're good.

She sat there with a sour look on her face, but there wasn't much she could argue with here.

"Now, I need to tell you about the relics," he said.

CHAPTER 9

Azalea snuggled her legs up under her bum. Her mind was fighting itself. She wanted to hear about the relics so badly, but she hated that she was cooperating with *him*.

"So, what are these relics?"

"I just need to send this report. At least if something happens to me tomorrow, they'll know where to look," he said with a new lightness in his voice as he finished typing.

"Why, what's tomorrow?"

"I'm going to retrieve the crane relic. I believe it's in an unopened tomb in China," he said as if he was planning to go down the road to buy a new coat, not Indiana Jones himself into a secret tomb.

"Am I going with you?" she asked hopefully.

He shut his computer and moved toward the fire, removed Faraday from his chair, and placed the cat on his lap. Azalea sat across from him, hating her damn curiosity.

"No, not tomorrow. It's too soon." He rubbed the white diamond marking on Faraday's head.

She felt his tension but didn't move, deliberately not letting her shoulders slump to give away her disappointment, though he probably felt it. She didn't really want to go with *him*. But an adventure to a secret tomb on the other side of the world sounded like something she shouldn't pass up.

"So this is illegal what you're doing? You're stealing these relics?"

"Yes. But for a cause I strongly believe in. Protecting these relics is more important than any law."

She watched him stroking Faraday. A little jealous the cat had remained sitting on him. "Why is that?"

"Because if they're out there for anyone to find, they could get into the wrong hands. It would affect the entire world." Torin looked into the fire.

He appeared calm and collected, but she felt how highly strung he was. She couldn't be sure if it was because she was there, or if it was nerves for the mission tomorrow.

"What do the relics do exactly? What do they look like? How many are there? What are you doing with them? Why does the Archmage even want them?" The questions rushed out, and for every one, several more popped into her head.

"I'll let you know everything in time. For now, we'll start with the basics, some of which you may already know from rifling through my notes—" He raised his eyebrows at her then looked down at the cat and stroked his head. "I started researching the relics over eight years ago when I was in prison," he said as if he were an old man retelling stories of his youth, not a twenty-four-year-old mage on a treasure hunt.

She felt a hint of guilt seeping out from him and realized why. He was thinking about the deal he took to do this job for the Archmage instead of staying in prison for murdering her dad. That was the reality of it: He had murdered her father, Samael Blackbourne, head of the House of Snakes, and his punishment was traveling across the world looking for treasure.

She swallowed back her hatred and curled her hands into fists, pressing them into her legs to not show her anger, though he must have been able to feel it burning out of her. She had to suck it up because she needed to hear this.

He frowned and ran a hand along the stubble of his jawline. If he felt her wave of hatred, he ignored it and continued, "It became my obsession. Besides studying and training to pass my mages' exams, I spent every spare minute reading any ancient text I could get my hands on, trying to piece where the relics had traveled through history. But being over ten thousand years old, stories have watered down over time, and the relics passed through so many hands. Some were easier to find traces of than others, depending on the records, and where they ended up. But I followed them down every rabbit hole I found."

Azalea sat silently, metaphorically on the edge of her seat, physically, nonchalantly lounging in the chair. A little half-smile curled at the edge of his lips. He saw right through her, and all she could do was scowl back.

"I won't bore you with the details of my research. All you need to know is there are twelve relics. They are all made of jade and are small enough to fit in the palm of your hand. Each is in the shape of a different animal chosen by a god or goddess to represent their House."

"You mean there were twelve magic Houses before?" She was surprised she hadn't read about that anywhere.

"Yes, thousands of years ago there were twelve, but now there are only eight. The others were lost, though vestigial magic can still pop up from them today." He looked into the fire, the flames sending flickers of shadows and light that softened his features.

There was so much she didn't know, but she didn't want to get too off-track or sound too keen. "So, what are they for?" she couldn't help but ask.

"I was about to tell you." He scowled.

"Sorry." She stuffed her hands into her hoodie pocket. Wishing she hadn't come down in her pajamas. He probably couldn't take her seriously dressed like this.

"The relics are the keys to an ancient gateway built by the gods."

Yes, this was more like it. "Which goes where?" she squeaked out and pursed her lips shut quickly.

Torin frowned. "It is a gateway to the Echo Dimension."

"What? How did I not know that was a thing? Why is there a gate? What would happen if the gate opened? Is there a gate to the Shadow Dimension too?" She unfolded her legs and couldn't help but lean forward. This sounded like a big deal.

"It's not common knowledge and for good reason. If the gate were to open, it would flood the world with Echo Magic so strong it would burn out anyone who tried to use it. We don't know what level of destruction it would bring, but it wouldn't be good. As far as I know, there isn't a gate to the Shadow Dimension. If there is, it's been lost."

"Holy crap. Why would anyone want to do that? Why is there even a gate? Why are there keys?"

Despite all her annoying questions, Torin remained sitting patiently, dressed all properly while she was dressed for bed. It was clear he was fighting his instincts and was on his best behavior to get on her good side.

"It was how some of the gods left this world to go to the Echo Dimension. As for the keys, records suggest they were ceremonial, a way for every House to partake equally in the departure of the gods."

"Okay..." She nodded for him to continue.

"The only reason someone would want to open the gateway to the Echo Dimension is for power. They could control when it happened and be prepared but take the world by surprise."

"That's insane. But why does the Archmage want them? I mean, she seems pretty evil, but I don't take her as someone wanting to control the world."

He took in a deep breath as if choosing his words carefully. "I like to think she is doing it to preserve an important part of our history and to protect the relics."

Azalea held in a snort. "You're in denial, Torin. She stabbed my brain with her fucked up magic; you saw it. You don't know what that felt like. She is not a good person."

"I know what it feels like, and I know exactly what sort of person she is." His voice was controlled, holding back his restrained anger.

Azalea swallowed. For a split second, she felt bad for him. No one deserved that level of violation, not even her enemies.

"I have no choice but to trust her. I had no other option but to do this. I'm aware she isn't the best person to have them, and I'm taking measures to make sure the collection is never fully assembled. I will hide the last relic so they can never be used together."

His eyes drilled into her, and a chill ran down her back. He had about as much choice in the matter as she did.

"Wouldn't the relics be safer if they remained lost?"

"Yes. They would be. But you may have noticed, we humans have a funny flaw where power and knowledge hold more importance than logic or the safety of the world." He leaned his head against the back of his chair, and she noticed how tired he looked.

She pulled her legs back up to her chest and rested her chin on her knees. "I'm not sure I want to find these relics now."

"Sorry to say it, but you don't have a choice. We're in it together now, and the sooner we get it done, the better." He offered a weak smile.

"And you actually think you can find them all? How many do you have?"

"I've got six of them: the owl, the dragon, the snake, the fox, the bee, and the phoenix."

She had to admit that was impressive, and she was starting to feel bad about all her drama that had distracted him over the past months while he was working on this seemingly impossible task. "Did you find them all?"

"No, I didn't get them all. The Archmage already had the owl in her collection. The snake, I believe was liberated from your Uncle Fabian before I arrived. That's the reason they banned him from here. He tried to blow up the place to get it back. Obviously unsuccessfully." He exhaled out his nose and shook his head slowly.

Somehow Azalea hated the Archmage even more.

"I got the dragon relic in Iraq last year, that was my encounter with the bashmu. I hadn't quite expected the mythical guardian creatures to still be alive, but that's something we need to watch out for. I got the bee relic from Topkapi Palace in Istanbul, no guardian creatures there. I just liberated it from the display. And the fox relic, I found in a temple in Kyoto, Japan."

She forgot to blink, her eyes fixed on Torin, wondering what might be next. "No mythical creature there?"

"Actually there was. A kitsune, but it was rather friendly and let me take the relic. It must have known I had no ill intentions for it." He waved it off as if it were nothing.

This was nuts. There were mythical guardian creatures for real? She took a stabilizing breath. "And you know where the others are?"

He shook his head. "Not all of them. Tomorrow I'm going for the crane in China. Then we are just missing the fish, the winged bull, the eagle, the white deer, and the raven. I've got a rough idea of where two are, but I still need to narrow it down, and fast."

"Bloody hell." She slumped back in her chair and let her legs hang down. His mission really was crazy. She almost felt sorry for him, but then she remembered her dad and why he was dead. A fresh wave of hatred crashed over her. It was always at the forefront of her thoughts now, simmering there, wanting to burst out and rage at him, blame him. But it was getting hard to keep it up.

"That's enough for tonight." He tipped Faraday off him and stood up, his face unreadable, yet she felt his nervousness and the pressure looming over him.

She swallowed down her hatred. "Thank you for telling me. At least I understand now." She wanted to know if he needed help tomorrow, wanted details on the crane relic, and where he was going in China. She wanted to know how dangerous it would be—but she couldn't bring herself to ask. She shouldn't even care. He was the one who said she couldn't come; she wasn't ready.

He nodded and went back to sit at his desk. "I'll be gone in the morning. I don't know when I'll be back." He glanced up but quickly looked away before meeting her eye. It was clear he was hurting, too.

She didn't know what to feel anymore. She was torn between the Torin she knew, who was working on an impossible task for all the right reasons, and the dark side of him she knew so little about.

"Okay." She rose from the chair and tapped her leg to signal Faraday to come. As she started up the stairs, she shoved her hands into her hoodie pocket. She couldn't bring herself to wish Torin luck or say goodbye.

CHAPTER 10

The next morning, Azalea awoke to find Torin gone, her first chance to relax in peace. She made a smoothie, but it wasn't nearly as good as Van's. It was eerie being in Torin's place alone. It didn't feel like home, and she missed Van and their cozy living room nook and her cave-like room. Admittedly, her new room was much nicer. The bed was like sleeping on a cloud, and the room actually had a window with a view. She could see all the way down the north side of Mint Street and across the Barracks. Plus, there was a fireplace, an actual fireplace, in her bedroom!

She'd seen the room before. It had been a dump, and he'd put a lot of effort into doing it up—for her. It was a nice gesture.

She wandered down to Torin's office after washing up from her smoothie and discovered thousands of files with sticky notes on top.

It seemed he had left her every one of his research files from the last eight years. She wanted to find out as much as she could, but the sheer amount of paper was daunting. Why did he even print these off?

She flicked a random file open. For what was essentially a treasure hunt across the world, it came with a lot of paperwork.

At least the fieldwork aspects would be fun. But she was determined to help and spent two hours flicking through the files. The more she read, the more she could see why he was under pressure from the Archmage if it took this much work to find each relic.

She flicked to a page about the crane relic. Torin's scribbled sticky notes suggested it was beneath the Mausoleum of the First Emperor of China: Qin Shi Huang. It sounded interesting, a tomb that housed a secret replica palace and underground necropolis. The next page suggested a mage was buried within the tomb over two thousand years ago and he might be the one with the relic.

Azalea pored over the notes. Her heart dropped when she got to a sticky note that read *guardian creature?* The page was about an aoyin. A four-horned bovine creature that ate humans.

Why was she not there with him? It sounded amazing! Maybe not the flesh-eating cow part but the lost tomb part.

He probably had it all under control, but she couldn't help the nervousness bubbling under her skin. She shook out her shoulders. She was just being silly. Of course, he would make it back. Without her morning training, she couldn't shake off the feelings of restlessness and pent-up energy. What she needed was to get out of here for a bit.

Torin could be gone for days. Maybe she could find out something about soul bonds and how to break them. Brainwave: the library at Blackbourne Manor! RoRo and her mum had invited her to come anytime; she might as well make the most of it. She uncovered her phone from a pile of folders as Faraday sat on another stack with his paws dangling over, watching her intently.

Azalea: *Hey mum. If the offer still stands, can I come for a visit to Uncle Fabian's today? I need to get away from here for a bit.*

Mum: *Of course love. We've been worried about you. I'll send Fabian to get you now. Xoxo*

Her mum was doing a good job of keeping her distance and letting Azalea deal with things on her own, just like she asked. The space to breathe away from home was just what she needed, and her mum was safest away from Azalea.

Azalea: *Great. Cya soon.*

Too easy. Getting out of the Tower might be just what she needed to pull out of her slump. She darted upstairs and changed out of her old jeans and into her slightly nicer black jeans—she was going to a posh house, after all. She pulled on a warm maroon sweater, retied her ponytail, and kissed Faraday on the head as he settled onto her bed.

"You hold down the fort, Faraday. I won't be long."

He opened one eye ever so slightly, then tucked his head under his paw as if to say, *bugger off already.*

She dashed back downstairs and put her warmest puffy winter coat on. It had been freezing the last few days, and although it had stopped snowing, she wasn't sure what the weather was like at the manor. She didn't even know where in the country it was.

Her phone vibrated in her pocket.

Fabian: *Meet me in the tunnel in five.*

Azalea: *cu then.*

She was nervous about seeing him. He hadn't exactly been happy when they parted the other day. But she was proud of him for not losing it and trying to murder Torin or drag her away. He had to know this was her only option, and she had to deal with it herself.

Stepping beyond the door, her breath misted in the late morning air. The brightness overwhelmed her other senses; she blinked and took in the sounds of traffic beyond the tower and gaggles of voices within. She missed having the handy secret entrance down to the underground complex across from her old flat. Here she had to contend with the spirits and tourists and weather every time she wanted to go out.

But right now, more important than avoiding spirits and tourists was avoiding the residents of the Tower of London: House of Owls mages, her ex-classmates, and anyone who now looked at her differently knowing she was from the House of Snakes.

She dashed past the chapel, this time pulling in her aura like a magnet to her body and avoiding all people that could be spirits. She went around the White Tower and refused to enter the Complex via the Barracks, instead opting to go into the hospital and down to the tunnel that way.

Fortunately, there were no guards on the way down she had to explain herself to. With a flushed face and feeling slightly out of breath, she made it to the tunnel before Fabian.

The drip, drip of water in the dank tunnel sent goosebumps up her arms. This place was creepy, and in the near silence, she realized she could no longer feel Torin's presence. She savored her own emotions, enjoying the fact that his weren't in there confusing her.

A silent rip appeared in the air, spreading down like fraying fabric as an arc formed and a head popped out.

"Hello, Uncle Fabian," she said with intentional politeness.

"Azalea, good to see you're still alive. Come on." He didn't make any move to leave the shadowy door. Fair enough, he had been escorted off the Tower of London grounds by guards and wasn't exactly welcome here being banned and all. At least she knew why now.

She froze in front of the Hollow, and her mouth went dry. The smell of ice and snow brought back sickening memories from the week before.

How she had cut into the Hollow then was beyond her. She barely had the strength to cut into it now, or maybe it was more of a mental barrier. Either way, it terrified her. Her uncle must have noticed.

"It's okay, just get back on the horse." He flicked his head toward the shadowy tear.

She nodded and took his hand to step into the void, an endless space of nothingness dimly lit by the light of the mysteriously spongy floor. The door sealed behind her, and she was left in the eerie blue glow of the Hollow, the sub-dimension between earth and the Shadow Dimension. She stepped closer to Fabian, unable to shake the feeling that maybe there were gallu in here. Unlikely, but not impossible.

She held her breath until Fabian cut another slit in the darkness and opened a doorway to a winter wonderland. She stepped out, blinded by the beauty of the landscape. It wasn't snowing, but the air was still and peaceful, the ground was a blanket of whiteness, and somewhere near, the trickle of water under ice bubbled and gurgled away.

They were somewhere in England still, but she knew this place was hidden with serious wards and protections, so it was hard for outsiders to find it.

"Welcome to Blackbourne Manor," Fabian said as his hand swept to the enormous iron gates with brick pillars. "Well, not actually the manor, but the gate. We have to walk up, sorry.

Colin Yates, the groundskeeper, dropped me off on his way out."

"A walk sounds perfect," she said, already feeling revived by being out in nature again. She hadn't realized how stifling it had been in the Tower until she remembered the vast freedom of the countryside, and for the first time, she felt homesick for her mum's cottage.

Fabian did something with his elemer and pressed his hand to the gate, which swung open, and they walked in.

They strolled up the gravel driveway, but it felt like walking on eggshells for Azalea, just waiting for Fabian to bring up one of the many issues he had with her.

"What was up with that spirit going through you?" Fabian asked.

Great, he picked that one to start with. It wasn't something she wanted to get into with him. She still had no idea why the gods had chosen her to be a gateway for the spirits. She especially didn't want him to know that Torin was bound to her, and their bond and combined power were the reason it was possible in the first place.

"Um, not sure about that yet. But I'm working on it. I've learned how to draw my magic in so they can't sense me most of the time. But I was too weak the other day."

"That isn't normal." He frowned but left it at that.

It was about a ten-minute walk to the house, but Azalea didn't mind at all. Fabian didn't bring up Torin or the gallu or anything. They just walked in uncomfortable silence, which she could deal with.

Azalea's eyes grew wide as the house drew closer. It was like a fairytale country house with white stone walls and a collection of Rapunzel towers around the edges.

What was even more amazing was the tent city sprawled across the lawn.

"What is this? A music festival?"

"I wish. No, these are the families I've taken in from the House of Snakes from all over the world. All of them are running from the House of Ravens and Korbyn's murderous rampage to wipe us out. Hopefully, it won't be for too long, this—" He waved his hand at the mini village. "Along with this bloody money pit of a house is draining me dry."

"There's a lot more of them than I would have thought. How many are hiding here? Do you have a plan for taking down the Ravens?" she asked with sudden confidence.

"I don't know, at least twenty families and plenty of other people. No plans for retaliation at this stage, but we're working on it." He offered no more information, and frankly, she wasn't ready to know. Today she was just looking for information on the soul bond. One problem at a time.

"So, this is where my father lived?"

"Yes, you came here once, you know?"

She shook her head as they made their way closer to the house. She didn't remember that; all she knew was her father had kept her existence a secret from the whole magical community. He hadn't been married to her mother, and she was surprised to hear she had been allowed here. A shiver ran through her, and she wrapped her arms around herself.

They got to the front door that had some dead-looking trees in plain pots on either side.

"Can you take me to RoRo?" she asked, hoping she would be outside in a garden somewhere. It was highly likely. After that, she would find the library.

"Certainly."

He was probably ready to get her out of his hair. He walked them past the front door and around the back, between some buildings and past some horse-less stables. They came to a glass greenhouse with an arched roof and solid metal frames.

He opened the door. "She'll be in there somewhere. Good luck."

Fabian marched off, and Azalea eventually found RoRo right at the back between the maze of ceiling-high cucumber vines.

"What a lovely surprise!" RoRo exclaimed when she spotted her granddaughter.

Azalea couldn't help but smile and throw herself into RoRo's arms. "It's nice to see you, RoRo."

"And it's good to see you up and about," RoRo said, but Azalea didn't miss the hints of concern in her voice. She knew her mum and RoRo hadn't wanted to leave her at the Tower, but they also knew what she had to do.

Azalea stepped back from RoRo and smiled, running her hand over the leaves, and they curled toward her.

"Here. Help me with this." RoRo handed her a pair of secateurs. "You can help me prune back these cucumbers. I gave them a little too much of the good stuff, and they're out of control."

It wasn't like RoRo to lose control of her magic to this extent. She must be more frazzled than she let on.

Azalea worked quickly as RoRo chatted about all the people living out on the lawn. How they had each escaped the House of Ravens' attacks and were working together now to take them down.

Azalea wiped the sweat from her forehead with her sleeve, thinking about her bond with Torin.

RoRo must have asked a question because she was staring at Azalea as if waiting for a response. "Sorry. I must have drifted off there. What did you say?"

RoRo knew a lot about magic, so she might know something about soul bonds. It was worth a shot.

"Oh, nothing important, dear, just rambling about cucumbers. What's on your mind?"

She took the opportunity. "So, I was reading a history book from the library. It's very old and dated, but they talk about soul bonds as if I should know what they were. Have you heard of them?" She glanced at RoRo. Hoping it wasn't too much of a weird question.

RoRo looked up thoughtfully. "Oh yes, I haven't heard about them in some time. Few people will talk about that these days, a very unpopular subject. The soul bonds were a spell reserved for the nobility, but they're all ashamed of it now."

"Why's that? Wasn't it a good thing?" She chewed on her lip as she stared at a vine, forgetting what she was doing.

"Depends who you talk to about it. It was a sort of test. Back before Victorian times, marriages were about making good matches, connecting the right families to increase their wealth. Though at some point a trend started where some rebellious wealthy people wanted to marry for love." RoRo put a hand on her hip.

Azalea rubbed her neck. *Marriages?* "Well, that sounds nice."

"It wasn't. It became a test of a couple's devotion to one another. To prove if it really was love, some demanded a soul bond. Then, if one person was just after their fortune, or seeking to climb in society, they would show their true colors and back out. Usually, it was the richer person who demanded the test." RoRo went back to her pruning as she talked.

"So they did it to tell if their fiancée was a gold digger?"

"Spot on, my dear. But it was also a truly romantic way to prove true devotion to one another. Many did it willingly as it brought significant advantages to a genuine love match."

This couldn't be the same thing Azalea and Torin had.

"What sort of advantages? And what about the ones faking it? Did they do the test?" Azalea stopped pretending to trim things and focused on RoRo.

"The advantage was unimaginable power for the couple. And as for the ones faking it, usually, if it was false love or deceit for money, the money grabber of the party would back out without doing the test. It was used more of a threat than in actual practice." RoRo snipped a large vine that dropped to the floor with a thud.

Azalea swallowed. "But what happened if they went through with it and failed?"

"Why both parties would die, of course." RoRo turned to her.

Azalea stood there blinking. *They died?* "Bloody hell. That's a bit of a risk."

This didn't make sense. She and Torin weren't in love, and technically she had been dead when he supposedly bound her back to her body and accidentally to him. Maybe he was wrong about this?

"Yes. But to many, it was worth it. When it was true love, the couple would perform the ritual to bind their spirits, pledging themselves to one another; body, soul, and magic. It's very romantic. But hasn't been allowed for over a century so it's hard to know as there are no recent accounts."

This couldn't be what they had. Could it? Torin had tried to call back her spirit to her body, but somehow they got tangled.

It was a necromancy spell he did, not one for love. Her pulse raced, but she tried not to panic.

"I read the bond must be sealed. How is that done? I didn't find it in the book?" Her voice was higher than she intended.

"By the marriage, or likely the consummation of the marriage. If the couple survived the soul-bonding ritual, they were then married soon after, and the bond became sealed." RoRo nodded at her cucumber plant in approval.

At least they hadn't done that, and there wasn't any chance of either of those things happening. Her cheeks heated at the thought of it.

"That doesn't sound so bad." Azalea bit her lip.

"No, it's quite lovely, actually. Once bonded, the couple had heightened powers. It was said they could sense each other and in rare occasions draw on one another's powers. Because of this, some couples were the most powerful mages on earth. Many people didn't like that."

Azalea chopped at a cucumber vine a little too intensely. "Is that why it's illegal? Did they become dangerous?"

"Society deemed them dangerous and said they caused a lot of trouble. It seemed they preferred the deceitful marriages rather than the bonding ritual."

"What did the ritual actually involve?" Maybe she could rule it out. He would be happy about that, but they would be back to the drawing board on whatever their bond was.

"Oh, it was very dangerous. One member of the couple had to die, and the other would call back the spirit to bind it. In order for it to work, the souls had to be compatible in spirit and magic. They had to be very sure indeed."

Azalea held back a gasp as she felt her face drain of blood. She gripped the secateurs but stopped pruning.

"Are you alright, dear? You're white as a ghost." RoRo held the back of her hand to Azalea's forehead.

She couldn't speak and couldn't help it as the secateurs dropped to the bench. She stepped back to lean on the table behind her.

"Azalea, you're worrying me. What is it? Here sit down." RoRo pulled a crate over, and Azalea sank onto it.

"Nothing, RoRo." Her voice was shaking. She had to pull it together.

"What's happened, Petal? You can tell me."

"I'm still recovering my magic. I'm fine," she lied. Everything did not feel fine.

A strange look spread across RoRo's face. "So, how are things being apprenticed to Mage Dumont? Are you getting on yet?"

Azalea kept her face as neutral as possible. She took in a sharp breath and squared her shoulders. "He's away, but we're getting on with things. Mostly I'm avoiding him."

"I talked to your friends Danni and Maiken about him at great length when we waited in the hospital, and they told me his story. His father is the one to blame, you know. He was just a boy." RoRo went back to her pruning but watched Azalea out of the corner of her eye.

Azalea didn't trust herself to talk. She knew all this, but she wasn't ready to face it or think about it.

"Has he been kind to you?" RoRo asked.

Azalea forced herself to stand up and focused hard on a plant in front of her. "Yes. He's been fine, but it's clear he wants to get rid of me. The feeling is mutual."

"You need to forgive him if you have any hope of getting through this apprenticeship and surviving the Archmage. You will need each other."

Azalea stopped and slowly turned toward RoRo.

"Hello?" Her mum's voice sounded from somewhere behind the cucumber jungle.

"Over here!" RoRo called out.

Azalea didn't ask anything further, rather glad of the interruption.

Her mum found them and wrapped her in a big hug. "I'm so glad you made it, love."

The tattoo on her chest pulsed with a gentle warmth. She wasn't sure if it meant Torin was in trouble, or if it was because he was far away. Either way, she had a strong urge to get back to the Tower.

CHAPTER 11

Torin glanced at his watch. It was 6 am on the dot as he shut the door behind him and breathed in the damp chill of morning air. After crossing the Tower green, he exited through the side gate to the walkway along the Thames. He walked quickly to help wake up. He'd spent longer than he wanted to last night explaining his mission and the relics to Azalea. But it was time well spent.

He nearly forgot she hated him the way she'd leaned in, hanging on his every word. Maybe she would make a good apprentice after all. She was interested at least, asking all the right questions, and almost seemed willing to put aside their pasts, or remain in denial, to get on with the job. They could make a good team. He smiled to himself. It had actually been fun sharing his progress with her, and he realized how lonely his job really was.

Torin twisted his neck from side to side and limbered up his shoulders that were aching with the weight of his backpack, heavy with small tanks of oxygen for his trip. He wasn't taking any chances.

His magic hadn't fully returned, but he had little choice in embarking on this mission now. He would find the crane relic alone. He'd thought about bringing Azalea along. She seemed keen, but this one was too dangerous.

The main danger was the potential presence of thousands of trapped spirits. Plus possible booby traps: not limited to cascading sand traps, automatic crossbows, underground rivers of mercury with noxious fumes, a sealed chamber, presumably with no breathable air, oh, and a mythical guardian creature, an aoyin, protecting the tomb of the ancient mage who was buried with the relic. He hoped all of that was mythology. At least he didn't have to worry about her and getting the relic.

He rounded the corner to the old St. Dunstan in the East church. The same place he'd brought Azalea back from the dead. A shudder ran through him as he walked up the brick steps through the overgrown doorway. The place gave him the creeps now, but it was the best spot to cut into the Hollow to save magic.

He sliced into the dark void and stepped inside. The world fell away, and he was left with a rare peacefulness, something hard to find in the city.

He cut out of the Hollow. His boots crunched on dead leaves as he stepped out into Jingshan Park in Beijing, China. He fought his way out of the shrubbery he'd appeared behind, hoping they wouldn't rip his warm, puffy jacket. A couple walked by, giving him disapproving looks.

So far, so good. His breath misted around him, and he remembered his pollution mask in his pocket. It was afternoon, around 1 pm, but the air held a thick yellow tinge that made the city hazy and overcast, even in the daylight. He slipped on the mask, welcoming his warm breath rather than the polluted winter air.

He picked up his pace through the park. The footpaths were freshly brushed of snow, and large piles sat around the edges of the gardens. He checked behind him, half expecting a squad of mages to jump out and arrest him for illegal International Hollow use. But Jingshan Park was one of their weak points. Because of ancient magic here and in the Forbidden City, it was hard to accurately monitor magic or Hollow use in the area.

The best plan was to get out of there fast. He headed for Tiananmen Square and the National Museum of China. He wanted to wait until nighttime before he went to get the relic, so he might as well do some research first. There was always the off chance the relic was in the museum, but not listed in their archives. The museum was known for housing many of the country's cultural relics, so if it was going to be anywhere, it would be here.

Beijing was just as cold as London, and Torin dug his hands deep into his pockets and crossed the road directly in front of the Gate of Divine Prowess, the north gate of the Forbidden City. Its red stone walls and turned-up golden roof eves blurred into the murky air. Tourists poured out of the giant open doors to cross the wide paved road that split the frozen moat. Though he had been there many times, the ancient palace never ceased to amaze him; it held even more secrets than the Tower of London.

His feet were growing numb, even with his wool socks. He upped his pace and followed the wall of the moat until he headed south.

He spent the rest of the day at the museum. But, as suspected, there was no sign of the relic, though he had learned a little about the mythology of the aoyin. Nothing useful, only that it was when they separated from their souls, they turned into violent creatures that had a taste for human flesh.

With a few hours to kill until he needed to leave for Xi'an, he avoided the tourist food streets, instead opting for a Hutong alleyway with a hole-in-the-wall courtyard restaurant where he could sit down. He sank into a cushioned wood chair and inhaled the fragrant steam of the hot green tea. Eventually, warmth came back into his limbs from his last walk, and he ordered the touristy option of the Peking duck, because, when in Rome. The succulent duck with crispy skin and delicate pancakes was just what he needed to revive himself and psych himself up for what was up next.

He didn't want to leave the steamy warmth of the little restaurant, but he forced himself out and went behind a large van to cut into the Hollow.

Once in the Hollow, he focused hard on the coordinates he set himself, recalling every image he had ever seen of the area, every map, and every drawing, even the ones from ancient scrolls.

Then he cut his way out into the darkness of night, a cloak of shadows already conjured around him to conceal his presence. He stepped out. It was cold enough to snow, but the air was pleasantly clear, though it smelled similar to the Hollow, like snow was over the horizon somewhere. He had come out in a paved area, clean and crisp, with neat lines and orderly barriers—a ticketing area.

Getting his bearings sorted, Torin walked toward the dark shadow of the pyramid-shaped hill that blended into the night in front of him. He needed to go up the pyramid to get directly above the chamber he aimed to enter underground. Going into the Hollow to find a new place straight down was tricky, but the closer he was to it, the better.

He avoided the stationed guards, who all looked very bored, and ascended the stairs halfway up the mausoleum. It was surreal to actually be here, especially after all the research on the man who created this gargantuan monument. The bloke must have been nuts to create a replica palace below ground, as well as the Terracotta Army buried less than two kilometers away. More than six thousand life-sized warriors, officials, and even horses had been created out of terracotta to accompany the Emperor in his afterlife.

Though it was the darker side of it Torin was worried about; the Emperor might have created replica warriors to avoid sacrificing an army, but there were plenty of sacrifices in the tomb Torin now stood on: concubines without sons, hundreds of craftsmen who worked on the secret necropolis, and mages—all trapped inside, forced to accompany their emperor into his next life.

He pushed a finger into his palm, checking this was real, imagining their ghosts cooped up for over two thousand years, all losing their marbles together. He betted the Emperor wasn't among them—not when he was this well prepared to die. Ironic, since he would have been the one to pass on, leaving the rest as spirits with their unfinished business in his city of the dead.

Torin jumped over the wall of the stairs, landed a short way into the rows of bare-limbed fruit trees, and checked the coordinates on his phone to make sure this was the spot he selected. The tomb of the mage should be directly below.

A stick cracked, and Torin darted around. A chill crawled up his back, but he brushed it aside.

He took off his bag and pulled out the mask attached to the oxygen tanks inside and slipped it over his head, so it hung at his chin; it was the type climbers used going to high altitudes. Hopefully, it was enough to keep him going in the stale tomb—he shook off a shudder, not wanting to think about it. Good thing he wasn't claustrophobic.

Shaking out his hands, he stretched his neck from side to side; it was time to do this.

He sliced back into the Hollow, then once inside thought of the coordinates and the location that had been directly below him and made another cut. His blade hit something solid.

The rough texture of rammed earth told him this wasn't a good spot unless he wanted to face plant into a wall. Closing the cut, he walked a few meters within the Hollow. Though it wasn't necessary to physically move within the Hollow, it helped with mentally moving a few meters to make a new cut. This time, the blade sliced into empty space.

The smell of stale, earthy air seeped into the Hollow as Torin cut a larger doorway. It was warmer than outside and warmer than the Hollow. He slipped the mask over his mouth and nose to be safe and turned on his head torch before poking his head out of the Hollow. No way he was stepping out of here until he knew he wasn't walking right into a trap or a cavern about to collapse.

As his beam of light hit the walls of a room, he did a mental risk assessment. He could feel the edges of the Hollow wanting to close, quavering beneath his hold. With his hand pressing the silky shadows back, he craned his head out to run the light around further. It was a simple room with four stone walls and various boxes and chests scattered around. It was no bigger than a double car garage, but against the farthest wall was a large, raised box; that had to be the tomb of the mage. It shimmered light back like it was metal.

He reached into his pocket and tossed out a golf ball, purposefully chosen to set off any motion detector traps. It bounced loudly on what sounded like a wooden floor.

Nothing happened, so he used a shadow rope to collect the ball and bring it back to him.

Taking in a deep breath of oxygen, Torin raised a solid shield of shadows around him. He wasn't taking any chances as he stepped out of his safety net of the Hollow. The doorway closed, and he was left in the muffled silence. It was the quietest place he had ever been. A shiver ran down his spine, there were spirits here, but without Azalea's presence, he wasn't sure if he would actually see them. He preferred not to. They were harmless after all, but being trapped down here all this time wouldn't have left them in a good state.

His ears pulsed in the silence. He took a step forward, and all hell broke loose. A deafening THUD, THUD, THUD hit his shield. He ducked and raised his arm over his head.

His barrier held strong. He waited a good thirty seconds after the thudding stopped, his heart beating in his ears like a drum, then let down his guard. The sound of clattering wood echoed around the chamber.

Reaching down, he picked up a short arrow with a broad metal tip, then glanced to either side. Embedded in the walls were rows of wooden crossbows, all with bronze trigger mechanisms. Deadly and aimed at whoever walked across the room. Shields to maximum. He stepped forward, noting how odd it was to have a wooden floor. It looked like someone had built a wooden deck over the entire room, almost like a bedroom for the entombed person at the other end.

A creak in the floor sang out, and a hammering of bolts hit his shields once more, absorbing into the shadows before clattering to the floor as Torin released them. That was one booby trap he could deal with. It didn't look like there were any sand traps or rivers of poisonous mercury to contend with. The sand traps were probably in the hallways outside, so he'd avoided that.

He made his way across the floor that sang out with each step as arrows pelted him but were ineffective against his shield.

Ornate chests surrounded the bronze tomb. If this was the Emperor's tomb, they would be filled with treasures of jade and gold, but he was hoping this was the mage's tomb. As a trusted adviser of the Emperor, the mage held a position of high authority during Emperor Qin Shi Huang's reign; it was said he voluntarily sacrificed himself to attend the Emperor in death.

Whether or not that was true didn't matter. What mattered was that the crane relic was somewhere in here, and Torin's bet was in the giant bronze coffin.

The silence shifted, and Torin was instantly on edge as if the pressure in the chamber had changed. He tucked himself into the corner between the tomb and a chest, cloaking himself in shadows. He switched off his head torch.

It was pitch black, pure darkness, and it was unnerving.

A slit of blue light appeared, floating in the middle of the room. Then footsteps.

"Torin. I know you're in here. Don't attack. I come in peace."

Torin's heart plummeted to his feet. His father had found him.

Torin remained hidden as the light grew into a larger slit, then into a doorway, and a man stepped out.

"Interesting place he's got here." His father waved his torch beam around. Torin remained frozen in the corner, back to the scared boy he used to be, while trying to focus his brain on useful thoughts.

"Come now, Torin. I saw you outside getting the exact spot on the ground, and I know you must be in here."

The question was, how did he know he was even coming here? The only people who knew about this mission were Aza-

lea, his boss Brandon, and the Archmage. He was sure Azalea
hadn't been talking to his father, so that left the other two.

If he didn't come out, he would remain the same scared
little boy for the rest of his life. He needed to face his father,
and more than that, he needed the answers he'd been waiting
years for. He'd been too distracted after the gallu hunt to
think of anything close to coherent. But now his mind was
clear, and this was his chance.

"What are you doing here, Father?" Torin turned on his
head torch and stepped from behind the tomb. His father
stood in the center of the room. He also wore an oxygen
mask, his gray beard peeking out below it. He squinted into
Torin's torch light, his solid black eyes avoiding the strong
beam as they changed back to light blue.

"Torin my boy. Lovely to see you," he said as if he'd conveniently forgotten about turning Torin into a murderer, ad-
mitting he killed Torin's mum, disowning him, and vowing
to kill his student.

Torin glared at the man. "Can't say the same. Answer the
question."

"Straight to the point, very well. I heard about your mission and thought you might need some assistance. I mean no
ill will." He held up his hands in defense and squinted into
Torin's light as if this were just a game. "This is a chance of a
lifetime, as I am sure you understand yourself. I should love
to be part of history in the making."

"Like hell you would. You've come to take the relic. Who
told you I would be here? Why do you want the relics?" Torin
carefully kept the tomb at his back and his eyes on his father's
hands. One held a torch. One held his elemer, the same elemer

he had stolen from a shaman years ago—it was powerful, and he wouldn't underestimate his father or his motives.

Korbyn stood with his shoulders back and his chin held high. "I swear I'm not here to take the relic. I just want to help you."

"Why?" Torin narrowed his eyes.

"Isn't it obvious?"

Nothing was obvious with his father. There was always a game in play beneath the surface. "Spit it out. I don't have time for this."

"I told you the other night. I want the girl. The offer still stands. Hand her over to me, and all will be forgiven. I will reinstate you as my heir, and you can come back to the House of Ravens. You have proven yourself more than worthy, boy. You are a powerful shadow mage. You have earned a place at my side."

Torin wanted more than anything to smash a hole in the ancient wall and throw the stone blocks right at his father's smug head. He could smash it into the ground like a watermelon and think nothing of it. But he was smarter than that. It was also what his father would expect from a son of his, and he refused to be that person.

Be smart, Torin. He still needed the relic before he could get out, and he couldn't afford to be provoked and lose his shot. Plus, there was no scenario where he would actually hand over Azalea. His father could never know about their bond.

"I am considering your offer. But right now I have things to do," Torin said bluntly, hiding any emotion in his voice.

"And I am here to help. What's the next step? Have you found anything yet?" Korbyn walked toward him. Torin kept him in his torch beam as he strode up and rapped his knuckles on the metal exterior of the tomb.

Torin frowned. He could use the extra help to get into the tomb. He could use his father, then get the answers he had waited so long for, about his mother's death. He just hated the idea of working with him.

Hmm. Time to change tactics. His father's last memories of him were from when Torin was sixteen, for all his father knew he was still that weak, terrified boy. He could use that.

"Fine. Help me get the lid off the tomb." Torin tested the lid with a shove, but it didn't budge.

He ordered his father around to the other side and directed him to use fine sheets of shadows in the same way as Torin to edge into the seals of the tomb and press the lid up from the inside. It wasn't difficult magic, but it took concentration and coordination to do it at the precise same time to raise the lid at the correct angle.

Sweat beaded on Torin's head, but he ignored it. Refusing to show weakness or admit he hadn't fully recovered from nearly burning out the week before.

Slow and steady, they raised the lid, and a hiss of air whooshed out, breaking the seal. Torin was glad of his oxygen mask, he wasn't so keen on breathing in stale tomb air, or ancient mold spores. He thought of the 'curse' on Tutankhamun's tomb when Howard Carter opened it. It hadn't been a real curse, but still, you never knew with ancient tombs.

Together, they set the lid down in the center of the room.

Torin didn't take his eyes off his dad. "Don't get any ideas."

"Wouldn't dream of it, son."

Son, how many times had Torin wished his father would say that word? Now he hated it, fake and spiteful coming from his father's mouth.

Torin shone his light into the inner tomb. The outer wall was bronze, but there was also an inner wall of stone, and then a coffin at the center. There wasn't extra space for trinkets or treasures. The relic had to be in the smaller coffin.

"Stay where you are," Torin warned as he raised a shadow shield around himself and wasted no time in vaulting into the tomb.

CHAPTER 12

At least the lid was too heavy for one person to shut him in.

"You don't need to worry about me. I have no intention of harming you. We're on the same side," his father said from outside the bronze coffin.

Torin ignored his lies and set about examining the corpse. His hands were shaking, but he had to block his father out and get on with the job. He would deal with him after. First, he took a few photos, in case he upset anything, and for historical records—not that anyone would see or ever know he had been there.

The mummified skeleton was drowning in a sea of partly broken-down robes. Flashes of gold and blue caught his eyes, but he was only interested in one thing: What was in the dead mage's grasp?

Torin's hands shook even more as he pried open the skeletal fingers and plucked out a small statue.

"Shit," he mumbled to himself. It wasn't the crane. He rolled the rough terracotta artifact over in his hand, and his breath hitched. It was a bull with four horns and fangs—an aoyin.

A ghostly howl reverberated across the room.

"What did you do, boy?" his father hissed.

"Not the relic. Shit." He moved to put it back, but his father grabbed it from his hands.

"Too late to put it back now. We might as well keep it. It'll be worth a fortune." His father grinned at the ornament.

Torin jumped from the tomb. "Put it back! It's cursed."

His father frowned as the relic crumbled in his fingers.

"Shields up," his father ordered in his Head of the House of Ravens voice.

Torin didn't need to be told what to do. He raised his shadow shield instantly and moved to the other side of the room. His father did the same.

Taking off his headlamp, Torin set it on the tomb, so it faced the other half of the room with them hidden behind the light in the shadows.

A shape grew up from the wooden floor where the crumbled relic lay, building on itself from nothing until it rose into a massive, larger-than-life terracotta bull.

"It's an aoyin," Torin told his father as he moved to the other side of the tomb, on the opposite side of the creature.

"A what?" his father whispered and crouched down beside him.

Torin peered over the top. He hadn't actually believed an aoyin would be down here after all this time. "A guardian creature."

"That's very obvious. How do we vanquish it?" His father shot him a disapproving look.

"It can be destroyed with light or Echo Magic. I'm not exactly sure how." Torin reached into his bag, pulled out a flare, and set it off, throwing it right under the creature.

The demon ox charged at the wall to escape the blinding flare, its hooves crashing through the wooden boards, sending ancient dust and earth into a thick haze. Its stone hide had turned to white straw, and its eyes were blood red and wild. Blood stained the four horns in two rows that topped its broad head, and in the place of the usual flat teeth of an ox were hooked fangs that protruded like daggers from its foaming mouth.

"That didn't help. You need to think through your actions, boy," his father scolded him like he was still a student.

Torin held his tongue, anger simmering in his blood as he ducked down. He had half a mind to push his father in front of it; that would sort out one of his problems.

The aoyin hadn't spotted them yet. It snorted showers of dust and thrashed around, kicking the walls with its back legs.

"How's your Echo Magic these days?" his father asked.

Normally he could use a bit of Echo Magic in a pinch, but he was still weak, and anything he did wouldn't stand up to this creature. Now was not the time to lie about it. "Not strong," Torin answered honestly.

"It's lucky I'm here then, isn't it? You tie it down with shadow ropes, and I'll take care of the rest," his father whispered as chunks of rock ricocheted across the room.

"What are you going to do?" Torin pulled his father down as he stood up. "We need a plan."

Korbyn stared him down. "This is the plan. Just do as I say."

His father stepped out, and Torin had no choice but to follow. He was a kid all over again, terrified of letting his father down and following instructions blindly.

"Now," his father ordered.

Torin threw out solid shadow ropes and looped them onto the horns of the ox. His arms were nearly yanked out of their sockets with the pressure, but he focused and threw wide strips of shadows over the thrashing back of the ox and pulled in more magic, forcing them down on the beast.

His father crept around the back of the aoyin until he was near its side. Part of Torin wanted the beast to kick his father in the head, to end this once and for all. But the other part of him was soft, and he didn't want to admit it, but he needed his father's help to get this over with.

His father's stolen elemer blade glowed faint white, and as he inched closer to the ox, the light in the blade built in intensity like the full moon concentrated into one strip of brightness.

Why hadn't Torin thought of that? He couldn't wield fire or any other sort of light magic well, but the power of the moon was always behind the House of Ravens.

The light caught the demonic ox's eye, and it yanked at the shadow ropes. It was strapped to the floor but struggled hard, slowly backing toward his father. Torin dug his feet into the solid floor, holding the ropes tight.

"If you have a plan for that, bloody well do it soon," Torin said through gritted teeth. This wouldn't hold forever.

The beast's eyes flashed wildly as it thrashed forward and smashed its head against the tomb, denting the bronze facade only slightly.

"Hold it still, boy," his father yelled. His elemer was suddenly as long as a sword and glowing even brighter white. He lunged forward and pierced it into the side of the beast, hopefully where its heart would be if it had one.

A harrowing scream ripped from the creature's foaming mouth. But it didn't go down. Torin fought to maintain control of the ropes. He reined them in tighter, forcing the beast closer to the ground.

"Again," he shouted to his father.

His father lunged, and a spray of black blood spurted out, showering them both in the foul-smelling liquid of something long past dead. Torin tried not to gag; even through the mask, he could smell it.

His father looked smug as the ox closed its eyes, and its head lolled to the side.

"That wasn't much of a fight." Korbyn wiped his sword elemer across the straw-like fur of the creature's back.

Torin didn't relax the shadow ropes, but the creature jolted its head up and flicked the shadow back to Torin like a wave and knocked him backward.

Torin skidded across the splintered wooden planks and jumped up. *Shit.*

The ox snorted through its nose like a cartoon bull and knocked Korbyn off his feet. The monster seized his father's leg in its predatory jaws.

The aoyin's fangs embedded deep in his father's leg, and it shook its head as if trying to rip off the limb. Torin blasted it with deadly pointed shadows, and it let his father go. It raged around the room as the shadows that pierced its hide dissolved into nothing.

Torin was calm and clearheaded, a benefit of not caring about the victim. If it was Danni, Maiken, or Azalea, he would be panicking.

He ignored his father's groaning, walked up to the tomb, and vaulted inside, grabbing the head torch as he dropped in. If this thing was really guarding the relic, it should be more interested in protecting it than eating some bloke that tasted like poisoned leather, he could only assume.

Wasting no time, he rifled through the pockets of the corpse. "Sorry, mate," he said to the long-dead mage. Hoping he had left the tomb and wasn't haunting it. But a chill at the back of his neck indicated differently. He looked around but saw nothing.

Torin moved aside a scrap of gold cloth sitting on top of two rib bones to reveal the glint of a smooth green stone crane, so light it was almost white.

It was cold to the touch; he pressed it against his cheek to be sure. Yes, this was it. It wasn't a replica or a trick. The chill of the jadeite was real, and he felt the pulse of ancient magic from within the stone.

The coffin shook with the reverberations of the demon ox hitting the bronze barrier.

Torin stood up. Maybe his father had bled out.

"Is this what you want?" he said to the ox as it rammed into the coffin again, its lips foaming red with blood, its eyes storming as they locked with Torin's.

A prickling raised all the hairs on the back of his neck, it seemed to understand him. It stopped and tilted its head to the side. Limping around the corner, it eyed the metal as if looking for weaknesses or the right angle.

His father pulled himself up on the side of the tomb. His eyes were black and determined. He raised his elemer sword, and a flash of light streaked through the air, and the ox's head rolled across the floor. Torin raised his arm but was doused in a waterfall of black blood. The head bounced into the darkness as its enormous frame fell to the floor with a solid thud.

His father stood up and brushed himself off, despite being unable to remove any of the foul-smelling blood he was drenched in.

"May I see it?" his father asked as he limped over, using the bright sword as a cane.

The head rolled to a stop at the base of the tomb. How the hell was this man still standing?

"No, you may not." Torin swung his legs onto the edge of the tomb, pulled out a black velvet bag from his pocket, and dropped the relic in it before pulling the drawstring and tucking it into his inner pocket.

"You're welcome," his father said.

"I didn't thank you."

"No, you were going to bloody well leave me there to be gored to death and eaten by a fucking carnivorous bovine."

"I had no such intention, Father. I knew it would be distracted if I tried to take the relic. It worked. Don't pretend you didn't come here for the same reason I did. I'm not giving it to you."

"I told you I wasn't here for the relic. I won't take it from you." What was this fake act? Had he lost that much blood? Torin glanced at his father's leg, swiveled around, and quickly dropped from the tomb, careful not to have his back exposed too long.

"Show me your leg."

His father didn't protest. He lowered himself to the floor and let Torin examine him.

His calf was mangled pretty badly, but it hadn't seemed to hit any major arteries or anything.

"What is it you want then, Father?" Torin asked as he took the first aid kit and a spare t-shirt from his bag and began bandaging the leg enough to get him out of there.

"I already told you." A slip of anger crept into his voice. "I want you to come back home. I want the girl to settle the oath I swore. I don't go back on my word."

"I won't give you Azalea. She doesn't deserve this. I'm sorry, Father, but I will be turning down your offer." It felt good to say it.

He leaned back and smirked as if Torin had agreed to everything. "I am not concerned. You'll come to see the right path soon enough. I will give you a week to decide, then I will find you. After that, I will come for her myself. This is the olive branch I am offering. Don't be so hasty in throwing it back at me."

Torin pulled the t-shirt tight on his father's leg and knotted it. A strong urge to murder him rose again. It would be so easy to do it. All he had to do was put his hand on his father's chest. He was sitting right there. *Just do it. Do it, and she will be safe.*

But he couldn't. This man had murdered his mother, had basically bragged about it as soon as he knew Torin was leaving. Still, it wasn't right, and it wasn't a solution.

"Why did you kill Mum?" Torin looked his father right in the eye.

A heavy silence filled the air.

His father's eyes narrowed. "I didn't mean it when I said that to you. I was angry and was trying to hurt you. You poisoned me for the gods' sakes and ran off to join the enemy. What did you expect me to do?"

Torin didn't believe a word of it. The memory of the morning when he left was burned into his thoughts, especially his father's words. *I killed your mother... She made me weak. She was going to betray me... That's what happens to people who get in my way, and you'll pay for this, boy.*

He would never forget those words and never trust his father again.

Torin would play along. "How did she die then?"

"You know how. That *Snake* murdered her, the Viper. You did the family proud; you avenged her death the right way. You have no reason to be ashamed."

"There is no evidence to say he did it. They say he was helping her escape you. They say it was suicide, but I know it was you."

His father let out a laugh that echoed around the cavern. "This was always a problem with you, boy. So naïve. They are our enemies. Of course, they want you to think that."

"You're not denying it."

His eyes, which were all black from using magic, drilled into Torin's soul. His fingers curled into fists, and Torin saw the man he remembered waiting to burst out and show his true colors. "I don't have to explain myself to you."

He confirmed at that moment what he had known all along—that it was all true. His father had killed his mother, had lied about it, and made Torin kill an innocent man because of it.

Now, all he had to do was get the man to admit it when someone else was there to hear. He needed evidence.

The air in the chamber grew thick, putrid with the smell of that thing's blood that crept beneath his mask.

Torin stood up as a shudder coursed through him and took a controlled breath to allow himself to walk away from something he really wanted to do.

"I won't be coming back, Father, and I won't let you take her."

He cut straight into the Hollow. His ears were pounding with blood and the wild magic burning inside his head. He had the relic, and he was going home. He stepped inside, but as the doorway closed, his father got in the last word.

"You want to know what happened to Kira, don't you? Give me the girl, and I'll tell you. Meet me at the—"

The doorway sealed.

CHAPTER 13

It was freezing out, and the night air poured into Torin's office as Azalea propped open the door with her foot. Van and Jade shuffled past her with the last of the boxes, most of which were plants she practiced her Echo Magic on. It was probably a little late in the evening to be moving, but at least they were getting the job done.

"Thank you so much for your help. Just dump them down there, it's fine," Azalea said as Van and Jade left the boxes against the wall by the stairs.

Jade's gaze scanned the walls of Torin's book-lined office that took up the whole first floor of the Devereux Tower. "This place looks amazing. I'm glad you moved somewhere so nice."

"Hmmm," Azalea replied, not wanting to explain her situation, though Jade probably already knew from Van. "How about a cuppa? I've got some pizza I can heat too." Azalea hoped they would want to stay. She could work out where to put all the plants later.

Jade peeled off her full-length black, winter jacket. Underneath she wore a black wool dress and black tights. Van brought an opposite splash of color with bright pink yoga tights and an oversized white sweater.

"My fingers are freezing. Tea and pizza sound perfect," Jade said with a wide smile.

"Yes, please, I'm famished." Van nodded in agreement. She had never been to Torin's place, and Azalea knew how interested she was in seeing inside the tower, so wouldn't deprive her of a tour while Torin was away.

Azalea led them upstairs to the second floor, made up of the spacious living room with red Turkish rugs and numerous wood coffee tables, and the large kitchen with black stone bench tops that curved around the shape of the tower wall. A large circular dining table was at the center of the polished wooden floor. While the kettle boiled, they dashed upstairs to the third floor to the bedrooms.

Van stopped in the doorway, nearly dropping her box of plants. "Oh my gods, you have a fireplace. This place is amazing! Can I get expelled?" Her hand flew to her mouth. "I didn't mean that."

Azalea laughed along with Van and Jade while she showed them the rest of the place.

After the tour, they sat in the comfy red and green gingham chairs by the fire and dug into the pizza Azalea had reheated. Fabian had been kind enough to buy it for her on their way home that afternoon.

They chatted for an hour, and Azalea decided she liked Jade; it was good that Van had a nice flatmate to replace her.

"I told you before that I wanted to come to London to study art, but I didn't realize quite how expensive it would be here. I'm going to have to up my commission if I'm going to stick around," Jade said, looking slightly worried.

"What sort of work do you do?" Azalea asked.

"Digital art mostly to sell online. My specialty is chibi characters and animals. I'm doing especially well with stickers right now, but I love doing custom commissions."

"Ooo, that sounds so cool! I'd love to buy some stickers!" Van said.

Jade showed them her gigs online. Her artwork was amazing, especially the animals.

As if on cue, Faraday pranced up and put his chin on Jade's knee. "Looks like someone wants to be a model for me, aye Faraday?" Jade rubbed his head.

"That's just what he needs, more attention," Azalea joked, but she could already imagine Faraday as a cute chibi sticker.

"That's awesome you can work online. I'm trying to do that too. I fix up and customize pocket watches to sell, but I am sucking at keeping up with it. I don't get many orders, and I'm way behind with my online uni work, so I wonder if I should just take a break and stick to the boring data entry job."

"No, don't do that! Your watches are so lovely. People need them!" Van said. Azalea wasn't sure about that, but it was nice to have support.

Azalea showed them two watches she had been working on. She'd already fixed up the mechanisms. They were both smaller than average, and she'd added hand-painted backgrounds of luminescent stars, which she rather liked herself. Watches were fun, but they didn't pay the bills. Her part-time data entry kept her expenses under control. Fortunately, the money from the gallu hunt had already come through and was split evenly between her and her classmates. Livia got Elam's share. Azalea had paid back Fabian for the rent he covered for her first few months, but other than that, she wasn't planning to spend hers. Torin insisted she didn't need to pay rent, but she put aside the gallu money in case he changed his mind. She didn't want to owe him.

Van gifted Azalea a housewarming fruitcake, and they dug into that while Van went into far too much detail about a boil she had lanced at the hospital the previous day.

"As much as I love hearing about boils, I'm not sure I can handle much more medical talk with my fruitcake," Jade mumbled through a full mouth.

Van giggled. "Sorry. I get carried away sometimes! So, can you really tell the future, Jade?" She sat with perfect posture as she reached for her tea.

"Sort of. Sometimes I get visions or say random stuff about the future when I don't plan it. But divination is more like finding answers to questions, not necessarily *seeing* the future."

"How do you know the answers?" Azalea tilted her head.

Jade shrugged. "I kind of just see symbols or random images of things. I can't always interpret what it means, but sometimes it helps. The person I'm reading will often have more of an idea than me. I'm not very good at it. Haven't put in the practice. I can show you if you want."

Van's eyes went wide. "Yes! Do Azalea first."

"Okay, thanks. It could be useful." Azalea gave a weak smile and nodded; she'd take any help she could get. Her nerves jittered wondering what Jade might uncover.

"Come on then." Jade flitted onto the rug by the fire and patted the space in front of her for Azalea to do the same.

Azalea joined Jade on the floor and rested her hands on Jade's outstretched palms. Van sat behind her with her chin perched on her hands, grinning wildly.

"Just breathe like normal and focus on whatever question you want answered. You don't have to tell me," Jade said softly.

Azalea's hands grew sweaty, but she let her shoulders relax seeing Jade close her eyes with a small smile on her lips. Letting her eyelids shut, Azalea took in a deep, peaceful breath.

They sat in silence for several minutes. *How can I find the answers about the soul bond and the spirits?*

She cracked open her eye. Jade's brow furrowed with tiny beads of sweat.

Jade pulled her hands away and gasped.

"What is it? Are you okay?" Azalea rested her hand on Jade's knee.

Jade took in a shaky breath. "Sorry." She gave a weak smile. "I'm not very good at this. I didn't really see much, just lots of shadows, which isn't unusual. But then this book appeared. It was dripping blood, and the way it popped up scared me. Then I was in the Great Desert of Dreams, and I snapped out. Sorry, that was silly of me to freak out."

A book? Oh dear. Azalea swallowed. "I'll get you some water. What did the book look like?" She got up and dashed to the kitchen.

"The book was black. It had blank pages, and then there was the blood. Sorry, that was not helpful." Jade leaned against the sofa.

Azalea bit the inside of her cheek as she stood at the sink. Just great, the Shadow Atlas was once again the unwanted potential solution to her problems. She didn't want to have to put her trust in that vile book that kept screwing her over. She wasn't even sure what its motivations were. Was it just an evil book for the sake of it? Unfortunately, it seemed to know a lot.

She took the water over to Jade and perched on the edge of the gingham armchair. "And what about the desert? What does that mean?" Azalea remembered the desert clearly from when she got her tattoos and met the goddesses, Ereshkigal and Ninhursag. She wasn't in a hurry to go back there.

"Maybe it's a sign you will find the answers you seek in your dreams. Have you had any unusual dreams lately? Maybe something prophetic?"

"No. I don't think my dreams are overly prophetic." Azalea shook her head, though there had been that one about the raven.

"I'm sure the answers will come to you. It will make sense in time, but sorry, I wasn't more helpful."

Azalea tried not to frown, seeing how Jade's hands were shaking. That bloody book was upstairs. She wondered if it could have tapped into Jade's magic somehow. Creepy thing. "Thanks for doing this. How about some more tea?"

Van was already pouring Jade a cup when a bang came from downstairs. Azalea twisted around. She sensed Torin the moment he walked in.

"It's just Torin," Azalea reassured Jade, who was looking a little pale, well paler than she normally was. Maybe Van had updated her new flatmate on the many scandals at the Tower after all.

Solid footsteps came up the stairs, and Torin trudged in. Azalea nearly dropped her teacup at the sight of him.

"Holy shit. What happened to you?" Azalea put down the tea. He was covered in dried blood, so dark it was almost black. His jacket was torn, and white feathers leaked out of his sleeve and trailed down the stairs behind him. He dropped his backpack at the top of the stairs and stripped off his jacket. His fitted gray t-shirt was stained with blood and clinging to him, showing every contour of his toned chest. Wow, his gym routine was really working. She realized she was staring, and her cheeks heated.

"I'm fine. It's not my blood," he said as he noticed Van and Jade staring. "Evangeline, nice to see you."

Van stood up and walked straight up to him. "Are you sure isn't your blood? Do you want me to check you over?" Van went straight into healer mode, looking him up and down, her elemer out, ready to scan him. Jade remained by the fire with wide eyes, probably unsure of what to make of the situation.

"I'm fine. Just in need of a hot shower." He let Van scan him without even arguing.

"You're all good. Jade and I will get out of your hair so you can shower." Clearly, Van wanted to know more but restrained herself.

Jade nodded and shuffled over behind Van.

"Sorry, I didn't introduce you. Torin, this is Jade, Van's new flatmate. Jade, this is Mage Torin Dumont."

Torin waved a blood-covered hand, sending a stench of death across the room. "Nice to meet you. I'm sure you don't want to shake my hand."

"Nice to meet you too," Jade said, quickly covering her mouth.

Azalea did the same. "What the hell is that smell?"

"You don't want to know," Torin said. "Excuse me, ladies." He grabbed his bag and headed upstairs.

"We'll show ourselves out. Just tell me later what happened! I bet it's a good story," Van whispered.

Jade, still looking a little woozy, said goodbye and followed Van downstairs.

Azalea sprinted up the narrow, spiral staircase, hoping to catch Torin before he got in the shower. He was just about to shut the door.

"What the hell happened? Are you actually okay?"

"Wouldn't you know if I wasn't?" A smile parted his lips.

She felt a burst of warmth radiate from him. He was in a rare, good mood.

"I take it you got the relic then." She couldn't help but smile as she was drawn into his energy.

He patted the pocket of his bag. "I certainly did."

"And you cut up a herd of elephants to get to it? How is there so much blood on you? Did you walk through the Tower grounds like that?"

"I used a shadow cloak to get back here and it was just the one elephant." He smirked.

Azalea's eyes grew wide. "Was there *actually* an aoyin?"

"Did you *actually* read my notes?"

"Of course I did."

"Let's just say it's a day for miracles, then." He shut the door with a grin.

She let out a breath. So he had the relic. That was one thing going their way. Next problem, should she tell him about the Shadow Atlas? Maybe wait till after he'd had dinner to tackle that one...

☽ ☽ ☽ ● ☾ ☾ ☾

After a mediocre dinner of sausages and fake mashed potatoes, Azalea rinsed the dishes, and Torin made a pot of tea. It was almost too easy to slip back into old ways. She gritted her teeth and remembered what Torin had done, willing her anger back to the forefront of her mind.

He frowned into the teapot and brought the tray over to the sitting area by the fire. Azalea took her time stacking the dishes in the dishwasher before reluctantly dragging her feet over to where he sat. She didn't want to tell him about the Shadow Atlas but knew she needed to. It was their best shot at finding the relics, and she had a feeling it knew about their bond. Hopefully, he would tell her about the relic hunt first, so she could put off the unpleasant task.

She folded her legs under her as she sank into the old chair. Torin poured a cup of tea and handed it to her. His eyes had dark rings under them, but at least he wasn't covered in blood anymore.

"So, my father turned up," Torin said as she took a sip of tea and did her best not to spit it out like they did in movies.

"Oh." A shiver trickled down her spine.

"He offered me the same thing. Turn you over to him, and he'll accept me back as if nothing ever happened." His expression gave away nothing and his emotions were all mixed up.

Azalea's pulse pounded in her ears, instantly imagining scenarios where he turned her over. "And are you going to do that?" Her fingers dug into the arms of the chair.

"I won't turn you over to him. I told you that." He sat up straight, taken aback as if appalled she would even suggest it. She felt his anguish roll through her and shelved her fears for the moment.

She swallowed hard and pulled her knees up to her chest. "I'm sorry. I didn't mean to suggest that. I'm just scared."

"I know you don't trust me right now, but I won't let him come anywhere near you. This is the safest place you can be," he spoke forcefully like he really meant it. His sincerity washed over her, and for a moment, she felt like no one could touch her.

"So, what did you say to him?" She set her tea on the stand beside her to keep from spilling it.

He leaned back in his chair. "I asked him for the truth."

"About?"

"My mother. I wanted to know if it was true... if he killed her." He ran his hand over his head.

A flicker of his pain sparked across the room and into her. Her breath caught in her lungs. This was news to her. Torin's father had blamed her own father for the death of his wife. But Fabian had said that wasn't true, and she wanted to believe it. But she never suspected Korbyn Dumont would have murdered his own wife. If he had, it made sense, and gave Torin a legitimate reason not to return to the House of Ravens, which selfishly worked in Azalea's favor. She could trust him, knowing he wasn't on his father's side.

"And did he do it?" she asked.

Torin nodded and looked into the fire. "Yes. He didn't say it outright like he did last time, but he might as well have. I know him, and for a split second, I saw it written across his face. He did it, and I will get proof." He shook his head slowly, and she felt his pain deep in her chest.

They sat in silence. She had no idea what to say. Azalea wondered if she should find some whiskey.

"I'm sorry," she said.

Torin closed his eyes and rubbed his temples. "I suppose I already knew, really. I just didn't want to believe it was true. It doesn't matter now, going back wouldn't be the right move, even if..." He stopped himself.

"Even if what?" She studied his face. A spark of hope jolted off him, and she tilted her head curiously.

"It's probably nothing. More lies, I suspect."

Now she needed to know. "Just spit it out."

"It was something he said; that he would tell me what happened to my friend Kira."

"What do you think happened to her?"

"There was an incident when I left. I wasn't sure if she survived. But his comment made it sound like she might be alive. Either that, or he was just baiting me. Baiting me, most likely. But if Kira was alive, someone would have heard something. Danni would have told me... unless she was undercover working for my father, or a prisoner... or she did die..." He spoke with fast breaths, his brow wrinkled in concern.

"What was the incident?" Azalea refused to give in to sympathy blindly.

Torin looked into his tea as a cascade of guilt surged into Azalea, a common emotion with him. But this was different. It was entwined with deep-seated regret. It had been his fault.

"What did you do to her?" Azalea whispered, wondering if she actually wanted to hear. Learning more about his dark past wasn't exactly going to help their partnership.

"It was an accident. I'd only used the hand of death on a person once before, in self-defense. It was an accident," he repeated.

"The hand of death. So it is real?" Azalea tried to recall what it actually was. She'd read about it, and the guy in the book was a hero from some myth.

"It's real. I've only used it three times, and I'll never use it again."

That would explain why he was so tense whenever they touched. He was probably scared he would kill her, though his hatred of sharing magic was probably a big part of that as well.

"Did you use it on my father?" A chill shot through her with the realization.

He nodded. "It is fast and peaceful." His voice wavered as a solid wall of misery and remorse slammed into her. It ripped at her heart, forcing her to feel his torture.

She didn't want to hear this or feel this. She didn't want to know the details and to have the image of her father in her mind and how he died. She wanted to leave that slate blank.

Her throat grew tight and she knew she needed to leave the room. She couldn't face telling him about the Shadow Atlas. After this conversation, it felt like she would be betraying her father's trust. She could consult the Atlas alone tonight.

"I've got to go," she said abruptly, tears welling at the corners of her eyes.

"I understand." Torin stood up and gave her the courtesy of looking away while she silently crumbled. She swallowed back the tears and rushed toward the stairs.

CHAPTER 14

A hum of unfamiliar magic crept around Torin, and he
threw back the blanket, too hot with the fire still going.
He must have imagined the magic, or perhaps it was in his
dream. He glanced at his phone. 4 am. He swung his legs out
of bed to go get some water.

The hairs on the back of his neck raised as he passed Azalea's
door. He stopped. There it was again, a wave of magic. His
blood raced as he strained his senses. Another wave.

Torin flung open the door to her room. "What the hell are
you doing?"

"Nothing." She sat bolt upright, guilt rolling off her.

He scanned the room. "I could sense the magic through the
wall, Azalea. It woke me up," he snapped.

"I was going to show you, eventually. I promise," she said with
an apologetic look. She was wearing a thin black spaghetti strand
top and pajama bottoms; her cat sleeping beside her was a tightly
rolled black ball. She took a breath and pulled something out
from under the quilt.

"You might as well look at it then." She twisted her mouth
nervously.

He took a step closer. It was a small black book with a snake
emblem on the front, she flicked it open to the first page.

Torin took in a sharp breath, feeling as winded as when he fought the aoyin.

"*The Shadow Atlas*. What the fuck." He stared at it and moved around to get a better look but didn't reach out for it. Her father's pocket watch rested next to her and she turned the page to a map.

"This book is what my father has been searching for for years. It's one reason he hates the House of Snakes. He thinks they stole it from him." His heart was racing as he spoke. He was sure people had died in his father's hunt for this book.

"It was my dad's, but I don't know where he got it. I found it before I came here. My mum kept it hidden from me. She thinks it's dangerous," Azalea said.

This idiot girl had no idea the value of this book or the danger. "Your mother is right." Torin held out his elemer and waved a stream of shadows over the book, testing it. The book absorbed the shadows instantly, and he stepped back.

"It feeds on Shadow Magic," he mumbled to himself and began pacing the room.

"And it likes this watch. That, and blood." The watch sat on her knee, and she held up her palm with a fresh cut across it.

"Blood? You fed it your blood?" Torin didn't even try to hide his shock. Azalea tensed. He could feel hints of her fear, but she placed her hands calmly on her lap.

He took deep breaths to remain in control of his anger. He didn't want her to be afraid of him. He knew what it was like to live in fear. "Do you know what this is?"

"I don't know. But it can help us; that's what I've been trying to work out. I wanted to show it to you. I just didn't know how." She nibbled at her lip.

The risk of having a dark object like this in his house was extremely high. Who knew what magic it had or what it was capable of? He had to determine if it had control of her. "Is it sentient?"

"Maybe?" she mumbled.

"This is a black grimoire. It could be from the Shadow Dimension. I don't want to alarm you, or actually, maybe I should." His voice grew louder. "This book you seem so attached to could be anything. It could have a demon inside. Did you even think about that?"

He regained his composure, taking in a slow breath. "Why didn't you show me this sooner?"

Azalea swallowed. She was probably considering the possibility she had been conversing with a demon this whole time. Her face paled.

"I was scared you would react like this, and it told me not to tell anyone about it." She wrung her hands in her lap.

He ran a hand across his head. If he wanted to stay alive in the foreseeable future, he was going to have to watch her like a hawk.

If this book had some influence over her, that would explain a lot. Why she thought she could bring her dad back from the dead and how she accidentally let the gallu into this world.

She inched back on the bed, leaning against the iron frame, and now looking appropriately frightened. "Could it really be a demon?"

Torin continued to pace. He needed to keep moving to think. "Maybe. Or it could be spelled to deliver fixed responses, or someone could be at the other end with a paired book. It could be anything. How does it communicate?"

"Mostly through maps. It shows me places but never gives clear information. Sometimes it writes back, but a lot of the time it talks in riddles. It enjoys insulting me. Here, I can show you some riddles."

She moved, and Torin darted toward her, ready to throw her down on the bed if she touched that bloody book again.

She raised her hands. "Calm down. I'm just getting my phone." She reached for her phone on the bedside table. But he felt the fear rolling off her. This wasn't what he wanted.

Torin clenched his fists. Azalea was going to be the death of him for sure.

He didn't know what that book was capable of, and he didn't want to look at it anymore. "Cover that thing up."

"What I was going to show you was the riddle it just gave me, along with the map of an island."

"For what?" He stopped. Her fear changed to excitement and hope. The burst of feelings was so sharp they almost took over his anger.

"I asked it where the relics are." Her eyes locked on his with confidence.

He took in a sharp breath through his nose. "You what?"

"I know it sounds crazy, but it just knows things. I think it knows where the relics are. I'm trying to help."

"Let me get this straight. You told a book that is probably filled with dark magic about our extremely secret mission?"

"No. I didn't tell it. I just asked it where the relics are."

Torin rubbed his fingers on his temples. Why couldn't life just be easy? Why couldn't he just get a decent night's sleep without adding some crazy new thing to his insane list of problems?

"What did it say?" he asked, doing his best not to reach over and strangle her.

"Here. I took a photo." She shuffled over on the bed and pulled Faraday toward her, presumably to make a barrier between them so Torin could sit on the other side. He reluctantly lowered himself, suddenly aware of her closeness as she passed him her phone. It was a photo of the open book with blood-red calligraphy across its page.

An island of birds that time has forgotten,
A deceptive creature, misleadingly rotten,
Where two cliffs part, you'll find a road,
Marked above by stones in code.
A cave beneath a long white cloud,
The Taniwha waits, strong and proud.
Its eye sees through deceit and lies.
Are you worthy of its prize?
Ancient spells and magic bind,
Undone by one who's strong of mind.
Free this creature from the key.
The fish in stone will set it free.

"It's a riddle," Azalea said.

"No shit." He read it another two times. The fish in stone was definitely referring to the fish relic, one he already had an idea of where it was, and this only confirmed it.

She leaned forward. "Do you know what it means?"

"I have an idea." Blast her being right. It certainly knew things, but that didn't mean it wasn't a demon or something.

"You going to tell me?"

"Were you going to tell me about this book?"

"Actually, I was. I wanted to tonight, but after all that talk about your dad and Kira, I chickened out. Then I thought I'd try to find something useful before I showed you. I'm sorry I hid it from you, but I don't want to lose it. Please don't take it from me."

He felt her fear like a storm cloud sparking between them and remembered how upset she had been before they went to bed, yet she was still trying to help.

"I won't take it, but we need to work out what it is. This is dangerous, Azalea. You need to understand that if we use it, there could be consequences."

She nodded. "I understand that."

"And I need to know I can trust you."

"You can trust me. I want to help." Her inviting gray eyes met his, and he was drawn into the depths of her sincerity and her drive to want to help.

He nodded. "Good."

"Okay. So what about the riddle?"

Shuffling back on the bed, he leaned against the iron headboard, so he wasn't just perched on the edge. His body felt heavy with the need for sleep, but this was more important. "Did it show you a map?"

"Yes. Here." She leaned closer and swiped the photo across. It was an island, and now he knew exactly where it was. This confirmed all his research.

"So?" she asked after he stared at it long enough to collect his thoughts.

"It's about the fish relic. It's on an island off the coast of New Zealand."

"How do you know that?"

"These two lines: *A deceptive creature, misleadingly rotten,* and *The Taniwha waits, strong and proud* show the guardian creature is a taniwha, which is from Maori mythology. *A cave beneath a long white cloud,* Aotearoa, the Maori word for New

Zealand, it means land of the long white cloud. I'd already narrowed down my search to New Zealand. This confirms it, but I wasn't sure where. *An island of birds that time has forgotten* narrows it down to several islands on my list. I'd have to check, but there were a few islands recorded that are bird sanctuaries. We need to see which island on the map matches up, but I have an idea which one it is."

Azalea was beaming. "So it was right?"

"Don't look so smug. We don't know where this information is coming from or who else knows about it. This could be how my father found me for all we know. And if he's looking for the relics, we need to get them quickly."

"Oh. Did he say he's looking for them?"

"No. But I'm sure he is. Let's talk about this tomorrow. I need sleep." Torin rubbed his hands over his face.

"Um, there was one more thing."

Torin fought back the urge to groan. Instead, he shut his eyes and leaned his head against the cold iron of the bed. "What," he said sharply.

"Sooo, I kind of asked it about our soul bond as well."

Torin's eyes shot open. His teeth ground together, and he did his best not to reach out and strangle Azalea right then and there.

Clearly, she sensed that and shuffled to the very edge of the bed, not so subtly.

"Sorry." He didn't actually want her to fear him. "What did it say?"

Azalea passed him her phone once more.

Your answer lies in desert sands.
A plane beyond your mortal lands.
He who dreams and conquers night.

Knows where to take your sacred plight.

Sweet dreams, mageling...

"The answer is in our dreams," Torin whispered to himself. The riddle was clearly referring to Zakar, the god of dreams and patron of the House of Ravens. He glanced at it again. "It calls you mageling?"

A blush spread across her cheeks. "Sometimes when it's in a good mood, it does. But you might be right about the dreams."

He was surprised she was being so helpful after the talk they'd had before bed. Perhaps she was turning over a new leaf.

"Why do you say that?" He removed any anger from his voice.

"It's something Jade said. She's from the House of Winged Bulls, and she did a reading on me earlier. She saw a book in her vision and freaked out, which I assumed was the Shadow Atlas, which, by the way, is why I was asking it. But she also saw the Great Desert of Dreams. That's what you mean, right? That's where I went when I got my mark of the gods."

She looked down at her toned arm and ran her finger across the watercolor snake tattoo that wound around her forearm and over the smooth skin of her shoulder. It had grown since he'd last seen it, and it was beautiful.

He pulled his gaze away from her and looked at the cat—still sleeping. If Jade saw those things in a vision, it could have been the book manipulating her magic in order to get to Azalea. "Yes. The Great Desert of Dreams is a realm of the subconscious and where you would have met the goddesses from your Houses."

"When I take that elixir potion when I pass my test to become an apprentice, could I go back there and find this god Zakar?"

"In theory, yes. But I don't want you to take the elixir, it's too dangerous for you to do that right now with your spirit problem and all. I have a much easier way. I have dream magic, remember?"

"You do?"

"I'm from the House of Ravens. It's our signature magic. How could you not know that?"

She shot him a thorny look. "Well, sorry if I'm half asleep and don't know everything about magic. I've only ever seen you use the same sort of Shadow Magic that I have, with shadows."

"I've used sleep magic on you before if you would recall." He stared right back.

She backed down, her eyes falling where the book lay under the covers. "So you can use your dream magic to take us to the Desert of Dreams?"

"I will take myself there and find out."

"No way. I want to come too. I'm in this as much as you are. Can't you take me with you?"

He didn't need the added worry of her in his dreams as well. "I could, but it's easier if I go alone."

"Why?"

"*Why?* Because I'm your teacher and apprentice master, I don't need to tell you why. You should just do as you're told."

She glared at him.

He sighed and stood up. "Go to sleep. We're both over-tired. We can talk about this tomorrow."

"You're not going to go to the Desert of Dreams now, are you?" She looked up at him with pleading eyes. He felt how much she didn't want to miss out.

He shook his head. "No. It takes a great deal of magic, and I know when to admit I need rest. Unlike some people."

"Just don't go without me."

"I won't." He softened his voice. He didn't need her panicking all night. "Put that book somewhere safe for now. I'll lock it up somewhere tomorrow." He stood up and stopped at the door. "Goodnight, Azalea."

"Night, Torin." A smile parted her lips.

He smiled back with a strong awareness of his racing heartbeat as he shut the door.

CHAPTER 15

Fabian was already half pissed. He took another sip of his pint and stared at the dark paneled wall in the corner of the booth he had commandeered for the past week. This was the fourth night in a row he sat in this lousy pub in the arse-end of the world, hoping Kat Emerson would show up. He felt, and probably looked, like a loser who had been stood up every night.

The pub was in Cornwall, in a small seaside town of no consequence, and had some sort of generic name like the Pig and Whistle, or Goat and Cock, or whatever two words the long-dead pub bloke had thrown together. But he knew she would show up. She used to come here once a week. But he didn't know what day anymore.

She had taken him here once when they had been... close? No, they were never close. When they had been better acquainted, that is. She had grown up with her family in this pointless village, and she came here to escape. As far as he knew, there were no mages or magic users in this area at all. That's why she liked it here.

The words on Fabian's phone blurred together as he scrolled through mindless internet drivel What a waste of his bloody time. At least he wasn't thinking about his financial situation and how much the house was falling into extreme debt. Damn, now he was thinking about it. He looked around. The same blokes as the previous nights were draped over the bar looking like they wanted to kill themselves. A few couples came in for dinner and sat in the other booths, but none stayed long. It wasn't exactly an inviting atmosphere.

Another pint down, and Fabian was ready to call it a night. She wasn't coming. He headed for the dingy toilet before he attempted a drunken Hollow opening.

As he unzipped his fly, he felt the cold press of metal on his neck.

"Fabian," a female voice purred in his ear.

"Kat? My long-lost love. That better be you," Fabian said, unimpressed by the slur in his voice.

"You're bloody lucky it is. You're off your game, Fabian. I could have cut your throat while you stood there like an unprepared initiate with your cock in your hand."

The pressure on his neck was gone, and he did up his fly, just to be safe. "Actually, I hadn't gotten it out yet. Do you want me to?" He turned and came face to face with Kat. Her dark intense eyes were just how he remembered, heavily bordered in eyeliner and drilling into him like she wanted to kill him.

"Finish taking a piss and meet me inside."

He leaned against the half wall by the urinal with intentional casualness and a brilliant, non-drunk demeanor. "You're not here to kill me then?"

"We'll see." She swept around, her long braid of black hair flicked behind her like a whip, he recalled she wasn't opposed to whips. Her coat swished around her in a breeze of her once-familiar perfume, something flowery he always liked.

"I missed you, Kat!" he called after her as she stormed out the door. Now he really needed to take a piss, but this time he looked behind him before he tried again. She was right about one thing: He was unprepared. Maybe he should drink less? No. He scoffed. A ridiculous notion. Clearly, that wasn't the answer.

By the time he made it back to his table, Kat had a pint and was sitting up straight and proper in the tatty booth. She looked exactly like a trained assassin should, toned, sexy, and dressed in black. It was not subtle. But everyone here knew her as Kat, the little girl who used to pick seashells, or whatever it was kids did when they grew up by the sea. He had no fucking clue. Either way, no one batted an eye at them.

"I take it your presence here means you are ready to listen to me now?" Kat asked.

"You stabbed me. I demand an apology." The first thing that popped into his mind. An issue they probably needed to clear up. He slumped into the booth opposite her and waved to the barman for another drink. The barman frowned and ignored him.

"You wouldn't listen, and you were the one who attacked me. I *actually* wanted to talk to you." Her smokey eyes drilled into him.

He snorted. "That's not how I recall events."

"As the sober one in both instances, I trust my judgment and *my* memory a hell of a lot more than yours."

He leaned forward, avoiding the sticky patches on the table. "Well, I'm here, and I'm listening now."

"Is that so?"

He nodded, wondering what she had said to the barman to turn down a paying customer such as himself. "So what was so urgent that had you chasing me that night?"

"You first. Why are you here right now, waiting for me like a pathetic alcoholic?"

He let her insults slide off him; she hadn't meant that. "I believe you might have information that can help me."

"And why should I help you?" she asked.

"Because you miss me and desperately want to win me back?"

"You are insane. Just to jog your memory. We were never actually together, and the last time I talked to you, you called me a traitorous slut and blamed me for your brother's murder. Which, by the way, I had nothing to do with."

"Ah yes, messy business that. Turns out the culprit was your number one student. Sorry, I never made that connection," he said sarcastically.

"You don't need to be an arse, Fabian. You knew me. I would never do that to you."

He looked down at his hands. "All I know is I can't trust anyone. Especially Ravens."

"And this is your way of asking me for help?"

"I am sorry, Kat. I know you had nothing to do with Samael's death. I've successfully narrowed my rage and revenge plans into a healthy resentment against Torin Dumont. You don't need to worry about me. I accept your apology and forgive you for stabbing me."

"I didn't apologize."

"Well, I accept it nonetheless."

"I forgot how bloody infuriating you are."

"But it's attractive, right?" He really should shut up if he actually wanted help.

"Why are you here Fabian?"

"I'm looking for a book. I recall you mentioning it before. The Shadow Atlas?"

She tilted her head. Clearly, not what she had been expecting. "Korbyn never found it. It's still missing."

"Oh." Fabian slumped back in the booth and twisted his blue spinel ring around his finger. Her confused look didn't lie. She didn't know where it was.

"That was all you wanted to ask me?"

"It's important I find the book."

"Why?" she asked.

Why? He had no idea, really. But when Rowena Sharp said something was important, he was inclined to believe her. Somehow she always just knew, and if Korbyn Dumont wanted it this bad all these years, it had to be important.

"I honestly don't know. Is he looking for anything else? Something important by chance?" he asked.

"Yes, actually. It's what I wanted to talk to you about the last time," she said.

"The time when you stabbed me?"

"Yes." She leaned in, not acknowledging the stabbing. "It's the relics. Korbyn is after them."

"Ah yes, the relics. I was supposed to mention them too... What are they?"

"Gods, Fabian. Do you not know anything? The relics the Archmage is collecting at the Tower."

"Still not following."

Kat slammed her drink down, looking like she wanted to punch him in the face. Fabian leaned back a little.

"The twelve jade relics. They open a door to the Echo Dimension, and the Archmage is getting them together. I have no idea why, but Korbyn wants them for himself. Once they have them, he's going to take the collection. I'm sure of it."

"Okay. This sounds bad. But why tell me?"

"Because you have friends at the Tower of London. I can't talk to anyone there anymore, but someone needs to be warned. He cannot get the relics; he will destroy the world."

Fabian squeezed his eyes shut. This was a lot of information he hadn't expected.

"Those conniving Owls stole my jade snake ornament." He suddenly put two and two together. His snake must have been one of the relics, and they'd taken it when he was getting it valued at a shop in Eagle Tower. He knew it was the Owls. He'd seen them following him that day but was too slow to realize what they were up to.

Kat's eyes were stern and serious. "Maybe but listen. You need to tell someone. They can't put them all in one place. It's a disaster waiting to happen."

"Fine. I'll tell someone. How is she even collecting them? If they're old enough to open the Echo Gate, shouldn't they all be lost or buried somewhere?"

"That's why she has Torin. He's finding them for her."

Fabian's stomach plummeted to his feet and threatened to vomit up all his carefully drunk beer. He fell hard against the booth.

"Fabian? What is it? Why are you frozen like an idiot?"

He swallowed hard, suddenly feeling a good deal soberer than he wanted to. "The Archmage made my niece Dumont's apprentice."

"Oh." Kat took a large swig of her beer. "She must really have it out for them."

"That's an understatement. That makes a lot more sense now. It sounds like she needs them both. I need to get my niece out of there as soon as possible." Azalea was in far more danger than he thought.

"I can help."

"And why should I trust you?"

Kat furrowed her brow. "Because I know Korbyn Dumont better than anyone. I know what he is capable of, and he's too dangerous. If he gets his hands on the relics, the whole world is fucked. Magic won't be a secret anymore, and who knows what creatures might come through from the other side? Anyone with Echo Magic would be helpless."

He glanced around. The surrounding booths had emptied, and no one was close enough to listen in. "So, what do you need?"

"I need you to warn someone at the Tower of London, and we need Torin to come back. Torin never wanted the job, but the House of Ravens needs a sane leader."

"Sane? You want me to help Torin Dumont become the head of the House of Ravens?" He snorted.

Her eyes locked with his, dead serious. "Yes."

"No fucking way. But if you're planning on taking down Korbyn Dumont, I'm in." He leaned right in and whispered, "As long as it doesn't conflict with my revenge plans for Torin."

"There are more important things at stake than petty revenge. Man up, Fabian."

"I'll have to think about it." It would take a lot for him to give up his 'petty' revenge. The bloke had killed his brother and gotten away with hardly any punishment. But keeping Azalea safe had to come first. They needed a plan. Korbyn could never get his hands on those relics, and he wasn't about to leave Azalea in the crossfire.

CHAPTER 16

I t was overcast and dreary outside, but Azalea wanted to be out there, or anywhere rather than holed up in the tower. Ever since she'd revealed the Shadow Atlas and the new info about the fish relic to Torin, they had been researching and planning their trip to Little Barrier Island, New Zealand, non-stop for the last two days. They'd only be there for one day, but they needed to be prepared.

"Did you print off the maps?" Torin barked as he rummaged through a stack of paper that had nothing to do with maps.

"Yes, I put them in the folder where you asked me to," Azalea said through gritted teeth.

She had spent the morning trying to keep it together, but she'd had enough of being pushed around and yelled at by Torin, who clearly didn't believe they were ready for the relic hunt, despite having done everything on his list. Plus they had gone over all the research about taniwha—which turned out could be a water spirit, a serpent, a sea monster, a dragon, a shark, or a giant eel—she wasn't sure she wanted to find out for certain.

She was just there for Torin to yell at to do things. She wasn't even being helpful anymore, and it was still morning; they had hours before the evening when they planned to leave.

Azalea left Torin searching for his maps and grabbed her stuff for the gym as they had originally scheduled. She crept downstairs and stood in the doorway.

"I'm off to the gym!" she yelled before Torin could argue. It was clear he didn't handle last-minute planning well.

The late morning workout was just what she needed. No one was there to dart her dark looks or frighten her off. It was certainly better than attending morning training, though not as fun.

After a solid workout, she left the gym, dragging her feet. She didn't want to go back to Torin's place to be yelled at. Maybe Erik was free? He should be at home this week studying theory for his metal smithing apprenticeship while his trainer was off sick. Her mind flicked to the last time he kissed her outside her flat, sending a wave of heat through her. Yes, seeing Erik was an excellent idea.

She exited the underground Complex via the stairs up to the Barracks and slipped outside before anyone had the chance to recognize her. Cutting through the small alleyway, she darted through the cars on the north side of Mint Street and knocked on the door to Erik's place before she could back out.

A tall, muscular man with ash blond hair like Erik, only much older, opened the door. A little girl peeked out from behind him, Erik's sister. Azalea remembered her from the hospital when she first came to the Tower.

"Hi. Is Erik home?" Azalea asked, suddenly nervous and wishing she hadn't come.

The man's eyes drilled into her. He must have known who she was. But the girl giggled and hovered behind the door shyly.

"What do you want?" he barked.

"I'm Azalea, sir. I'm in... I was in Erik's class."

"ERIK! Someone's here for you," the man called in a deep bellow over his shoulder.

"Um, thanks," Azalea said, unsure where to put her hands or how to stand.

"I know who you are," he warned. "Just don't get my boy into trouble."

"I don't plan to," she said, taken aback.

Erik's dad glanced out the door. Probably to see if any nosy neighbors would see her there.

She let a breath out of her nostrils. She wouldn't be intimidated. "What project are you working on? Erik said you're working on something to do with magic staffs?" Azalea broke the awkward silence. She'd seen the rows of strange staffs down in his forge and wanted to know what they were for.

"Erik should keep his mouth shut if he knows what's good for him," his father said, clipping Erik across the back of the head as he walked past.

"Oi, what was that for?" He rubbed his head, then spotted Azalea. He tilted his head in surprise, and a smile spread across his face.

Butterflies rushed to her stomach. Good to know she could catch him off guard. But his father didn't look happy, and Azalea's cheeks heated knowing she might have put her foot in it.

"You know better than to be talking about my projects with strangers." He frowned at Erik and marched back inside, and Erik's sister ran off.

"Sorry about him." Erik rubbed the back of his neck. "We're not meant to talk about his project, top secret and all."

"Thanks for the warning. It can't be that secret if you're taking randoms down to his workshop." Azalea frowned.

Erik shrugged. "He doesn't tell me anything, anyway. What are you doing here? Missed me?"

"I needed to get out of the house." She bit her lip, pushing down the nerves and not wanting to admit she wanted to see him.

He leaned on the doorway. "Mage Dumont grinding you down already?"

"Something like that." She didn't want to go into details, and there was a lot she couldn't tell him about Torin's work. It was best to not bring it up. "You want to go somewhere?"

"Sorry, love. I can't. Got lunch with the classmates planned since I'm home and all. I would invite you, but you know..."

"It's fine." She wrung her hands together in front of her. "Another time."

"It's nice to know you want me." Erik grinned and ran a hand through his hair.

She spun around with a quick wave. "Bye, Erik."

"Wait." He pulled her back. His lips crashed into hers. She didn't even have time to work out what was happening or kiss him back before he pulled away and ran his thumb over her bottom lip. "Want to come over one night and hang out?"

Her head was still whirling from the kiss. "Yes," she said without thinking.

"Perfect. How about tomorrow night?"

"Sounds good. What did you have in mind?"

"Leave that up to me." He kissed her softly, then pushed her gently out the door. He winked and shut the door in her face.

What was that? Whatever just happened, it looked like she'd signed up for a date. She turned to the street, unable to wipe the smile from her lips. Damn her desperation, making her look needy.

The last resort was now the library. A few hours researching everything she could about the House of Ravens wouldn't be wasted time.

))) ● (((

Nerves jittered under Azalea's skin, making it hard to keep still. She glanced out the window of Torin's office. Despite it being 3 pm, the sun hadn't seemed to have risen properly. She sighed, watching Torin slam books onto his desk and stuff supplies into his bag. But even his last-minute grumbling couldn't bring her down. Her afternoon in the library proved quite relaxing; she'd even had a nap in a chair and was pumped for the relic hunt and traveling across the world in the blink of an eye. Who wouldn't be? The answer to that was Torin.

"Let's get on with this," Torin growled as he put a torch in the front pocket of his bag and slung it on his back.

Azalea tucked her dad's pocket watch into her bag for extra luck and patted Faraday on the head before heading out. They left the Tower and power-walked at Torin's power-walking pace to St. Dunstan in the East. Torin stopped abruptly at the iron gate. A shudder ran through her. She loathed the place, but it had the strongest natural magic around for cutting into the Hollow with minimal exertion, so she blocked out her surroundings and focused on sticking close to Torin, just as he had instructed her to several times before they left.

She half-expected his father to jump out from behind a tree and throw a bag over her head or something. A shiver trickled down her back, and she hugged her arms around herself.

Torin cloaked them in shadows and looked around before slicing into the Hollow. "In," he ordered.

Azalea took a deep breath, ignoring her hammering pulse. She would not let her fear rule her, and she wasn't about to show Torin just how terrified she was of entering the Hollow once more. If he could feel it, he had the decency to not bring it up.

The chilling breath of the Hollow beckoned her in as her legs did what her brain didn't want to. She stepped in. Torin was right behind her, not wasting any time.

"Since we are traveling so far from our point of origin, it will help if we both focus on the destination when I make the cut. Got it?"

She nodded, then closed her eyes and forced her mind to focus on details she had learned that day about New Zealand. Torin was so close to her that they were nearly touching. An unfamiliar sensation filled the surrounding space, like a warm blanket of static electricity covering every inch of her skin. It was a pleasant tingling that made her feel both powerful and comfortable, like a puzzle locking into place.

She opened her eyes to see Torin staring at her strangely. He could feel it, too. The narrow space between them buzzed with energy like tiny sparkles of lightning. Without a word, Torin cut through the darkness and into a window to a new land before them.

Torin stepped through, and Azalea followed close behind, taking a breath of fresh air. It was much warmer than London; it was muggy, and she could smell the earthy dampness of a nearby forest and the saltiness of the sea. The quacking of ducks disturbed the peace; they weren't happy to be so rudely woken.

She followed Torin out of the Hollow into the early morning darkness. It should be around 3 am NZ time, and they walked through the silent main street of a small town and down to a marina. She stepped onto the gently rocking pontoon. A mix of yachts, small boats, and big, speedy-looking boats were tied up in neat rows, all bobbing along with the sleepy morning current.

"We are getting picked up by the water taxi soon. Don't talk to the driver, and don't tell him what we're doing. If he asks, we are checking on a university experiment that got its funding cut, and we need to get to the island secretly to finish our work." Torin glanced around.

She could feel he wasn't scared, just on high alert. "Got it." Though it didn't seem like a very believable cover story. It was a shame they couldn't just go in the Hollow to get to the island, but it was naturally warded against the Hollow somehow.

As if on cue, a large, cheery man lumbered up the ramp that went down to the boats, he waved enthusiastically.

"You Torin?" he asked, in what Azalea now recognized as a New Zealand accent, though much stronger than Jade's. Torin didn't have a chance to answer, as the man was already vigorously shaking Torin's hand.

She grinned at him. "Hi, I'm Azalea." He shook her hand, squeezing it half to death as she tried not to wince.

"Nice to meet you both, Poms I see. Love the Pommys. Better get a move on, gotta get out of here before it gets light." He clapped his hands together and marched off, his large frame sending waves out with every step on the pontoon.

Torin nodded to her, and she set off after the boatman as a lightness spread through her chest, excited for the boat ride.

"Sorry, I didn't even introduce myself. I'm Pete. My boat's called *Pete* too in case you were wondering, so I can't lose it, you know?" He chuckled to himself, and Torin didn't answer. "So anyway, I'll drop you on the other side of the island and come back in four hours?"

"Yes, if that's not too much trouble," Torin replied.

"No trouble. I'll go fishing till I need to pick you up. Get us some snapper for dinner, aye?" Pete grinned.

Azalea zoned out as Pete asked Torin a million questions, glad she wasn't the one having to deal with it. It was funny watching Torin forced to interact with someone so animated and sociable.

Pete's boat, *Pete*, was tied up to one of the floating walkways. Azalea eyed it suspiciously. It was metal and covered with layers of gritty, solid salt with an added stench of fishiness about it.

She'd been imagining something like a clean, white, taxi-type boat with lights on top; but this would have to do. It only had two seats at the front and no roof, just a small salt-covered windscreen and a ratty-looking canopy. Hopefully, it was hole-free.

Torin frowned at the boat as they got in, but he booked it, so he could hardly be surprised.

"Hang on!" Pete yelled as he started the motor, and a plume of black smoke filled the air and shattered the silence of the still morning.

They held on tight, standing at the front of the boat and chugged out of the bay and into open water. It was too bumpy to sit on the seats. Azalea's arms threatened to rip from their sockets as she gripped the metal bar above her head, and her feet scrambled to stay put as Pete pushed the small boat to full speed. She felt Torin's hand on her back as she regained her footing with a more solid stance. She didn't fancy a swim in the dark, unfamiliar ocean and was glad he had her back.

They crashed along at full speed in the blackness of the night. Azalea's stomach fluttered, and she was ultra-awake with adrenaline. Torin, beside her, was the opposite. He gripped the rail intensely, all somber and serious. Every now and then, she felt a wave of unease roll off him.

Everything around them was sea-spray and inky ocean. She had no idea how Pete knew where he was going, but by the grin on his face and his easy grip on the steering wheel, she felt like they were in safe hands. Either that or he was plain mad.

They bounced and flew off the waves, airborne. Azalea couldn't help but whoop loudly each time they fell back down to crash onto the water. She'd forgotten what freedom felt like.

Clearly, her joy didn't extend to Torin. His face turned deathly green while both hands were in a white-knuckled grip locked to the rails above and beside him.

After what could have been an hour or more, Azalea was almost disappointed to see the dark mass of the island appear in front of them. They took a wide berth and went around to the far side. There were a few tremendous crashes as the boat slammed into the swell with knee-rattling force, and they lopped over the last sizable waves as they slowed down. Torin looked like he was ready to jump overboard. Azalea loved the feeling of her stomach dropping as they fell off the edge of the wave crests.

As they came in close on the other side, the sea flattened, and Pete slowed the boat to a crawl. The island was the dark silhouette of a floating forest with a fringe of beach around the edge and stark cliffs cut from the trees like sliced cake.

Pete brought the boat in close, digging the front into the sand, then cut the motor. The silence echoed in Azalea's ears. She adjusted the new volume to the tune of the gentle lap of the waves, followed by a shrill screech that smashed right through the relaxing quiet and made her twist her head.

Azalea looked at Pete and Torin in panic. It sounded loud and very close.

"That's a kiwi, nothing to worry about. It's just calling out to its mate," Pete said.

"You mean that was a bird?" *Not a taniwha, at least.*

He laughed. "Nothing but birds on this island, mate... except the weta and the tuatara."

Azalea had no idea what a weta or a tuatara was, and maybe she didn't want to know.

Pete dropped them off with a friendly farewell, promising he'd be back on time.

Azalea spun around on the sand, taking everything in. "That was so fun."

"If you say so," Torin grumbled.

She wouldn't let his mood bring her down, though she still felt the edge of his sea sickness, which must be a lot worse for him. But they had made it and only had a short while to wait for sunrise.

"You okay?" she asked Torin. His skin looked almost gray in the starlight.

He just nodded but then ran to the edge of the sand to throw up. She handed him a water bottle when he returned. His unease mixed with queasiness sent a brief dizziness over her.

"I don't like boats," he said, accepting her offering.

"Never would have guessed," she said sarcastically but with a smile. Hopefully, he would come right soon.

They sat on the beach, Torin with his head between his knees and Azalea squishing her feet into the soft grains, enjoying the sensation of the sand trickling between her toes. It was easy to forget they were on a mission.

She nearly jumped from her sandy seat when a squawk cracked through the air. It was just a flock of rowdy parrots screaming at one another. Then from behind her, as the sun filtered faint blueness into the sky, the morning chorus of bird-song grew louder, rising beyond the trees and sending goose-bumps up her arms.

It was as loud as a real orchestra, but with one sound echoing above all the others, a low and mournful cry that crept from the trees, raising the hairs on the back of Azalea's neck. She froze, trapped in the mystical call. Surely that one wasn't a bird? The notes rose and fell in rich alien tones.

"Are they the spirits of the forest? Is that a taniwha?" Azalea whispered. She could feel the magic pulsing through the forest around them.

Torin shook his head. "No, they're birds, Kokako. One of the protected endangered species on this island."

She waited for a break in the melodic call, drawn to it like a siren. "It feels like magic." She closed her eyes, taking in the sound.

"Let's get moving. It's light enough now." He looked a little better.

The sun rose high enough that she could see the green of the trees around the edge of the forest.

"This way. *Where two cliffs part, you'll find a road. Marked above, by stones in code,*" Torin recited the line from the riddle and nodded to what could be a path. He had identified the trail from satellite maps, and there was a pair of distinct boulders that looked similar to the ones right ahead.

The beach stopped abruptly at the path which was much steeper than the 2D map suggested. They pulled their way up some rough clay steps fashioned from rocks and tree roots.

Azalea's hands were dirty with yellow clay when they emerged onto the forest floor.

They followed what seemed to be a goat track, rather than an actual path for about an hour. The damp earthy smell was strangely comforting, reminding her of home, of her mum.

"That's gotta be it." Torin wiped his forehead. Even he, in all his gym-body glory, was breathing hard from the uphill hike.

Ahead of him, a massive wall of stone grew out of the lush forest like an alien spaceship that had landed there. At the base was a narrow gap between the rocks that did not look at all inviting.

A cave beneath a long white cloud... The Taniwha waits, strong and proud.

She didn't see a long white cloud, only trees, and she sure as hell hoped there was no taniwha. Torin went straight for the entrance that looked like it might be a doorway to hell if this were a horror movie.

Anxiety crept over her like an unwanted centipede running down her spine, and she repressed a shudder.

He shot her a cheeky smile and leaned on the edge of the rock to the dark hallway of doom. "You good?" He casually plucked a sprig of leaves from a nearby plant and placed it in his pocket.

"Yup. Just dandy," she said in a too-high voice. *Good one, Azalea. Way to look calm.*

"We'll go a short way in and let our eyes adjust."

"Wait, we're not using torches?" Her chest froze up. She knew she shouldn't be scared. She had learned to embrace the darkness, after all. *Shadows were her friends.* But it brought back memories of the shadows at night taking over. That feeling of having no control was what made her limbs freeze and not want to go into that cave.

"You'll be fine. Just stick close to me and do as I say."

She tried to lighten the mood. "Yes, professor."

Torin didn't even argue back, just quirked an eyebrow at her and climbed down into the darkness without hesitation.

You can do this. It's just a dark cave, with a potential monster waiting for you... It's fine...

She followed Torin in. The cool dampness of underground air chilled her skin. The light from outside was dim but brightened up the tunnel enough to make out Torin in front and large rocky walls around her. It wasn't too cramped. Even Torin could stand straight without leaning over.

The earthy floor was dry, but as they moved further into the cave, trickles of water meandered down the slick stone walls and dripped from the ceiling, converging in a thin stream at their feet.

The darkness weighed down, and as they turned a corner, she lost the light from the entrance. The blackness was so all-encompassing it suffocated her. She tried not to panic but froze, reaching out for the cold stone wall to ground herself. She wished she could get her torch out and light everything up. She took a deep breath, closing her eyes, waiting for what her mum called her 'forest sight' to kick in.

Torin's footsteps stopped. "You're doing good. Just up ahead, it's lighter." His voice jolted her blind gaze straight forward.

She swallowed and followed his voice. He must be able to feel her fear if he was acting this nice. After a slow minute of baby steps through the darkness, his shape formed in front of her, and she let out a shaky breath as the walls of the tunnel lightened.

"Thanks," she said, relieved he had waited for her.

She turned another corner, and a huge cavern opened before her. Torin appeared at her side. Her ears strained in the semi-darkness where a constant drip, drip of water and scuttling sounds on the walls made her skin crawl. A splash echoed.

"Can you see them?" Torin asked. She felt a thrill of childlike excitement spring off him.

Her eyes adjusted, and she looked around the cavern. The walls seemed to come alive with lights illuminating the underground room like a cathedral of stars, and the massive stalactites hanging from the ceiling were chandeliers mysteriously lit in the darkness.

"Holy shit," was all she could think to say. It was a private universe painted across the ceiling. Her heart sped up as she took it in.

"Can you see now? Follow me to the edge of the wall where it's safer." He gestured for her to follow. His voice and his energy were all confidence.

The stars on the ground rippled, trembling until they blurred away. *Oh, it was water. A reflection.*

Carefully stepping on the soft, sandy-ish floor, she avoided the jutting rocks and followed Torin to the edge of the cavern.

With their backs against the cave wall, Azalea took in her surroundings. It was a huge open space with a black lake covering most of the room.

"Are the lights magic?" she whispered.

"No," he scoffed as if she should know. "They're glow worms. Use them to see where all the edges are and remember the exit."

"Do you think the taniwha is here?"

"I don't know. If it is, it will be in that lake. We might need to lure it out. Just promise not to do anything stupid. You'll follow my instructions." He stared at her, waiting for an answer.

Azalea swallowed. That did not sound like a fun thing to do or a good idea, but she wanted him to see she could be useful and competent. "I promise," she said reluctantly. "But shouldn't we just look around to see if we can find the relic first?"

"You go up on that ledge and see if it's there." He pointed to a rocky outcrop nearby. He was trying to get her out of the way. But she might as well look; it couldn't hurt.

She climbed her way up a few meters to the ledge above Torin and looked over. Beneath the rock were dangling beads of light pulsed. Revolting. He was right; the lights came from strange blobby worms.

"Put a shadow shield up and stay there," Torin ordered.

She didn't argue. Instead, she did what he said as he inched toward the water's edge and placed a small woven basket half in the water, then put the sprig of leaves he picked outside the cave right on the top.

He began chanting in some ancient language, and she crouched, remaining as small as possible as the words reverberated their way around the cave way too loudly.

Then absolute silence.

Things in the mirror-like lake moved. Logs and sticks drifted like ghostly ships in an invisible current. Large ferns and bits of rotting forest joined the flotilla as a whirlpool dragged everything in the water into its vortex.

"Are you doing that?" she whisper-yelled down to Torin.

He backed up a little and gave a sharp jerk of his head to say no. He didn't take his eyes off the water.

The whirlpool shifted toward them unnaturally, its black hole creeping near the edge of the lake. Azalea held her breath, body tense and wondering if she should move closer to the exit, maybe stand in the tunnel ready to run.

A log bobbed to the surface. Moving against the current, it drifted into the bank, perching like a waiting crocodile. The whirlpool drifted back to the center of the lake, but the log remained.

Torin inched forward. Azalea had a strong urge to jump down and pull him back. But that wouldn't help either of them. She could feel his focus and control; he knew what he was doing.

He pointed at the log, and Azalea peered forward, trying to see what he was looking at. Her eyes were drawn to what sat on top. The relic. It sat there riding the log, a tangle of small vines holding it in place.

Torin stepped to the water's edge. Azalea held in a scream as the log stretched and crackled with movement like tree branches splitting.

"Get out of there," she yelled, scrambling down the rock to pull him back if she had to.

The log transformed before her eyes. Sticks creaked out to form legs, and a reptilian head emerged from the front to become a massive and terrifying lizard.

She crept behind Torin, silently urging him in her mind to move the fuck away from the creature.

Its ancient body was covered in lichen. It crouched on its belly with clawed legs out to the sides. Its eyes were black and reflected the glowworms' stars like trapped universes. It turned its head toward Torin, and Azalea spotted a third eye on the top of its head. A low growl rumbled from its throat.

Yup, this was the Taniwha.

CHAPTER 17

Torin remained perfectly still, and Azalea wanted to scream at him to move. But she had promised not to interfere and to do as she was told. It was so hard.

The mix of dinosaur, crocodile, log monster looked Torin up and down as if it wanted to eat him.

The whirlpool violently shifted toward them as the taniwha swung its meaty tail, knocking Torin's feet out from underneath him. He was tossed into the air, landing at the water's edge. Azalea darted forward and grabbed Torin's shirt. Her heartbeat shot up as he reached out for her, and she managed to grab his hand. Sparks of determination and the fizz of magic raced between them as she hauled him back from the inky spiral.

Slipping on the slick rock, she fought, using all her weight to heave him out. The taniwha stood still and cocked its head as if waiting to see what would happen. She pulled Torin enough to free his leg from the grip of the dark water, and his muscles bunched as he fought to scramble across the slimy rock.

Azalea moved as far back as she could and hit the cave wall. Scuttling feet darted over her. She screamed. Ancient-looking, giant insects with armored bodies and too many legs swarmed over the wall with long feelers reaching out into the darkness. She shifted closer to Torin, brushing off her shoulders and head to make sure they weren't on her, imagining the horrible bugs dropping onto her head and getting stuck in her hair.

"They're just weta; they won't hurt you." Torin ignored the alien insects and focused his dark, determined eyes on the taniwha.

"I don't care what they are, there are millions of them." She shuddered and forced herself to pay attention to the real problem.

She swallowed the fear that was possibly coming from both her and Torin. It was getting hard to tell whose emotions were whose. The three-eyed beast rushed at them, its claws scraping loudly on the rock. She hauled herself onto a ledge, and Torin scrambled up behind her. Her heart was beating wildly, but she felt a rush of excitement from him.

The giant lizard rushed toward them, dragging its belly along the ground. It lunged at their ledge, its solid head hit the stone like an earthquake as the rock cracked and shuddered, and the stalactites around them fell and shattered.

"Move!" Torin dropped down a level from their perch and scrambled along the rock wall on a thin ledge that hung above the black water.

Azalea followed closely, trying to ignore the weta and focus on clinging to the slippery rocks. The taniwha turned and splashed into the water and came out on a patch of ground just below them.

Torin helped Azalea onto an outcrop where they crouched on the solid ledge looking down. "We're going to go down there. I'll make it sleep while you grab the relic. Got it?"

Was this really a good plan?

"Trust me, Azalea. Can you do that?"

She wanted to trust him. But how could she after everything? "I don't know," she whispered as panic rose in her chest.

"I won't let it hurt you," he said with absolute confidence.

His eyes said the same, and she felt it in her soul, or maybe it was from his. Either way, he meant every word. He wouldn't put her in more danger than himself.

"Okay, I trust you. But if I get eaten by that dinosaur down there, I'll be coming back to haunt you." She took in a shaky breath; it was time to have a little faith; she wanted to trust him.

He smirked. "I wouldn't expect anything less."

Torin's elemer morphed into a sword of shadowy flames. It glowed with scintillating shade, not fire, somehow light and dark at the same time. She didn't have time to think about backing out.

"Once I give you the signal, you'll have about two seconds to run down and grab the relic. Got it?"

She swallowed the acrid fear building in her throat. Why had she begged to go on this mission? Why was she even trying to be his apprentice? Torin was already lowering himself to the ledge below. He waved the sword in soft fluid motions, mesmerizing the beast as he got into position.

Torin leaned over the edge, right over its monstrous head. Its face craned up to him, its central eye focused on Torin as its breath washed over them like the salty breeze blowing from the crest of a wave. It was so close it could have snapped him up right then if it wanted to, but Torin reached out his hand, and the creature almost purred into it. A heavy rumble filled the cave as its eyes slowly closed.

"Now," Torin whispered.

Cool signal, professor.

Her sarcastic thoughts were all that was keeping her from running out of the cave screaming. This was absolute craziness, but she trusted him and slid down the rock face, heading straight for the creature.

She reached its side, using its cold ladder of scales to climb onto its back. Her heart pounded in her ears as her skin brushed against the cold-blooded flesh of a mythical monster. *Just wait till Isaac hears about this.*

The taniwha stood like a statue under Torin's control, and her confidence grew as she reached for the huge white spines that formed a ridge down its back. She used them to clamber up its body to the neck as its flesh squished under her boot. There it was, the tiny relic wedged between two spines.

On hands and knees, she shuffled closer to its head and reached for the relic, but it was tangled in tightly woven vines. She grappled with it, wrestling with the natural ropes, but they tightened as she pulled. It wouldn't budge. The muscles of the creature tensed and shifted, nearly knocking her off its back. She grabbed hold of a spine.

It settled, but there was no time to muck around. She pulled her elemer from her belt and sawed at the strands. Time slowed with every agonizing sweep of her blade. With the last ping of a vine being sawed through, it gave way, and she grabbed the fish relic.

Cold and smooth against her palm, she shoved it in her pocket and twisted, holding her breath as she slid down the bumpy scales. Her feet crunched into the sand on the opposite side, and she sprinted toward the exit. Thundering footsteps shook the earth as it lumbered somewhere behind her. Torin must have broken contact with the beast.

She looked back to check on Torin.

"Run," he yelled.

She did just that, sprinting for the tunnel, dodging the low points on the wall, and avoiding weta.

Torin was breathing heavily and stomping behind her. Bursting into the forest and the bright morning light, she continued for what seemed like hours, running until she made it to the cracked rock path to the beach with Torin close behind.

With screaming legs, she tumbled down onto the sand and hauled herself up. Not stopping till she reached the distant cliffs at the end.

Only then did she collapse. She flung her bag down and lay next to it, not caring about the sand in her hair or the rocks digging into her spine. Torin came to a halt next to her and flopped onto his back beside her. She was still clutching the relic. It felt stupid to risk their lives for such a tiny stone fish. She ran her thumb over its scales, its body coiled around a perfectly round ball.

They lay there for several minutes recovering their breath, both looking back constantly to make sure the taniwha hadn't followed them.

"So, what was in the basket?" she asked between breaths.

"A peace offering of a small branch and a rare black Tahitian pearl, one with some very ancient magic linked to the sea."

"A pearl?"

"It's what it wanted most. Now it's free of the cave. An equivalent exchange, so to speak."

"You traded with it? Then why the hell did it attack us?"

Torin rested his hands under his head. A buzz of happiness washed over her. "It needed to test us, to see we were worthy. When I made it sleep, I showed it our true intentions. I couldn't lie to it. It accepted the gift and let us leave. I imagine it must be bored in a cave all those years. It probably wanted a bit of excitement. Gods and creatures find their fun in tormenting mortals. Always remember that."

"It didn't feel like it was letting us take it, and why do you look so happy? We nearly died!"

"We found a relic. Do you know how rare that is? How impossible our task truly is?" Torin beamed.

"At least I know what makes you happy now. Doing impossible things." She shook her head at him but allowed herself a little smile as she rolled the small jade fish in her palm before handing it to Torin.

Her first relic hunt was a success.

"And you did it," Torin added.

"Did what?"

"Passed your initiate's test. You did exactly what I told you to do, and you trusted me."

She turned her head to see him staring up at the sky, the hint of a smile on his lips. "Does that make me your apprentice now? I didn't even use any magic."

"I think you've more than proven yourself." He turned his head to look at her. "I know what you're capable of. The test wasn't about magic. I know your abilities better than anyone."

A lightness flooded her chest. Why was she so happy? This wasn't even what she wanted. She didn't want to be his apprentice; it was only temporary. But she let the pride rise through her.

"Thanks, Torin." She meant it, and she hoped he felt it.

"We'll just hold off on the official apprentice ceremony until we know what's up with the spirits and the gods' plans for you. You still need to drink the elixir of the gods, a potion similar to when you received the mark of the gods. But I don't want you getting trapped alone in the Desert of Dreams."

"Oh. Neither do I." She was with him on that. She'd learned her lesson after taking the potion spontaneously to get her mark of the gods. She wasn't about to jump into that again.

The trees exploded as the taniwha ripped through the small track. Azalea and Torin both jumped up. The taniwha lumbered down the cliff, tearing off big chunks of clay as it slid on its belly onto the beach.

Blood pounded in Azalea's ears as they heaved themselves up. Her heavy legs found a new wave of energy, and she sprinted over the sand faster than she ever would have thought possible until they were at the edge of the cliff behind a huge boulder.

But the taniwha ignored them as it went straight for the sea and slid into the water like a sleek otter. Its body was no longer like a log, but a lithe, blue iridescent sea serpent that moved in undulating waves across the glassy surface of the deep blue ocean. The water glowed around it, and it left a trail of luminescence in the waves as it splashed and frolicked, then disappeared.

Azalea stared out across the vast ocean, wishing with all her heart to catch one more glimpse of the insane creature. Torin was at her side, doing the same, and everything felt right for one second. Although she didn't want it to, and everything was, in fact, still very wrong.

But something had changed between them, and both of them knew it. They needed to find out what the gods wanted with them.

"I think we need to pay a visit to the Great Desert of Dreams," she said without looking at him.

"You might be right."

CHAPTER 18

T orin trudged out of the Hollow to a hidden corner behind a tree at St. Dunstan in the East. A hazy yellow fog hung around the streetlamps and skeletal trees, the light wavering as he tried to stay up straight. The smell of car fumes hung in the freezing night air, making Torin feel more seasick than before, and the smell from the plastic bag containing the freshly caught fish Pete had given them wasn't helping.

"You alright?" Azalea swayed the plastic bag beside her. It appeared their boat ride back had the opposite effect on her. She was buzzing and full of life; whereas he had been drained and wanted to throw up on the rosebush he was hovering over.

"Give me a minute," he said.

She was probably enjoying his misery. He leaned over and took a few deep breaths until the nausea passed. Something about doing magic made motion sickness much worse. He failed to remember that every time.

He checked his phone. There was a message from an unknown number:

Kerridge's at the Corinthia tomorrow 1:30 pm. KD.

Torin's stomach roiled once more. His father would not wait. But Torin would give him one last shot to own up to what he had done, and this time he would have it on record.

Torin straightened up and checked his watch; it was 11 pm. Good, close to midnight was when his magic was at its strongest. They had to get this visit to the Desert of Dreams over with and find some answers tonight.

Azalea was looking at him strangely as she handed him a bottle of water from her bag, and they walked in silence back to the Tower. After tomorrow, she wouldn't be safe.

ɔ ɔ ɔ ● (((

Torin had showered and was making sleep tea when Azalea wandered into the kitchen wearing a cute purple dressing gown. Her hair was tied up high in a messy bun, and her skin was pink from showering. As she walked past to grab a cup, the smell of her moisturizer coiled around him sending a pleasant warmth through his chest. *What was she doing to him?* He turned back to the tea and poured himself a cup.

He leaned on the kitchen counter, and his hand went to the fish relic in the pocket of his black dressing gown. The cool green stone had a calming effect; he wasn't quite ready to part with their new treasure yet.

"Are we going to do this thing?" she asked. Nervous energy surrounded her, and he was only adding to it.

"I don't have any better ideas." He sipped his tea. It was too hot, and he burned his tongue. *Good one.*

She poured herself a cup of tea from the pot, not even asking what was in it. "So, how does it work?"

"You won't have to do anything, just go to sleep. We will do a body scan meditation that will induce theta brain waves, and at that point, I'll transport both our subconsciouses to the Great Desert of Dreams."

"And you've done this before?"

Not since his training, and not like this. His eyes shifted away from hers. "Not in a while, but yes."

"What aren't you telling me? I can feel there's something you aren't telling me." She added cold water to her cup and leaned back on the counter.

"My father trained us to use dream weaving as a form of torture. He had us practice on each other. The idea is that you defeat your prisoners in their dreams, play on their deepest fears and amplify them beyond nightmares. Wear them down so they don't know what reality is anymore."

"That's horrid."

"Normal dreams I can control, but the Great Desert of Dreams can be different. Just be prepared," he said firmly. This wasn't something to be taken lightly.

"That isn't all, is it?"

He didn't want to mention how he was terrified he would have to touch her. Dream weaving worked best with physical contact, but if he was asleep, he didn't know if he had control over the hand of death. In the daylight, he was fine. He'd learned control, but this was going into uncharted waters.

When he first got to London, he'd avoided sleeping next to anyone. It wasn't worth the risk. Danni had set him up on numerous blind dates, all women within the magical community, and a terrible idea. He didn't get any second dates, let alone sleep with any of them.

But when he rediscovered drinking and bars as a haven away from the Tower, he also discovered women—women who had nothing to do with magic or the Tower or his father. And he made the most of it, made up for nearly eight years of being in prison.

But even when he was blind drunk, the fear of the hand of death never went away. He never brought women back to the Tower or slept over at their places, always slinking from their bedrooms in the night like a cowardly rat. He was the arsehole who never called. But no amount of drunkenness would have him risk their lives, and he was too fucked up to make any real connections.

Yet here he was, risking Azalea for purely selfish reasons, to break a bond. He swallowed and took a sip of his tea. He had to tell her.

"Well?" Azalea said, watching him over the top of her cup as she blew on the steam.

"I've told you about the hand of death. I can control it, but it's my emotions that fuel the magic I consciously keep in check. I don't know what will happen in the dream. If I lose control of my emotions in there, I could hurt you. That's why I wanted to go by myself."

There he said it. Now at least she wouldn't want to come.

"How would you hurt me? Wouldn't it just be in the dream, not in real life?"

"Yes. But I need to be touching you to have the connection to draw you into my dream."

She twisted her mouth side to side as if she hadn't thought of that. "Oh?"

"If I'm touching you, I can kill you by accident." He wanted to make that point very clear.

She put down her cup and looked at her hands. This was it. She was going to back out. "I only know what you've already told me about the hand of death, but I know you, Torin. I know you wouldn't do anything to hurt me."

"But what if I can't control it? What if I hurt you? I've done it before. I killed my best friend for gods' sake. I loved her, but it wasn't enough." Panic rose in his chest. Why didn't she get it?

Azalea looked up and held his stare, her eyes soft and understanding. "I know, but you were young, and now you're a mage. You also brought her back."

"I never found out if she was okay afterward. You know this, Azalea." He forced himself to sip his hot tea. He'd need it to get to sleep under this sort of pressure.

She drained her cup and put it next to the sink, then crossed her arms. "We don't have a choice, so stop trying to scare me, and let's just get it done."

He felt the uncertainty rolling off her, but her face was determined.

"You're sure?"

That was the opposite effect of what he wanted. He had warned her at least, and there was no getting out of this now.

"You won't hurt me, Torin. I know that."

He didn't know that.

She let out a near-silent breath and tapped her fingers on the bench. "So we have to go to sleep. In a bed. Together..."

"How did you think we would get into a dream?" He turned from the sink and folded his arms. Enjoying her discomfort just a little.

A blush crept across her cheeks as she pivoted away. "Never mind, let's just go."

"Fine. My bedroom then." He drained his tea and walked upstairs before he could back out.

He heard the clatter of her cup in the sink, then her footsteps on the stairs.

She appeared at his door, lingering in the entrance. The best way to do this was to treat it as any other teaching exercise. Not make it awkward, despite the fact that it already was.

"You lie on that side. I'll put on a guided meditation, then do your best to fall asleep as normal. That's all it is. We can link hands, and I'll bring you in once we're both in the same dream state. Got it?"

She nodded and marched up to the bed and sat down, her back rigid.

He was suddenly glad they had private quarters. This was wrong on so many levels, one of which was she being his apprentice. Being caught in bed together would have them both in deep shit. Plus, he was sure she was seeing Erik, and he wouldn't approve of them sharing dreams. Not to mention anything could happen if they went into a dream together, and they didn't know what it would do to the soul bond. For all he knew, it could draw them closer and strengthen their connection.

"It'll be fine, Torin. I'm okay with this, but I'm going to steal this blanket because my feet are cold." She dropped her dog slippers to the floor, lay on top of the covers, and pulled the green quilt folded at the end of the bed over her. At least she was being nice now. The relic hunt had done them wonders.

He swallowed. She was handling this far better than he was. He started the meditation app and clicked off the lamp, throwing them into the dull light from the streetlamps outside.

He lay next to her on top of the covers and closed his eyes. He followed the soothing voice in the app, relaxing his facial muscles, then his neck, his shoulders, his torso, and all the way down his legs and arms until his limbs felt like they weren't attached. But his muscles tensed whenever Azalea moved the slightest.

He held his breath and inched his fingers to the side as he reached out to find her hand. Her breath hitched at his touch, but she entwined her fingers with his confidently and squeezed them as the fizz of magic sparked between them. The magic wasn't as shocking now.

Her pulse was steady under his palm, but he'd done nothing to alter her heart rate, nothing to put her in danger. His magic was under control.

He was suddenly very awake, and he suspected so was she. He lay there in the dark, trying to focus on the meditation, but all he could think about was the softness of her hand linked in his and the seductive trickle of magic running between them.

He got himself under control and focused on slowing his heart rate and breathing and felt her pulse do the same. His eyes were heavy, and his limbs were once more floating like they weren't even there.

Suddenly, he was awake. But he wasn't in his bed. The sun blazed down from a vibrant blue sky, and around him, desert sands shifted in undulating waves as if they were alive.

"We made it!" Azalea said.

Torin nearly jumped out of his skin, not realizing she was next to him. Excellent. His subconscious had brought them both to the right place.

Enormous steps of the pyramid rose behind him, and he faced Azalea, who was staring at him.

He realized why. He was dressed in the classic Desert of Dreams menswear, a loincloth. *Just great.*

Azalea looked like a goddess in a wrapped dress that rippled like water and flowed around her form in a very alluring way.

His breath caught. He'd never appreciated just how beautiful she was in the waking world. As she twirled around, admiring her dress, her long brown hair danced around her, and her smile went right into her silvery-gray eyes, making them sparkle. That was the difference here, her smile. He'd never seen her this happy in real life, and it made her glow in a whole new light.

She beamed at him. "Wow. You're ripped—I mean... your tattoos. They're amazing. Is that a snake skeleton?" she asked, staring at his leg. Then clamped her hand over her mouth. "Sorry. I didn't mean to say all that out loud."

He smiled. He could take that as a compliment.

"It's a dream. You can't always control what you say," he said. Though, usually, he could but only with years of practice. It was always funny going into other people's dreams, but this was the first time he'd accepted someone into his. He chose not to comment on the snake tattoo. Hopefully, she would forget about that when she woke up.

"Time to find our answers." He faced the temple and marched toward it. The glow of the two suns burned down on his back. He always thought it was strange that Zakar lived in a desert of endless sunlight when he was the god of the night. To each their own.

Azalea caught up to him, her bare feet padding silently across the sand-swept marble path that gave off no heat. "What do we do? Ring the doorbell or something?"

"Something like that."

They made it to the giant stone steps, and Torin picked up a clay bowl at the base. Azalea peered around his shoulder, trying to get a look. He showed her what was in the bowl.

"It's a carved bird?"

"It's a whistle." Torin put the wooden bird's tail to his lips and set out a trilling melody that was eaten by the desert wind. He placed the bird back and sat at the base of the steps with his legs out.

"Now what?"

"Now we wait," he said.

They sat for an unknown amount of time. His dream body felt floaty and relaxed, the opposite of his tense, overstressed mortal body. He preferred the dream version of himself.

Azalea hummed next to him, swaying gently. He remained still, watching the glitter of sand swirl in eddies.

"Are there other gods here?" Azalea asked as she picked up a handful of sand off the step and let it trickle slowly through her fingers like a fine waterfall.

"No. They only come when they are summoned."

The wind picked up. The sky turned a deep scarlet as one of the suns dipped below the horizon, leaving only the red giant in the sky and pitching the sand blood red.

"That's not ominous," Azalea said lightheartedly.

The sand churned in front of them. Torin shielded his eyes as they crouched by the pyramid step. Faster and faster, the sand whipped around until a great cloud of it collected in front of them like a giant swarm of flies.

Was this Zakar? He had never requested to meet a god before. The last time he was here was when he took the elixir of the gods for his apprentice test. Maybe Zakar wasn't happy they came.

"We seek the god Zakar for guidance!" Torin yelled into the gust. Wind thrashed in all directions, but the solid-looking sand swarm in front of them remained stationary.

"I don't think it's friendly," Azalea called over the roar and pulled on Torin's arm. "We should get out of here."

For once, she was the voice of reason. He was about to wake them up when the swarm morphed and folded in on itself like a flock of starlings working in unison. Azalea gasped, and Torin remained frozen as it spread into two enormous wings, and from the center, the head of a dragon emerged.

The sand folded itself into a solid mass of a dragon, and it set down on the marble path with a deep rumble that shook the earth.

"What message do you wish to relay to Zakar?" A deep voice boomed from the dragon's mouth.

"We wish to ask Zakar if we can communicate with the gods, Gula and her son Damu of the Shadow Dimension. Can you call them?" Torin yelled.

The dragon let out a roar, took off into the sky, and disappeared. The wind stopped, and the suspended sand fell to the ground in a fine, exfoliating rain.

Torin slumped back down on the step. "I don't know if that was good or bad."

"It didn't seem angry at least." Azalea spun in a circle, smiling out toward the desert. "Do we wait?"

Before he could answer, the world whipped up into another storm of sand as the dragon spun itself back into existence, and Torin stood up again.

"The gods you seek have agreed to meet."

Torin let out a breath.

"You will return tomorrow at the hour of the moonrise."

Before he could thank the dragon, he blinked and found himself in bed. His toes were freezing, and his dressing gown was half open, leaving his middle exposed and cold.

He suddenly remembered what had happened. Azalea. She hadn't moved. Not bothering to turn on the light, he felt along the bed until he found her and shook her shoulder.

"Azalea, wake up." His skin was sweaty and flushed, and his hands were shaking.

Please wake up.

"Alright, I'm awake. Jeez." She rolled over to face him, and in the low light, he could just make out her sleepy eyes and her hair spread over her shoulders, all fluffy and tangled.

He let out a shaky breath and fell back onto the bed, and the blood that had drained from his face returned. "I thought I'd hurt you." He breathed and rubbed both hands over his face.

"Well, good job you didn't." Her voice was low and sleepy. "That was incredible. So, back tomorrow night, then?"

"Looks like it." He sat up to lean against the headboard, trying to forget the brightness of the dream and the way Azalea had looked at him in there—happy. It wasn't real.

The bed moved; she must have gotten up. "Um, so I'm going to my bed now. Night."

"Night." He could see the faint outline of her form.

"Shit."

"What?"

"I've got my date with Erik tomorrow night."

So she was seeing Erik. His stomach hardened. "I can go alone."

"No. It's okay. I'll tell him we can do it another night." She shrugged.

"Good. We can get this over with."

As the door closed he smiled to himself, secretly glad she chose him over Erik. He was being petty and knew it was the bond, but didn't care. He switched on the light, too awake to go back to sleep now.

CHAPTER 19

Torin wasn't home when Azalea woke up. She could still sense him somehow, so she guessed he hadn't gone too far. Maybe the gym or to his office to catch up with his supervisor Mage Brandon Guildford to tell him the good news about their relic hunt.

After another attempt at a breakfast smoothie, this time a little better, she made her way down to Torin's office where she found a note on his desk telling her to go through his research on the Lost City of Petra. That sounded fun. It was the next place he had narrowed down to find a relic, but apparently not narrow enough.

After two hours of reading, she had come to the same conclusion Torin had. They didn't have enough to go on. Her eyes fell to the safe where Torin had locked away the Shadow Atlas. She knew it would have the answers, and he had given her the code. But she had also promised Torin she wouldn't consort with it unless he was present.

His revelations that the book might be a demon or connected to some evil person had her jittery just thinking about touching it again.

She went against her instincts—she would not open the safe—she would wait for Torin to get back from wherever he went, and they would look at it together.

She sighed. This was a waste of time. Standing up and stretching, she spotted her boxes. Faraday followed her around the tower for the next hour as she found new homes for the plants and practiced various Echo Magic techniques in boosting them as she went; just because she wasn't studying Echo Magic anymore didn't mean she wanted to forget how to use it.

With hands on hips, she looked out her new bedroom window through a mini bamboo forest she had created and decided a workout at the gym was a good idea. She couldn't face doing any uni work or sitting down to do fiddly watch repairs; she needed to do something active.

She had just changed into navy blue yoga tights and a long-sleeved white top when Isaac called. Sitting on her bed for a quick break, she caught him up on all the craziness.

"I'm proud of you for not defaulting to the Shadow Atlas," Isaac said after the long recollection of events, minus the dream trip, of course.

"Thanks. I'm trying to cooperate with Torin to get through this, but it's so hard." She wished she could explain why, but it was too risky talking about the bond, and she didn't want to admit the Shadow Atlas was adding more tension. She swore she could feel it pulling at her somehow, like it was at the edge of her psyche, nudging her to go get it.

"I better get back to study. Call me if you need to chat again, okay?" Isaac said.

A lump formed in Azalea's throat. She wished he was here now. It felt good to have someone to talk to. She ended the call, promising herself she would spend more time with Isaac once this was all over.

$$\text{☽ ☽ ☾ ● ☾ ☾ ☾}$$

The visit to the gym was non-eventful and challenging—exactly what she wanted in a gym session. She left sweating and with legs made of rubber.

She nearly slammed into Erik as she rounded the corner, into the main hallway of the Complex.

She steadied herself, not so gracefully against the wall. "Hi."

"I was hoping I might find you here." He leaned in, his gaze set on her lips.

A fluttering sensation darted through her stomach. "Shouldn't you be out metalworking or something?"

"My instructor is still sick. Thought I'd grab a late lunch at the caf. Wanna join?"

Azalea checked her phone. Still no messages from Torin, and it was past lunchtime...

A tightness spread across her chest at the thought of going into the caf. "I dunno. I'm not exactly popular around these parts if you hadn't noticed."

"It's after lunch. It'll be empty now. Come on, I'll protect you if anyone gives you shit." He flexed a bicep and winked at her. He grabbed her hand, and she let herself be pulled along, though she never actually agreed to it.

Her stomach clenched as they entered the caf. The room was bright and sunny with warmth drifting down from the fake sky ceiling as if the real sun was shining. A few sparrows had found their way in and flitted around the shallow part of the pond, having a nice bath next to some giant sunflowers that had popped up around the edge. Maybe she could grow some of those in her room?

Erik waved an arm across the empty tables spread across the room. "See, no one here."

"Alright. I can stay for a bit. But if Torin calls, I need to get back," she said as part of her exit strategy.

They ordered sandwiches and coffees and sat at a picnic table near the pond.

Azalea took her first bite, then her stomach dropped as Livia and Millie sauntered in. Well, Millie sauntered, Livia trudged, looking sad and defeated.

Azalea's sandwich went dry as chalk in her mouth. Maybe she should go talk to Livia? She hadn't gone to Elam's funeral the week before because she knew she wasn't welcome. Had she left it too long?

But Livia spotted her. Her slouched shoulders straightened up, and she charged straight for Azalea.

"YOU!" Livia bellowed, pulling her elemer out as she ran.

Azalea shot out of her seat and threw up a shadow shield, hiding herself from Livia.

"I think she's mad," Erik said sarcastically as he slowly rose and stepped around the shield.

"Not helping," Azalea said through gritted teeth.

Erik held his hands up. "Livi, calm down. It wasn't her."

"She killed Elam!" Her words came out in sobs.

Azalea lowered the shield and was ashamed that she didn't stand up for herself. Instead, she hid behind Erik as he stepped toward Livia, forcing her backward. Millie stood with her arms folded, glowering at Azalea.

Swallowing hard, Azalea moved to Livia's line of sight but out of reach. "I'm sorry, Livia. I didn't want any of this to happen. I tried to save him." She wished more than anything he was still there.

"Show me!" Livia demanded. "Let me in your head and prove it."

Azalea's breath froze in her chest. No way she was letting anyone into her head ever again. The memory potion she took every day took care of that problem, but she wasn't about to test it.

"I'm not going to do that. But it was your grandmother's choice to keep me around. She wouldn't have done that if she thought I did it. I'd be dead if it was my fault, and you know it." Azalea tried to appear calm and not make this worse.

"She expelled you from our class. You're nothing but a lousy shadow witch. *A murderer,* just like your new shadow mage *master*. I knew you two were scheming together."

"We aren't scheming. We're doing exactly what the Archmage told us to, and if you want to be her little spy, go ahead and tell her that." That reminded Azalea about spying on Torin for the Archmage. Maybe she should bring it up with him again.

Livia let out a humorless laugh. "You have no idea what she's planning."

"Livia!" Millie barked and frowned at Livia so seriously, she was almost unrecognizable. Livia's eyes widened, and she looked around as if she knew she'd slipped up. Her gaze briefly flicked to Erik.

What *was* she planning? Livia stood, wide eyes looking to Millie for help.

Azalea felt the probe of Livia's magic chipping away at the edge of her mind. She wouldn't get through, but it was time to take the high road and walk away.

"I think I'll leave now," Azalea whispered to Erik.

"Don't try anything, Livia." Erik remained in front of Azalea, and they backed around the fountain.

"Oh, no you don't!" Livia summoned water from the pond and morphed it into ice daggers and launched them straight at Azalea and Erik.

Azalea threw up a shadow shield, quick enough to catch the ice, leaving embedded spikes sticking out of the solid dark wall. An ice shard stopped right in front of Azalea's face—a close one. She exchanged a look with Erik, and he let out a breath.

"That was bloody close," he said, quiet enough that Livia couldn't hear.

Clearly, neither of them had been expecting that level of force.

"I don't want to hurt her," Azalea said.

"Neither do I. Do you know how to do shadow ropes?" Erik asked.

"Yes." Azalea nodded. She'd practiced them several times but in her bedroom trying to lasso her lamp. This was a little more pressure.

"Lower the shield. I'll send two fireballs to distract her and Millie, then you knock them over with the shadow ropes—tie them to a table or something, then we'll run."

Azalea nodded. She dropped the shield, and Erik threw his fire. Shadow magic streamed from Azalea's elemer as she willed the ropes of darkness to separate and pin the girls to the ground as gently as she could.

But the shadows slammed into them hard, knocking them off their feet and winding around the table legs so Livia and Millie looked like giant insects tangled in a non-geometrical spider's web.

"I'm really sorry!" Azalea yelled as she ran.

Erik followed her. "See you guys in class!"

They sprinted up the stairs and all the way to Torin's tower. She dodged several spirits as she passed the chapel, careful not to touch any this time.

The shadows must have held because they weren't followed, and hopefully, they would just dissolve away and free the girls now that she was further away.

Azalea checked her bag for her keys, realizing that in her haste to leave for the gym after her phone call with Isaac she'd forgotten them. She looked around to make sure no one was watching, then shuffled out the loose stone in the wall where Torin hid the spare key. He changed the spot regularly, but it was necessary since Azalea had forgotten her key more than once in the last week. She unlocked the door.

Erik held it open. "I better get back to studying."

"Me too." Her heart was racing. She licked her lips and met Erik's gaze.

He leaned in and kissed her. His fingers tangled in her hair, and he pulled her in. The adrenaline pumping through her veins had her arching into him, wanting more.

He let her go and pulled away, not looking anywhere near as flustered and hot as she felt. She rubbed the back of her neck, frustrated he had stopped.

"Maybe we can continue this tonight," he said as more of a statement than a question.

Something she wouldn't say no to right now.

"Oh, crap!" She gave an aggravated shake of her head.

He traced the line of her cheekbone with his thumb possessively. "What?"

"I forgot. I need to reschedule." She chewed her bottom lip. "Is that okay?"

"You're not just blowing me off, are you?" He pulled his hand back, studying her as if he was trying to decide for himself.

"No. I really wanted to come over." She touched her lips briefly.

He held his hands up and stepped back. "Then why can't you come? What's the problem?"

"Something came up. Sorry."

"Let me guess. That something is Mage Dumont?" He turned away to look out over the stone wall.

"You know I don't have a choice."

"Stop apologizing all the time. It's fine." It didn't sound like he was fine. He smiled, but it was forced. "How about Saturday night? No Torin Dumont plans that night?" he asked with notable sarcasm.

"Sounds good." She ignored his tone. Saturday was two days away. That should give her time to get their dream trips out of the way and go back to normal sleeping.

He stepped back and gave a half-arsed wave. "See you then."

Azalea went inside and slumped into her chair across from Torin's computer, letting her bag fall to her feet. He still wasn't home, but there was a note on her book.

Out for the afternoon. Continue working on the Jordan relic. If I'm not back by 3 pm, meet Maiken at her apartment.

Why all the secrecy? She got out her phone.

Azalea: *Got your note. Where are you? Are you doing something dangerous? Is it to do with a relic?*

He messaged back straight away.

Torin: *No and none of your business. Just do what I say without questions for once.*

If he was up to something dodgy without her, she wanted to know. Though she was bound to feel it if something bad happened.

Azalea: *Fine. But I can't find anything on the Jordan relic. We need to use the Shadow Atlas.*

Torin: *Don't use the SA till I'm home. Just practice channeling magic into the ruby.*

That did not sound like a good idea.

Azalea: *By myself?*

Torin: *I trust you know how to recognize burnout by now.*

Azalea: *Okay. Stay safe.*

She sent the last message and cringed. *Stay safe.* She didn't want him to know she wanted him to be safe. She still hadn't forgiven him. Somehow, they'd fallen into some sort of unspoken truce, and she wasn't sure she liked it. It was like everything he had done kept slipping from her memory. Even when he was being a grumpy bastard yelling orders at her, things had somehow drifted back to the way they were before.

Hopefully, whatever he was up to didn't interfere with their plans to go back to the Desert of Dreams tonight. Faraday bounced down the stairs and hopped onto her knee. She scooped him up and put him on her shoulder as she went to get the ruby. A few hours of channeling magic would be good for her.

CHAPTER 20

Torin did his best to not make eye contact with Danni as she taped the cold mini microphone to his chest right next to that cursed moon tattoo that matched Azalea's. He looked around the calming white and gray conference room to avoid Danni. It had perfectly arranged rows of maroon chairs, with light blue curtains drawn to the sides of the tall windows, and vases of white flowers that sat on angular podiums.

He turned to the table covered in Danni's surveillance equipment, where they sat at the back of the room. The lad she had brought along to assist was typing away furiously and switching between screens on multiple devices.

"Just because I'm asking for your help doesn't mean I forgive you and Maiken for lying to me about who Azalea is. You set the both of us up to crash and burn. I killed her father for fuck's sake. Did you think that she would ever forgive me for that?" Torin said quietly as he did up his shirt over the mic. If she noticed his tattoo, she didn't mention it.

"I'm sorry, Torin. I thought maybe you could help each other. But I'm going to keep apologizing until you either get sick of me or until you believe me." Danni gazed at him, her green eyes begging for his forgiveness. "And I mean it, I am truly sorry I lied to you both."

"You keep doing that then." Torin stood up and shrugged on his blue sports jacket and continued to not look at her. Of course, he would forgive her. He just wanted to drag it out a little more, so she realized how much she'd hurt them both.

"Eh, hem." The assistant cleared his throat. "Um, it's working now."

"Good," Torin said, hoping it hadn't started recording earlier.

"Right. You're ten minutes early. Get out there before your father arrives." Danni gave Torin a friendly shove toward the door.

Torin checked he had his phone, wallet, and elemer, then left the conference room and walked into Kerridges, doing his best not to look for the Paranormal Justice Unit agents that Danni had scattered around the restaurant. He thought he spotted two, one on either side of the white columns, and quickly averted his eyes to take an interest in the deep green ceiling above. Danni would remain in the conference room to monitor and record their lunch.

Torin followed the waiter to a curved booth of rich, maroon leather. Two chairs sat opposite him, but he preferred the more solid option and chose the booth facing the door.

His phone buzzed in his pocket.

Azalea: *Got your note. Where are you? Are you doing something dangerous? Is it to do with a relic?*

Nosy girl. They exchanged messages for the next five minutes as he waited, and he specifically told her not to use the Shadow Atlas until he was back. Whether she listened to him was another matter.

They'd have to check it tonight before their visit to the Great Desert of Dreams. After what he was about to tell his father, she wouldn't be safe after today.

This was the last shot for his father. The problem was he had almost seemed human at one point in the tomb in China. But Torin had to remind himself that the man was a master manipulator.

Torin told Azalea to go to Maiken and Danni's place if he didn't return, slipped his phone back into his pocket, and checked on his elemer again; just to be safe.

Korbyn Dumont marched into the restaurant as if he owned it. Berating the waiter for making him wait several seconds before being taken to his table.

"Torin, a pleasure to see you," his father said, offering his hand as he arrived at the table. He wore a three-piece suit and carried his customary raven-headed cane. Torin noticed the elemer his father stole from the shaman tucked into his belt.

Torin stood up and shook his father's hand, going along with the charade. "Father."

"You always were such a serious boy." His father chuckled.

Torin took in a calming breath. He was here to be diplomatic, but firm. He would not let his anger overcome him and put more people in danger. He just needed his father to admit to killing his mother, then he would finally have some evidence.

"I just want to talk. No trouble," Torin said.

"Very well. Straight to the point." His father held his hands up in surrender. He seemed to be in a good mood. The old man must be assuming Torin was going to join him. This meeting was sure to go downhill quickly.

The waiter brought two glasses of red wine his father must have ordered. No way Torin was drinking that.

"I take it my offer about your old girlfriend, Kira, changed your mind about giving up the girl?"

"Is Kira alive?" Torin asked.

"Are you going to come back and join us?"

"Tell me first." He had to assume she was still alive; otherwise, why would he bring this all up?

"Yes. She is alive. But you'll have to come see for yourself, son."

She was alive. Words he had been waiting years to hear. Words that absolved him of murdering his best friend. Words that set him free. He could have hugged his father if he was sure it was true, but a small part of him said not to believe it just yet.

There was nothing about this man he could trust. He could be using Kira to lure him back in. Either way, he wouldn't abandon Azalea or his mission. He would take down his father from the outside; today would be a step toward that.

"I'm glad to hear it. I'm sure she did well under your training," he said, not wanting it to sound like he cared.

His father frowned and put down his wineglass mid-sip. "You are coming back? That is why you came to meet me. You wouldn't dare be stupid enough to show up without the girl, would you? I saved you from that bull creature in that tomb." The vein in his father's head twitched, and he slammed his fist into the table.

"Tell me what happened to Mother." Torin didn't flinch.

"You know what happened to her, you ungrateful beggar," Korbyn spat.

Torin sat there calmly taking a fake sip of his wine. He needed something more on record. He needed his father to say it.

"You killed her," Torin stated.

Korbyn leaned back in his chair. "I see now what you've become, a slave to the Owls, a slave to the PJU. You are no son of mine, and I take back the offer. I'm coming for the girl, and I'm giving you the courtesy of leaving this room unharmed because I like this restaurant, and I know people are watching. But trust me, it won't happen again."

He stood up and threw his napkin on the table so dramatically Torin could have laughed if he wasn't so on edge. His father was a fucking joke in his own disillusioned world.

Torin reached for his elemer, just in case.

"Admit that you killed her. You told me once before; own up to it like a man," Torin said, louder than intended, and the restaurant fell into hushed silence.

Korbyn slammed his palm on the table. "I slit her throat and watched her die. Is that what you want to hear, son?" he hissed under his breath, his eyes locked on Torin's and seething with rage.

Torin's muscles stiffened involuntarily, so shocked at the outright admission and bluntness that he didn't react. He'd said it—the horrible truth after all these years.

Korbyn prodded Torin hard in the chest with his cane. "You think you're better than us, but the same blood runs in our veins."

"I have my mother's blood as well, and she sure as hell deserved better than you," Torin growled. He sat up straight, his hand on his elemer; shaking so hard with restraint, he wasn't sure he could keep it up.

"Goodbye, son. I'll be seeing you and your new girlfriend very soon." His father chuckled and turned his back to walk out.

Torin's heart drummed in his ears, blocking out all logical thought and reason as red-hot anger took over. He picked up a chair and threw it at his father who turned just in time to raise his arm and a shadow shield against it. The look in his eye was priceless. He hadn't expected such a petty response, and Torin shouldn't have done it. Faced with immediate regret, he realized too late they were in the center of a restaurant in a non-magical part of London in the middle of the day. He couldn't get into a fight. But it was too late. The blood was already pounding through his veins.

"How dare you raise a hand at me!" Korbyn yelled.

Spikes of shadows shot from his elemer and hurtled toward Torin as he flipped the table and ducked down. The thud of the razor-like shadow daggers spiked into the table instead of his flesh, as his father intended.

"She deserved better than you!" Torin said, loud enough for his father to hear.

"She deserved what she got. She was weak and holding me back. You're just the same. A disappointment."

Torin roared and hurtled toward his father, only to be whipped around and smashed into the floor. He groaned and looked up to see his father cutting into the Hollow.

Struggling against whoever was pinning him down, Torin twisted and thrashed, but multiple arms held him as he fought to reach his father; he had to stop him from leaving.

"See you soon." His father sneered as the Hollow closed.

Torin didn't care about his morals or oaths to himself anymore. He would use the hand of death right now if he could get close enough and reopen the Hollow in the same place to catch his father.

The room filled with PJU agents. They were closing in on all sides. Torin twisted and flipped himself over so fast, the hands had to let go of him. He ripped his elemer through the air, dragging it into the Hollow roughly, and launched himself at the cut before it was even open. But hands gripped his legs, and he smashed onto the floor once more.

"Get off me," he roared, battling against them. At least two men were holding him down, with one sitting on his back. Someone held his face squished against the wooden floor, spit dribbling from his mouth as another took his elemer from his hand.

"It's clear," a PJU agent called.

Danni rushed over. "We got what we wanted, Tor. I'm so sorry."

He closed his eyes and gave up his struggle; it was too late. His father would be long gone now.

His hands burned with the need to kill, the hand of death beckoning him to use his curse once more. Closing his eyes to the surrounding rabble, he waited for his blood to cool, not resisting the agents as they held him down.

This would be a huge cover-up job because of him. He cringed at the thought; the room was filled with non-magic people who would need some House of Owl mind erasing—something he could have prevented if he'd kept his head clear.

Danni came back once he was calm, and he was allowed to sit up unrestrained.

"Maiken just called. Azalea is at our place going mental saying something has happened to you. Care to explain?"

"No," he answered bluntly.

Shit. Their bond was getting stronger if she felt his anger across town. He checked his phone and had lines of notifications, messages, and missed calls asking what happened to him and demanding he call her.

"I told her to go to your place if I wasn't back by 3 pm."

"It's not three yet, and that's not what this is, Torin." Danni tapped her booted foot against the hardwood floor. "She was distressed and convinced something had happened to you. Maiken said she was about to leave and come looking for you herself. I take it this means you two made up?"

"We've come to an arrangement. But she hasn't forgiven me, understandably," he said, hoping she would drop this.

"That doesn't explain her reaction."

Time to run away. Torin shrugged and stood up. "I have no idea. You'll have to ask her. Let me know if you got enough evidence against my father when you go through the recordings. I've got things to do."

He marched out of the restaurant, leaving the PJU team to clean up his mess. Anger still simmered beneath his skin, too close for comfort. This had to be enough to build a case against his father. If there was a next time, he wouldn't hold back.

CHAPTER 21

Azalea dressed in her good pajama bottoms, the ones with frogs on them, and put on a comfy t-shirt. This was the night. They were heading back into the Great Desert of Dreams, and her heart was drumming in her chest at the thought of it.

After the afternoon she'd had, she was exhausted enough to crash for days. Torin's secret meeting with his father had her storming down to Maiken's door, demanding answers like a crazy person. It had been hard to think straight, let alone get out coherent sentences with the psychotic levels of anger and hatred screaming down the bond from Torin, not to mention the tattoo on her chest burning painfully.

Maiken probably thought she had lost it. For someone who supposedly hated Torin, Azalea was doing a good job of looking like a crazy girlfriend, rather than his apprentice. But she couldn't help it. He could have just told her where he was going, so she could have been mentally prepared, at least.

Nervous energy prickled over her as she walked across the landing to Torin's room. It felt weird to even go in there, let alone sleep there, but it also felt natural. It was the bond brainwashing her somehow.

She hovered in the doorway for a second before walking up to the bed with artificial confidence and sitting down. He'd changed the duvet cover. It was now plain gray cotton with white and gray pillowcases. Maybe he missed the prison vibes. Azalea had brought her pillow and patchwork quilt from her bed to make herself more at home. On his side of the bed, the fire was crackling in the open grate.

"You ready for this?" Torin asked without looking up from his phone from his spot on the edge of the bed.

"What? To meet a couple of gods in a dream conference a sand dragon set up for us. Sure, why not?" She dropped her pillow on the bed and shook her head; this was absurd. A flicker of a smile broke the edge of Torin's lips as he turned to meet her eyes, and she couldn't help but smile in surprise.

She hugged her pillow to her chest. "Are you okay?" The rage from earlier was still in him, simmering under the surface.

He swung around and arranged his pillows to lean back on them. "I'm fine. I'm sorry I didn't tell you what I was doing. I didn't think it would affect you like that."

"Okay. Maiken's suspicious of us though." Azalea shrugged. She didn't want to go over the same conversation they'd had when he got home. At least she understood why he was so angry. "Can't do much about that now. Should we get on with this then?"

"Yes. But let me do the talking this time, okay? It takes years to master conscious control in a dream." Torin crossed his arms.

Her face heated a little. Her memory of their last dream together was still clear, despite Torin telling her she wouldn't remember it. A vivid image of his god-like body was now pressed into her mind, and she blushed, remembering her comment about how ripped he was and then rambling on about his tattoos. Tattoos. A snake tattoo...

"Wait. Didn't you have a snake tattoo in the dream?" Her gaze moved to his leg. It was covered by black tracksuit bottoms, but the memory became clear. She was sure that was real. "Do you have a snake tattoo?"

"I'd hope you wouldn't remember that." He rubbed his hand down his face. "Let's get on with this. Lie down."

She hopped on the bed and sat cross legged facing him, desperate to know if it was true. "You're not getting away with it that easy. Tell me why you have a snake tattoo?" No way she could fall asleep if she was wondering about that.

"Because—" He slid down the bed to lie down, leaning on his elbow, looking at her like he wanted to make it obvious who owned the bed. "I may have experimented with necromancy when I was younger."

"Well, well." She paused, and he held her gaze like he was challenging her. "A bit hypocritical, aren't you, professor?"

"Please don't call me that." His expression was serious, but she felt a mix of emotions sparking off him that she couldn't pin down to identify.

"Please don't change the subject. It must have been more than a little experimentation. Why do you have a big tattoo like that, and I don't? You're not even from the House of Snakes."

"You're right. It was more than a little experimentation, and let's just say my attempts at necromancy was more successful than yours."

"You mean with Kira? You've been having a go at me all this time when you did exactly the same thing?" She had the sudden urge to hit him with her pillow. But she figured that wouldn't go down well, and she desperately wanted to know details.

"It was a completely different situation. I knew what I was doing. I researched it for years, not a few weeks like you, and it worked, or I think it did." He went quiet for a second. "Plus, I brought you back, didn't I?"

True. But he failed to mention his level of necromancy training. "When did you get the tattoo?"

"It appeared after I did it the first time, and it is a constant reminder never to do it again. One I didn't listen to when you came along, obviously." He fell back onto the pillow and looked at the ceiling.

"What happened to Kira?" she asked cautiously.

"It was an accident. I was angry and desperate. I didn't even know I'd stopped her heart." His Adam's apple bobbed in his throat. "Apparently, she's still alive. Though it was my father who told me, so I don't know if I should believe him."

"That's great that she might be alive," Azalea said, not sure how to deal with this information. "Well, I like the tattoo." She swung her legs around and lay down, looking straight up as she pulled the blanket to her chin. Wasn't that interesting? The truth about not-so-perfect Torin Dumont revealed.

"Thanks. Now go to sleep." He switched off the lamp and put on the meditation app.

The room was lit by the soft glow of the fire, and suddenly Azalea wasn't sleepy. "Hey, Torin?"

"What?" He sounded annoyed.

"I'm nervous about meeting the gods. What if they can't undo our bond or the spirits-going-through-me-thing?"

"Don't think like that. We'll find a solution." His words weren't convincing, but when his fingers met hers, she felt he meant it.

"Go to sleep," he said.

)))●(((

The yellow sun burned down on Azalea's exposed arms with billowing waves of heat, closer than it had been last time. The red sun was nowhere in sight. She couldn't help but admire her dress again. Dream fashion was fun, though not something she'd ever wear in real life; she couldn't get enough of the way the silky blue material brushed over her skin, slinky and cooling, but also flattering. She'd never felt pretty in dresses, but this one was a winner.

She looked up, wishing she had sunglasses. They were right in front of the epic pyramid. Torin was in his skimpy loincloth again, and Azalea stared at his toned muscles and amazing tattoos. His arms and back were covered in bold ravens, stars, and galaxies, but around them were delicate jasmine flowers that blended into the background so you almost couldn't see them. The snake skeleton was by far the most impressive; its glowing white bones contrasted with his dark skin and almost seemed raised, like a 3D snake about to crawl off his leg.

"Pay attention. We don't know when they will turn up. We need to be alert," Torin said.

"Got it." Azalea whipped her head around to scan the area. She would do her best not to speak and say something she would regret this time. This dreamscape had a way of making her brain cloudy with a lot fewer filters than usual.

A man appeared in front of them without a sound—the strange alien man from Azalea's near-death experience—Damu, god of healing, and son of the goddess Gula of the House of the White Deer. He loomed over both of them with a tall and gangly gray frame. His face had sharp angles and an unreadable expression.

"I follow your call children of the night," Damu said.

"Thank you for meeting us," Torin said, not at all fazed by this deity standing right there in front of them.

Azalea kept her mouth shut and stared up in awe.

"Tell us what you did to us, why we are bonded, and why Azalea is a doorway for spirits," Torin said, demanding, rather than asking.

"She agreed to a price to return. This is the price."

"She didn't know what she was agreeing to," Torin said.

"It is the way," Damu said calmly.

"How do we break the bond?" Azalea asked, quickly forgetting she was supposed to keep her mouth shut.

"With death, the bond shall break."

Ignoring Torin's disapproving huff, she asked, "Like if we kill someone it breaks, or more like if we die, it breaks?"

"Your deaths will release you."

"As in, we both have to die, or one of us dies?" she asked, not sure why she wanted to know since dying wasn't a plan for either of them.

"Either."

Azalea casually shrugged at Torin. "So we could die?"

"Not a wise choice. Death would be preferable to the pain of such a bond breaking. The one left behind will quickly wish for death."

Hmmm. Not ideal.

Azalea tilted her head, studying Damu's strange features. "There must be another way."

"Death is not always a permanent state. You of all people should know this, Azalea Sharp. Death brings new life."

So, they could temporarily die to break it? That also sounded like a terrible idea. Even her dream body felt nauseous thinking about it, but Torin looked concerningly interested. She needed other options.

Torin shot her a look that said, *stop talking*. "The bond isn't sealed, is it? Does that make a difference?"

"This is the reason it can be broken. Once it is sealed, there is no return."

"How do we seal the bond? I mean, hypothetically, so we don't do it." She suspected she knew the answer but wanted to know for sure.

"When you lie together as one, the bond will be sealed."

A flush of heat ran through her, and it wasn't just embarrassment.

"You set these bloody rules. There has to be another way to break this. Tell me," Torin demanded.

"There may be another way. Liberate enough spirits; it is possible for us to break the bond."

"So you were lying," Torin said bluntly. "You *can* break the bond if you want to."

"If we receive the spirits," Damu said with a small bow of acknowledgment.

"Why did you make Azalea a gateway for spirits? What do you want with the spirits? Why did you do this to us?"

"It was your bond that allowed this rare event to happen. I merely took advantage of a bond waiting to be activated, and I used the shared power you generate. It allowed me to link you to the Shadow Dimension. It is a rare thing."

"But why?" Azalea couldn't help but ask.

"The City of Stars has been decimated by spirit wraiths, the gallu. They consume spirits in the Shadow Dimension, and they are gone forever, and the wraith are never satiated. The balance is unstable. I am setting the balance right."

"Fine. Whatever. How many spirits until my debt is paid?"

"One thousand more spirits and the debt will be considered paid. After this, we will break the bond if you so choose."

"Too many. No way. That will kill her!" Torin's fists clenched at his side, and Azalea instinctively reached for his hand and unwound his grip, forcing her fingers into his to try to balance their emotions and calm him. Their skin glowed white where their hands joined. Torin looked down, clearly horrified, but didn't pull away.

Azalea squeezed his fingers as she felt his magic trickle into her, and in return, she pushed hers through to him, sending calming thoughts with it. His shoulders relaxed a little, and he looked back at Damu.

A sly smile crept across Damu's thin gray lips. "If you seal the bond, you will both be strong enough. If you do not, it is hard to say. Perhaps she will survive, perhaps she will not."

Azalea contemplated the idea. She might be up for collecting the spirits, not the bond-sealing part, but maybe if she spaced them out, it wouldn't take as much of a toll sending that many spirits through.

Torin shook his head as if he knew what she was thinking.

"Ereshkigal will be most pleased if you agree to this. Every spirit is valued," Damu said.

Azalea tilted her head. "What does she have to do with this?"

"Ereshkigal is queen of the Shadow Dimension and ruler of the City of Stars. All that we do is in her name."

"Why does she want the spirits?" Torin's warm brown eyes narrowed.

Damu's expression remained tranquil. "She is their guardian, their protector. She wants them to come home. To find peace. For the city to be alive once more."

Azalea nearly snorted. A city alive with dead people sounded rather contradictory.

"What about the gallu? What's being done about them? And what happens once a gallu is captured in our world? Are the spirits set free? Do they go back to the Shadow Dimension?"

"So many questions. But you are so young and ignorant. I will answer them for you. Ereshkigal is sending the gallu to your world so the humans may capture them and prevent them from returning."

"She's sending them to our world on purpose?" Azalea moved to take a step closer to this Damu knob, but Torin pulled her in closer to him.

Damu nodded slowly. "It is a good plan."

"No, it isn't. You used me to do that!" Azalea spat. "They kill people and take their souls. How does that help anyone?"

"The answer is the answer to your other question. Once the gallu is captured, the souls it consumed return to the Shadow Dimension. Some do not make it back; it is unclear why. But many are returned, and the undamaged ones may return to life in the City of Stars."

What the fuck? This was all some grand master scheme of a goddess who wanted her city filled. At least it took a little blame off Azalea. She was just a pawn in this bizarre game of the gods.

"How is she sending them through?" Azalea asked.

"She has means of manipulation on earth. We do not know all her divine ways, and we do not question her wisdom. But I have seen the spirits return myself. Her plan is working."

Despite the thought of all those gallu on earth and how sick to her stomach it made her, Azalea couldn't help but wonder if maybe her father was okay. Could he really be in the Shadow Dimension, living a whole new life? The thought was strangely comforting. Hopefully, the City of Stars wasn't some sort of euphemism for hell.

"Is my father there?" She had to know.

"I do not know your father. It is a large city. It is possible he is there."

That was enough for her. A glimmer of hope. "Why didn't the gallu with my father's spirit recognize Torin? Why didn't he warn me who he was?"

Torin tensed beside her.

"I cannot answer that. Gallu do not retain all the memories of the spirits they consume. It is possible it did not know, or it chose not to reveal this, or it could only focus on the powerful memories of you."

"Oh," Azalea said.

Torin let go of her hand and crossed his arms. "Azalea, you can't be thinking of taking this deal. It's too dangerous."

"Just trust me, Torin. I can handle it, and we don't have another option other than us dying, so just let me do it."

She felt the absence of his touch, but his power still ran through her. She felt his emotions tangling with her and confusing her thoughts. She had to override them and listen to her brain. This was the right thing to do.

"I can't stop you. But for the record, I think this is a bad idea, and I'm sure I'll be a lot angrier back at home than I am here. So get ready for it," Torin warned.

Azalea smiled and turned to Damu. "You have a deal. I'll do it. I'll send you the spirits, but I'll be sending shit ones, so don't get fussy."

Torin stood there frowning.

"All lives are valued equally. Ereshkigal will be most pleased with you Daughter of Snakes. My time is up. I bid you farewell, children of the night."

"Glad that's settled," Azalea said.

Damu clapped his hands as a great wind of sand whipped up.

The next thing she knew, Torin was looming over her in the bed, shaking her shoulder; in the dim firelight, his eyes were dark from both the magic and his current mood.

"Why did you agree to this, Azalea? It could kill you!"

"But it also might *not* kill me." She rubbed her eyes, trying to wake up.

He shoved a pillow behind him and sat against the headboard scowling. "I could strangle you right now. You never listen."

"Technically, you didn't tell me not to." She rolled over sleepily to face him and closed her eyes again.

"Since when do you care about technicalities?" He nudged her shoulder and a spark of his magic forced her eyes wide open. "Hey, wake up, this is important."

She frowned and rubbed her eyes. "Look. If we do it, they will break the bond. It's exactly what you wanted."

"What's the point if you're dead?" He slid back down the bed and stared at the ceiling.

Was this Torin actually caring, or was it the whole 'one left behind will quickly wish for death' thing?

"Well, I guess I'll go live in Star City, or whatever it was." She joked but felt the weight of his seriousness. He really didn't want her to die. Her heart was beating hard against her ribs. Despite being able to feel his emotions, they were confusing, and she had no idea what he was thinking or how he felt about her.

He sat up again, and waves of frustration rolled off him. "Death isn't a joke, Azalea. There's no guarantee you will go there."

"You were the one who didn't want to live like this. I thought you'd be pleased!" She forced herself to sit up, now wide awake.

He ran a hand over his head, and she turned to face him, sitting cross-legged, just able to make out his strained expression in the firelight. She found herself wanting to be closer to him, wanting to run her fingers over his tattoos.

What? Get a grip, Azalea!

Since waking up, she couldn't get the feeling of his power merging with hers out of her mind. It was like her magic was seeking it out here in the real world. The feeling washed over her again, the way his magic wove into hers and made her feel so alive, so powerful—her blood raced.

She pulled herself out of her daydream to find Torin looking at her in the same way she was trying not to look at him—like he wanted to kiss her.

"The bond is affecting our judgment." He broke the moment, jumping out of bed as if there was a spider in it.

A little insulting. "You're probably right. Did you read my mind or something, or was it the emotions thing?"

"Call it intuition." He moved to the chair by the fire.

She needed to get out of here now, or things would get very insulting or very inappropriate. One thing was evident: their bond was getting stronger, and there was no way they could let that happen.

What she needed was a serious distraction.

CHAPTER 22

Azalea's nerves buzzed, wondering what Erik had in mind for their rescheduled meet-up, or maybe hook-up, at his place. Two days had passed since her visit to the Desert of Dreams, and she craved a distraction more than ever.

Putting as much distance between herself and Torin hadn't been easy, not while they lived together. She escaped by doubling her training time at the gym, forcing herself to do uni work in her room, and getting research and Shadow Magic study done while he was out of the house. It had proven to be a productive two days.

She still had to train with him in Shadow Magic, but she was getting stronger again, and they were careful never to touch, except when he taught her how to use pressure points with sleep magic to knock someone out. That had been worth it. They remained entirely professional, and she successfully knocked Torin unconscious once, though she suspected she may have borrowed some of his sleep magic to aid the process.

She looked in the mirror at the bags under her eyes and wet hair, wishing she could magically dry it. Air magic wasn't exactly her forte, or at least, it wasn't safe experimenting that close to her head. As she dried her hair with a boring hairdryer, her thoughts turned back to the next relic hunt. It was hard to stop thinking about it.

They had made good progress, and it had been a win for Azalea when Torin gave her permission to use the Shadow Atlas to ask about the Jordan relic, under his supervision, of course. And as a result, they had one more riddle to work off of; it played over and over in her head.

Beneath a cold evening sun sits a camel of stone.
A Guardian beast, a serpent, a throne.
Fire lizards basking will show you the way.
A warning to those who search in the day.
By glow of pink light is when you must seek.
Do you dare take the prize, or are you too weak?
Those dark of heart and bound up in greed
Will fail at their task. In the dust, they will bleed.
Those pure of heart, who seek to protect
Can handle the key, they alone may collect.
Know your intention before you contest.
A griffin is deadly when guarding her nest.

A griffin! That was the part she was excited about. They had narrowed down a specific place where Torin was confident they would find the relic and had already planned a trip to the Lost City of Petra in the next few days.

Faraday jumped onto the bench, knocking her out of her planning. She rubbed his chin, then finished drying her hair that went halfway down her back. She wanted to do something different with it for once but didn't know what.

After trying to do a fancy twist thing, she gave up and settled for straightening her hair and leaving it down. Faraday sat watching her from the shelf next to the sink.

She put on a little makeup, then sprayed on some natural floral perfume RoRo had made; jasmine and orange blossom, then dabbed on some lip gloss. That would have to do. They were probably just staying in and watching movies, after all.

She didn't have much wardrobe choice, so went for her good black skinny jeans and a nicely fitted green top that she forgot she had.

Stepping out of her room, she narrowly avoided crashing into Torin as he came out his door, and he nearly tripped over Faraday.

"Where are you off to?" He backed up a few steps, arms folded across his chest.

"Just Erik's." Her heart rate sped up. She pulled in her aura, hoping that would hide any emotions to give away how flustered she was.

A microsecond of something flashed through him, then it was gone. She wasn't sure what it was; jealousy, anger, fear, frustration—she couldn't tell.

"Don't walk through any spirits on the way there. Is he coming to get you?"

"I know, and I won't... yet. He's coming to get me, despite living two minutes' walk away." She swung her bag over her shoulder and smoothed out her hair self-consciously.

The muscles in his jaw tightened. "Are you forgetting about the part where my father said he was coming for you? You aren't safe outside this house."

"I know. But Erik is well-trained in defensive magic, and the Phoenix guards are stationed near his flat as well, so I'll be perfectly safe. You'll know if something happens to me, anyway." She raised her eyebrows. He knew all this. Why did she have to spell it out?

"Just don't say anything around him about what we're doing. I don't trust him."

"I know you don't, and I'm not stupid. I won't say anything," she snapped.

"He could be spying on you for the Archmage. Be careful," he said.

Azalea met his glare as hot anger raced through her. "Hold up!" She stormed up to Torin, hands on her hips. "He's not a fucking spy! Did you ever think he might just like me?"

Torin held his hands up in defense. "Sorry. I didn't mean it to sound like that."

"Yes, you did." She glared at him, feeling his irritation. Good.

"I apologize. I just mean I wouldn't put it past the Archmage to use him to get close to you," he said without a hint of genuine apology.

"He isn't." She couldn't think of a better comeback, and the back of her neck prickled at the off-chance Torin could be right.

"I take it back. He's not a spy. Have a good night then." He stomped down the stairs and went straight to the kitchen while Azalea went down to the bottom floor to wait for Erik near the front door.

Faraday sat next to her expectantly. "You go back upstairs, Farry. Keep Torin company, I'm not sure when I'll be home," she told the cat with a kiss on top of his head. Hoping she might spend a night away from this place.

Erik was on time, and the walk to his house was uneventful, with no ghosts or assassins. One win for the night.

"My lady," Erik said as he opened the door for her and took her coat, all gentlemanly-like.

"Thank you, kind sir," she said with a smile, determined to put Torin and this stupid bond out of her mind. She was well aware she might just be using Erik, but if it took her mind off everything else, she deserved to have a little fun after months of nothing but stress and drama.

Van, Isaac, and RoRo had been telling her to do that all week—do something for yourself, have fun, relax a little. She was listening to them and doing just that.

"Where're your dad and sister?" Azalea asked as he closed the door on the chill of the night, and she took off her damp boots and followed him down a short hallway.

"Gone to Bath to stay with my aunt for the weekend, a bit of a getaway."

She couldn't help being relieved knowing his dad wouldn't be there. "And you didn't want to go?"

"Rather be here with you. You hungry?"

"I am. Something smells good. Did you cook?" He led her into a small dining room where the four-seater table was set up for two, complete with lit candles. This was more than she expected—admittedly, she had low expectations: beer and pizza while watching TV.

He grinned at the spread of food set out in the center of the table as if he made it himself. "No, but the Italian restaurant did a good job."

"Looks great." She wasn't about to complain; it wasn't like she could cook anything decent.

"Let's dig in then." Erik shoved a large portion of pasta onto his plate, and Azalea sat down and helped herself to a salad. They chatted away like they were still in class together. It felt natural and was a relief to relax. She didn't eat too much but had a sufficient amount of beer with the meal, as did Erik.

They moved into the small living room, and Azalea fell onto the old gray sofa, feeling quite at home. Erik swung himself over the back, landed next to Azalea, and handed her a bottle of beer.

Despite not having worked Erik out yet, she had to admit he'd impressed her tonight, and she couldn't help but wonder what he saw in her. It could be the fact that she was the newest thing around or that he was embracing his rebel streak and being the 'bad boy' dating the shadow witch. She didn't think that was it. So the most likely answer was he wanted to get in her pants.

He started the movie, *Thor: Ragnarok*, and moved closer, his leg pressed up against hers. She swallowed, realizing how nervous she was.

As the movie went on, he draped his arm over her shoulders, and she snuggled into his side. He occasionally ran his fingers through her hair, causing her breath to hitch every time. He was so chilled, so relaxed. She wished she was more like that. Yes, he was still an arse a lot of the time; that part of him might never change, but she liked him. It was simple as that.

He kissed her on the cheek and jumped up to get another beer. Her heart rate spiked at the little kiss sending warmth to her belly. "Want another one?" he asked.

"Yes please." She bit her lip and watched Erik as he breezed out of the room.

Suddenly, a sharp pain and heat pulsed across her chest. The moon tattoo over her left breast seared her skin. She pressed her hand to it and sucked in a breath. Torin. Something wasn't right.

"You okay?" Erik said, only a few meters away in the tiny kitchen.

"Fine. My drink just went down the wrong way." She patted her chest, pretending to cough.

She picked up her phone from the coffee table and messaged Torin.

Azalea: *Are you okay? I thought you weren't doing anything dangerous tonight.*

Eric came back and handed Azalea the open beer. "Everything okay?"

"It's just Torin. I wanted to check he wasn't in trouble."

Erik let out a snort. "I'm sure Mage Dumont can take care of himself."

She wanted to say he couldn't, or she could feel he wasn't okay. But she didn't. "He can. I just wanted to know he's okay."

"You're not his mum or his girlfriend." Erik took a swig of beer. Torin was certainly a sore point between them.

"I'm not. I'm his friend, and I'll message him if I want to," she said stubbornly.

"You're his student." Erik pointed out.

"Well, you're messaging Livia all the time." She pointed to his phone which was blinking with notifications.

"Her brother died, and she's my friend."

Her fingernails dug into her palms at that jab. She ignored Erik and pulled the soft blanket over her but didn't offer any of it to Erik. She stared at her phone, willing Torin to message her back. The pain in her chest dulled. He was probably fine.

But maybe another message to be sure. He was the one who said they had to be extra vigilant.

Azalea: *Are you okay? Please don't tell me you went on a mission and didn't tell anyone where it was. Message back.*

She had promised Torin not to call anyone when she thought he was in trouble after the incident the other day. Danni and Maiken were already suspicious of them. They'd be crazy not to after several occasions where Torin and Azalea had inexplicably come to them when the other was in danger. They needed to come up with a cover story or explanation soon.

They had another beer each and started the next movie, the first *Iron Man*, when Torin finally replied.

Torin: *I'm fine. I'm watching a movie.*

Azalea: *Oh. Ok. Me too. I thought I felt something. Just ignore me.*

Erik frowned at her phone. "He's alright, then?"

"He's fine," Azalea said and relaxed back into the cushions.

"Are you pissed at me?" Erik asked.

"No," Azalea said.

"Good." With a sly grin on his face, he leaned in slowly, maintaining eye contact as he lowered his lips to hers, causing her to part them. His hand slipped into her hair and trailed down the back of her neck, sending a shiver down her spine.

This was the distraction she needed. His touch set her skin on fire, and she pressed into him, wanting more. Her hands snaked under his shirt, encircling his waist, pulling him closer.

"I take it this means you like me." He broke away, grinning.

She brushed her lips across his. "I like you, Erik." *She certainly liked him right now.*

"Good."

She grinned back.

"Want to take this to the bedroom?" he asked.

"Yes. Yes, I would," she said honestly, with a strong awareness of her racing heartbeat.

Without warning, he scooped her up, and she squealed, latching onto his neck and giggling as he carried her out of the room. Hopefully, he wouldn't drop her halfway down the hall. His coordination in the dark wasn't great as he bounced off one wall before finding the bedroom and depositing her ungracefully on the edge of the bed, leaving them both in a fit of laughter.

"So you want to do this, then?" he said as he climbed onto the bed beside her.

She didn't need convincing.

They faced each other. His gaze lowered to her mouth as she shuffled back on the bed, and he followed.

"This is probably a bad idea," she muttered as he lay next to her and pulled her in close.

"I think it's a fantastic idea." Erik trailed a finger down her abdomen, finding its way to her jeans and slowly unbuttoning them.

Her eyes suddenly shot open with a thought. "You can't mix magic by having sex, can you?"

It had been so easy for her magic to mix with Torin just being near him. She didn't want to be surprised with yet another weird magic thing.

He sighed. "No. Sex is just sex and unless you turn it into some sort of ritual, your magic will be fine." He pulled her closer to his chest.

"Okay good. Just checking." She smiled into his kiss.

He pulled away. "Where'd you get the idea about mixing magic?"

Not now. "Nowhere," she answered quickly. She eyed the lamp, self-conscious because she didn't want Erik to see the tattoo on her chest and ask about it. He rolled her over in one quick move and turned off the lamp, plunging the room into pleasant darkness. She pressed her lips to his once more, no longer fearing the shadows, and gave herself over to him.

Time went by as if the outside world didn't matter anymore. She forgot all those things she wanted to escape, just for tonight, and it was bliss. Her magic simmered under her skin the whole time, sparking with heat, and she kept it all to herself, giving in to what came so naturally between them.

Afterward, they lay in the dark, sweaty and satisfied. But that little voice couldn't help but tell her it was only temporary. She moved to the edge of the bed to find her clothes and slipped on her shirt to cover the moon tattoo. She should probably get back.

"Stay with me tonight," Erik whispered, the warmth of his fingers stroking her back before he found her wrist, guiding her back into bed. It took little convincing.

He pulled her in close, his arms wrapping around her in a safe cocoon.

"I'll stay. Goodnight, Erik," she whispered back.

"Goodnight." He kissed her neck, and she let the lightness in her chest spread through her entire body. For once, she fell asleep feeling good about things.

CHAPTER 23

Azalea dashed past the chapel. She still had ten minutes to get ready before Torin expected her in the office. She was in an especially good mood this morning; the sun was even peeking out from behind the clouds to shimmer on the damp pavement.

"Young Miss!" a man in torn clothes called out to her.

"Oh, crap," she muttered and sped up to dodge him before he blocked her way to the courtyard. His raggedy appearance meant he was a ghost; the Tower wasn't open yet for tourists, and he certainly didn't look like he lived there.

"I seek your council!" the man called out.

"As do I," another shouted.

And before she knew it, a gathering of spirits had formed, scattered across the entrance to the courtyard and Torin's tower on the other side of the chapel. She skidded to a halt.

"You are the one," an old woman said in awe. She lurched forward, and Azalea darted to the side, looking for a way around the growing group.

She nearly got through when a small boy at the end caught her leg.

Stumbling forward, Azalea's breath was stolen from her chest for a split second as her heart convulsed, and the boy disappeared. His memories washed over her. He was a nobody, an orphan, and had died coughing at the back of a hospital with a group of young children around him.

At least she could feel a little better about it now, knowing he might be in the City of Stars. No time to mourn. She shot straight through the group and made a dash for the stairs before the rest of them could catch up with her.

Torin already had the door open and was looking pissed. She stumbled up the steps as he glared down at the spirits.

"Piss off the lot of you," he shouted. Looking very much insane to anyone nearby who couldn't see spirits.

He hustled her inside and slammed the door, locking it with the bolt and the key, then mumbled something to check the wards.

"I didn't do it on purpose that time, I promise." She pressed her hand on her chest, trying to catch her breath. Faraday greeted her with a "brrrrp" and wound around her legs, overly lovingly. He wanted food.

"I know. You're late," he said and went back to his desk and turned his glare on his computer.

She pointed at the clock. "I'm not late yet. I've got six minutes."

"And you still have to get ready. You're late."

Whatever. She wouldn't let him wreck her good mood, and she would make sure she was on time, just to spite him.

She ran upstairs and had a one-minute shower, tied up her hair, and dressed in jeans and a soft blue sweater. No time for breakfast. Faraday howled at her from the bed, so she dashed down to the kitchen and fed him, noting an empty whiskey bottle in the sink, then ran down the stairs back to the office.

There was no time to catch her breath, but she landed in her chair opposite Torin at exactly nine am on the dot.

"Morning, Torin." She smiled at him, hoping to start the day again.

He mumbled something like good morning and threw a book in front of her. "You need to learn about griffins."

Griffins! They were going to Jordan tomorrow to find the relic. Hopefully, it wasn't too much to learn on that short notice.

"Is there likely to be a griffin guarding the relic still?" Her hopes went sky high. Imagine seeing a real-life griffin!

"Maybe, but don't look so happy about it. They are fiercely territorial and not something you want to meet while stealing from their nest."

"Oh. What makes you think it's there?"

"The two lines in the riddle *A warning to those who search in the day* and *By glow of pink light is when you must seek.* Griffins sleep during the day and leave at dusk to hunt, that's the hint."

"Right." She started reading. The more she read, the more she didn't want to meet a griffin after all. They might look beautiful with the head of an eagle and the body of a lion, but they sounded like real bastards.

Torin went upstairs, presumably to make coffee for his hangover by the sounds of his banging and the kettle boiling. Azalea took the chance to check her phone.

Erik: *Hey you didn't stay for breakfast.*

Azalea: *Sorry. I was nearly late as it was. Thanks for last night.*

She got a message back straight away. He must be studying from home again.

Erik: *come stay anytime ;)*

She might actually take him up on that. It was the best sleep she'd had in a while. She checked the rest of her messages. There were several from Van and Isaac, and one from her mum, checking if Azalea was still alive. She messaged her mum and told her she was fine. She'd taken to twice daily updates so Leda and RoRo wouldn't worry about her. Then read the messages from Van.

Van: *Dinner at our place Wednesday night. Bring Erik if you want. I've already invited Isaac, and Jade is going to attempt a roast lamb, but I'm not sure she knows what she's doing. Come at 7. Bring wine!!!*

Azalea: *Sounds good. I'll be there with the wine and maybe Erik.*

She messaged Erik, and he responded instantly that he would be there. Doubt suddenly crept over her. She wasn't sure what this thing between them was but didn't want it to get too serious, too fast. Not when she had so many other things to worry about.

Finally, she got to Isaac's messages, all of which asked her to promise she would be at the dinner because he planned to go but didn't want to show up if she wouldn't be there. Azalea smiled at his desperate messages. It was clear he liked Van. Azalea assured him she would be there.

"Put your phone away," Torin barked as he sat back down. Only one cup of coffee. He was clearly in a bad mood. Things finally felt back to normal, at least. It made him easier to hate when he was like this.

"What's got you so pissy this morning?" she asked.

He slammed a book down. "You need to learn to control your emotions instead of sending them out across the universe."

"*I* need to control my emotions? You're the one throwing the tantrum." She had no idea why it was bugging him so much today. Was her unusually bright mood bringing him down?

He closed his eyes and ran a hand over his face. "I didn't have a good sleep."

No shit. His eyes were bloodshot, and he looked extremely hungover. Probably best not to point that out to him.

"How do you suggest I work on controlling my emotions?" she said, trying to set the tone to maintain the peace for the rest of the day.

"The same way as spirit warding. Pull in your aura. But do it while you're meditating, so it becomes second nature and you don't have to focus on it," he said in a more reasonable, teacherly manner.

"Okay. I'll work on it," she promised. It was something she'd already been trying but clearly not getting good at. "Now, what else do I need to study before tomorrow?"

"Here." He handed her the maps they had already marked out. "Drill the locations into your brain. We won't have much time, so we need to get through all the caverns quickly."

She nodded and got straight to work.

"And Azalea."

She looked up. "Yeah?"

"Don't stay over at Erik's tonight. We both need a good sleep for tomorrow." He looked back down at his work and ignored her once more.

She frowned and went back to her map. If she didn't know better, she would say he was jealous.

)))●(((

The next day, Azalea sat at the kitchen table with Faraday, watching from the chair next to her. They'd done as much preparation as they could for their trip this afternoon, and both her and Torin were on edge. The bread was dry in her mouth as she forced herself to eat the ham and cheese sandwich. Sandwiches never tasted as good when she made them herself, but she was avoiding the caf, or more accurately, all the people who ate there.

The nerves were getting to her. She did her best to pull in her emotions as Torin walked past without a word. It was clear he was stressed, but so was she, and his mood hadn't improved much from the day before. At least he wasn't hungover for their trip.

She forced down the rest of the sandwich and trudged downstairs. Her bag was all ready to go, but it was the waiting that was hard.

Her first relic hunt had gone well, but what was to say the second one would as well? She didn't want to let Torin down or screw up and do something stupid. She just hoped there wouldn't be any griffins or spirits waiting on the other side of the Hollow for them.

"Let's head out," Torin said as he lifted his backpack.

They walked in silence to St. Dunstan in the East; Azalea pulled her backpack in tight. It looked like they were going camping in the middle of London, both dressed in hiking trousers with waterproof winter jackets, hiking boots, and backpacks.

Torin cut into the Hollow, and they stepped out; Azalea marveled at the unbelievable sight. A valley of rose sandstone was gouged out below them; ancient cliffs were dotted with caves, both natural and manmade—the Lost City of Petra.

The sun, low on the horizon, sent a pinkish glow over the chasm of the valley, casting deep shadows that contrasted with brilliant brightness in the stone. No wonder it was called the Rose City.

"The camel rock should be just over there." Torin looked up from his GPS and nodded to a rock that resembled a seated camel.

They had the Shadow Atlas to thank for that one: *Beneath a cold evening sun sits a camel of stone.* Azalea missed the demonic book's presence when she was away. She wished Torin would let it come with them, but he said it was too dangerous.

She remained upbeat as they walked toward the camel. They needed to find the right cave before sunset, but not too soon, in case the griffin was still in there. They walked silently.

Azalea nearly squealed out loud when she spotted some glowing red lizards sun baking on a rock as they neared the camel.

"'*Fire lizards basking will show you the way!*'" she repeated the Shadow Atlas's tip and tried not to startle them with her excitement. They were cute little lizards. They had round faces like geckos, but the tiny mohawk of fire up their backs gave away their magical nature. She'd read a myth about griffins the day before, saying they liked to pick up fire lizards and throw them into a forest to start a fire and flush out prey. Torin confirmed this was still a problem today, and countries with griffin populations had task forces dedicated to covering up their fires and maintaining their secrecy as they were protected animals.

She poked Torin's arm and pointed more out with silent excitement.

He nodded, clearly not sharing her enthusiasm for the creatures, and walked right to the edge of the cliff and pointed down.

She nodded, and they quietly set about scrambling down the cliff face. Her finger strained, grasping the natural handholds in the rock as they made it down to a ledge and shuffled along the narrow path. It was about half an hour before sunset, so they were right on time, *if* it was in one of the many caves they had in front of them. They weren't big caves like the taniwha one, just hollows in the sandstone gouged out by sandblasting and weather. Peering into the first few, cautiously, they found nothing.

Though it was much warmer than London, the breeze picked up, and she was glad of the windbreaker she wore. She scooted around the edges of a jutting rock, careful not to look down. The drop was probably the height of a one-hundred-floor building, and she had no wish to find out how good Torin was at throwing shadow ropes down a cliff at speed.

They scrambled across the narrow ledges of the cliff from cave to cave. She noticed Torin hadn't looked down once and wondered if he wasn't a fan of heights.

"This one's bigger," Torin whispered as he poked his head around the corner of a rock Azalea was making her way toward.

A stillness settled as she entered the cave. Sheltered by the angle of the entrance, the wind dropped away, but the glow of the dying evening sun shone through lighting up the small room perfectly.

Torin went ahead, peering over a pile of debris at the end. Azalea padded over with cautious footsteps to see it was just a pile of sticks and a big log.

Motioning for Azalea to come in further, Torin pointed to some markings he'd spotted. He examined the soft stone walls, and Azalea took photos as part of her assigned job, then wandered closer to the back wall. She heard a faint noise and froze.

She peered into the pile of sticks. It wasn't just debris. She sucked in a breath—there was a nest at the center, filled with straw and animal hair. But her eyes fell on the three fat, squeaking, roly-poly balls of fur and feathers in the nest.

Baby griffins!

She couldn't help but let out a squeal of delight. Something Isaac would have teased her for if he were there. But these were the cutest bundles of fluff she had ever seen. She took some photos to show him.

They looked more like giant kittens than birds or mini golden eagles mixed with baby lions. They were fuzzy and fat with tiny beaks and adorable wide, black eyes, rimmed with gold; their pointed, feather-covered ears stuck out the tops of their heads like radars.

Their little wings were too small to lift them, but it didn't stop them from flapping them like crazy. Two of them half rolled, half ran out of their nest and straight up to Azalea, squeaking and chirping. She held her cheeks in her palms as they bounced around her feet, nipping at her shoelaces.

Just as she crouched down, Torin appeared next to her, making her jump. Their little front bird feet were scratching at her shoes, trying to climb up her legs.

"DO NOT touch those!" He pulled her back. The kitten birds rolled off and started play-fighting each other. Torin's eyes widened, and pure terror rolled off him. "We have to get out of here."

A throaty growl arose from the cave entrance, followed by an ear-piercing squawk. Adrenaline shot through her—they were standing between the griffin and her chicks.

CHAPTER 24

Azalea scanned the fierce-looking griffin from top to bottom. It was equivalent to facing a lion or tiger, but far more terrifying because she knew how smart this creature was.

This thing was massive. Unlike the kittens, its face was all eagle, zero cuteness. Its golden eyes blazed with rage as it opened its sharp, hooked beak and let out another piercing squawk. Azalea and Torin stood frozen as it raked its large taloned foot across the ground and spread its wings so wide they blocked the entrance of the cave; gold glinted off every feather.

Its body shimmered in the sunset, sending blinding flashes of light into their eyes. Torin moved in front of Azalea as the baby griffins, happy their mum returned, squawked for food, jumping up and down on Azalea's feet, their tiny sharp talons scratching her legs.

She tried to hush them, sure it was working their mother up further. Torin backed into her until they were right against the cave wall. Off to her side, there was a gap in the rocks, and Azalea inched closer. She discovered a dug-out area around a corner with a stone chair, hidden from the angle they entered.

It was the relic. Sitting there on the chair like it had been waiting for them. It was deep green and in the shape of an eagle spreading its wings.

She could lunge over to reach it but was sure the griffin would get to her first. Azalea's hands shot to her ears when the baby griffin, still inside the nest, started making an alarming, high-pitched squeaking sound. The other two at Azalea's feet shut up for a second, then began their calling again. Azalea glanced at the nest to see a huge black cobra waving over the helpless griffin who was trapped there.

"The griffin!" Azalea cried as she moved toward it without thinking. His pointed ears pinned back on his head, and he flattened into the nest. The snake reared up with its full hood swaying over the terrified creature.

Azalea took off her jacket and swung it in front of her, creeping toward the snake without making any sudden movements.

"Azalea," Torin hissed. His eyes pinned on the bigger problem at the front of the cave. It wouldn't help them if the snake killed the baby while they were there. She had to try to help it. Crouching, she moved toward the nest.

She slowly drew her jacket in front of her, using her elemer to access the Echo Dimension. She focused her mind and forced a breath of air to float her jacket gently down onto the snake's head where it sank into a pile.

She let out a breath, her heart still racing as she dashed forward and scooped up the baby griffin, but the snake moved under her jacket and shot out at her before she had time to react. Fiery pain flared through her wrist. She flicked her arm, but its fangs had already left her flesh. She stumbled backward, clutching the baby griffin to her chest. The snake sunk back into the nest and under her jacket.

Torin took the baby griffin from her and placed it on the ground as her vision began to swim. His arms were around her as she sank to the floor, her eyes desperately trying to focus on the mother griffin, making sure it didn't go for Torin while he was distracted.

He turned her arm over; his magic warmed her, as his fingers ran over the soft skin on the inside of her wrist. She tried to sit up. There were two distinct puncture marks on her left wrist right in front of her snake tattoo's face, perfectly positioned on either side of the crescent moon it pointed its tongue at.

"Sorry," she mumbled, knowing Torin would be pissed off at her. The baby griffin stumbled onto her lap. It was warm and soft and gently rumbling in gratitude—she could only assume.

"It's okay, we can fix this. But we need to go now." Torin pulled the griffin off her lap and pushed it toward its mum. "Sorry about that," Torin mumbled to the griffin with a small bow.

Azalea giggled. She knew it was totally the wrong time for it, but that was cute. She slapped a hand over her mouth. "Sorry. I'm feeling a bit woozy."

The mother griffin folded her wings back, so they were streamlined across her gold-flecked body and tilted her head to the side. She began making a cooing sound from her throat; the babies responded in kind. The baby griffin Torin set on the floor ran to its mum. They cooed at each other, the other two scrambled over themselves to join their sibling.

At least they were happy.

"Come on, let's go." Torin went to help her up. But she grabbed his arm and pulled him down to her level.

"Wait. The statue is in the alcove behind the nest. Get it first." She swayed slightly, but she didn't want this mission to be a bust because of her.

He glanced behind for a split second, then his eyes flicked right back to the griffin. She was ignoring them for now, turning her large body to drag in a very dead donkey from some-where outside the cave.

She lay down the same as a female lion would with the donkey in front of her and started ripping smaller chunks of meat, depositing them on the floor for the little ones.

"At least she won't be hungry now," Azalea said. Trying to remain positive and ignore the shaking in her limbs that was spreading to her whole body, along with the feeling that she might be about to die.

"Azalea, stay focused. The relic doesn't matter. I need to get you back now." Torin's eyes were wide with fear. She could feel his concern for her.

This was her fault. She was messing up the mission. Suddenly the mother griffin was in the cave, just a few feet from Torin, and cold terror sunk into her bones at the thought of that razor-sharp beak ripping him apart. But the griffin didn't make a move. It let out a low warbling sound from its throat and then turned and trotted back to the donkey and sank down next to the kittens.

"What was that?" Azalea asked. But as she spoke her wrist tingled, and her arm felt light as air. Her vision cleared. Torin's hand rested on her back, tingling with magic, and he didn't move it as she sat up straight.

He leaned over as she turned her wrist. The puncture marks were no longer red and raised, but pink and shiny like old scars.

Azalea touched her wrist with shaking fingers. "I think she healed me."

"Maybe it was all a test." Torin frowned as he ran a finger over her wrist, studying the marks as if he couldn't believe it.

Her breath hitched at his touch, his magic calling to her, and she did her best not to close her eyes and look like a weirdo soaking it in. She bit her lip to distract herself.

He pulled his hand away; he had to have felt it too. He cleared his throat. "You okay now?"

Azalea nodded and stood up to prove it. After an initial wave of dizziness, she rolled her shoulders back to prove she was stable. "I'm good. Now what?"

"Let's grab the relic and get out of here." Torin's eyes darted to the griffin family, who were still eating.

"You sure? I feel like we should ask her or something?" Azalea whispered, not wanting to make any sudden movements in case the griffin's altruism wore off.

"I think she gave us permission. But to be safe, I'll watch her. You grab the relic." Torin nodded his head toward the crevice.

"Yes, sir." She gave a silent salute and grinned at Torin. He rolled his eyes but smiled back. Something about nearly dying, and then not, put her in a rather good mood.

Stepping cautiously, she backed into the wall and slid across until she reached the carved seat. She held her breath and looked away from the griffin for a split second as her fingers wrapped around the small jade eagle and felt a buzz of energy rush through her.

She held her breath and crept back to Torin and placed the jade relic into his palm.

The griffin watched every move they made as if she knew what they were doing.

"Time to go," Torin said.

"Wait! The snake has my jacket."

"No." Torin grabbed her arm. His fear barreled through her, sharp and acrid, hitting the back of her throat and making her gasp.

"It's okay. I won't go over there." She reassured him and peeled off his arm, surprised at the force of his reaction. But she was sure the griffin was letting them take the relic. She could have easily attacked them by now and just a few more seconds wouldn't matter. Azalea stood a safe distance from the jacket and gently levitated it off the snake with carefully focused air magic. But the serpent was gone. She looked around and checked in the nest. She shook the jacket, just in case the giant snake was lurking in the sleeves somehow, but it was definitely gone.

Torin cut into the Hollow. The griffin family paused as the shadowy gateway opened. Azalea stepped through first, and Torin followed.

As the shadows surrounded her, Azalea yelled, "Thank you!" to the griffin. She swore she heard an echo of friendly chirping as the doorway closed.

They exchanged a look as soon as they were safely inside the Hollow.

"Holy shit, that was intense." The chill of the air and the calming blue light let her relax her shoulders, she hadn't realized she'd been so tense.

"And you thought it was a good idea to walk up to a deadly snake and pick up a griffin cub while its mother was watching?" Torin ran a hand over his head, shaking it in disbelief. His skin was tinged with blue light from the floor, and the scar on his eyebrow was bright.

"It was a test. She wanted to know if we were worthy of the relic. It's like in the riddle, '*those dark of heart*'... blah blah blah. It was proving we were worthy to take it."

"And that's what you were thinking when you walked toward that nest? You were certain?"

"Well... no. But I had a feeling. I can't explain it, but I knew it was the right thing to do. I couldn't let that adorable critter get bitten by that snake."

"I'm just glad you're okay." He didn't look at her, but she felt the relief rolling off him. He really meant it.

"Thanks for having my back." Azalea felt a lightness in her chest. She relished the feeling of not having poison running through her veins. "It worked out well at least."

Torin shook his head as if he didn't believe it had happened. "I think we're lucky you have a soft spot for helpless creatures."

"You would have done the same thing," she said.

He looked away and held his elemer up. "Before we go home, I've got something to show you."

Azalea followed as he cut out of the Hollow and found herself in a massive stone chamber. Sunlight spread in a bright, door-shaped column across the floor, leaving everything else shadowy and dull.

"What is this place?" Her voice echoed as her eyes adjusted. The room wasn't just a black void, eerie light filtered from an entranceway on the other side, and the walls weren't dark, but shades of pink with swirls of black marbling carving through the walls and high ceiling.

"It's a royal tomb," Torin said. "Come on, it should be time."

A tomb? Time for what? She followed Torin through the huge stone pillars framing the entrance. They were still in Petra. The place was magnificent, and because it was made of the earth, it didn't feel completely owned by man. It held a wildness of the elements about it. Ancient spirits were there but were far too old to bother anyone. They almost felt the same as the magic in the relics.

Torin and Azalea stepped out into the dusky light, high in a valley of ancient tombs. A natural valley with temples carved into the very walls of the earth.

She looked up behind her and saw the facade of the tomb they stood in; it was as if the rocks were alive, the sunset breathing life into a city of the dead. Its curved pillars and carved arches glowed red with the blood of the earth.

There were people lower on the cliffs, packing up their market stalls for the day. There was a sudden rush to get down to the valley floor.

"Why are they all rushing like that?" Azalea asked.

"Just wait."

They sat on a rock and watched as the sun slid below the cliffs on the other side of the valley, and the rose tint extinguished from the earth, replaced with dull shadows. A fresh chill crashed over Azalea, and she pulled her jacket around her.

Suddenly, people poured from the doorways in the cliffs and onto the flat platforms where the markets had been. They walked with purpose, greeting each other and sitting down at stalls as if they owned them.

She glanced at Torin to see him enthralled by the sight below. Behind them, a drumbeat sounded, and Azalea shuffled back against the wall as a procession of drummers and official-looking people streamed from the empty tomb past them.

"They're spirits," Azalea breathed.

"I'd read about this, but never thought I'd see it," Torin said. He wasn't scared, just fascinated by them, and his calmness wore off onto Azalea. She didn't have to be scared. They didn't know what she was.

She sat with her muscles tensed, hoping none of them would look at her. "Who are they?"

"Royalty, the spirits of travelers, Romans, Nabateans, Bedouins; all lost souls that have come together in this place."

"They actually look like normal people. How are they like this?"

"It's a mystery. But if you're ever in need of somewhere to harvest lots of spirits..."

"You mean you're okay with the deal?"

"No, of course not. But I'm showing you there are options. This is one, but I want you to think about it long and hard."

Azalea's stomach flipped. They could do it, break their curse with this number of spirits on tap.

"I'd also like you to think of the consequences. Say you sent away one spirit every day, just one. That would mean stopping your heart once every day. Say you did that three hundred and sixty-five days a year. Then, to reach your quota of one thousand spirits, it would take nearly three years to break the bond. Three years of stopping your heart once every single day."

His logic ticked over in her brain. When he put it like that, it sounded horrible and dangerous.

"Look down. There are probably over a thousand spirits down there. Can you imagine every single one of them passing through your body? Each time, feeling that same horror as your heart stops and your breath catches in your chest. Every time wondering if it will kill you?"

Her heart beat fast, thinking about it. Why was he saying this? She'd already agreed to it. "I know you don't want me to do it.

But we're low on options here." Azalea watched more and more spirits trail past.

"Right. I want to be very clear about this. I don't want you to do this. It is not a good deal." He looked her right in the eye, so she could feel his conviction.

She licked her lips and looked away; she could do this. It might take longer than she thought, but it was possible. "It's a way out. It solves one of our very large problems."

"It's not worth the risk," he said firmly.

"Of course it is! You said it yourself, we can't keep this bond. It's illegal, and it's making us act weird. Clearly, you hate it. You can't stand being around me, so let's start this spirit countdown, and get it over with."

"No." He shook his head and set his jaw. His determination and stubbornness slammed into her.

"Why not?" she said through gritted teeth.

"Because I don't want you to die," Torin snapped, then looked off into the distance. A stream of bejeweled, royal-looking spirits marched past, not giving them a second glance.

Azalea didn't know what to say. She'd been expecting a lecture about responsibility or solving this some other way. "I might not die," she whispered.

"We will find another way." He lifted his hand toward her shoulder, then dropped it.

Gods, this man was confusing. He'd done a 180 on this bloody soul bond in a matter of days.

"In the meantime, I'll gather a few spirits, just in case we don't." She was sorely tempted to reach out and grab the nearest spirit to prove her point, but she knew that would put them in danger and spontaneous decisions didn't seem to work in her favor.

"Or you could not. Come on, mageling, let's go back." He didn't look at her, just hopped off the rock they were sitting on.

That damn book was wearing off on him. She turned away from the spirit community, and Torin ordered her to find their way back via the Hollow.

CHAPTER 25

"This is exactly what you need, Azalea. A night off from all the stress of being Dumont's apprentice and a catch-up with us lot." Van handed her a glass of red wine, then topped-up Isaac's, who looked like he might have already had a few.

Azalea leaned back in the yellow armchair at her old flat as the smell of roasting lamb and potatoes drifted around the room. Van peered over Jade's shoulder as she seasoned the roast veggies, and Isaac sat across from Azalea on the sofa, half sucked into the mountain of cushions behind him. The room had a pleasant warmth to it with the heat of the oven and the boiling pots on the stove. Being with her friends for a cozy dinner felt just right for the drizzly Wednesday night, and Van was right. She needed to take some time out from all this craziness, but it was also a chance to see if Jade had any more prophecies up her sleeve. She didn't trust the Shadow Atlas, and a second opinion might be a good thing.

"She'll be fine," Van said with a wave, but shot a look at Jade, who was taking out more pots from the cupboard.

"Just let her go. She'll work it out." Azalea smiled as Jade whizzed around the kitchen in a blur of gothic lace.

Van folded herself into the sofa next to Isaac, so her legs rested against his, which sent a coy smile across his face.

"How're things with Mage Dumont?" Van asked.

"Pretty good," Azalea said. Not even a lie. They were on good terms after the trip to Jordan two days ago.

"You don't have to pretend with us. You can tell the truth," Van said, and Isaac nodded along.

"No, I really mean it. Things are good. It's just a little intense being there all the time. The work is good, and Torin is fine mostly, but it's hard to sleep, so I've slept at Erik's house the last two nights." She didn't want to say why it was hard to sleep. That Torin being right there in the room next door was driving her mad. It was nothing against him for once, but the bond was making boundaries rather difficult, and it was getting harder and harder to block him and his emotions out. She couldn't even escape him in her sleep anymore. He was there in her dreams being all flirty and seductive in his stupid loincloth in the desert, nothing at all like the real Torin. But it was sure as hell confusing reality for her.

"What?! You're sleeping with Erik!" Van yelled and threw a cushion at Azalea, who instinctively blocked it.

It threw her out of her Torin fantasy. A good thing too. She couldn't keep thinking about him that way. It was wrong on so many levels.

Azalea took a sip of her wine. "Did I forget to mention it?" At least that was out of the way now. She hadn't been sure how to bring up her thing with Erik in conversation. Where was he anyway?

"You conveniently forgot to mention that in the several times we've spoken this week," Isaac said. She had thoroughly updated him on the trip to Jordan and made him delete the adorable griffin photos after she sent them to him.

Isaac continued, "So what? You've just forgotten what a dick he was to you when you got here?"

"Yes actually. I have blocked that out and am focusing on the good things about him."

"Like what?" Isaac poured more wine into his and Van's glasses on the coffee table.

Jade came over and perched on a kitchen chair. "I don't want to miss out." She glanced back at a pot with a banging lid and ignored it. Van craned her neck, frowning at the kitchen.

"Other than you lot, he's one of the few people on my side in this whole bloody tower. He's got my back, and it's kind of a nice feeling," Azalea said. It was true, she might not be in love with the guy, but he had proven himself a worthy ally.

"Aw, Zaley. I know it's been hard. I'm glad you have him, but we've always got your back if you need us too," Van said as she launched herself off the couch and onto Azalea in a big hug.

Azalea hugged her back, glad she'd put down her wineglass a second before. Van had clearly had a few drinks already as well.

"Thanks, Van," Azalea said as Van peeled herself off with a warm smile on her face. Azalea glanced at Jade, wondering how to ask if she'd do a reading.

"So, is he a good shag?" Van asked.

Azalea's eyes widened; she blinked, then tossed a cushion at Van's face, but she darted out of the way.

"I am not talking about this anymore," Azalea said.

"I can do a reading if you want to find out how it will turn out?" Jade said.

Well, that was convenient. Though it wasn't her future love life she was interested in.

"Yes!" Van squealed as she fell back into the sofa and shuffled closer to Isaac, whose arm hovered on the back nearly touching her. *Just go for it, Isaac.* Azalea tried to tell him with a look. But his face tinted pink, and he didn't move his arm. She could tell he wanted to. Maybe after a bit more wine.

Azalea raised her eyebrows at Jade, hoping she was easily swayed. "I don't know if that's a good idea. Erik will be here any second. How about a non-romance reading instead?"

"No. This is more fun! Come on!" Van pleaded.

"Are you sure, Jade? I thought you weren't keen on divination." Azalea wasn't sure she wanted to know anything about her future love life. Cryptic prophecies about the future, yes. Romance? Not so much.

Jade shrugged, not focusing on the dinner anymore. "Just because I don't want it to be my lifelong career doesn't mean I don't know what I'm doing sometimes," she said, with a slight slur in her words.

Azalea noticed the empty wine bottle by the kettle. What the hell? Might as well give it a go. How much could divination actually tell about the future when there were always different paths?

"Fine, let's do it then," Azalea said. The wine was already giving her that carefree feeling she'd been seeking for days. Moving to the kitchen table, she perched on the chair opposite Jade and held out her hand.

Jade ran her fingers over the lines on Azalea's palm, different from what she tried the last time.

"This is your love line," Jade said as she ran a finger over the crease that stretched across her hand closest to her fingers.

"Okay..." Azalea said, wondering why she agreed to this and hoping Erik wouldn't come in right now, or that maybe Jade would get a useful vision.

Van peered over Jade's shoulder, and Isaac stood next to the table with his arms crossed, looking very skeptical.

Jade's finger glowed white, and she cut into the Shadow Dimension with the elemer in her other hand. Azalea hadn't even noticed. The line of Azalea's palm turned a brilliant pulsing red as Jade rested her elemer on the table and held Azalea's wrist gently. Brushing her other finger across the red line, Jade pushed the magic into Azalea's palm, and it heated with a soothing warmth.

Jade looked up. Her eyes were all white and locked onto Azalea's.

"I see two shadows on the path of your future. One, a great love; a love that can transcend the stars or burn you to ashes. The other, a shadow that will lead to betrayal and torment." She paused and tilted her head to the side. "—or rebellion and passion."

Azalea's heart squeezed in her chest, and she tried to pull her hand away. *Why did she think this was a good idea?*

Jade continued, "You spoke to the god, but it is another who has the answers in the sands."

That was more like it. But Jade snapped out of her trance and shook out her hand.

"A god?" Azalea asked.

Jade shrugged. "Sorry. The sight is kind of vague. I get crossed wires sometimes."

Another god? Going back to the desert wasn't exactly an appealing idea.

"Two loves!" Van squealed.

"That's not what she said," Isaac said.

"Shit, the roast!" Jade scraped back her chair, racing to the oven. A plume of steam billowed out as she opened the door. "All good! No need to panic," she called over her shoulder.

Azalea didn't have time to process whatever that premonition was when a loud knock came from the door, and she rushed up to get it. She'd have to tell Torin about the other god soon, though.

"Hello, love," Erik said as she opened the door. He grinned and planted a kiss that tasted like beer.

She pulled away. "Hello, you," she said, as he handed her a bottle of red. She didn't look at what type of wine it was; red was red as far as she was concerned.

She took Erik's hand and pulled him into the living room, which seemed to put a big smirk on his face. Van jumped up straight away and hugged Erik, then poured him a glass of wine.

"Don't you two have class tonight?" Azalea asked, looking between Jade and Erik.

"Nope. Wednesday is now counseling night. Me and Jade went last week, and tonight it's Livia and Millie. Trust me, they need it more than us." Jade nodded along with Erik.

Azalea's heart twinged thinking about Elam. She hated that she'd caused the girls so much pain. Even if they were bitches, they didn't deserve this. But it turned her mind back to what Livia had said last week: *You have no idea what she's planning.* Maybe she should mention that to Torin...

She pushed it from her mind. Tonight was about being happy and getting drunk enough to sleep without dreaming, hopefully in Erik's bed and far away from Torin.

The roast turned out to be amazing. They got through four bottles of wine with dinner and moved on to shots of terrible tequila that Van pulled from the depths of the cupboard.

Jade fit in like she'd always been there and, thankfully, had no more premonitions for the rest of the night.

It was well past 1 am when Azalea checked the time on her phone. Jade had just gone to bed, and Isaac and Van were preoccupied with each other on the sofa.

Empty shot glasses sat in front of Azalea on the sticky table as Erik held up the bottle of tequila.

"One more for the road?" he said.

"No thanks, I'm good. We better get to bed. You've got class and I've got a... thing, I need to do..." She trailed off, thinking about how shitty the next day would be, dealing with Torin and the Shadow Atlas while hungover. Plus, she needed to tell him they might need to talk to another god.

Erik raised his eyebrows. "A thing?"

"Yes, a thing. It's important," she slurred. Just because she was drunk didn't mean she was about to spill the beans on everything.

"Come on. Just tell me what you're up to with Dumont. I won't tell. Promise." He leaned in and kissed her gently, carefully, like he wanted to get information out of her. His hand slid up her inner thigh.

"You can't seduce me into telling you," she said, smiling onto his lips, then pulled back.

He narrowed his eyes and poured another two shots. "Fine, don't tell me. Just do another shot, and we can go."

It was easier to do the shot than argue. Azalea shuddered as the tequila hit the back of her throat, and she immediately reached for a chaser of cola and downed half a glass as bubbles fizzed up her nose.

She'd have to deal with the hangover tomorrow, but for now, she'd blocked out Torin and could enjoy the numbing drunken haze. Even better, she could stay with Erik tonight.

CHAPTER 26

Azalea kicked the door twice to get it to open and trudged into Torin's office, not looking forward to the rest of the morning. At least inside, she could block out the blinding sunlight she'd had to endure from her walk of shame across the Tower grounds at 8 am.

"Miss Sharp, how lovely of you to turn up." The Archmage's biting voice jolted fear straight to Azalea's core, like she'd been touched by a spirit.

Azalea stood there frozen as the Archmage strode toward her. Her cane punctuated her steps. Azalea fought the urge to scurry away, knowing it would make matters worse.

The old woman reached Azalea and shook her hand. "I don't know if Torin was holding out on me." She shot him a sharp smile that was lethal on the edges. "Or if you are just better at this than him, but either way, the two of you make an excellent team. Just like I told you, two shadow mages are better than one." Her icy-blue eyes sparkled at Azalea with mirth.

In that look, Azalea could see the way the Archmage appeared to her family. There was a soft side buried far beneath the surface. One that the woman took great care to hide from those not dear to her.

"Um, thank you." Azalea stood there blinking as her brain tried to process the Archmage's good mood.

Torin leaned back in his chair with crossed arms, looking a little too smug, but she could feel the unease rolling off him as the Archmage marched over to Azalea's seat at the desk and sat herself down.

Azalea shrugged off her coat and slunk to the end of the desk, trying to blend in with the armchair behind her and wishing she could curl up in it and go back to sleep. Her head was pounding, and she desperately needed a cup of coffee and a shower, but at least the Archmage seemed pleased with their relic collecting so far.

"I wish to review the relic plans now," the Archmage said as she folded her hands neatly onto her crossed legs.

"Of course, Archmage. We have our next target to pick up this week," Torin said as he handed over the list of relics.

A target this week? That was news to Azalea. Their plan for the morning had been to ask the Shadow Atlas for new targets.

The Archmage's face remained blank as she read through the list. Azalea remembered what Danni told her about the Archmage's parents being executed. She tried to picture the woman as a small girl, orphaned and alone, shunned by the residents of the Tower. She couldn't see it. She might have seen a hint of what was beyond the cold shell this witch had molded around herself, but if there was an innocent child in there once, she was long gone now.

"Your father is after the relics as well. We cannot let him find any or take the ones we have. You have made good progress, but you need to work faster. I do not want this to turn into a battle, and I do not want anyone to get hurt." She sounded like she meant it. "What is the current status?"

"We've found three relics in the past two weeks: the crane, the fish, and the eagle. Plus, we have the bee, the fox, and the dragon I found last year," Torin summarized.

He'd only given Azalea basic information about how he got them as if she'd be bored hearing about it, despite her asking multiple times. She knew the dragon relic had been from his run-in with the giant snake monster, the bashmu, in Iraq. His leg had been screwed up for weeks, but he refused to talk about it. The bee he'd apparently gotten—no, stolen—from a palace museum in Istanbul, and the fox he got in Japan.

"Yes, and I have three other relics in my collection, but it is all meaningless unless we have the entire set. There are three to go, and you will not let me down now. What is the next one?" The Archmage's eyes drilled into Torin, but Azalea noted the flash of concern behind them. She was scared.

A sudden chill shot through Azalea, and Torin glanced at her.

"The winged bull. It's in Greece, and we're preparing for our trip now." Torin rolled his shoulders back and met the Archmage's eyes.

Um... it was? Azalea stepped closer to the desk. Was he bullshitting the Archmage, or hadn't he told her about this one? Either seemed plausible. Her head pounded against her skull. Why did they have to do this now? She ignored the pain and focused on studying the Archmage. Her skin was dull, and her eyes, though sharp and as piercing as usual, were sunken into her face like she hadn't slept.

Torin gave a sharp, decisive nod. "After that, it's just the white deer and the raven to go."

"I'll take care of the raven." The Archmage glanced at the small gold Rolex on her wrist with a frown.

Torin masked his surprise well, but Azalea saw the split-second widening of his eyes and felt a jolt of shock run through him. "You know where the raven relic is?"

"I have an idea." The Archmage's lips narrowed to a thin line, but she didn't offer any information. "Bring the next relic to me as soon as you retrieve it. Do not let me down." She narrowed her eyes at Azalea. "I need a word with you, Miss Sharp. Mage Dumont, if you would be so kind as to give us some privacy."

Azalea's stomach tightened, and the walls of her mind shot up. Torin frowned but left the room without another word.

"You have been here several weeks now. What have you learned?" Her words were curt but didn't hide the desperation behind them.

"Well... I've been learning how to use the Hollow." Azalea stood with her hands folded in front of her. Not wanting to offer up any real information.

"Don't get smart with me, girl. You know what I mean." The Archmage frowned.

Azalea knew exactly what she meant. "Torin wasn't lying. He's planning a trip soon for us to get the winged bull relic."

"Has he mentioned any plans for the relics once he has found them?" The Archmage's eyes drilled into her, but she didn't resort to mind magic.

"Only that you will keep them safe here in the artifacts gallery," she said, making it as believable as she could.

"Anything else?"

Azalea shook her head.

"Good. Keep watching him." The Archmage stood up. Perhaps she was testing Azalea, or perhaps she believed her. Whatever it was, she gave Azalea a nod and let herself out without telling Torin she was leaving.

Azalea slumped into the seat the woman had vacated and let out a breath as Torin's heavy footsteps thundered down the stairs. He must have heard the door.

"Good of you to finally turn up." Torin marched over to his desk and slammed a drawer shut.

"Don't take it out on me. I'm still forty-five minutes early. Why did you say the relic is in Greece? We don't know that yet."

"No, but it's somewhere in that area, and I had to give her something. Get the Shadow Atlas. I plan on finding it now. We need to move fast."

"Can't I have a shower first?" Azalea asked and wished she hadn't as a wave of anger crashed into her.

"Just do it," he snapped.

She held her tongue, despite wanting to argue. She didn't because behind that mask of anger, she felt the desperation bleeding off him. This was important. Her fingers clicked against the safe buttons, and the door snapped open. The book called to her immediately and silently, willing her to feed it.

She placed the familiar black book with the snake emblem down on the table, then without hesitation she flicked her elemer out and drew forth the shadows, spiraling them around herself and into the book as if it were the most natural thing in the world. Then she cut the tip of her finger and dripped blood onto the open page. The parchment absorbed its food greedily; she stared, mesmerized by the red ink swirling around the paper.

A hand latched tightly around her biceps. "That's enough," Torin growled.

Azalea blinked and pushed the chair back. She'd hardly noticed herself continuing to call the shadows, but the book was happier now. The room was dulled to a soft darkness, shadows blocking out everything except the desk, and Torin standing next to her.

"You need to be careful it doesn't control you," he said harshly. His voice masked a strong sense of fear and worry.

"Sorry, I'm not exactly in the best state to be doing this right now," she snapped.

"You knew what we were doing today. It's not my problem you spent a weeknight night out drinking and shagging Erik," he snarled.

A harsh silence stung the air as Azalea processed what he had just said. He might as well have called her an alcoholic whore.

"Fuck you, Torin," she said coldly but with full control. "I'm going to have a shower and start the day over again, and it would be better for all of us if you weren't such a dick when I return." She stormed off with the Shadow Atlas tucked into her chest, not waiting to see or feel his reaction.

꒰ ꒱ ꒲ ● ꒡ ꒢ ꒣

Torin slumped into his office chair and rubbed a hand over his face as Azalea stormed upstairs. She was right; he had been a dick and was way out of line. Too bad she had taken the Shadow Atlas upstairs. He needed to find the next relic and yesterday.

Leaning onto his desk, he stared at the relic list. Only three to go. It was feeling more possible than impossible now—they might actually complete the mission to find them all. He sipped his cold coffee and pushed the cup to the corner of the desk. Revolting.

Poring over the research for the winged bull relic for the millionth time didn't get him anywhere. He needed the Shadow Atlas and Azalea's help, though he hated to admit it. Half an hour went by before her heavier-than-usual footsteps clumped down the stairs.

She scowled as she came in holding a glass of water and a hot drink; he took in the dark rings under her eyes and her paler-than-usual skin that made the freckles across her cheeks stand out. At least he wasn't the hungover one for once.

"Azalea, I'm sorry about what I said before," he said sincerely.

"If you've got a problem with me drinking, then spit it out. But it was just dinner for fuck's sake, and I'll remind you that you drink a hell of a lot more than me, so you're hardly one to give advice." She glared at him as pure rage and disgust rolled off her. Her long brown hair was still wet and trailing on either side of her shoulders in neat twists.

"I was way out of line. I'm sorry, and I don't have a problem. The Archmage just got under my skin. Can we start over?" It wasn't the drinking he had the problem with, but he didn't want to admit to himself what was really keeping him awake at night and certainly wouldn't say it to her.

She marched over to her chair opposite him at the desk, slammed down her drinks, and planted herself down with her arms crossed. "She asked me about you."

"Oh." He had suspected as much.

"I covered for you and said you planned to give the relics to her, and that we were going to Greece. Are we?" she demanded.

"I don't know. It's just a vague idea at this stage. Thanks for covering for me. And I'm truly sorry about the way I talked to you. Can we start over?" he asked again.

"Yes. But I'm still mad at you. I know she's a bitch, but never take it out on me again." She dropped it far more quickly than he expected. Perhaps she knew it was her spending time with Erik that was bothering him, and she didn't want to bring it up either.

Torin would do his best to keep his mouth shut in the future, but he felt like he got off with that way too easily. "I won't."

"Good. Let's just get on with this. Don't want to keep the dragon woman waiting," Azalea said sarcastically. She slammed the book onto the desk and slumped into the chair but didn't open it. "I need to tell you something."

There it was. She'd done something stupid.

"What?"

"The Archmage is up to something. I don't think we can trust her," Azalea said.

Torin sat up straight. Not at all what he was expecting. "Why do you say that now?"

"It's something Livia said to me. She said *'you have no idea what she's planning.'* But it was the way she said it, her face changed, and it looked like she'd slipped up," Azalea said.

"Wouldn't put it past her. But concerning if she might be planning something soon."

"That's not all." Azalea took a sip of her water, clearly reluctant to say whatever it was.

Torin narrowed his eyes, his back overly straight in his chair, waiting for the next bad news to hit him. She'd released more gallu, or summoned some sort of new demon, or made a deal with another god. It was never good news with her.

"Jade had another prophecy moment last night."

"How lovely." He exhaled through his nose.

Azalea bit her lip and looked at him. "I think we need to go back to the Desert of Dreams."

"Why?"

"Her vision said *'another had answers in the sand.'* So I'm guessing that means we need to go talk to someone else?" She looked like she wanted to say something more but sat back in her chair instead.

Great, just what he needed on top of everything else. But they couldn't ignore a prophecy handed to them like that. "Let's worry about that later. For now, we'll get the Shadow Atlas to find us the next relic so we can go get it tomorrow. Then we can go back for more answers." One problem at a time was all he could deal with right now.

"Fine." She opened the Shadow Atlas and cut her hand, letting blood drip onto the page.

CHAPTER 27

The sun was brighter than Azalea had ever seen it, and the sky was a tranquil blue canvas. They were in Paphos, Cyprus, and the air smelled of sea salt and distant winter mixed with goats and dust from the dry earth they'd stepped onto from the Hollow. The Shadow Atlas had been kind enough to give them a riddle that was easy enough to match with Torin's research, it wasn't Greece, but he'd been in the right area.

Antiquities in shops abound,
The winged bull can be found.
Travelers seeking treasures of old,
Paphos is where your story unfolds.

Maybe the Shadow Atlas was starting to like her. It was an obvious riddle, and it had called her *beautiful mageling*, though she was certain it didn't have eyes, but bonus points for pointing them to a holiday spot in Cyprus.

Azalea let her shoulders relax at the freedom of leaving the Tower. A good night's sleep had done them both wonders after a shitty day of bickering at each other and researching everything they could about antique stores in Paphos until late last night.

"Fresh start?" Torin asked cautiously.

Azalea felt his remorse about the way he'd spoken to her the day before. It was so strong she couldn't help but let it go and forgive him. It was better than his overwhelming guilt hovering over both of them. Plus she wasn't sure she wanted to know the real reason behind his outburst.

The Archmage's presence certainly had a negative effect on people, but it didn't explain his arseholery, but she was willing to forget about it for the sake of the mission. One they needed to be on good terms for; their cover was as a newlywed couple. A newlywed couple, who apparently loved antiquing on their honeymoon.

"Fresh start," Azalea replied with a nod. She couldn't help but let her excitement bubble up at the thought of exploring a new place.

Torin took her hand, and Azalea held back a gasp as magic rushed between them. She did her best not to lean into him at the draw of it. His magic was hot in her veins, burning its way straight to her heart and injecting her with new life.

He did his best not to react as well, but she knew he felt it. Holding her left hand up, he slid a ring with a bright green stone onto her finger.

"Aren't I meant to say yes first?" she teased as her heart raced with his magic.

"I assumed you would, *beautiful mageling*." Torin smirked and let her hand drop. She shouldn't have mentioned that part to him.

"This isn't exactly how I pictured my honeymoon," she mumbled.

"Might as well make the most of it while the Archmage is paying. That is a demantoid garnet in the ring. It's meant to provide protection," he said with a hint of a smile. The sea air and bright skies must be getting to his brain too.

"It's pretty. I'll try not to break it," she said, admiring the glow of the bright green garnet, and noticed the interesting inclusion inside that looked like a starburst spraying out from the center.

A sea bird of some sort squawked, gliding past on a gust of wind that rushed up the white cliff they stood on. The sea was a brilliant turquoise below them, and Azalea breathed in the salty air that had a slight chill to it but felt downright tropical compared to London.

Azalea could still feel Torin's magic pulsing through her blood. She'd need to sort that out before they went into the town in case the shadows made a surprise appearance.

"So this is your dream honeymoon, then?"

"Hardly," Torin said. "I never imagined having a honeymoon. But I would love to check out the Archaeological parks and some of the neolithic sites."

She tried to ignore the uneasy feeling of his magic under her skin. "You sure know how to show a girl a good time," she teased.

"And what would you do if this were actually a holiday?" he asked.

She shrugged. "Go skydiving?" That would be a buzz.

"Count me out of that." Torin scrunched up his nose.

"Just as well antiquing is our only activity." She glanced around. No one was near them on the cliff top they'd appeared on. Azalea faced out to sea and blasted streams of shadows from her elemer to ease the pressure of magic.

"Sorry, your magic was a bit much," she said, relishing the release.

"Better to do that now than in town." He shot a flock of shadowy birds out of his elemer. They twisted into the sky like a swarm of bees, folding and dancing in waves of undulating motion that were hard to turn away from.

She looked up in awe. "Wow, you have to show me how to do that."

"Let's get on with the mission," he said impatiently, but a flicker of a smile passed his lips.

Neither of them mentioned just how much power had built between them in those few seconds. Azalea's plan was to ignore the fact that their bond was getting stronger and follow Torin's lead and remain in denial.

)))●(((

They spent the afternoon wandering the beautifully paved streets of Paphos amongst the old and new buildings, staking out every market and antique or trinket store they came across. By dusk, Azalea's feet were aching, and she was ready for either a bath or a glass of wine.

Hopefully tomorrow they would have more luck. Despite being exhausted, she was also nervous about having to spend the night in their honeymoon suite. Fortunately, the hotel room was large, and there was a big sofa she planned to claim as her own.

The sun sank below the horizon, and the sky shifted to a mix of soft pink and orange as they walked through the old town area down a narrow walking street of cafes and restaurants lined with outdoor tables and chairs on either side. Clinking glasses and happy voices sounded all around them, and the aromatic smell of garlic and grilling meat had her mouth watering. A tweak of unease from Torin nudged at her.

He darted her a sideways look. "What did you tell Erik you were doing?"

"I didn't tell him anything. It doesn't exactly sound like hard work if I say, 'I'm off to Cyprus with Torin to pretend to be tourists, see you in a few days,' and not explain why. I just said we were working." She bit the inside of her cheek, hating that she was basically lying to Erik.

"Fair enough. This is the closest I've come to a holiday since..." He trailed off.

"Since when?"

A cozy warmth trickled off him that she'd never felt before. "Since my mum was around. We went to Spain when I was about eight."

"Must have been a nice holiday." It was nice to see him happy about something for a change. From what she had seen, his holidays usually involved fighting some sort of guardian monster.

"Yes, it was." A smile tweaked at the corner of his mouth.

They got back to the hotel as the moon tipped over the edge of the roof like it was sitting on it. Palm trees lined the grand entranceway, and Azalea had to pinch herself as she walked through the towering doors into the sparkling atrium. This was by far the fanciest place she had ever been.

Torin didn't seem to notice the five-star opulence. He had picked the hotel purely based on its proximity to the Tombs of the Kings he wanted to visit for fun, and a part of her liked to think he wanted to spend up large to get back at the Archmage, just a little. Though he never said it.

Azalea's eyes fell on Torin as he held open the door to the elevator for her. The corners of his mouth tilted to form a smile and she wondered what he was thinking about. Her eyes stayed on his lips. *What would it be like to kiss him?* She imagined what his lips would feel like against hers, what the spikes of his short hair would feel like under her hand.

She swallowed and darted through the door with a quick thanks. Not something she should be thinking about, especially when she was sort of with Erik, though they had yet to discuss what that was.

But she couldn't help wondering what the bond would do if they got that close. How would she even know if her feelings were real, or if it was all the bond? The way they shared magic felt amazing, different from any other connection she'd ever had.

She snapped out of it when Torin stopped and she nearly slammed into him, realizing they had left the lift and followed the long hallway to their room at the end.

Torin gave her a sideways look and followed her in. Her cheeks grew warm, hoping he hadn't sensed what she had been thinking about.

Their suite was amazing. The spacious living area boasted a plush three-seater sofa, one she planned to fall onto the moment she got changed, but her attention was captured by the balcony and the picturesque ocean view. She slid open the door, inhaling the salty breeze, and gazed down at the sprawling complex of pools, illuminated walkways lined with palm trees, and rows of inviting deck chairs.

After a moment, she retreated back inside. Torin stood, resting his hand on the back of a dining chair near the balcony door. "You should take the bed," he offered.

"I'll just take the sofa. It's not like you can even fit on it," she replied, making her way to the sofa and leaning on the backrest.

She could tell he wanted to be a gentleman, but he was way too tall to fit on there, and they both needed a decent night's sleep. Diving into the bed that looked like it was made of clouds was tempting, but she wasn't going to go there, and suspected he wanted to keep his distance as well. Sharing was not an option.

"Okay. Goodnight then." He turned awkwardly and marched into the bathroom.

"Night," Azalea squeaked out, cursing her voice. She suspected he'd gone in there to avoid arguing. She was in a luxury hotel and away from all the bullshit at the Tower. She was going to bloody well enjoy it, and she could easily do that sleeping on a luxury sofa. She jumped over the back and flopped onto the soft cushions.

CHAPTER 28

Azalea did her best not to make eye contact with Torin the next morning after a very intimate dream she'd had about him. She dressed in jeans and a nice white blouse with a few pretty ruffles that were suitable for holidaying, then sat on the couch and messaged her mum and RoRo in their group chat with photos from the day before. Torin sat at the white circular table, mumbling into a tourist guidebook marking all the shops and markets they hadn't been to while eating the fruit he'd cut up from their complimentary fruit bowl.

She ignored him and his mumbling and sent a message to Isaac, updating him on their lack of progress the day before, and also made him feel jealous of her mini holiday while he was busy studying, just as she should be doing. He was the only one who she confided in about the mission; she needed someone to share with to maintain her sanity.

A message from Fabian popped up.

Fabian: *Please check in. Are you okay?*

Nice of him to care.

Azalea: *I'm fine. You could just ask my mum.*

Fabian: *She went home.*

"She what?" Azalea said aloud.

"Who did what?" Torin said, with a mouthful of apple.

"My mum. She went back to the cottage," Azalea said as she texted.

Azalea: *Why? What did you do?*

Fabian: *I didn't do anything. She wanted to go back to the forest.*

Azalea couldn't deal with this now on top of everything else. She sent a message to her mum telling her to go back to Fabian's where it was safe and another to Fabian saying to go get her mum. Both were as stubborn as the other, so she suspected nothing would come of that.

"Your mum okay?" Torin asked.

"Yeah. I think so. I'll deal with it when we're back." Azalea helped herself to an orange and ripped the skin off in big chunks, a little rougher than necessary.

She barely tasted it. It was hard to relax with so many things on her mind.

Torin tucked his guidebook under his arm. "Let's get going."

"Let's." Azalea twisted her fake wedding ring and plastered a counterfeit smile across her face. She was going to enjoy today, gods dammit. They were newlyweds looking for the perfect honeymoon memento to bring home and that was final.

☽ ☽ ☽ ● ☾ ☾ ☾

One hour and five shops later and Azalea was ready for a divorce. They were in a district for magic-friendly shopping, which she'd imagined would be thrilling and super magical, but not with Torin and his meticulous scanning of every shelf as if he were conducting an archaeological survey.

Azalea held in a groan of frustration. She'd already checked those rows and knew the relic wasn't there. He just didn't trust her. This was more of a bookshop than an antique shop, anyway.

She drifted over to a stack of leather books and toward the bottom of the tower a book caught her eye: *Spirits Here and Beyond*. The spine with the creepy eyes caught her attention. Once she opened it, she forgot all about the relic hunt.

"Torin, come quick."

He appeared at her side with several books teetering in his arms. "What?"

"It's a book about spirits! Look here." She pointed to the page with pictures of spirits being absorbed into a body and going out the other side like a door. The next picture was of the same person, but with a sword and the spirits going through that instead.

Torin leaned in close.

"What's she holding?" He narrowed his eyes.

"A sword," Azalea said. "You said the shopkeeper was a historian. Can we ask her?"

"Yes. Do it." Torin's interest appeared to match her own.

"Excuse me. Do you know what this is?" Azalea asked, placing the book on the cluttered counter as a ginger cat watched from a document tray.

"It is the spirit blade," the gruff woman in a bright purple dress said as if it was something everyone knew.

"And what is it doing?" Azalea asked, doing her best to remain polite.

She gave a dismissive wave of her hand. "Sending spirits away."

"To where?" Torin squeezed in next to Azalea, so his arm rested on the counter.

"The Shadow Dimension." The woman stared at them blankly as if they should know that.

Azalea glanced at Torin and felt like he was thinking the same thing. *Why didn't Damu just give them this sword?*

"Of course." Torin nodded along. "Out of interest, what is the story behind this sword? And do you know where it might be? Sounds like an interesting artifact."

"Everyone knows of this story." She was gruff but apparently happy to tell them. "The gods gifted this gate-person to connect between worlds. Each time a spirit travels through them, they are marked to be recognized in the Shadow Dimension when it's time to go through."

"What do you mean, go through?" Torin pressed.

Azalea swallowed hard. It was just a story, not necessarily what was happening to her.

"The tales says that if the spirits go through this gate-person, the last one will take them through with them."

"And when is that?" Torin leaned further over the counter.

"When the time is right."

Torin clasped his hands together. "Could you be more specific?"

"It is just a tale, Mister. They don't give out numbers. Each story is different."

"Amuse me," Torin dared her.

"Some say one hundred thousand, some say fifty, some say one thousand. Whoever is telling the story makes up a number." She chuckled. "My Ya-Ya always said one thousand; she was certain of it."

"Thank you. We'll take this book." Torin closed it and gave it a pat.

Torin paid for the book, leaving the others he'd selected behind, and they left.

"He said the bond would break when we got all the spirits, not that I'd go to the Shadow Dimension with them." Azalea's mouth was dry. Why was nothing ever simple?

"Never trust the word of gods." Torin was walking so fast that it was hard to keep up. "Damu has a lot of explaining to do."

"We're going back?"

"Yes, and we're going to find that bloody sword, but first we need that relic, and I think I know where it is." Torin's tone was sharp. She could feel his determination mixed with a hint of anger.

"Not in the magic area?" Azalea said.

"No. I was wrong. It has to be in the old town, in the market we went to, but disguised, maybe there was a spell on it that we missed."

They strode back to the market, sidestepping past people, shifting through souvenir t-shirts and cheap handbags until they got to a shop selling hand-crafted pottery and trinkets.

"How do you know it's here?" Azalea stuck close to him as they squeezed past a crowd of tourists leaving the shop and greeted the shopkeeper as they walked past—a short, squat man with a forest of chest hair spilling out of his low buttoned shirt—he acknowledged them with a grunt.

They made their way to a back corner, obscured by cluttered shelves.

"Because something tugged on my magic here yesterday, but it didn't seem significant. Maybe we can find it together. Give me your hand." His eyes locked on hers, silently asking her to trust him.

She raised an eyebrow but lifted her hand. He had better know what he was doing.

The intoxicating buzz of his magic tapped into her skin the second they touched. Her grip on his hand tightened as she closed her eyes and told herself not to sink into the magic.

"Focus," he whispered in her ear.

A pleasant shiver trickled down her spine and her eyes shot open. She avoided looking at him as she pulled her magic in tight. Calming her breathing, she focused her mind into a meditative state, doing her best to block out his closeness.

"Send a tiny amount of magic out, not shadows, but an invisible stream to seek other magic. Imagine the power symbol for the lighthouse. I'll do the rest." His breath was so close she could smell the peppermint tea they'd had earlier.

His magic pulled at hers, and she let it flow out of her, seeking something beyond her body.

"Got it!" Torin said as he gave her hand a firm squeeze and let go.

She opened her eyes and wiped her sweaty palm on her jeans.

Torin crouched down, focused on the bottom shelf where a small winged bull of deep green jade sat among a collection of porcelain animal figurines.

"Do we just grab it?" Azalea crouched next to him.

"It seems too easy." Worry knotted Torin's brow and rolled off onto Azalea, making her more jittery.

"How about I grab it, then if something happens you can deal with it?" Azalea suggested.

Torin continued to stare at the relic. "No. I'll get it. I don't want you getting hurt."

"I've hardly been any use. If something happens to me, you can fix it. If something happens to you, I'm basically useless. I'm supposed to be your apprentice. Please let me do something." She bit her lip.

"Remember, just the other day, when you got bitten by that cobra?" He raised his eyebrows.

"A test cobra. I was perfectly fine." She corrected. Her thumb ran over the shiny puncture marks on her wrist as she fought off a shudder.

She reached into her coat pocket, pulled out her leather gloves, and slipped them on. "We can't just crouch in this shop forever staring at it."

"Fine." He let out an unsteady breath. "Just be careful."

Azalea nodded furiously. She could do this. All she had to do was pick up the relic.

Torin rose and took a step back, his elemer in his hand as he scanned the shop, then gave Azalea a sharp nod.

She backed up a little and reached out with her gloved hand. Her fingers wrapped around the tiny, winged bull, and she held her breath. Nothing happened. She looked up at Torin with a smile and shrugged, then stood up, holding the bull at arm's length.

"Now what?" Azalea asked.

Torin held out his open palm, and she placed the jade relic in his hand. "Time to go home."

Azalea's heart sank. She wanted to stay in this sunny land where no one knew who she was and where there were fresh fruit and soft towels waiting for her every morning. She didn't want to face cold London and her variety of problems.

A loud bang rattled the shelves, and Azalea froze; her eyes darted to Torin. He put a finger to his lips and crept to the end of the aisle on the left side of the shop and peered around.

He stepped back, his eyes wide. A rush of his fear blasted over her. He waved his hand for her to back up, and she followed where he pointed to the far end of the aisle.

A loud snort was followed by clomping footsteps, too loud to be human. Torin rushed back to Azalea and gestured for her to follow him as he moved silently.

What is it? She mouthed silently.

He put his finger to his lips again.

She swallowed hard. But followed until he put his hand out for her to stop. They both peered around the next row of shelves, and Azalea saw it. She covered her mouth to stop herself from crying out.

It was a monster with a giant bull head planted on top of a muscular humanoid body. The shreds of a shirt barely clung to its hairy chest, and she realized it must be the shopkeeper. It walked on two massive, hoofed-feet, sniffing the air as it went and letting out angry snorts.

She held her hand over her mouth, not even daring to breathe as it passed the other end of their aisle. Her heart raced in her chest as the bull passed, and she stuck close to Torin as he edged forward.

Suddenly, Torin's hand wrapped around hers, and they darted for the front door.

Her pulse pounded in her ears. She didn't look back. But the creature roared, and the shelves tumbled toward them like dominos.

Azalea dashed out of the way. All around her, trinkets and antiques crashed to the ground in a deafening avalanche. Torin yanked her forward as a shelf crashed behind her, sending a blast of air through her hair.

"Get to the door!" Torin yelled.

Azalea didn't need telling twice. She scrambled over a fallen shelf, and Torin lifted her down the other side. An inhuman roar bellowed behind her, and she glanced back, wishing she hadn't. The bull-man scraped his hoof across the cracked tiles and charged at them, his eyes wild and red.

Adrenaline pumped through her legs, and she shot out the door Torin was holding open. She sprinted up the cobbled street with Torin right next to her. Behind them, tables and chairs from restaurants crashed into walls as the beast raged.

"This way," Torin yelled, his gray coat flying behind him like a superhero's cape.

She didn't slow down as they turned the corner, and he yanked open a random door to a brick warehouse-looking building. The thunder of hoofbeats was so close, but she didn't dare look back.

Azalea flew through the door, and Torin slammed it behind them. He locked it and cut into the Hollow straight away. The monster's weight slammed into the door; it wouldn't hold for long.

Azalea threw herself into the Hollow, and Torin rolled in behind her. The slit shut, and she closed her eyes. Her breath was heavy, and her chest burned. She'd never run that fast in her life, and she was glad for all the training she did. It probably saved her life.

"What the fuck was that?" Azalea's hand went to her chest, wondering if she'd ever breathe normally again. Her heart thundered like it might explode.

Sweat poured down Torin's forehead. He wiped his eyes and shook his head. She felt the disbelief rolling off him.

"It was a minotaur. I wasn't sure we were going to get away." He let out a shaky breath, reached into his pocket, and pulled out the small, winged bull of deep green jade. He cradled it in his hands as if it were a baby bird that might jump out.

"A minotaur was not one of the scenarios I was expecting. The Shadow Atlas didn't even warn us." She leaned over, her head close to Torin's, taking in the fine features of the wings and the curve of the tiny horns on the bull's head.

"I didn't expect it either," he admitted. A look of pure relief shot between them.

Torin grinned. "Well done, mageling."

"Good teamwork, professor." She giggled. There was something about nearly dying that made her a little crazy.

He narrowed his eyes at her, and she smirked to herself; though she had to admit, the mageling thing was growing on her.

Torin pocketed the bull. "Let's get back to the hotel for our stuff and head home."

"What about the minotaur? Won't it hurt people?" Azalea asked, suddenly feeling bad about the street and the shop getting wrecked.

"From what I've read, minotaurs are cursed men, usually set with a task. If its task was to guard the relic, it won't hurt anyone else. I'll make an anonymous call to their Paranormal Justice Unit, and hopefully, they can catch it and set it back to its human form. I wouldn't worry about it."

"And maybe we can make a few donations to the local restaurants courtesy of the Archmage?"

"Good thinking." He patted his pocket and pulled out the book he'd bought before, checking it was okay.

))) ● (((

It was nearly midnight before they made it back to London. Azalea's phone was at 2% battery, but it blinked out when she tried to send a message to Erik saying she was home. Oh well, she would just message him in the morning.

She couldn't find the phone charger in her bag and gave up and changed into her pajamas. She caught a glimpse of the vibrant green ring Torin had given her; she rather liked it. She slipped it off her left hand and moved it to the ring finger on her right. She might as well wear it till he asked for it back. A light knock sounded, and she opened the door to find Torin still fully dressed and looking anxious.

"We need to go back to the Desert tonight," he said with a wave of reluctance rolling off him.

Azalea scrunched up her eyes. She just wanted to sleep. Well, sleep without having to go on another mission *while* she was asleep. That couldn't be very rejuvenating.

"Let's get it over with, then." She wanted answers more than she needed sleep. Pulling her patchwork quilt off the bed, she wrapped it around her shoulders, then followed Torin to his room. He wasn't wearing a shirt, but she was too tired to even sneak a look and appreciate his firm muscles and amazing tattoos. She could do that in the dream. At least it would be easy to get to sleep this time. After walking thirty thousand steps around Paphos and sharing her magic, it felt like she could sleep like the dead and nothing would wake her.

CHAPTER 29

As soon as Azalea's head hit the pillow, she was out. She awoke almost instantly, surrounded by desert sands and the giant pyramid at the end of the familiar marble path. A welcome blast of hot air sent her long brown hair dancing in the wind.

She felt Torin before she saw him and almost had to break into a run to keep up with him as he took off at a march toward the structure.

Her limbs were floaty like she could just sway her way up to the steps, or maybe glide her way there. She'd have to ask Torin how to go about such advanced dreaming techniques when they got home. Right now, he would either ignore her questions or call them silly and tell her to be quiet. It was so hard to be quiet in this dreamscape; words bubbled to her mouth like champagne, all wanting to pop and burst from her at the same time. But she could be restrained. How hard could it be?

Torin began yelling before they even got to the steps. Clearly, he was having brain bubble issues too.

"Damu! Come speak to us! We summon you now."

Azalea skipped up to him, tilting her head as she examined the snake skeleton tattoo winding up the back of his leg, around and around. It really was beautiful.

She fought the urge to link arms with him and skip to the pyramid steps. It was such a lovely day. The two suns were glowing like fireballs in the sky, which was exactly what they were. Perhaps it was the lack of sleep and the fact that dream walking took energy that was making Azalea not care so much about the outcome of this meeting. Damu probably wouldn't show up, anyway, and getting back to proper sleep sounded like a delightful idea.

The ground shuddered, and the sand roiled up in a great wave, then settled again, leaving the enormous sand dragon in its place.

"Hello, dragon!" she called out. Even though it was made of sand, it was spectacular. She'd read about dragons in one of Torin's books. They used to be fairly common in the world, but now there were none. A pity. She'd rather like to meet an actual dragon one day. Apparently, they could travel between dimensions, which also made her wonder why none had returned to earth. Because of humans, probably.

"Be quiet," Torin hissed.

Azalea smiled at him and waved to the dragon as it lowered itself to the ground, folding its front legs in just like a cat. Its back legs followed it down. But something else moved.

"Oh, crap," Torin muttered.

"What? Who is he?"

A tiny man hopped off the dragon.

But as his epic strides brought him to the marble path, it became apparent he was anything but tiny. He was so big, in fact, that he would certainly give The Rock a run for his money. Definitely a god. He had a classic god beard and muscles on top of muscles beneath his perfect golden skin.

"Snap out of it, Azalea," Torin said.

She pulled her eyes away to look at Torin. "What?"

"I said—he's the god Zakar, so don't speak unless he asks you something. Okay?"

"Yes, sir," she said as seriously as she could. Wow, Zakar himself. Was this good or bad?

"I greet you, children of the mortal realm," Zakar bellowed in a larger-than-life voice as he stopped in front of them. He was twice Torin's height, and that was bloody tall.

Azalea strained her neck as she gazed up at him and fought to keep herself from speaking before Torin.

"We thank you, great Zakar. We were seeking the god, Damu. But are honored by your presence."

Okay, so maybe it was good Torin was the one doing the talking.

"What is it you seek from Damu?"

"We seek information about a sword. The spirit blade we believe it is called. Damu cursed Azalea here to channel spirits to the Shadow Dimension, but he failed to tell us this sword might be able to do the same thing. If we can get it, we can spare her the danger of being a gateway for the spirits."

The god's brow crinkled into a shiny gold frown. "I know of this sword. It was I who forged it. Ereshkigal took advantage of my children, so I left behind a weapon to protect them. I am sorry she is using you once more."

"Can we find it?"

"It still exists. But it will not fulfill the same role as a human conduit. There is a reason the girl was chosen."

Azalea let out a defeated breath. Well, it had been a nice idea.

"Why?" Torin said.

"Ereshkigal does nothing without reason. That is all I know."

"Where is the sword now? Can we find it?" Azalea asked, unable to keep quiet any longer.

"I see it in the dreams of one man."

"Maybe we can find him," Azalea whispered to Torin.

Torin nodded. "Does he have a name? Where can we find him?"

"For generations, the sword has been passed down. It hangs on the wall of a great study. You have seen it before, young Torin."

Torin's expression changed to obvious shock or realization. It was hard to tell, emotions felt different in the dreamscape.

"I know where it is," Torin said.

Azalea jumped up and down and clapped. "Where?"

"My father's study." He groaned and tilted his head back as if looking for the answers in the stars they couldn't see.

"Oh."

"I do not recommend retrieving it. It will not help your plight," Zakar boomed.

"Do you have any suggestions on what might help our plight?" Azalea asked.

"You are stronger together than apart. Do not waste the gift of power," Zakar said, staring down at them like a school principal on steroids.

That wasn't exactly helpful advice or an option for them. She let out a heavy dream sigh. Back to the drawing board, it was.

"Was Damu lying when he said he would break our bond if Azalea fills the quota of spirits?"

Zakar threw back his head with a deep belly laugh. "A god would not lie. But there are many ways to interpret spoken promises."

"Thanks, anyway," Azalea said with a smile.

Surely it was time to go to real sleep now. Hopefully, she could just stay sleeping once this dream ended.

"That is not all. You need to claim the last two relics. The future path is unclear. You lowly mortals are the catalysts for change—nothing in the future is certain."

"Do you know where the last relic is?"

"It is not far but guarded by the barghest."

Torin's eyes lit up. He knew something.

"We thank you for your time," Torin said, giving nothing away.

"I am always amused to speak with mortals. Your brief lives are filled with such tragedy and drama. It keeps me young to hear of your troubles. I must ride my dragon now. He is in need of recharging in the fires of the red star. Farewell, mortals."

He marched toward his dragon and took off in a great flap of sand that briefly blocked out the suns.

"We need to get back and get the next relic tomorrow."

"Can't we just sleep?" Azalea groaned.

"We're asleep now. It will have to be enough."

It hadn't felt like she'd slept at all. Even in her sleep, she felt sleepy. But he was right, getting the relic before his father was far more important.

⟩ ⟩ 🌖 ● ◖ ◖ ◜

"What the fuck is this?" a voice woke Azalea from her unfinished sleep.

She rolled onto her back, groggy and unable to will her eyes open. Maybe she had dreamed it?

"Azalea!" Erik yelled, and she was jolted from her sleep as the warmth of the blanket was ripped away.

She jolted upright, her mouth dry and her voice croaky. "What the hell, Erik?"

"What the hell do you think? You tell me you're going away, and you don't say where. Your phone is off, and I had no idea where you were, and I find you in bed with *him!*" Erik loomed over her, clutching the blanket as if he was about to rip it to shreds.

Torin was already out of bed, his elemer in hand, his chest bare, and his eyes locked on Erik.

"Oh," Azalea said, trying to get her brain to lock into gear. So, this looked bad.

"This isn't what it looks like, Erik. Calm down," Torin said, not very convincingly.

The vein in Erik's forehead looked like it might explode as his eyes flicked to the tattoo on Torin's chest. "I don't care what it is. I'm not dealing with this anymore."

"Just let me explain." Azalea's heart raced as she tried to comprehend what was going on. She jumped out of bed, grabbing her elemer as she got up. At least she was wearing respectable warm pajamas. That had to count for something. Though Torin was shirtless and had a sheen of sweat over him.

"Fuck you both. I don't want to hear." Erik threw the blanket on the floor, but Azalea was fast and flicked her elemer to send a blast of air to slam the door shut.

Erik turned and glared at her. His hands were in sealed fists, with smoke smoldering from the gaps between his fingers.

"Nothing happened, Erik. I was learning dream magic." She stepped toward him and reached for him, but he backed away with his hands up.

He rubbed a hand over his forehead and closed his eyes. "And that's supposed to make me feel better about it?"

Shouldn't it? "I'm sorry. Let's just talk about this." She wiped her sweaty hands on her legs.

Azalea glanced at Torin, and he gave her a clear look that said, *leave me out of it.*

Erik saw the look, and his fists turned into flaming balls. "You don't just go into dreams with random people. That's not even your House's magic, so stop lying to me."

Erik was clearly on the edge of losing it. Torin inched around the bed toward him.

"Just listen, Erik. Please. I didn't mean to sleep here all night. My magic was drained, and my phone was dead. I'm sorry."

"Pathetic excuses." He held up his hands and closed his eyes. When he opened them, the fire vanished as he shook his head slowly. "You know, when the Archmage asked me to keep an eye on you, I jumped at the chance." His fiery eyes locked onto hers.

Azalea's stomach dropped to her feet.

"I actually liked you Azalea." Erik laughed, but there was no humor in it. "Here I am. A fucking idiot being cheated on." He dropped his hands to his sides and shook his head.

"I didn't cheat on you, Erik." Azalea tried to keep her voice calm. She didn't know what to say. Her mind was cloudy with sleep, and she'd never seen Erik mad like this.

"You're nothing but a dirty slut, and I'm done," Erik spat. His glare shot ice through her heart, and she stepped back as if he'd hit her.

"Don't speak to her like that." Torin stormed forward and shoved Erik against the door.

Erik's back slammed into the wood. But he just smirked. "What are you gonna do about it?"

"Torin, stop." Azalea latched onto Torin's bare arm and pulled him back, ignoring the warmth of the magic that flooded between their skin.

"Fuck you both. You two deserve each other." Erik threw the door open and stormed down the stairs.

Azalea let go of Torin's arm and swallowed hard as tears pricked at the corners of her eyes. *What had just happened?* None of it had been real, and Torin was right. She bit her lip to stop it from shaking.

"Azalea," Torin said softly.

She grabbed her blanket off the floor and pulled it to her chest, avoiding Torin's eyes. "You were right about him. Happy now?"

"Of course I'm not happy. Are you okay?" She could feel him just a few feet away in the dim light, the pity rolling off him so much she wanted to throw something at him. But this wasn't his fault.

"I'm fine. Just leave me alone." She bit her trembling lip and went back to her room. Faraday appeared on her bed as she fell onto it, taking deep shaky breaths to calm down.

She didn't blame Erik for being mad, but it hurt just how quickly he had turned on her. Had he ever actually liked her? He sounded like he had but was only with her because the Archmage told him to be. Her vision blurred, and the heat rose in her as she tried to fight off the tears. The words '*dirty slut*' played over and over again in her mind.

Unfortunately, she didn't have the luxury of being able to wallow. They needed to get the last relic on their list and find that sword. She couldn't trust any of these gods and their games, so it was time to take things into her own hands and sort out this mess she'd gotten herself into.

She set an alarm and slept for another hour, then pulled herself up, got dressed and made a cup of tea as if nothing happened, and trudged down to the office to consult the Shadow Atlas.

CHAPTER 30

Azalea walked down the stairs and into Torin's office as if nothing had happened. As if Erik hadn't just broken up with her from whatever their lie of a relationship was, as if she hadn't just been by the Mediterranean Sea the day before, and as if they hadn't spoken to Zakar himself.

Today she had to stay focused and block the rest of the bullshit out. This was their last relic. Their last chance to maintain control and they sure as hell weren't letting Torin's father get to it first. This one was their security and the last piece in the puzzle that decided who held the power. They had to get it and hide it well.

"You ready to do this?" Torin asked.

"Yup," she lied. Her body was heavy; her heart was heavier. She wasn't ready at all, but she had to get on with this. Erik wasn't worth wasting her energy on.

Torin already had the Shadow Atlas out on his desk, but it was sitting well away from him, and he was wearing leather gloves like a paranoid weirdo.

"It's not going to poison you," she said, feeling hints of fear rippling off him. Maybe she had gotten *too* used to it, or maybe he was right, and it was using its mysterious powers on her. Whatever it was, they didn't have much choice. They needed the book, and whatever its ulterior motives were, they would have to risk it and find that out later.

"Okay, you lump of a book. Give us what we need, and it's extra blood for you for breakfast." She sliced into her hand with her elemer and dripped a few red droplets onto the first page. Strange how this now seemed normal.

She wrote out a simple request about the white deer relic they were after next.

Torin shuffled his chair a little closer as Azalea leaned over the book. Blood red ink seeped onto the aged paper and around the edges a border of gnarled trees grew onto the page, looking like something from a dark fairytale story.

Hello, mageling...
A Wisty wildwood, where the barghest await,
Enter the shadow to discover your fate.
The two knotted trees will show you the way.
The beasts in the darkness may lead you astray.
A balance in stone in the land you know best,
Your heart must be pure or there you will rest.

"You know what it means?" Azalea asked as she took a photo of the riddle.

Torin nodded. "Zakar mentioned barghest. They are endangered, only found in one place: Wistman's Wood."

"What's a barghest, and can we go there this morning?" Azalea said. Better to get this over with than drag it out. Time was not on their side, or rather, nothing was on their side right now.

Before Torin answered, the letters shifted on the page of the book, scattering and rearranging themselves into a new riddle.

Magic in peril by creatures of Night,
Know who to trust, or prepare for a fight.
The twelve keys together can open the gate,

Whether hidden or used, will determine your fate.

"'*Hidden or used,*'" Azalea repeated. "Why the hell would we use them?"

"I think it's just a warning. Though we're going to need a damn good hiding place. But we shouldn't talk about this in front of the book. We can't trust it, no matter how much it's helped us recently." He slammed it shut and shoved it straight back into the safe.

"I'm well aware of the fact, thank you. But it's usually right, even if it's for misguided reasons."

"Let's just get the relic and then deal with hiding it later. We're going to have to wing it."

She smirked. "Torin Dumont, winging it. I never thought I'd see the day."

"Azalea, you have no idea how much winging it I do day-to-day." He shot her a roguish smile and pushed back his chair.

Well, you learn something new every day, and he was in a very good mood now. Azalea wasn't about to do anything to jeopardize that. She wanted to ask him what the Archmage would do if she thought she and Torin were together. She was certain there was a rule about masters and apprentices not sleeping together. But she also knew how desperate the Archmage was to get the relics. Perhaps she wouldn't mention it for now. They could only hope.

"So what can I do to get ready, and what's a barghest? I feel like you're avoiding that particular detail."

"You pack our bags and see if there's any steak or meat of some sort in the freezer."

"Do I want to know why?"

"Barghest are dogs straight from the Shadow Dimension—guardians of the underworld."

"And they like steak?"

"I have no idea, but I hope so."

)))●(((

Azalea cut into the Hollow, and Torin cut out. Ethereal mist hid the damp moor, with only the silhouettes of gnarled trees giving away the woods. Everything smelled of recent rain; wet earth mixed with the dank, rotting smell of the nearby forest.

"This way," Torin said.

Azalea followed him into the fog toward the specters of miniature oak trees. The closer they got to the woods, the more it felt like she was entering a Grimm Brothers' fairy tale. Moss draped over rocks like sheets covering old furniture, and water dripped from beards of lichen suspended from the trees like tattered curtains.

They didn't get the torches out, opting to let their eyes adjust to the darkness of the mist despite it being the middle of the day. Azalea did her best to keep up with Torin's quick pace. He seemed to know where he was going, but every rustle of wind or crack of tree branches had Azalea raising her elemer. It wasn't until she spotted the border of tiny glowing mushrooms that she relaxed. They shone like little rainbow glow sticks and reminded her of her mum's forest, of home. Perhaps the goddess Ninhursag was watching over her here as well.

The peace was short-lived when Torin stopped, and she saw why. *'The two knotted trees will show you the way.'*

Before them stood two ancient trees curved toward each other over the path, forming a perfect arch of interwoven branches. The braids were so symmetrical, they must have been guided with magic. Long strands of lichen hung from the arch; a veil covering the path to the unknown darkness behind.

"Let me go in first," Torin whispered.

"You can go in first, but I'm coming with you."

"I expected as much." He didn't argue, just pushed aside the living curtain revealing a narrow path of darkness.

Why did their quests have to involve dark tunnels? Azalea took a deep breath and followed him in. At least this one wasn't underground and wouldn't involve any weta.

Trees on either side closed in, folding over at the top with their gnarled branches interwoven like a rustic cage on all sides. They had no choice but to follow the narrow path further into the forest.

A low growl rumbled through the misty air, and Azalea jumped as a dangling strand of lichen touched her arm. Torin came to a halt in front of her, and she nearly slammed into his back.

He stood dead still.

"What is it?" she whispered.

The low rumbling growl grew louder and was joined by a second creature.

Azalea sucked in a breath. Her legs froze on the spot, half of her wanting to blend into the trees like a ghost, the other half wanting to sprint off as fast as she could. But she wasn't about to leave Torin there.

Raising his elemer slowly, Torin sent out silent tendrils of shadows in front of them. Azalea did the same. Cutting into the Shadow Dimension and summoning the shadows was now as easy as breathing to her. For a second, she wished Erik was there. His fire magic would be pretty handy right now, but then she remembered what a dick he had been.

Though none of that seemed to matter right now, not when the silhouette of two giant dogs prowled out of the mist.

Torin raised the shadowy ropes in front of them, crisscrossing to make a lattice shield they could see through. Azalea moved closer to him, though it was hard on the narrow path. She wanted to help attack if need be, not get stuck hiding behind him.

"You brought the steak, right?"

"Yes, but it's stewing steak. Do you think they'll like it?" Azalea flipped her bag to her front and dug out the packet of meat.

"Just throw the bloody steak!" he hissed and stepped to the side.

Azalea stared into the glowing red eyes of the barghest. The dogs were massive, like mastiffs mixed with Great Danes, mixed with dire wolves that were genetically engineered to be twice the size of a normal dog. Their shaggy, dark fur dripped with water. She was surprised they weren't growing moss and lichen like everything around there.

Ripping the bag open, she tossed a handful of the cut-up meat as far as she could, then held her breath. The beasts dove for it, their tails whipping back and forth like giant sweeping brooms. One let out a happy, booming bark, and suddenly they were as innocent as playful puppies.

Azalea let out her breath and cracked a shaky smile as the mist cleared a little. Her heart was still racing, but the dogs were on the ground happily wolfing down the meat.

"Maybe they were just hungry?" Azalea whispered.

Torin didn't respond as they watched the two dogs devouring the chunks of meat.

She took in her newly unobstructed surroundings. A stone altar stood at the center of the clearing, kind of like a large birdbath but flat like a sundial without the dial.

Azalea threw some more meat before the dogs had time to look up.

"We need to get to that altar. The relic must be around there somewhere." Torin inched toward the dogs.

Azalea stuck close, tossing the last bits of meat to them as they went past. Hopefully, that would keep them happy. "Nice doggies."

One looked up and glared at her with bright red eyes, then its tongue lolled out to the side, and it let out a happy bark so loud Azalea nearly fell over. Her heart thundered in her chest, but the beasts didn't seem to want to eat them.

She focused on the altar. They got there with no issues; no booby traps, no vines jumping out to capture them, no dogs suddenly turned evil.

Azalea knew better than to touch the stone. She would await Torin's instructions. No way she was getting blamed for touching the wrong thing this time. "What's it do?"

"It must have a button, or a switch or something. Maybe it's activated by magic?" Torin said, more of a mumble to himself than Azalea.

"The riddle said, *'A balance in stone in the land you know best; Your heart must be pure or there you will rest.'* Maybe it needs to balance something to give us the relic. Like if we put something on it, that's the same weight it will pop out?" Azalea said.

"You might be onto something there, but it won't work with just anything."

"Try a rock?"

They both looked around, and Azalea picked up a slimy rock from the base of the altar. "Should I try it?"

"Go on then." Torin sighed, clearly not believing it would work.

It didn't. It just sat there like a rock.

"If it's a test, we might need to leave something valuable," Torin said.

"You got any money? I've got ten quid," Azalea suggested, swinging her bag around to search for it.

Torin rummaged through his bag. "I don't think it accepts cash."

"What about this?" Azalea pulled out her father's pocket watch. Her heart ached at the thought of giving it away. But this was more important than silly sentimental attachments.

"You can't give that away, Azalea; it's too important to you." A rush of guilt rolled off him. That watch was certainly a trigger for him. At least if she gave it away, he wouldn't have to feel that every time he saw it.

She glanced behind to see the two dogs sitting like statues, not moving a muscle, just staring.

Before Torin could talk her out of it, she placed the pocket watch on the altar and pulled her hands back.

The altar shuddered, and the center sank as a set of metal scales rose; old-fashioned like something you'd find in a Victorian pharmacy. Her watch sat cradled on one side, and on the other was a tiny white deer.

Torin moved to her side, probably to make sure she didn't reach out and grab it. She was glad she didn't because the scales started slowly tipping one way, then the other.

They finally stopped, and they were dead equal.

Azalea held her breath, waiting to see if it moved again. When it didn't, she looked to Torin. "Is it safe?"

"I don't know." He reached out and scooped the little white deer up before Azalea could take in a breath.

They stood there frozen, waiting for something to happen. Azalea's eyes slid to the dogs. One let out a deep bark, and she nearly fell flat on her face from the fright. Torin caught her under the arm and steadied her.

"I think it's okay," he said. She felt his relief mix with her own and couldn't help but smile.

The dogs seemed to approve of them. In unison, they flopped onto the ground, rested their chins on folded paws, and shut their eyes.

Her eyes settled on the tiny white deer relic. The white jade was pretty and quite different from the other relics. "Is that it?"

"I guess so." Torin frowned at the altar scales. "Want to try to get your watch back?"

She bit her lip, wondering if it was worth the risk. "Don't you think it would want to keep it as payment?"

"I think it was a test. You gave up something important to prove we were worthy of receiving the relic. It would have taken it back into the table if it wanted to keep it."

"And you're willing to take that risk?" Azalea said, surprised he was even considering it.

"I can't let you leave it here."

Her heart rate shot up.

"Okay, get ready to run." Torin reached out.

Azalea stepped back, her muscles tense. Should she let him do this? Her chest ached at the thought of leaving the watch in this cold, creepy forest. In a strange moment of clarity, she realized she would rather lose the watch than Torin, but it was too late.

His hand darted to the scale, and a flash of light flared around him. His eyes rolled into his head, and as if in slow motion, he toppled backward.

Azalea staggered forward but was too slow to catch him as he fell, taking her down as he went. Her back slammed into the hard earth. Torin's shoulder dug into her gut, knocking the wind out of her. She gasped for air and heaved herself to the side as Torin lay still on the ground.

"Torin. Wake up!" She shook him, and his head lolled to the side.

The dogs didn't even blink.

She grabbed his hand and closed her eyes. Pushing her magic into him, willing him to be okay.

He sucked in a breath and groaned.

"Thank the gods for that." She let out a breath of relief and rested her hand on his chest. Her heart thundered, and she could feel his doing the same.

"Got the watch." He smiled and tucked it into her palm.

"Thank you, Torin." She draped herself over him in a big, pathetic hug. Her magic met his with a fuzzy warmth as the gap between them closed. She didn't care if he didn't want to be hugged, or that they were meant to stay apart.

"At least the dogs didn't bite me," he said with an awkward laugh that danced through her.

She pulled away as he sat up and looked down to see if he was injured. "Me either. Are you okay?"

"I think so. Maybe it was a warning. Let's get back before something worse shows up."

"Agreed." Azalea smiled as she helped Torin up.

They set off into the creepy tunnel of trees with him leading. The smile he threw back at her sent butterflies cascading through her stomach.

Azalea silently scolded herself for such an over-the-top reaction to a smile. But their win had her floating on air, and she was certain Torin felt the same, like their good moods were bouncing off each other and being boosted. A dangerous thing with extreme emotions. But for now, she would enjoy their success.

CHAPTER 31

Azalea fell into bed that night feeling like she could sleep for a week. Faraday curled up on her stomach as soon as she lay down. Without the energy to move him to roll into a more comfortable position, she just lay there on her back.

For once, everything was going as planned. She let her eyes close.

❯ ❯ ❯ ● ❮ ❮ ❮

The world around her faded; she was in the lobby of the House of Eagles Tower. Though she'd only been there once, she remembered the magical forest at the top of the skyscraper well. Glowing lanterns bobbed up and down around the trees, and streams trickled under moon-shaped bridges; the water was alive with glowing silver fish that sparkled like glitter.

This must be a dream because her limbs felt nice and floaty, and there were giant griffins wandering around wearing top hats.

A bundle of rolling, baby griffin kittens nearly bowled her over as they tussled their way past her before the three of them bounced up to chase each other's tails. She giggled as one cub bounded over to her.

"You can't trust the Archmage. She's working with the House of Ravens," the little cub said in a clear voice that shocked Azalea so much, she nearly fell into the stream.

She crouched and ruffled the kitten bird's head. "And what would you know, little cutie?"

"I only know what you already know." It purred.

Some people drinking coffee at a nearby table frowned at her. She glanced around. *Super weird*. She stood up, and the griffins rolled off to attack their mum.

The sky turned dark outside, and the glass walls lit up with galaxies and stars.

Why was she here?

A chill settled in the air. She walked through the paths of silver trunks of birch trees and into a corner where weeping willows dangled their tendrils of leaves into a moonlit pond, leaving ripples of bioluminescent sparkles where the tips touched.

Yellow fireflies lit the air like fairy lights and led her to the pond and its soft grass; there was a person on the edge of the water by the reeds.

"Azalea," the familiar voice greeted her with surprise.

The fireflies had led her to Torin. She smiled, glad to see it was him and that this wasn't turning into a horrible nightmare, like so many of her other dreams did.

"Hey, Torin. Didn't expect to see you here," she said, suddenly noticing the large raven with one eye from another dream sitting on a branch above her.

"Me neither." Torin sounded a little confused.

She eased onto the soft grass next to him and relaxed back on her elbows, and he did the same, glancing up at the raven with a smile.

"I've never been here," Azalea said, breathing in the fragrant night air.

Torin continued to watch the raven. "Danni took me here when I first moved to the Tower. It was my favorite place to go when she set me up on blind dates."

"You took your dates here?" Azalea said defensively. It was her dream, after all. She could be jealous in a dream if she wanted.

He laughed. "No, I escaped the dates. I came here to hide. There's something about this spot."

"Something magical?" Azalea laughed. Everything here was magical.

He shot her a look, and she laughed again, and he joined in.

"I wouldn't mind if you took me for a date here," she said, suddenly full of confidence, though her feelings were all jumbled up, but this place was extremely romantic.

"I wish I could, Azalea," dream-Torin said.

Even in a bloody dream, she couldn't stop herself from blushing. "Really?"

"Of course," he said as if it were obvious.

"Well, why not? Nothing's stopping us. Look, we're already here," she said boldly.

"You know why. We can't risk sealing the bond."

"This is a dream. Who gives a shit! Just give me this dream dammit!" she shouted to Zakar, or whatever other god was spying on her dreams. She wanted to forget about Erik, she wanted to give in to whatever it was she was feeling about Torin, and she wanted to have some fun.

Then she remembered what the griffin cub said.

"I need to tell you something." She eyed the raven above them.

"Don't worry about the raven, she was my pet, Licorice," he said, as if lost in memory for a second, then turned back. "What was it you wanted to say?"

Of course, he had a raven as a pet. She focused on the message before she forgot it in a dream fog. "We can't trust the Archmage. She's working with the House of Ravens."

"How do you know?"

"A baby griffin told me. But it makes sense. It explains why your father hasn't tried to attack me, why he hasn't tried to get the relics from us, and how she knows where to get the final raven relic."

He paused, staring out across the pond before he answered. "We already knew we couldn't trust her. You could be right. Despite your information coming from a griffin, it makes sense."

A wave of happiness washed over her. Things were making sense, and Torin was looking very appealing right now. "But it's just a dream. We don't have to worry about that now."

Torin chuckled and turned toward her. "You're right. It's just a dream."

"So what should we do in this dream?" she asked suggestively.

Her heart nearly froze in her chest when he leaned over and tucked a strand of hair behind her ear.

"Something I've wanted to do for a long time," he teased, his face dangerously close to hers.

"Then do it," she whispered.

He brushed his lips across hers, pausing as they barely touched. A rush of dizziness washed over her. His mouth was against hers, so perfect and soft, it could only be a dream—and so light it sent shivers sparkling along her skin.

She let down all her usual defenses and moved toward his warmth, letting her bare feet twine around his legs as he pulled her in. His hand slid around her head; his mouth dipped to hers.

Their kiss deepened. It wasn't gentleness either of them wanted.

Her fingers slid under his shirt, tracing his muscles, and every place she touched lit up with magic, wild and electric. It sparkled between them like a smoldering fire waiting to erupt, sending waves of energy through every cell in her body.

He pulled back and nudged his nose against hers as his warm fingers grasped her waist and rolled her onto her back. He hovered above her with a whisper of a smile on his lips. She ran her hand over his broad chest, knowing their shared tattoo of the knot and the moon was right beneath her fingertips.

"You have no idea how long I've wanted to do this," he said.

Shivers ran over her skin at those words. He actually wanted her.

"I want it too." She hadn't realized how much until that moment, until she allowed herself to look into those dark eyes and see the truth. See what he hid so well, what she was too afraid to look for.

He hesitated for an agonizing second.

Reaching for his neck, she pulled him onto her. No more waiting. She arched her hips toward him and bit back a moan as his body pressed closer.

The buzz of magic between them grew stronger, humming around them like a weird electrical aura as they tangled together on the grass. *What if something bad happened?*

But her concerns quickly turned to pleasure as her back pressed into the soft earth—

))) ● ((

Azalea yanked the pillow from behind her head and muffled a moan of pure frustration. She wasn't in a magical forest; she was in her bed.

She threw the pillow on the floor and shot upright, drawing in a shaky breath. Where the hell had that dream come from, and why did she have to wake up right then?

Collapsing back down on the bed, she strained her ears to hear if Torin was awake.

She didn't dare get up and get a drink of water like she wanted to; what if she bumped into him?

How could she look Torin in the eyes after a dream like that? It was so different from any others she'd had. She abandoned the idea of sleep altogether after that and tried to focus on blocking out anything to do with Torin. Instead, she rewound the dream in her mind and remembered what the little griffin had said: *You can't trust the Archmage. She's working with the House of Ravens.*

Deep down she knew it must be true, and unfortunately, it was too important to ignore. She had to talk to Torin about it. Tomorrow.

CHAPTER 32

Azalea mindlessly stepped up to the glass food cabinet in the caf and waited for Van to make her lunch selection. Her hand fell to the tiny locket on her neck, as if it had always been there. It had been sitting next to her father's pocket watch that morning on her bedside table, and she slipped it on. After the day before, and perhaps a little because of the dream, she decided she had tortured Torin long enough. She wasn't sure if she was ready to fully forgive him, but wearing the necklace he gave her for her birthday felt like a step in the right direction at least, a good luck symbol to celebrate their success with the last relic. Not that they'd told anyone about that yet.

"Did you not sleep well, hun?" Van said as she waved a hand in front of Azalea's face.

Whoops, she was blocking up the lunch line.

"I'm fine." Azalea selected a sandwich from the glass cabinet and followed Van to the cashier.

"Do you still have some sleep tea?"

"Yes, it's just these weird dreams," Azalea said, wondering where the hell Torin was. As much as she didn't want to face him today, she needed to talk to him about the Archmage. She'd eat the sandwich, then go back to looking if he hadn't messaged her back. The gym was the next place to check, though he couldn't have been in there all morning.

"I can interpret dreams for you if you like," Jade said as she caught up and the three of them walked to an empty picnic table in a quiet spot, away from the main thoroughfare of the caf.

"No thanks," Azalea said. The last thing she wanted was an interpretation of her newly apparent secret lust for Torin. With this damn bond affecting her sleep, she had little hope of retaining her sanity for long.

At that minute, Erik walked in, his arm draped casually over Livia's shoulder, and Azalea froze. He whispered something in Livia's ear, and she giggled.

What the fuck was this?

Azalea sat down and met Van's wide-eyed stare.

"Did you and Erik break up?" Van said.

Oh, right. She had forgotten to mention that.

"We were never officially together, but yes, and it's a long story." Had he gotten over her that quickly to move on to Livia, just like that? Her fingernails dug into her palms. She hadn't been in love with the guy, but it still hurt.

Van frowned, and Azalea looked down at her lunch, hoping Erik wouldn't notice her.

"Do you want me to go punch him in the face?" Jade said. Her dark eyeliner and death stare toward Erik made Azalea believe she was serious.

Azalea shook her head. "No, it's fine. Just let it go. Let's just eat."

"He's all over Livia," Van said, her hand curled into a fist on the table. "I can't let him do this to you, it's rude and ungentlemanly." Van stood up with a determined look in her eyes.

Azalea shot up, grabbed her sleeve, and pulled her back down, pleading, "Please, just leave it, Van."

"Why aren't we doing something? What happened between you?" Van demanded, looking most put out.

Her eyes were wide, pleading with Van. "We had a slight misunderstanding, and I don't want to end up causing a scene if we antagonize Erik any further."

"You're worried about him? You have to tell us now." Van leaned in.

"Fine, but it's not what it looked like. So don't overreact until I finish," Azalea whispered and lowered her head.

Van nodded. Jade was already eating, apparently not fussed if she found out or not.

"So, the thing is. I was sleeping in Torin's bed—"

"You were what!" Van yelled and shot up.

Azalea squeezed her eyes shut at the noise and didn't dare glance toward Erik. He had to have heard that and noticed they were there.

"Van!" Azalea hissed and pulled Van's sleeve to make her sit. "I said *not* to overreact."

"You were in Torin's bed? I feel like that's something you might have mentioned earlier and it's a legit reason to overreact." Van's hands were spread on the table, leaning in, extremely focused on Azalea.

"It was after a field trip for the Archmage, and we were both shattered. But he was teaching me about dream weaving, so we were in a dream together, which obviously requires sleeping, but I was so tired that I didn't end up back in my bed. Trust me, that's all it was."

"You were in a dream together. That doesn't sound like nothing to me." Jade shrugged as she bit into her lunch.

Why was this such a big deal? She could hardly explain that they were trying to get answers from crazy gods. Surely going into a dream wasn't as big of a deal as people were making it out to be.

"I wasn't aware you were on such good terms with Torin again. You must trust him a lot." Van's eyes flicked over her like she was trying to work something out.

Azalea's fingers went to the locket again. "I guess I do," she admitted.

Van noticed. "Isn't that—"

"Come sit with us, Jade." Livia walked over to their table. "You don't want this traitorous shadow bitch rubbing off on you. She'll only stab you in the back or get you killed." She stood next to their table with hands planted on her hips, her low-cut red sweater dress showing maximum cleavage; the look in her eyes was pure malice.

Erik sauntered up next to her and put his arm around her shoulders. Livia turned as he kissed her in a far-too-inappropriate way for the cafeteria.

Azalea nearly gagged, and magic coursed through her, threatening to burst out and strangle them both. She took in a deep breath and tamed it. He wasn't worth it. Plus, she felt terrible for what she'd supposedly done to him. He didn't deserve it, but he also didn't have to flaunt Livia in front of her like that.

Jade just smiled. "I'm fine, guys. I'll catch you in class." She took another bite of her sandwich. That wouldn't do her any favors with her classmates, but Azalea was grateful.

"Clearly, there has been a misunderstanding." Van turned to frown at Erik, very obvious about her disapproval.

Erik stared Van down, his eyes flickering with fire. "I caught her cheating on me red-handed. She was in his bed, for fuck's sake."

Okay, so he wanted to bring everyone into this. Just great.

His arm slipped from Livia's shoulder, and he shot a dark look at Azalea that made her want to leave the room instantly.

Livia folded her arms, clearly not impressed at how upset he was.

"I told you. Nothing happened." Azalea tried to keep her voice low, but people were staring. Why did it have to be lunchtime, and why the hell had she agreed to meet *here* for lunch? Peer pressure and her stomach won out over her better judgment once again.

He crossed his arms. "I'm not stupid, Azalea."

"Can we not do this here?" Her heart was beating faster, Torin could probably feel her panicking, and she hoped like hell he wasn't nearby about to storm in.

"Don't want everyone knowing your dirty secrets? You don't want them knowing you're a whore as well as a snake," Erik said loud enough for the whole room to hear. Which also meant the Archmage would hear the rumor soon enough if Erik hadn't already reported to her.

This was the Erik she'd first met, showing his true colors once more. It hadn't taken long for him to revert to full arsehole.

Livia smirked.

"Enough of that talk." Van shot up with her elemer out.

Azalea stood in case Van did something stupid. But it was time to leave. He was the one waltzing in here with another girl. It had never been her intention to cheat on him, and he was just doing this to be a dick.

"There's nothing between me and Torin. I told you that then, and it's still true now. I'm sorry you got hurt, but at least I can see who you really are now. Goodbye, Erik." She grabbed her bag and her sandwich, and turned on her heels, marching out with her back toward him.

Azalea nearly flinched when Van and Jade appeared at her side and linked arms with her.

"Just keep walking," Van insisted.

"You're a fucking idiot if you expect anyone to believe that," Erik yelled. "I've seen the way Dumont looks at you and the way you pine after him. It's fucking pathetic."

Livia laughed out loud, and Azalea shrugged off her friends and spun around, her hands at her sides, shaking with rage and the effort of not releasing her magic.

"Shut up now," she warned.

"Shagging your father's murderer. That's a new low," Livia teased.

Azalea flashed her elemer out and cut into the Shadow Dimension, her blood bubbling with anger, waiting to hulk out and smash Livia in the face with whatever came to her mind first.

But a firm grip encircled her hand and pulled her back.

"Calm down, dear. No need to get wound up. Take a few deep breaths." The familiar female voice led her away until the magic and anger in her veins simmered down.

Her hands were shaking, and the magic under her skin was waiting to be released.

The door opened, and Azalea found herself in the classroom, sitting on her old seat on the long bench.

Mage Shepard, Van, and Jade were staring at her.

"Sorry," Azalea mumbled.

"You did so well, dear. You didn't lose control or retaliate with violence," Mage Shepard said with a slight stutter.

"I thought you were going to rage out for a second there." Jade sat down next to her looking genuinely relieved.

"Nearly did," Azalea unclenched her fists as her phone buzzed in her pocket.

Torin: *You okay?*

Azalea: *So all it takes for me to get hold of you is a near panic attack. I'm fine.*

Torin: *I've been busy. See you at dinner tonight at Danni and Maiken's. I've got something I need to talk to you about.*

Azalea: *Same here. Did you not get my thousand messages looking for you?*

No reply. Typical.

CHAPTER 33

F abian had given up on the spreadsheet that wasn't adding up and sat staring into his bowl of chicken soup, wondering why Noodle, his adopted un-dead, pet skeleton snake, was sitting in his bowl blinking up at him with those giant, puppy-dog eyes.

He watched the ridiculousness of the snake happily circling in his soup, trying not to think about how taking in all these people and keeping up maintenance on this ridiculous house were sending him deeper and deeper into the hole.

But he couldn't do anything about it until they dealt with the House of Ravens, and they might have to do something sooner, rather than later, judging from what Kat told him about Korbyn looking for these mysterious relics.

He sighed and removed the fresh basil leaf from Noodle's tiny white skull as the snake swayed expectantly from side to side.

"I know you're trying to cheer me up, my friend, but sitting in my dinner isn't the best way to go about it." Fabian got up, grabbed a tea towel from the kitchen bench, and placed it next to his bowl.

"Out," he ordered the snake.

Noodle flicked his tongue in agreement, and his rib bones clattered over the bowl, spilling half the soup as he wound his way onto the tea towel and curled up obediently into a neat coil.

"Good boy," Fabian said. Noodle was a fact of life around here. Fabian had grown up having him around, and at least Noodle didn't talk back to him. Fabian had been the one to rename him Noodle and save him from his original designation as Sir Shadrack—a ridiculous name for a snake. No one knew who resurrected the small grass snake, but he had been part of the house for centuries, appearing in many of the portraits of Blackbourne ancestors for generations, an unofficial mascot.

Fabian frowned at his soup, then shrugged. Couldn't let good food go to waste, and Mrs. Yates, the housekeeper and cook, had clocked off early that afternoon.

His phone buzzed. It was Kat. He held it for a second, letting it ring so he didn't appear too keen. Then pressed *answer*.

"Well, hello there, Kat," he said in a most casual manner.

"Shut up and listen, Fabian. Meet me outside the gates of your estate in fifteen minutes. It's important."

"Anything for you, my Kat." But she'd already hung up.

Rude. Never mind, meeting Kat sounded a lot more fun than going back to his horrible finances, though she was sure to be bringing bad news. Hopefully, she hadn't turned on him and was leading him into a trap of some sort.

If it was a trap, he might as well look good getting caught. He drank straight from the soup bowl and quickly washed the dishes, then told Noodle to take a bath in the dishwater after he was done. He left out a fresh hand towel for Noodle to dry off on, then dashed upstairs to change out of his sweatpants and stained t-shirt. He threw on trousers, a respectable black, woolen sweater that suited him rather well, and a red scarf—because it was bloody freezing out there.

He grabbed the keys to Colin's old Land Rover and slipped out the kitchen door into the cobbled courtyard. His car was in the garage, which was more effort to access. Colin wouldn't mind him borrowing his truck to go up to the gates.

The old truck shuddered to life and bounced up the long driveway to the large iron gates. He ignored the expanding number of gers, tents, and containers on his front lawn. Fabian left the truck inside the property boundary and left through the small side gate into the great wide world of the unwarded lands outside his sanctuary. He shoved his hands in his pockets—should have brought gloves out.

He paced in front of the gate. The old weeping willow's skeletal branches dangled down to brush the edge of the small creek. He preferred the lush green version of the trees in summer. This had been a favorite spot of him and Samael when they were boys. They used to make bridges and dams in the small stream out of pebbles. He picked up a stone and tossed it in the water but hit the ice built up on the edge.

After Samael was gone, he regretted not having spent more time at the family house. Before, he had always been so keen to get away from it, and Samael had been more than happy to take on the responsibilities. If Fabian had been around that fateful night, he would have been there with Samael. Maybe things wouldn't have turned out the way they had.

A vibration of power shifted behind him, and he spun around to see two figures step from the Hollow. He held defensive shadows at the tip of his elemer, ready to respond to an attack.

"It's just me, Fabian," Kat said.

"Don't recall you saying you were bringing company."

"Because I knew you wouldn't meet me if I did."

"Who is she? Go stand in the light," Fabian ordered. He could just make out the second figure was female. Whoever she was, he didn't appreciate surprises or strangers.

"Go on then, just do what he says. He likes to think he's in charge," Kat said to her companion.

They both moved toward the security light perched on the stone pillar of the gate, and Fabian held his elemer out, showing he meant business. Though Kat clearly wasn't worried, she had her hands tucked into her leather jacket and her elemer rested at her hip. Her long black hair was tied in a high ponytail, and her eyes were dark with heavy eyeliner.

"So who's the extra, then?"

"Fabian, this is Kira Reid," Kat said. Both women were dressed in House of Raven black combat uniforms with lots of pockets and heavy military boots.

Kira stood with her arms crossed, an elemer held loosely in her fingers. Fabian took in her brown hair in tight French braids, her green eyes, and the sexy, confident look.

"Kira Reid as in, Kira? The same Kira that Danni has been looking for, for eight bloody years? That Kira?"

"She's the one," Kat said as if it were hardly news.

Kira shrugged unenthusiastically. "Well, now you've found me."

"It wasn't me looking for you. I couldn't give a shit if you were dead. In fact, I was rather hoping you were. Just to add a touch more tragedy to young Dumont's life. Unfortunately, here you are, alive, and apparently well."

This was unexpected and very interesting. Her stern look slipped for a second at the mention of Dumont's name. A touchy subject still? No doubt Kat would have kept Kira apprised on Torin's failure of a life.

"Charming," Kira said. She clearly would not go any further on the matter. Perhaps she didn't want the younger Dumont knowing where she was. That was a nice thought, knowing he had one up on Torin. Perhaps he could use that as blackmail material in the future?

"Why is she here?" Fabian asked, still holding his elemer, ready to react.

"I wanted you to meet her, in case something happens to me. She's on our side," Kat said.

Fabian tapped a finger to his lips. "And which side is that?"

"The side where we don't want the Owls or the Ravens to get their hands on all the relics. We came here to warn you, something big is about to go down."

"Big, like what?"

"We believe Torin is close to finding the last relic. When he does, there won't be any time left. You need to warn him and get him out of the Tower before he finds it."

Fabian had warned Azalea when Kat told him to last time, but apparently, they already knew Korbyn was looking for the relics. "Why are you telling me this? Why not tell him yourself?"

"Because he doesn't have any reason to trust me anymore," Kat said.

"And you think he trusts me?" Fabian scoffed.

"No. Idiot. Your niece is his apprentice, so if you explain the situation to her, she can explain it to him."

"Sounds like a lot of secondhand information by the time it gets to him. He's a suspicious bloke. I don't see why he'd listen."

"It's important. Danni Fletcher will vouch for me as well, but I know Torin isn't on the best terms with her right now. I tried to call her first, but her phone is off."

Fabian pulled out his phone and called Danni to make sure Kat wasn't lying. Her phone went straight to voice mail. "Checks out. But what aren't you telling me? What is Korbyn planning exactly?" Fabian paced, keeping a suspicious eye on both women.

"We aren't sure. Korbyn isn't letting anyone in on his plans anymore. We don't know what he's up to, but we suspect he is working with someone outside the House of Ravens. Someone powerful." Kira kept her elemer in her hand, standing like she was ready to fight, compared to Kat whose elemer remained on her belt, her hands still in her pockets.

He looked Kira up and down. "And why are you here?" She certainly looked the part of an assassin as much as Kat. Kat would have trained her well; of that, he was sure. "And where the hell have you been while everyone thought you were dead?"

"I've been in America with the House of Ravens, working undercover for the past eight years. Kat thought it would be a good idea to come back here for some ridiculous reason." Kira exhaled through her nostrils.

"It's not ridiculous. If Torin knows you're here, he will trust us. We need him on our side for this to work, and we need *you* to get him to trust us again." Kat crossed her arms.

Kira scoffed. "You think I'm the right person for the job? He literally stopped my heart and then abandoned me after he promised never to leave me. So excuse me if I'm a little pissed at him still."

Fabian grinned. This was gold. The girlfriend Torin had been looking for all these years was alive and well, and even better, she appeared to hate Torin as much as he did. This, he could get on board with.

"It wasn't like that Kira, and you know it. Torin did what he thought was right," Kat said sharply.

Kira slid her elemer into her belt and crossed her arms, staring out into the darkness. "By running away like a coward."

"I think I'm going to like you, Kira," Fabian said.

She glared at him with stunning, wide eyes. "Wonderful."

"Anyway." Kat frowned at both of them and flared her nostrils in obvious frustration. "Korbyn has rounded up Raven operatives from all over the place and is planning something tonight. We suspect it's to do with the Tower of London. But we won't get orders until right before the mission. We want you to get Azalea and Torin out with the relics as soon as possible, just to be safe."

"Shit," Fabian said. If Kat was right, he needed to get Azalea out now. "I'll try to call her."

"Get them to come here. It will be safest inside your estate." Kat's eyes flicked to the solid gates.

Fabian shook his head. "No way am I having Torin Dumont set foot on my property."

"Can't you just forget about it for now? This is more important than you," Kat said bluntly.

Kira remained standing quietly with her arms crossed.

"Can I just forget about him murdering my brother? Um—no. They can come to the gate. You can take Torin, and I'll take Azalea and the relics."

"We go where the relics go," Kat said.

Fabian tucked his elemer in his belt and rubbed his hands together to warm up. "And where is that?"

"I think we should discuss it with Torin. He's the expert, and he'll know better than us how the Archmage will react." Kat ran a hand through her dark ponytail, the hair trickled from her fingers like silk.

"I would think that would be obvious. She's insane. She will kill every single one of us to get the relics."

"Which is why we need to be somewhere safe." Kat threw her hands up.

"Which is why you came to me, isn't it? How do I know this isn't a setup and you'll give them straight to Korbyn Dumont?" Fabian stepped toward them.

Kira moved into a defensive stance. "It isn't."

"I've never lied to you Fabian. You'll just have to trust me." Kat guided Kira back.

Fabian stepped back. "You're asking a lot, Kitty-Kat. Let's just talk to Azalea and see if she can bring Torin here, okay? One step at a time."

"Fine." Kat guided Kira away further down the driveway.

Fabian called Azalea, and with every ring that she didn't pick up, he ground his foot deeper into the gravel. He pressed end and sighed.

"We have to get back now," Kat said, squaring her shoulders. She was nervous, not a good sign.

"Yeah. Conner's going to grill me for details if we're out any longer, and we want to keep this under wraps for now," Kira said.

"I'll keep messaging Azalea and calling till I get hold of her. I'll keep you updated."

Kat nodded. Kira sighed reluctantly.

"If we don't hear from them, I'll be back here later tonight to form an extraction plan," Kat said.

"It's a date," Fabian said as he called Azalea again, each ring feeling longer and longer than the last.

CHAPTER 34

T orin paced the space between the shiny white kitchen and the palm tree at the front door in Danni and Maiken's apartment, taking small sips from his red wine as he went, and wondering what the hell he was going to say to Azalea when she finally got there. After the crazy dream he'd had about her the previous night, he couldn't get her out of his head.

Danni was busy upstairs getting the girls washed up for dinner, and Maiken was in the kitchen, humming as she added things to a bubbling pot on the stove that smelled pleasantly of garlic and onions. He hadn't been listening when she told him what was for dinner.

He couldn't take much more stress after the day he'd had with his supervisor, Brandon, discussing the relics and trying not to give away the fact that they'd found the white deer when it had been in his pocket the whole time. He rolled the small relic over his palm in his pocket as he walked, letting the cool stone seep into his skin.

He'd nearly run out of the office at one point when he'd felt Azalea's panic levels rising but knew he couldn't appear at her side with every emotional hiccup she had. He'd ignored her messages all day as it was, and she wouldn't have been happy for him to just appear out of the blue.

He checked his phone.

Azalea: *On the way now. Just needed to grab some stuff.*

Then a sharp pain stabbed his chest. He did his best to remain upright and not attract Maiken's attention as his heart spasmed, and he nearly doubled over. Azalea better not have walked through that fucking ghost on purpose; he thought they were past that.

He was often wrong about things to do with people and emotions. This was probably no different, and he suspected these recent dreams and the bond were affecting his rational judgment.

He downed the glass of wine and joined Maiken in the kitchen.

"You alright, Tor?"

"Fine. Thanks. Dinner smells wonderful."

She smiled but clearly didn't believe him. No doubt there would be an interrogation about his well-being during dinner. They were playing the game where everything was fine between them. So far tonight, he hadn't brought up the whole Danni and Maiken lying to him thing. He still felt betrayed that they had let him get so close to Azalea, the daughter of the man he murdered.

"Wine's on the bench. Dinner won't be long." Maiken nodded to the bottle.

Gods, yes. Wine was the answer here. He was already feeling one percent more relaxed.

A knock sounded on the door. "I'll get it," Torin said, knowing it was Azalea.

He opened the door, and all his anger dissipated when he saw her. Her long, brown hair fell loose in soft waves over her shoulders, and she shot him a nervous smile. His eyes locked on her necklace—she was wearing the locket with the watch he'd given her; the locket his mother had given him as a protective amulet, not that he ever told Azalea that. He hadn't wanted to freak her out.

He couldn't help but smile at the locket resting against her collarbone. It had to be a good sign. He inhaled deeply—grounding himself, unintentionally taking in a breath of her perfume, orange blossom and jasmine. His pulse skyrocketed. She was just like in his dream, and he was having trouble separating what was real. For a second he felt like a teenager with no idea how to talk to girls. *What the hell was wrong with him?*

Faraday let out a long *reoooow,* forcing them both to look down and snap out of their daze at the same time.

"Hello, Faraday," Torin said as the black cat sauntered in past him with the lightest possible rub across his legs. It was only when he looked up that he noticed Azalea had her backpack on and was dressed as if she might be going for a hike in the snow, not to dinner within the Tower of London grounds.

"I need to talk to you," Azalea said, her voice urgent, verging on breaking into panic.

"What is it?" He frowned. Trying to decipher her emotions, but they were all over the place.

"Azalea! So lovely to see you!" Danni popped up from somewhere and hugged Azalea with extreme enthusiasm, over the top if you asked him, but she was trying to make it up to them.

Danni offered to take Azalea's coat, but she refused politely and took the coat off herself, keeping it with her bag by the front door like she might make a run for it.

"Food's ready," Maiken yelled.

He shot Azalea a questioning look, and she shot one right back that said they needed to talk. But Ava and Zoe burst into the room and spotted Azalea, both sprinting for her legs in a race to hug her first. For tiny girls, they sure were competitive.

Azalea laughed as they tackled her and gave them a big hug. "Come on, let's get some dinner." She put on a false smile as the twins led her to the table.

Tension levels were high as Torin sat down opposite Azalea. *Soon,* he mouthed silently to her.

Azalea bit her lip and gave a slight nod, but her eyes darted around as if she were looking for something.

"Before we start, Maiken and I would like to apologize to both of you for not telling you the truth about everything. All we wanted was a fresh start for both of you. We just wanted you to see each other for the people you were, not unchangeable actions of the past," Danni said, her eyes welling with tears already.

Maiken took Danni's hand into her own. She wasn't one to get overly emotional, at least. "It wasn't our place to make that decision, so we are very sorry."

"But why did you do it? You must have known we would find out," Azalea said.

"Too much happened, and when you needed help last year, Azalea, Torin was the only one who could give it. I was going to tell you, but then a little part of me thought if you could get to know each other, you could see past the hatred and forgive." Danni stroked Maiken's hand absentmindedly.

"We'd like to start over with you both if that's okay with you?"

Torin glanced at Azalea. She was fidgeting and curled a loose strand of hair around her finger; she still wore the green demantoid garnet ring he had given her, though on the other hand. Hopefully, the protection charm on it still worked. The girls sat quietly, not even listening as they shoveled spaghetti into their mouths.

Torin was about to speak when Danni cut in.

"And you know, it might have all been—"

"Do not say all for the best, Danni. Let's just leave it at that," Torin said. She didn't know just how much of a mess he and Azalea were truly in.

Danni snapped her mouth shut and nodded in agreement.

"I accept your apologies," he said. It was time to move on.

He felt resentment coming from Azalea, but she sat up straight and forced a smile.

"Me too. I forgive you both," she said, though it didn't seem as genuine as his.

"Excellent! Thank you both." Danni didn't seem to notice. She clapped her hands in excitement as if the gods themselves had just appeared before her.

Maiken's shoulders relaxed, and she took the lid off the pot of spaghetti in the center of the table and let Azalea and Torin help themselves. The girls were already covered in red sauce and were focusing hard on winding spaghetti around their forks.

Torin nodded to Azalea to help herself first. She was clearly agitated by something. Perhaps she was just hangry? All his thoughts escaped his mind, overrun by her growing anxiety.

"Azalea, what did you want to say?" He couldn't take the waiting anymore.

Azalea glanced at the girls as if checking they weren't listening and mindlessly scooped spaghetti onto her plate as she spoke. "I don't want to alarm any of you, but I just got a call from my uncle on the way over here." She handed Torin the serving spoon. He was careful not to touch her as she did so and filled his plate.

"Oh. What did he have to say?" Danni asked.

"He strongly suggested we get out of the Tower tonight. He said that the Ravens were up to something, and we shouldn't be here," she spoke carefully. Clearly trying not to cause panic in front of the kids, but that explained why she had her bag.

Torin's chest squeezed. He could feel the panic rising in Azalea and escalating his own anxiety tenfold. Danni and Maiken exchanged a worried look. No one was eating.

"Why didn't you say something sooner instead of letting me blather on?" Danni put her knife and fork down.

"I didn't want to butt in. He said we had time, that they probably wouldn't do anything until late tonight." Azalea nibbled at her spaghetti.

"Okay, let's stay calm," Danni said in a reassuring voice. "What exactly did he say?"

"Not much. He said he's on good terms with his friend, Kat Emerson, again, and that she knows something is happening tonight. She doesn't know what but suspects it's to do with the Tower. He said you would know who she is, and that Danni would vouch for her," Azalea said.

"Kat Emerson? What is Kat doing talking to Azalea's uncle?" Torin said.

"You know this Kat?" Azalea said, adding to the confusion.

"Yes, she was my teacher at the House of Ravens." Torin's memory flicked back to all those early morning training sessions. Mage Emerson, Kat, had been a hard-arse and terrifying, but she was an amazing teacher.

Danni ran to the kitchen counter, grabbed a bag of rice, and darted back. Torin noticed the outline of her phone through the grains.

Azalea frowned at the phone and the rice in confusion.

"The rice is to dry it out," Danni explained and continued. "Kat was Fabian's inside contact when he was my partner with the PJU, and she always had good intel. Their relationship was, let's say... less than professional. But Fabian assumed she just used him to get to his brother. After all that we lost contact with her."

"Kat Emerson was an informant back then?" Torin said, stunned that he never knew that. All that time he'd worked with Danni, she never let it slip that Kat might be on their side. Danni really was good at her job and so was Kat, apparently.

"Why didn't she call you instead of going to Fabian?" Torin asked Danni.

She pulled her phone out of the bag of rice and frowned at it. "It still won't turn on. I dropped it in the bath earlier. She might not think we trust her either."

"We don't really have time to discuss this. Shouldn't you all be leaving, like right now?" Maiken said.

Danni looked at Maiken, concerned. "What do you mean, *you*? Shouldn't we all be leaving?"

"If something goes down, I'll need to be here in case people get hurt. I can't leave my patients. But you should get out," Maiken said.

The girls had stopped eating and were following the conversation with wide eyes. No point in pretending now. Kids always knew more than they let on.

"We probably have time, it could all be a setup," Torin said, trying to formulate plans as he talked.

"Should we warn the Archmage?" Maiken asked.

"No!" Azalea and Torin both said at the same time.

Danni exchanged a confused look with Maiken. "Why not?"

"That's what I needed to talk to you about, Torin," Azalea said. He felt her anxiety spike through the roof, almost like when she walked through a spirit. "We can't trust the Archmage, I think she's working with the House of Ravens."

Torin's stomach dropped to his feet. "Why do you say that?" *And how had she come to the same conclusion as him?*

"I worked it out in a dream," Azalea said, and her cheeks turned red.

Torin took in a sharp breath. He swallowed; his throat instantly turned dry and raspy. "I suppose a baby griffin told you," he said, meaning it to sound funny, but it came out totally humorless.

Azalea's face turned ashen, and Torin froze, not wanting to believe it was true—that they had shared the same dream, and she had just worked it out too.

Azalea's cutlery clattered onto her plate as she pushed back her chair and ran to the bathroom. He could feel the panic radiating off her like a sun as she slammed the door behind her.

"What was that?" Danni glanced between Torin and the bathroom door as if it would somehow become clear.

Torin felt the blood drain from his face. It was true. They were in the same dream at the same time, without the intention, without direct contact—it shouldn't be possible. The details of the dream rushed over him in an unwelcome reel of vivid memories. The feel of her lips against his, the way she smiled at him, the way her fingers felt against his skin—it was all so wrong.

"I'll deal with it. Don't worry." Torin forced himself to stand, despite his legs feeling like they'd turned to jelly.

"Now I'm really worried," Danni said.

"Me too," added Maiken as she got up.

"Is the Archmage really working with the House of Ravens?" Danni asked.

Torin nodded absentmindedly. "I'm quite certain." If Erik told her about what he thought he saw between him and Azalea, they could be in real trouble. He had to talk to Azalea.

He went to the bathroom door and knocked lightly. "Azalea. It was just a dream," he whispered, not meaning a word of it. *It meant everything.* It meant their bond had gotten into them so deeply that they didn't know what was real anymore. It meant she knew how he felt about her. And, if he allowed himself a little hope, how she might feel about him. *Or* it was just a dream to her, and he was a fucking idiot.

He could feel her on the other side of the door. Her heart hammering away in her chest as if he was touching her, her magic instinctively reaching out to him.

"Azalea, just talk to me."

She opened the door a crack. "You were there, in the garden with the willow trees? That was you?"

"Yes, it was me," he said softly. Hoping Danni and Maiken weren't listening.

"You kissed me," she whispered, one eye peering through the gap in the door.

"You kissed me back." Heat flooded through him as his eyes met hers, and then she shut the door.

She was silent for too long. He leaned his head on the edge of the door frame. They really didn't have time for this.

"Azalea," he said.

"I don't want to talk about it now," she whispered.

"We don't have to. Let's just get out of here and work out the rest later. We need to get the relics somewhere safe and away from the Archmage."

She opened the door and stood with her hands awkwardly at her sides. He wanted to reach out to her but didn't dare.

"Yes. The relics." She avoided meeting his eyes.

Relief shot through Torin. At least she was talking to him, not slapping him in the face.

"If they're working together, then they have all the relics except our one. I need to go get them now." He was hyper-aware of her standing right in front of him. She was the same as before, but everything felt different, like a dimension between them had shifted. All he could think about was that kiss.

"Do you think they're planning to open the gateway to the Echo Dimension?" Her eyes went to his lips.

Warmth spread across his chest. She was thinking about it, too.

He swallowed, snapping his gaze away from her. "I don't see how that would benefit the House of Owls. They wouldn't be able to use their magic if they flooded the world with that much Echo Magic. Everyone would burn out."

He glanced back at her. Azalea leaned against the frame of the door and tilted her head as if she just thought of something. "Unless they had a way to protect themselves? Danni told me about the Archmage's parents being executed for trying to take over the council. What if the Archmage is doing the same? She wants to finish what her parents started and kill off everyone else, but she has a way to protect the ones who know."

"If that's true, we need to get the relics back and scatter them out. Hide them." Torin was aware of the space between them buzzing with magic. And so was Azalea. She turned her body toward him, and he could sense her heart beating rapidly, even though they weren't touching.

"Oi, what are you two whispering about over there?" Danni yelled.

Torin shoved his hands in his pockets. "Let's just go back to the table and make a plan. Okay?"

She nodded and walked past him. Now, somehow he needed to act like the dream had never happened.

They sat back down, not making eye contact. Danni and Maiken knew something was up, but he ignored the sky-high level of tension in the air.

"I'll go down to the artifacts gallery now and get the relics and replace them with the fake ones we use as decoys. It isn't too unusual for me to go down there at random hours. The guards won't care." Torin tapped his fingers on his thighs, eager to get away as soon as possible.

Maiken tilted her head. "Why do you need the relics?"

"We're close to having the whole collection. When all twelve are together, they can open the gateway to the Echo Dimension." Torin swallowed, hoping that wouldn't be the case.

Danni gripped the edge of the table and frowned at them. "The Archmage wouldn't do that."

"She would. Trust me." Torin risked a glance at Azalea who nodded in agreement. His heart skipped a beat feeling her strong solidarity against the Archmage.

"I don't see why she would. But let's not take any chances and get them out of here." Danni's gaze darted toward the girls.

"We just need to get out of here," Azalea said calmly, but Torin could feel her anxiety levels rising.

"Did Fabian say he had a plan?" Danni asked Azalea.

"He just said to meet him at the gates of Blackbourne Manor. Anyone know how to get there?" Azalea asked.

"I know where it is." Torin nodded, careful not to look at Azalea, though she could probably feel where his thoughts turned. Since that first visit so long ago, he had memorized the location of that fateful night. He didn't particularly want to go back there but also suspected Fabian would never let him in the gates. His vow to kill Torin still seemed to be on the table. At least he could get Danni, the twins, and Azalea there safely. He'd worry about himself later.

Azalea didn't say anything, but her cutlery scraped across her plate as if she were pushing very hard. Her feelings were too confusing to decipher; conflicted, angry, sad, hopeful? It was too hard to tell.

"Okay. Let's just finish dinner, nice and normal. We'll get a few things together to go on a nice trip. Does that sound good, girls? A nice trip to the countryside! We can see some sheep!" Danni said, far too enthusiastically, even for her.

The girls raised their eyebrows. "You said nice too many times, mum," Ava said.

"Let's go pack some toys," Maiken said and took the girls upstairs.

"Maybe we should bring Jade and Van, too." Azalea patted Faraday without looking down when he jumped on her knee.

"We can't warn too many people, it will look suspicious," Torin said.

"He's right. But warning them should be fine. It's normal to see you lot together, no one will suspect anything. What about Erik? We should tell him too," Danni said.

"No. I'm sure he'll be just fine," Azalea said, with obvious bitterness.

"Oh. Did something happen?" Danni asked.

"He's not on our side." Azalea shoved some food in her mouth, and he felt the guilt and humiliation roll off her.

Torin's gut twisted. Another thing to add to Azalea's list of things to hate him for. Even though Erik was a tosser, he still felt terrible about the whole situation. At least Erik had shown his true colors before it went too far.

Danni's eyes flicked between him and Azalea with a questioning gaze. She was too nosy for her own good.

A blast of sound began blaring in every direction. Torin slammed his hands to his ears. That was one way to end an awkward conversation.

"It's the attack alarm!" Danni yelled and raced upstairs.

Fuck. They were out of time.

CHAPTER 35

Wearing her black winter jacket, Azalea followed Torin toward the door. His gray coat swished around his legs. Who knew where they would end up tonight, but at least they'd be warm.

Azalea had planned ahead and pulled an empty sports bag from her pack and opened it for Faraday to jump in; she didn't want to lose him if they had to run.

"It's the attack alarm. Protocol is to go down to the Complex. Don't go outside," Danni yelled over the alarm. She had Zoe in her arms, the girl's eyes were wide and swirling with silver, and a bag stuffed full of kids' things on her back.

"Can't we get out somehow?" Azalea tried not to let her panic show as they gathered at the front door.

She'd had enough of a shock finding out that sexy-dream-Torin had, in fact, been real-life-Torin, but in a shared dream. Mortified didn't even begin to describe how she was feeling.

"The exits will all be covered by now. Our best bet is to go along with it." Danni looked around like she had forgotten something.

"Just pretend we aren't onto them," Torin crossed his arms.

It was amazing he could act so normal when something had shifted so significantly between them. But she knew he felt it, too. He might be calm on the outside, but she could feel the turbulence beneath his skin, the same as hers, writhing and flickering with burning magic, and something else; something she didn't want to acknowledge. But she'd seen the way he looked and her, and she looked back at him the same way. Like they should go get a room.

If he could act normal, then so could she.

"Where's the white deer?" Azalea kept her voice calm.

He tapped his jacket pocket, and she nodded. At least it was safe. She'd looked for it during her mad dash around their flat, trying to pack what was important, but assumed he must still have it with him. She packed everything that mattered to her: her father's watch, the Shadow Atlas, Gerald the dinosaur, and grabbed a change of clothes for both her and Torin, plus some cat food. She left the glass cat from Erik on her bedside table.

Maiken picked up Zoe, and Danni opened the door.

"Stick together," Danni said as they followed the flood of people dashing from their flats and down the stairs until they made it down to the Complex. Danni and Maiken were right behind them with Ava and Zoe in their arms.

House of Phoenix guards were hustling everyone into the cafeteria without explanation. Unfortunately there were too many of them, and too many people around to just whip up some shadows to hide behind and sneak out.

"Just go along with it. We'll find a way out later." Torin's hand was on the small of her back, sparking heat right through her core as they entered the familiar room.

It was warmer than usual and smelled of hot chips and Sunday roast but also of human sweat and too many bodies in one room.

Sticking close to the group, they found their way to the back wall of the caf and claimed a large picnic table. Azalea and Torin sat on one side with their backs to the stone wall covered in creeping ivy vines.

BOOM! A deafening explosion rattled the building. A few people screamed, and several ducked to the floor.

"What the hell was that?" Azalea said. Could the House of Ravens actually be attacking, or was this some sort of staged performance the Archmage was putting on for effect?

"I'm sure it was nothing." Maiken lowered Ava onto the seat between Danni and Azalea. "But I'd better get to the hospital in case anyone is injured." She shot an apologetic look at Danni, who just smiled in understanding.

"Don't forget to take your supplements and get some rest when you can. It might be a long night," Danni said as Maiken leaned down and kissed her, then kissed Ava and Zoe on their foreheads.

"Be good for Mum. It'll be like a big sleepover!" Maiken said.

"Bye-bye, Mummy," they said in unison.

Azalea's heart ached that Maiken had to leave, and here she was, being as useless as ever. They needed to find a way out. Maybe the Shadow Atlas could help? She spotted Van and Jade on the other side of the room and stood up to wave.

"Did you see anything?" Azalea asked as Van and Jade sat opposite her and Torin.

Jade shook her head. "Not on Mint Street. Just a few Phoenix guards running around. But we came straight down here."

"I was asleep. I had no idea what was going on until Jade dragged me in here," Van said.

"*Brrrrp.*" Faraday popped his head up and greeted Van and Jade, then coiled back into the sports bag with his favorite blanket. Luckily, it was normal enough for her to be seen with her cat around here.

"Cheeky bugger," Azalea said but was so relieved to have him nearby. Hopefully, he'd feel safe enough in the bag.

"What's happening?" Van asked.

"We don't know. It's possibly a House of Ravens attack," Danni said.

Azalea knew it wasn't.

The Archmage marched into the room as the alarms ceased. The rabble of voices instantly silenced. The only sounds were the waterfall splashing into the pond and faint yelling from above. She felt Torin tense up next to her, and it took all her strength not to reach out and touch him, to feel the pull of his magic. But she wasn't sure he'd appreciate that.

"I will have your attention," the Archmage announced, tapping her cane on the floor three times. "This is not a drill. We sounded the attack alarms as we are under siege from the House of Ravens. They are waiting outside our walls, but as long as we keep our defenses up, they will not take us.

"We ask that you remain down here until we give word that it is safe to return to your homes. In the meantime, we will provide food and bedding. There is enough room to spread out, so please get some rest. We do not require additional defense, but be prepared in case you are needed."

The Archmage's gaze fell across her family spread out across two tables near her: her daughter, Livia and Elam's mum, and a serious-looking bald man who must be their dad. Livia, who was sitting with Erik, and Erik's dad and little sister. Millie's family was at the second table with a bunch of kids and four adults who Azalea didn't know.

It was strange to think she was the matriarch of a large family. It was hard to think of her as anything remotely close to warm. But there must be another side to her. She'd once had a husband after all. She must have been nice to him.

The Archmage continued, "My number one priority is to protect the House of Owls and the Tower of London. We will all remain safe as long as we are together. That is all for now. May Enki protect us all."

"May Enki protect us," an echo of voices rang across the room.

Azalea's table didn't join the echo. Enki was the God of the House of Owls, and it seemed over half the people in here were House of Owls. The Archmage closed her eyes for a brief second, long enough for Azalea to see how exhausted she looked. But a split second later, she was standing tall and nodding gravely as she shook hands with a group of serious-looking mages surrounded by some very fit bodyguards from the House of Phoenix.

As the low rumble of concerned voices returned to the room, Azalea got out her phone to message Fabian and her mum. But there was no signal.

"My messages aren't going out," she mumbled.

"Must be a blocker on the Tower." Danni stroked one of the twins hair absentmindedly.

"They don't want us communicating with anyone outside." Torin checked his own phone.

Azalea was overly conscious of him sitting right next to her. Everything felt slightly wrong between them now, like she'd slipped into a different version of herself in a different timeline. This whole business with the dream had sent her well off balance, and she had no idea how to deal with it or with Torin.

"But why?" Van asked.

"Something isn't right here. We need to get out as soon as possible," Torin said, not explaining anything to Van. "Once everyone goes to sleep, we'll try to slip out to the tunnel by the hospital and get into the Hollow."

"We'll have to take out the guards down there. They have additional patrols watching that tunnel," Danni whispered.

"I don't think they will. I think it will be minimum guards. They'll all be up top for show since it's likely there is no real threat. Between me, you, and Azalea, we can take them out," Torin said.

Azalea nodded. She felt a swell of pride that he'd included her in the attack team.

Danni slid off the bench and began setting up beds on the floor for the girls beside them. Jade and Van went off to find supplies for their table.

"What about the relics?" Azalea whispered to Torin.

He rested his elbows on the table. Azalea did the same, leaning in so no one could overhear. Neither of them acknowledged the pull between them.

"As long as we have our one, they can't do anything. We have to hide it somewhere, so they never find it." Torin's brow furrowed.

"We can hide it with Fabian." She nibbled her lip, knowing it wouldn't be Torin's first choice, but it was the best option.

A low growl sounded from the back of Torin's throat.

"No need to get pissy about it. It's the logical place to hide it. The Ravens can't get into the estate. Right?" she asked. Torin had infiltrated there once. As much as she didn't want to know how, she needed to.

"They can't get in." He held her gaze in a challenging stare as if he had another option.

Butterflies exploded through her. She needed to stay focused. "How did you get in?"

"In a van for a party, it could never happen again. They're not stupid." He let out a breath through his nostrils in frustration.

A party. That's how he'd done it. He'd killed her father at a party in his own house. She had to remember that if she ever lost sight of what was important.

"I assume you got the Shadow Atlas?" His gaze darted to her bag beside her.

"Of course I did, and I got hit with some bloody ghosts on the way over there. I was so distracted." She hadn't meant to walk into them. But after the phone call with Fabian and the stress of it all, she hadn't noticed a benign-looking man bump into her. The other spirit next to him copied. She'd barely gotten away.

"I know. I felt it." Torin rubbed his chest.

Danni sat back down opposite them, giving them a strange look. "Spirits are still going through you?"

Azalea bit her lip and nodded, careful not to look at Torin.

"And what did you mean by you felt it?" Danni focused on Torin, using her professional interrogation stare.

"I didn't mean anything. I was being silly," he said.

Azalea nearly snorted out loud. Great cover, Torin. His expression was so serious it was hard to imagine him ever being silly.

Danni narrowed her eyes, but let it go. "Right, well, the girls are sorted for now. We need to monitor all the exits and establish who's going where before we try to leave." Danni was in full agent mode, something Azalea rather liked.

"I'll keep an eye on the Archmage to see who she talks to." Torin's gaze flicked to the other side of the room behind the fountain where the Archmage was deep in conversation with her new friends.

Van and Jade got back with extra blankets, sandwiches, and a monopoly set. They set up the monopoly board but didn't start playing. Azalea was assigned the hat, and Torin, the wheelbarrow.

They divided up the exits for each of them to watch for the next hour while trying to appear smiley and casual. Not something Azalea had ever experienced playing monopoly; she wasn't sure anyone ever had. Still, it was better than no cover.

The next hour was the longest of Azalea's life. A few people had gone to sleep around the room, but most sat at tables, too wired and afraid to sleep with the occasional explosion going off overhead. Danni was lying with the two sleeping girls beside the picnic table on some foam mattresses that looked pretty comfy. Azalea wanted more than anything to sleep, but no way in hell was she going to do that here.

She spotted Erik near the center of the room on a picnic table with his dad and sister. Livia was next to him. His eyes locked onto Azalea's, and he smirked as he pulled Livia into his side, tilted her chin toward him, and kissed her.

Vulgar and unnecessary.

She felt Torin shift beside her and a wave of disgust roll off him. At least it wasn't just her. But it only made her more aware of his presence. She could always feel his magic now as if it was a magnet trying to pull hers in.

Her thoughts flashed to kissing Torin in her dream, which escalated to her imagining kissing Torin in real life. She imagined kissing him right now in front of everyone. That would make Erik go wild for sure, but that was just petty. She wouldn't stoop to his level, and she certainty wouldn't try to kiss him. Even if she found she really wanted to. Not that she did... It was just the dream tricking her. *Was it hot in here?*

An awkward silence was building between them. She had to say something soon, or she was going to lose it. But she couldn't even face looking him in the eye anymore. That dream was so embarrassing and so hot. She couldn't stop picturing it. What did he even think of her for behaving like that? She was starting to think that it might be real, that she might actually feel that way about him. She was mortified just at the thought of mentioning it. They needed a change in subject.

Azalea took a deep breath. "There's something I forgot to mention."

"Spit it out then." It was clear he was on edge, too. Was he thinking the same thing she was?

"Fabian mentioned someone else was with him and Kat," Azalea blurted out.

"Who?" he said, not taking his eyes off the door he was monitoring.

"Kira Reid," Azalea whispered. Then held her breath. That was the girl Torin had been searching for for years, and apparently, she was alive and well. She had no idea how he would react. But she didn't want him to be too shocked when they got there and he saw her, either.

"Kira? My Kira?" Torin said.

Azalea felt the burst of hope rush out of him like a flood across the desert. She swallowed back her irrational disappointment at the *'my Kira,'* trying to rein in her emotions so he wouldn't feel them. Of course, he would be happy.

Danni popped up behind Azalea's shoulder. "What?"

"Danni! You scared the shit out of me." Azalea twisted around. Danni joined them at the picnic table. Van and Jade were watching in other directions, but Azalea could tell they were listening.

"Azalea said Fabian was with Kira." Torin's eyes were wide and full of hope. For his sake, she hoped it was true. Not a horrible Fabian trick to hurt Torin.

"I spent eight years looking for her with zero hints of a clue, and now she shows up? What did he say?" Danni leaned in.

"Um…" Azalea wasn't about to tell them how excited Fabian had been that Kira was there, and apparently, she was not at all keen to see Torin. But she couldn't take Fabian's word for it. His life mission was to destroy Torin.

"He didn't really say much, just that Kira Reid was with Kat." Azalea left it at that.

Torin let out a relieved sign. He'd just gotten proof that the girl he thought he might have killed wasn't dead after all. That had to be a good feeling; she wasn't about to make him feel bad again.

"Kat Emerson must have known where she was all along. They'll be trying to get Torin back on their side if they're really working against Korbyn," Danni said in a hushed voice.

"How do you know we can trust them?" Jade said. Poor girl, she was still trying to catch up on who was who, let alone who was on what side. Azalea didn't even know.

"We don't," Torin said. "But Kat was my teacher, and Kira was my squadmate. They are both good people. They're people I would have trusted with my life."

Danni cleared her throat and pulled her black coat in close around her. "But it's been eight years, Torin. People change."

"I don't know what they're up to. If it's a trap, or they want to work together for real. But we're low on options and don't exactly have a choice. You'll have to meet them and see." Torin's hopefulness drifted into Azalea subtly, like snow or ash, and it had a pleasant warmth to it that made her want it all to be true. To know they could trust his old friends.

Azalea sat bolt upright as Erik marched over to their table. She swallowed hard, not wanting to draw attention to any of them, or get into a fight. Erik leaned in close to Azalea's face, and she instinctively moved back, closer to Torin.

"If you're wondering if I told the Archmage about you two, I did," Erik whispered. But it wasn't malicious, more like a warning.

"Why are you doing this, Erik? Why were you even spying on me?" Azalea whispered back with newfound confidence. She didn't want to deal with this bullshit anymore.

"I didn't have a choice. My dad was under pressure from her, and he roped me into it to make our family more useful to the Owls. Whatever she wanted me to find out, she made it clear I didn't find it. I think she wanted to know if either of you were working with the House of Ravens. I told her the truth, that you weren't, you know that, right?" Erik's gaze darted around. People were watching.

Azalea's heart skipped a beat. This was unexpected, and it took her a few seconds to get her thoughts together. Maybe it hadn't all been a lie.

"I really liked you, Azalea. That's why I went off the rails, and I'm sorry I did. I just wanted you to know that I believe you.

But it's safer this way, for both of us." His eyes narrowed, and he glared at Torin.

Azalea leaned in closer, and Torin tensed beside her. Danni, Van, and Jade chatted quietly, but she could tell they were listening.

Her eyes met Erik's, and his softened like he was silently pleading for forgiveness.

"Thanks, Erik. Just be careful of the Archmage. Don't trust her, okay?" Azalea warned.

A lightness spread through her chest. At least he had a reason for doing what he did, and being close to Livia probably ensured his safety. She couldn't blame him.

"Will do. Now I'm going to make a scene, so we don't look too chummy. I've already been here too long. Um, and sorry about everything, mate." Erik gave a sharp nod to Torin.

"If you say so." Torin just narrowed his dark eyes at Erik, his jaw set firmly. Azalea felt the hatred rolling off him. They weren't going to be friends any time soon.

Erik suddenly stepped back with his hands up in defense, and a smirk replaced his sincerity.

"You two should be locked up until this is all over. We can't trust what side you're on." Erik's voice boomed so everyone could hear.

Azalea set her jaw and told herself not to react. It was fake, but it still stung. Murmurs of agreement rumbled through the crowd, and a few people stood up nearby.

"He's probably working on the inside," someone yelled.

Torin sat still as a statue, but she could almost feel him vibrating with rage. Erik knew how to piss him off. Azalea's hand crept to his under the table where no one could see. She took a breath as her hand folded into his and their magic merged. Her limbs grew light, and warmth radiated through her chest.

She sent a wave of calmness toward Torin, doing her best to ignore the jeers. His hand relaxed into hers, and surprisingly he didn't pull away.

"Gods know why the Archmage keeps them around, they're not even out there protecting us," another sneered. In the dimmed light of the cafeteria, it was hard to see who made the comments. Cowards.

"Don't listen to him," Van said loudly, playing along.

Jade grinned and gave him the finger. "Fuck off, Erik."

"Back to your seats!" a Phoenix guard yelled and raised a flaming hand, warning Erik to back off.

Erik just chuckled and raised his hands as he backed away.

Azalea let out a breath and was careful not to look at Torin as the magic built between them, but she didn't want to let go.

"That was super weird. What the hell happened between you?" Danni asked.

Van's gaze darted to Torin, and Danni didn't miss it.

Azalea looked down at the monopoly board. She didn't want to rehash this whole thing again.

"Just ignore him. Everyone's on edge." Torin released her hand and turned to Danni as if nothing had happened.

But Azalea felt Danni's eyes on her and couldn't help the blush that spread across her cheeks.

"What is up with you two?" Danni asked, not subtly.

"Nothing, just a misunderstanding on Erik's part," Torin said.

Torin's leg was close to hers, and she had to fight herself not to lean into his warmth.

She was starting to see what Erik might have been seeing all along. Maybe the bond between her and Torin wasn't as subtle as she wanted to believe. This energy buzzing between them was always there. She thought about him constantly, and now these dreams. Of course, others might notice it. They had to be more careful. She shuffled away from Torin slightly.

"What sort of misunderstanding?" Danni asked.

Fortunately, the Ravenmaster marched past, his face red with veins popping out as he stopped at the nearest guard. Azalea strained her ears to listen as everyone else pretended to be playing monopoly but were all doing the same.

"The ravens are gone," the Ravenmaster said in a panicked whisper while wringing his hands.

"They can't be gone," the guard growled.

"They bloody well are. Someone needs to tell the Archmage."

"You do it then. It's your fault they've gone."

"It was the explosions, but you know what they say… I'm not going to be the one to tell her," the Ravenmaster said and marched off. His face was red, and his eyes were wide with real fear.

Azalea swallowed. "What is it they say about the ravens leaving?"

"That the Tower would crumble to dust and great harm would befall the kingdom," Danni said. This time, she wasn't smiling when she said it.

"I think we should leave now. That news will distract the Archmage for a while," Torin said quickly.

"Let's do this then," Danni whispered, clearly pumped up for getting out of there.

"Which exit is best?" Azalea asked.

Van and Jade leaned in to listen.

"Van and Jade should go first, head down the main hallway, then you can slip into the hospital and down to the tunnel. Can either of you conjure a cloak of shadows?" Danni asked.

They both shook their heads.

"Okay, Azalea, go with Jade first. I'll go with the girls next and explain we're on the way to see Maiken. Torin, you go last with Van. Wait for us in the stairwell down to the tunnel."

Azalea conjured a shadow cloak over her and Jade, and they linked arms. Thanks to the low light, it was easy to sneak around the edges of the caf, slinking around the walls like a pair of ghosts, until they made it out. When the guard turned to talk to his colleague, they snuck past and made it into the hospital. Azalea headed straight for the stairwell and rushed through the door.

Her heart was ready to burst in her chest from the stress of the short walk.

"Wow, we made it." Jade grinned as they unlinked arms.

Her eyes suddenly went white.

"Jade, Jade," Azalea shook her gently. "Shit." She was having a bloody premonition.

Jade's voice turned to a low drone. "Magic in peril, by creatures of Night; know who to trust, or prepare for a fight. The twelve keys together can open the gate; whether hidden or used, will determine your fate."

The same bloody thing the Shadow Atlas said last time. She didn't like the sound of the twelve keys being together; they had to stop it from happening.

Jade slumped against the wall, and Azalea propped her up, so she didn't fall to the floor.

Danni burst through the door with Ava and Zoe in tow, looking ruffled and confused.

"Is she alright?" Danni asked.

Jade blinked and hauled herself up straight. "Sorry. Did I do it again?"

"You did," Azalea said, trying not to freak out.

Torin and Van burst through the doors. "We need to go now! Run!" he said.

Azalea pulled Jade up, and they thundered down the stairs and burst into the damp tunnel.

Two guards spun around and threw fireballs instantly. Everyone flattened themselves to the sides of the dripping stone wall.

"Keep moving!" Danni dropped the girls' hands and threw a fireball from each hand.

Torin sent out ropes of shadows before Azalea could react and tripped the two guards.

"Shield the others and get down the tunnel," he ordered Azalea.

Azalea instantly threw up a wall of shadows and ushered the twins, Van, and Jade behind it. Faraday had jumped out of his bag and was trotting along as part of the team. They dashed past the fallen guards and waited for Torin and Danni to join them.

Azalea felt Torin's magic spread through the tunnel. She wanted to go to it but restrained herself. What the hell was wrong with her?

Flashes of fireballs burst in every direction as shadows burst from Torin's elemer, surrounding them and whipping out with intense speed directed at their attackers.

"I believe you have something of mine." The cold voice of the Archmage echoed through the tunnel as the fighting stopped.

Torin and Danni were between her and the Archmage.

Azalea didn't lower the shield. There had to be a way out of this. They had to protect the relic.

Erik stepped out from behind the Archmage. His eyes were red like he'd been crying.

"Please Azalea, you have to hand it over. They've got my sister."

CHAPTER 36

F abian couldn't sit around this blasted house doing nothing while Azalea was right in the path of danger. He hadn't heard from Kat, and he wasn't going to wait around.

"Noodle, get off that. Go curl up by the fire," Fabian scolded as Noodle clattered across the kitchen bench onto the stovetop, heading for the gas burner with his small pot of stew bubbling away. He hadn't made it; he was just reheating it. Food was a pleasant distraction, not as good as alcohol, but he was refraining from drinking too much, just until this House of Ravens' business was dealt with.

Noodle continued toward the lit burner, so Fabian plucked the skeleton snake off, and the silly thing coiled around his arm like a bony vine, its thin rib bones gently scraping his skin as they went. It pinched a little but didn't break the skin.

"Bloody, snake," he muttered as he wandered down the hall into the drawing room.

He set Noodle down by the large open fire that was roaring away.

His phone buzzed. *Finally!*

Kat: *We've been sent to the Tower. Something's up though. We aren't attacking. I've been kept in the dark on this one. Kira and I are stationed at the South exit on the Thames. The Tower is* *in lockdown, but we haven't been given orders and are all on standby.*

Fabian: *I'll be there straight away.*

Kat: *Negative. Wait until we know what's going on.*

He didn't message back. No way he was waiting around, not when the Tower was surrounded, and Azalea was inside. He needed to get her out. And if the Ravens were about to attack, no one was safe anywhere.

"You stay there, Noodle. I'll be back as soon as I can." Fabian ran to the kitchen and took the stew off the stove. He burned his tongue, forcing a few mouthfuls down, then headed outside, knowing Rowena would still be up.

He dashed across the cobbles to the greenhouse, and sure enough, Rowena's silhouette was visible in the warm yellow light radiating from inside.

Panting, he threw open the door. "Rowena, it's time to get moving."

"They've attacked?" She put down her secateurs, and the glowing vine she had been holding slithered away from her.

"Sounds like they've got the Tower of London under siege or will have before the night is over. It's all hush-hush now, but knowing them, we need to prepare. I'm off to get Azalea now."

"Good. You have a plan to get her out?" She wiped her hands on her trousers.

"No." He raked his fingers through his slicked-back hair.

"Then go get Leda first. If you don't have a plan, you'll put the girl in more danger than she's already in."

Fabian sighed. She was possibly right. If the House of Ravens had the place surrounded, the Hollow tunnel would be sure to have extra guards. There was no way he could get in undetected.

But he could go there and talk to Kat, find out what was going on. At least then he'd have up-to-date info.

"Fine. I'll grab Leda. Then head to the Tower—"

Rowena frowned.

He continued. "—head to the Tower to talk to Kat before I do anything stupid."

"Good. I'll talk to the shaman, who's in charge of our wee village, and get everyone else warned. We can expect a lot of newcomers tonight. I'll make sure we're set up."

"Alright. See you in a bit then," he said, possibly too casual for going straight into the enemies' nest.

"You're a good man, Fabian." Rowena grinned and, before he could move, pulled him into a squeeze of a hug.

"You're getting dirt on me," he said.

She untangled herself and hit him with her gardening glove. "Off with you then."

Fabian didn't want to waste any time, but he had to go get Leda. She wasn't safe in her forest, despite whatever she said about her almighty goddess guarding her. It was far safer just to haul her off, so he didn't have to deal with rescuing her later.

He borrowed Colin's Land Rover again and drove to the gate. He took an extra minute to check the wards. The estate was protected with wards of embedded crystals in the walls and buried in the perimeter's ground, as well as blood wards on all the exits and entrances. He strengthened the blood wards as he left the gate and cut into the Hollow.

As he suspected, Leda was less than cooperative, even after he explained they were possibly going to be under attack the next day. Fortunately, her concern for Azalea and possibly a hint of common sense in that thick skull of hers had her packing up her suitcases full of herbs and teas, and they were out the door and back into the Hollow within thirty minutes.

He dropped Leda just inside the gate and handed her the keys to the Land Rover.

"You'll bring her back to me, won't you?" Leda's expression was strained. Sometimes he wondered why she never chose to be a mage. Why would you want to be so powerless?

"I'll bring her back," he said, and he meant it.

He checked his phone, just in case Azalea had messaged, but still nothing. They must have jammed the signals around the Tower.

But he had another message from Kat, so presumably, she was still on watch outside.

Kat: *Fabian. DO NOT come here.*

Disregard that. She knew him too well. Of course, he was going to turn up.

He sliced into the Hollow and let the chilling air draw him into the shadows. As soon as he was in, he focused on the exact spot outside the Tower where he wanted to go. He knew it well. A small brick wall near the entrance Kat should be by.

He cut out and instantly surrounded himself in a cloak of shadows, perfectly blending into the night air. Creeping low, he inched his way along the base of the wall. Kat was standing with her back ramrod straight, eyes darting around, waiting for danger.

He let out a low barn owl call.

Kat jerked her head around and glared in his direction. She knew that sound. He couldn't help but grin at the way she locked her jaw and the vein in her forehead twitched. Yup, she was pissed at him.

"Hey Kat," he hissed. Knowing she was close enough to hear. Fortunately, it was Kira Reid beside her. The other guards were staggered along the walkway but not toward the entrance.

"Piss off," she mumbled.

"Just let me in. I can get Azalea and the relics out," he whispered.

Kat marched closer, so her back was to him. "No. Not without a plan. Just fuck off until we know the full situation."

"Come on. I promise I won't even try to kill your precious Torin once they're out," he said, unsure if he meant that last part or not.

Kira didn't seem overly concerned. Perhaps she wanted Torin dead herself. Maybe there was a partnership of some sort in their near future...

"It's amusing you think you could kill him with us around," Kat scoffed.

He leaned closer to Kat and whispered, "Once this is all over and you're left a homeless, washed-up assassin, just remember, I will be there to be your hero. Who knows, I might even be willing to take you in and you can come live with me and Noodle in my giant house."

He swore he could hear her rolling her eyes somehow.

But Kat turned around. "I'd love to meet the famous Noodle. But a hard pass on moving in. Thanks."

Kira shook her head at the both of them.

Kat's radio cracked to life. "Patrol three to the southeast tunnel, potential hostile action."

"Kira, with me, Loyd, take our positions," Kat bellowed.

A man further down jogged their way.

"I'm coming. Let me come; he's getting close," Fabian said.

Kat put a hand on his chest. "If it's Torin trying to get out, we can help them. Just. Stay. Out. Here." She pushed him back into the shadows.

Fabian slipped behind the wall, mentally cursing her. He remained hidden within his shadow as Kat marched off.

Gods, he hated waiting. There had to be another way in.

CHAPTER 37

"Please Azalea, you have to hand it over. They've got my sister." Erik cowered behind the Archmage, hunched over like a beaten puppy. He looked like shit. The Archmage must have gotten inside his head. If it was anyone else, Torin might have felt sorry for them.

Torin reined in his shadow whips but kept his elemer raised. Azalea was behind him with a strong shadow shield protecting Jade, Van, and the twins.

"Back up," Torin said to Danni.

"Torin, give me the last relic, and your debt is paid. You will be free to live your life." The Archmage locked eyes with him and gave a sincere nod.

She was probably telling the truth. She might be detestable and manipulative, but he had never known her to lie. It would be so easy to hand it over and get his life back. But at what cost? Her upending their society, wiping out the council, flooding the world with deadly magic?

"Hand what over? Look, there must be some sort of mistake here. Torin hasn't taken anything, so let's just all calm down." A blue fireball smoldered in Danni's palm.

Torin moved backward with slow, careful footsteps.

"Azalea. Cut into the Hollow, now." Their best bet was to just leave while they had the chance.

"Don't." The Archmage slammed her cane into the floor so it echoed with a loud crack.

The twins were whimpering somewhere behind him, but he didn't take his eyes off the dragon woman.

"Let's just all stay calm." Danni's fireball expanded.

"You will give me the relic now." The air around the Archmage rippled, but her gaze darted between them. She didn't have any backup, except Erik. She probably didn't want anyone else to know what she was planning.

"We don't have the relic." Torin tested the waters. How far would she go to get it? Would she really hurt a child, or was it a bluff?

"Oh, I think you do." The corners of her lips curled into a tight smile as she raised her elemer and placed her hand on Erik's head. Erik's body jolted, and his scream echoed through the tunnel.

"Azalea, now!" he ordered again. But her shock rippled over him at the sight of Erik being tortured.

The Archmage stopped and turned to face them while Erik clutched his head.

Danni choked back a gasp of disbelief. It shouldn't be surprising to her. Danni had seen the way the Archmage treated prisoners, but doing it to one of their own was what she needed to see to believe this woman was insane.

"Let him go. Erik didn't deserve that." Danni's eyes were wide with rage.

"I got what I needed from him. Everyone has their part to play, you see. And Torin and Azalea have been my biggest assets until now. They have completed a near-impossible task that people have attempted for centuries." Her hand went to her heart. There was genuine pride shining from those normally cold blue eyes. "I thank you both for your service to the House of Owls."

Torin glared at her. "I wanted them kept safe. This isn't what I signed up for."

"I admit, you didn't have a choice in the matter." She nodded sympathetically. "But you ought to be grateful for the life I've allowed you to have. If it wasn't for me, you'd be rotting away in prison."

"I am grateful for that. But it doesn't change the fact that no one should possess all the relics. It's too dangerous. My father will use the first opportunity to take them and open the gate. Or you will open it and that's not a risk I can take. You will never possess all the relics," Torin said slowly, trying to buy time for Azalea to get her shit together and cut into the Hollow.

He could feel her magic reaching out to him from her shadows, stronger than usual. He could feel her guilt, her compassion for Erik and his sister; he could feel the slow despair creeping over her, waiting to ignite her into full-blown panic. She wasn't going to leave them.

"She's going to hurt my sister; help. Just give her the fucking relic!" Erik pleaded as he scrambled back to his feet.

"Erik is correct. As long as you cooperate and hand over the relic, I have assured him that his sister will remain safe. I know you have it. I know you and Azalea lied to me and hid your true memories, and I know how loyal you are to one another. Erik showed me a very interesting scene in Torin's bedroom." Her eyebrows raised like a disapproving grandmother, and her hand rested on her cane like she had all the time in the world.

Torin gripped his elemer, holding back the shadows that so desperately wanted to tear out of him and rip her apart for being so manipulative, for threatening a little girl.

"We don't have the relic," Torin repeated calmly.

He felt disgust from Azalea ripple his way. She wouldn't be able to hold her shield much longer. They had to get out of there before they were outnumbered. They could handle the Archmage and Erik. The other guards were still knocked out, and the Archmage would eventually call for backup.

If he wasn't so close to the Archmage, he could cut into the Hollow himself, but that would mean the others would have to drop the shield and put the kids in danger to get out. Not worth the risk. It was up to Azalea to make the right choice.

"I know you do. Refrain from lying and get on with it. I don't have all night," the Archmage barked.

"Please, just do it," Erik said.

"Torin?" Azalea pleaded.

He swore he could hear what she was thinking, though he knew it was just him feeling her emotions through the bond. She was about to give in.

Scenarios flashed across his mind; if they handed over the relic, the enemy would have the keys to the Echo Dimension gate. There was an infinitesimal chance the Archmage was being truthful and wanted to protect the relics and lock them away, but he very much doubted that now.

But to save the girl, all he had to do was hand over the relic. The Archmage still didn't know where the gate was, or how to open it. He, on the other hand, knew exactly where it was. Maybe if he went there first and destroyed the gate before anyone could get there, they wouldn't even have a problem to deal with.

"Get behind, Azalea," he ordered Danni as he flashed up his own shield and moved back a step, creating a little more distance. "Azalea, open the Hollow."

"Torin, please, don't leave," Erik begged. "I know you don't like me, just don't let my sister pay. Just don't leave."

Torin glanced at Azalea for a split second. He couldn't take that risk. He couldn't risk Danni and her kids for the off chance the Archmage might hurt Erik's sister.

"I'm sorry, Erik." Torin backed up, prepared for a fight with Azalea to get her into the Hollow and out of there safely.

"Wrong move." The Archmage flicked her elemer in a sharp arc in front of her, and a wave of invisible power hurtled through him, shattering all their shields and sending spasms of pain through every nerve in his body with electrifying vibrations of magic.

Torin clasped his head and crawled back toward Azalea and the girls. They were all huddled over with hands on their heads until the wave of magic subsided.

The twins whimpered, but Van and Jade had them wrapped up tightly in hugs, stroking their hair.

"I'm fine," Azalea reassured him. He glanced around for Danni.

"Looking for someone?" The Archmage remained in the same place as if nothing happened. But held Danni to her chest with an elemer blade to her throat.

Torin's heart froze, then kicked back into gear. "Keep the girls back," Torin said to Van. He crept forward, one slow step at a time, his elemer raised. "Let her go."

"I will if you give me the relic. You drove me to this, Torin. I didn't want anyone to get hurt. Especially not Danni here. She has done nothing to deserve this." The Archmage tightened her grip on Danni. She was a lot stronger than she looked, and she would have weakened Danni's mind to stop her from fighting back.

He had to give it up, even if it went against everything he had been working for. He knew what it was to live with the blood of innocents on his hands, and he wasn't about to add Danni to the list. He wouldn't turn into his father to get what he wanted.

New plan: Hand over the relic and destroy the gate.

"You can have the relic," Torin said. "But if you open that gate, it *will destroy* the world. Nothing can be worth that risk." He reached into his jacket and pulled out the tiny white deer. He felt Azalea close behind him and her desperation to hand it over and get Danni back.

"I assure you, I don't need advice from a disgraced shadow mage." The Archmage stepped closer, her icy blue eyes drilling into him, challenging him to provoke her.

"You'll let Danni and the girl go?" Torin asked.

"Yes, you have my word on that. Erik, you may go fetch your sister. Take her to your father, and meet me in my office. I have another job for you after." She waved him off with her hand.

Erik stumbled. "Thank you." He darted an apologetic look at Azalea, then spun around on the slimy stone before running off.

Torin took a breath. After everything he'd done to get to this point to protect the relics, here he was, handing over the last fucking one, right into the hands of the enemy. He tossed the deer relic to the Archmage. She sent out a jet of water that gracefully caught the relic and coiled it through the air into her palm.

"You did the right thing, Torin, and you are now free from your contract, as promised. I thank you." The Archmage gave a nod of recognition as she gripped the white deer to her chest tightly and released the blade from Danni's neck. Danni stumbled forward, and Torin caught her.

Azalea was at his side in an instant and took Danni's weight on her shoulder, leading her back, and shot up a shadow shield behind her.

"Keep your thanks. I didn't do it for you," Torin growled. He wanted to rip this woman's head off. His hands hummed with the dark magic he worked so hard to suppress, the hand of death. He wasn't going to give in to it now, not after this long. There was nothing that could compel him to use it again, no matter how much the dark magic sang to him. *She* certainly wasn't worth it, and the reality was, he could never get close enough to her to use it if he wanted to. That invisible resonance spell she used was too strong.

"Keep your wits about you, Torin. Change is upon us." The Archmage turned back toward the hospital and left without any further threats.

Azalea cut into the Hollow without him having to tell her this time.

"Everyone in!" he yelled.

Danni basically threw the kids into the dark void, and everyone else tumbled in after them.

The shadow door sealed shut.

"Everyone in?" Torin instantly felt Azalea at his side, her magic buzzing around him like an angry bee.

"I'm here," she whispered. She was shaking.

Van and Jade answered in unison, and Faraday let out the same yowl he made when he was hungry, which broke the tension a little. Danni had the girls bundled in a tight hug, kissing the tops of their heads.

Torin cut straight back out of the Hollow, just in case anyone followed them in there. It was better to get out fast to minimize any traces of their magic, which faded with every second.

"Everyone out," he ordered.

Azalea was slow to react and was last out, clasping the sports bag with the cat closer to her body. He gave her an apologetic look, but he had to get somewhere fast and close to save his magic.

"You okay?" Torin asked. The relief coming off her overwhelmed all her other emotions and his.

"Yup. You did the right thing, Torin. Don't blame yourself for losing the relic." She looked around, realizing where they were, and he felt a jolt of panic, but it didn't show on her face. Her features were serene and calm, despite the night they'd had.

"I might not have had a choice about giving up that relic, but I did about collecting them all. I never should have done it."

"You didn't have a choice in that either. Like she said, you'd be rotting in jail." She made it sound so simple, but the choice had been selfish. He took in the surroundings. Trees, naked of leaves, stretched into the night sky; the stars and moon were obscured by gathering clouds. Around them, the broken stone walls of the abandoned church melded with nature, the ceiling above long gone, destroyed by bombs in World War II.

"Where are we?" Van asked.

"We're down the road, at St. Dunstan in the East." Azalea swallowed as she looked up. He knew how much she hated the place. Dying wasn't the best memory to flash back to at a time like this, but it was the best place to leave from.

"What's the plan now?" Danni asked.

"I'm going to make sure they can't open the gate to the Echo Dimension. Azalea will call Fabian to pick you all up." Torin set a shadow shield around them, despite it being late and no one being around. Better to be safe.

"Open a gate to the Echo Dimension? That's what that relic does, and you handed it over?" Van said.

"He didn't have a choice, Van. He couldn't let the Archmage hurt Danni or Erik's sister."

"She wouldn't really have done that," Van said.

"Trust me, she would have. You saw what she did to Erik, and she's done the same thing to me and Azalea before. She could have killed all of us if she wanted to. You don't want to mess with her," Torin said.

Van's hand went to her mouth in disbelief.

"It's true. She's a monster. I didn't want her to hurt Danni or Erik's sister, and I know Torin did the right thing." Azalea shifted closer to him.

Danni's eyes burned with fire. "I can't believe I didn't see it before. She's done so much good for our society. She's so well respected and an amazing leader. It's just so hard to believe." She pulled the girls in close to her chest.

"I had no idea. I mean, I knew she was a bitch. But I didn't think she was insane." Van linked arms with Jade, and they huddled close together.

"She's scary as hell. Torin was brave for standing up to her as long as he did. I would have given in straight away." Jade shivered and shot Torin a smile of thanks.

"I can still fix this. Azalea, call Fabian now. See where he is," Torin ordered but saw she already had her phone out. The faster he could get them away safely, the faster he could go find the gate.

Azalea held the phone up but didn't call. "Fine, but I'm coming with you to the gate."

"No." Torin crossed his arms.

"Yes. You need me. Jade had another prophecy before, she said; *Magic in peril, by creatures of Night; know who to trust, or prepare for a fight. The twelve keys together can open the gate; whether hidden or used, will determine your fate.*"

Everyone looked at Jade. She shrugged. "I have no idea about half the bullshit that comes out of my mouth."

"So..." Torin said, thinking. This was taking too long. Maybe he should leave them all here or drop them at the gates to Blackbourne Manor. The problem with that was the Ravens could be waiting there now if their plans were already underway.

"We've already determined our fate by deciding not to hide the keys, apparently. It says to know who to trust. If you trust me, Torin, let me come. I can help," Azalea pleaded.

He could feel the determination radiating off her like sun rays. There was no way she would give in, and he didn't have time to argue. He had to admit, this would be easier if there were two of them. They could use their shared magic and destroy the gate before anyone even got there. Plus, she had the Shadow Atlas, and he might need that if he was wrong and they needed to narrow down the gate's location further.

"Fine. Call your uncle and get him to come here and pick this lot up and take them somewhere safe."

Azalea nodded furiously and swiped her phone on.

CHAPTER 38

Fabian's legs were cramping up from waiting behind the wall in the shadows. He wasn't made to sit still and wait; he was a man of action, of decisiveness, a man of pro-active-ness—fuck, he needed a drink. Sitting around and thinking was slowly killing him. What a terrible way that would be to die.

His phone rang. *Azalea.* He picked it up, careful not to raise his voice.

"Where the hell are you?" Fabian said.

"We made it out of the Tower." Her voice held an urgency to it.

Fabian shook his fist in triumph and let out a breath. "Thank fuck for that. I'm outside the Tower waiting. I've been trying to find a way in to get to you. Tell me where you are. I'll come now."

"You came to get me?" she said in a small voice.

"Of course I did." Silly girl, of course, he would come get her. Her situation with this whole Tower thing was his fault, anyway. He never should have brought her here. Not that he would admit that to her, or out loud, ever.

"Thanks. We're at St. Dunstan in the East. Danni and the girls and my friends need to get somewhere safe. Can you take them?"

"Of course. And I'm taking you too. Your mum and grand-mother are waiting at the manor."

She was silent for several seconds. "Just come now, please hurry."

The phone beeped, and she was gone.

Thank fuck for that. He didn't have to infiltrate the Tower or deal with any of the fuckwits inside.

He needed Kat to come back out.

Fabian: *Get your arse out here. They got out. I know where they are.*

No response. He paced for what seemed like an eternity, though his watch lied and said it was one minute. Maybe if he set an explosion outside the gate, Kat would come out. It was worth a try. He checked his pockets. There had to be something explosive in his jacket somewhere.

"Fabian," Kat hissed into the darkness.

He hadn't even noticed her slip off the path to his secret shadow hiding spot. That was her damn assassin skills. It was good she was on his side.

"Let's go. I know where they are. Where's your mate, Kira Reid? She's not up for a reunion with Torin?"

"We made sure the Archmage didn't have any backup so Torin and his friends could get out. I left her with Korbyn on damage control." Kat moved closer.

Fabian shifted between his feet to get the blood flowing back into them. "But you're coming with me?"

"Torin is more important than my job. I'll have to risk it. I bought myself a little time doing checks on the guards, but we can't be long."

"Good. You can stop me from killing him if he says something stupid." Fabian cut into the Hollow, not wasting any time. He might not agree with Kat's ideas about Torin being their savior, but at least they were on the same side.

He offered his hand to Kat from inside the Hollow, but she ignored him and stepped up and brushed past him with a smirk on her face.

Cutting out, Fabian pursed his lips, knowing he would have to hold his tongue just to get through the next few minutes without trying to murder Torin Dumont.

He stepped out of the Hollow with Kat at his side. He had to admit they looked pretty badass together, Kat in her sleek black outfit and military boots, her long black hair pulled into a high ponytail. Him in his long dark coat with heavy boots, not to mention his family heirloom rings that gave him a mysterious rich-guy vibe. Even though Leda said he just looked like a weirdo, he knew he looked cool.

Azalea's friends' stares only proved his point. He held in a smirk and put on his serious face. Though he didn't need to pretend once his eyes fell on Torin Dumont.

Blazing anger shot through his veins and into his hands. His elemer buzzed with magic, wanting to blast it right at Dumont's smug face.

Before he could react, Danni rushed up and hugged him, and he felt the cling when the two little girls attached to his legs. He squeezed Danni back.

"You okay?" He studied her face as she pulled away.

She nodded, but he could see the worry behind her eyes. "Maiken's still in there."

He crouched down and hugged the girls, which instantly simmered his anger down. It also made things easier. He wouldn't attack Torin in front of the twins. They didn't need to see the dark side of magic so young; there would be plenty of time for that later.

Azalea stepped up, not at all subtly, putting herself between him and Torin. "You came," she said with a weak smile.

"I always come. I'm not sure why you doubt me so much," he said. But he knew why. He was unreliable, and not someone who should be responsible for other humans. She was proof of that.

"Torin, I'm so glad you're okay." Kat stepped through the others, taking no notice of anyone else.

Torin cautiously stepped forward. "It's good to see you, Kat."

She wrapped her arms around Torin, and they stood in each other's embrace for far too long. Kat never hugged him like that. Somehow, he had to win her over enough to go back to the *physical* friendship level. Their frenemies-with-benefits relationship had been a good one, and they were a good team.

Fabian ground his teeth, forcing himself not to react to the man that murdered his brother. He didn't even notice Danni peel the twins off his legs. He stood there scowling with his arms crossed.

"Let's get going," he barked.

Kat focused all her attention on Torin. "Wait, we need to know what happened first."

"Are you really on our side, Kat? You want to take down my father?" Torin stepped back and stood far too close to Azalea for Fabian's liking.

Fabian took in a sharp breath; they better not be on friendly terms again. Not after everything that bastard had put her through. That was not something Fabian could handle, and there was something strange between the two of them, something to do with that spirit that went through her.

"We want you back, Torin. You're the only hope for the future of the House of Ravens. Korbyn is going to get everyone killed." Kat slid her elemer into her belt.

Torin's face was a blank mask. He didn't even react. It was impossible to tell what the bloke was thinking.

"Is it true that Kira is alive? She's okay?" Torin's eyes flickered with concern for a split second, showing his weakness.

"Yes, your whole squad is back. They've been stationed in America for years. But your father has called them all in. Something big is going down, and we need to stop him."

"She doesn't want to see you, *mate,*" Fabian said. He had to get one jab in at least.

Azalea gave him a warning look, and Torin glared at him. Not quite the reaction he'd hoped for.

"We know what my father is up to. We believe he's working with the Archmage, and we're going to stop him tonight." Torin kept his elemer low by his waist, but it was obvious he was ready to attack if need be.

Fabian took a step toward him. And yes, it was a challenge. "And what would that be?"

Torin didn't move or react, but Azalea stepped closer to the traitor. So close they were practically touching.

"They have the last relic. He's going to open the gate to the Echo Dimension. That's why we need to go now so we can destroy the gate before they get there. You need to spread the word that no one should use Echo Magic tonight, just in case we fail." Azalea's voice was confident and strong, so different from the girl he had left mere months ago.

"Are you fucking serious? That would kill anyone who used Echo Magic." Fabian's chest tightened. That certainly wasn't the news he had been expecting. He exchanged a glance with Kat. It was clear she hadn't been prepared for that either.

"Let's get going. Azalea, you're with me." Fabian stepped forward to grab her arm, but she jerked back.

"No. I have to go with Torin." She raised her elemer as if she thought she could fight him, silly girl.

Fabian ground his teeth. "No, you don't. Come with me."

"He needs me." Azalea stood her ground.

"What could he possibly need you for?"

"She's my apprentice," Torin said in a cool tone that grated on every one of Fabian's nerves.

"We don't have time for this. Just get us out of here, Fabian," Danni demanded. The girls were crying, and Azalea's friends were shivering.

But if they thought for a minute, he was letting his niece walk away with his brother's murderer, they were sorely mistaken. It was bad enough that she was stuck as his apprentice but following him to stop an inter-dimensional doorway from being opened was not an option.

Fabian locked eyes with Torin. Azalea slowly took off her bag and handed it to her old flatmate. Her eyes darted to Danni.

"Tell mum I'll see her tonight," Azalea said, and before Fabian could react, she cut into the Hollow.

Danni darted in front of him and twisted his arm around his back, so he was forced to spin around. When he turned again, she was gone. All he saw was Dumont's boot entering the void in the air.

"Fuck!" he yelled and strained against Danni's grip. "Don't you dare bring *him* back with you," he called after Azalea, unable to think of anything better to say.

He thrashed against Danni, and after several long seconds, she gave up and let him go.

"Don't follow them," she warned.

"It's too bloody late for that now, anyway, isn't it?" He fought the urge to stamp his foot like a child. He had no inkling of where they were going, and they would have left the Hollow by now. He couldn't track them.

"They know what they're doing," Danni said as the twins crept back to her side, cuddling her legs.

"She's right, Azalea is safe with Torin," Azalea's ex-roommate said, not that he had asked for her opinion. The goth girl next to her remained quiet. Her, he didn't mind.

"You better be right," he snarled. "Come on then, you lot. Let's get going."

He rang home to check the gates were clear and no one was waiting to ambush them, then cut into the Hollow.

Azalea was on her own now. He had failed.

☽ ☽ ☽ ● ☾ ☾ ☾

"Sorry about that. I thought it was better if we just got out of there. Fabian wouldn't have backed down," Azalea said as she pulled her coat in closer around her. The darkness of the Hollow pressed in on her more than usual.

"Good call. Let's get out of here before he follows." Torin cut out of the Hollow, and Azalea followed him with no clue where they were going.

Wherever it was, it was also nighttime; the glow of her locket watch told her it was 2 am in London when they left.

"Where are we?" Her whisper echoed in the huge vaulted room lit by warm yellow light. Her jaw actually dropped when she turned around and took in their surroundings. She crossed the marble floor, drawn to the edge of the balcony where she saw the grandest, most expansive room she had ever seen. The balcony railing was made of giant marble slabs, and over the edge at eye level were giant iron chandeliers hung from an immense domed ceiling that glowed with gold in every direction.

"In Istanbul. Do you have the Shadow Atlas?" Torin rubbed a hand across the stubble on his jawline.

"Course I do. Wait what? We're in Istanbul, like, in Turkey?"

"Yes, the gate is in Turkey. This is a stopover point to work out exactly where, then we're off."

"And where is *this*?" She spun around in the huge upstairs area, craning her head to take in the shimmering gold mosaics that covered the wall in front of them. This had to be a palace.

"Oh, right." Torin looked around as if it was obvious where they were. "This is the Hagia Sophia. There's very strong magic here for using the Hollow without draining our magic. It's a mosque, but we've got about an hour until the call to prayer. No one will come up here." His boots tapped across the ancient floor, and he lowered himself onto a stone bench.

"Okay..." This was crazy. *Focus, Azalea.* She followed him and sat down.

"The Shadow Atlas?" He raised his eyebrows in question.

"Right. But I thought you knew where we were going?" She pulled it from her backpack and set it on her knee.

"I do, but I'll take any help we can get. Ask it about the Echo Dimension gate." He rested his elbows on his knees, leaning over to watch her write.

She quickly scribbled her request with a solid helping of blood.

Between the standing Ts of stone,
A gateway from an ancient throne.
United the twelve unlock the door,
From which a magic flood will pour.
One death tonight, for an open door,
Another one, to shut once more.
From this death, a bridge will form,
Raining down the Echo Storm.
The choice is yours to shut the gate,
To sacrifice one more, or wait.
The future shows another way,
A harder path for those who stay.
For the good of the many or the good of the few,
Find out where your heart runs true.

Azalea swallowed hard. That wasn't at all what she'd been expecting.

"I think it's fucking with us again." She passed Torin the book. Their fingers brushed, and tiny sparks fizzled into the night air. But she didn't pull away this time and neither did Torin.

He flashed a small smile, his gaze briefly flicking to her lips; she held her breath as he pulled the book onto his lap.

She knew what was at stake here, but she couldn't get that stupid dream out of her head, especially when he looked at her that way. They needed to talk about it. She couldn't go on with this tension between them—like she was walking on eggshells, just waiting for something to happen, for him to blow up at her, to tell her how what happened in the dream could never happen again, or, in her new crazy fantasy, for him to kiss her.

She was losing it. But that dream had been so real, and he *had* kissed her; he even admitted he'd wanted to do it for a long time. But that was dream-Torin, not real-life-serious-Torin who wanted to break their bond.

It could be anything with him, but how could she know? His expression gave away nothing, and since the whole dream revelation thing, his emotions were confusing and gave no solid answers.

"I've got the place right. I'm sure of it." He pointed to a new page in the book.

She leaned over as a map bled onto the page. She hadn't even asked it to do that. "Where?"

"Gobekli Tepe, it's in the Southeastern Anatolia Region, near the Syrian border. It's been described as the world's first temple, and it's one of the oldest megalith sites on earth. The gateway is an enormous set of standing stones created by the gods when they left. When the relics are placed in there correctly, the whole thing will become a doorway to the Echo Dimension."

"And you think the Archmage and your dad know where it is?" She bit her lip.

He nodded and shut the Shadow Atlas. "I never told her where the gate was. But I wouldn't put it past either of them to have found it."

"What about the parts about death and sacrifice? That better not be about us."

"I've read nothing about a sacrifice in my research. But you know how blood magic strengthens any spell? A sacrifice is exponentially more powerful. I wouldn't put it past the Archmage to bring a goat along or something to be safe. Or, it could be the book messing with us," he said, probably trying to sound upbeat, but it did not come across that way.

"I'm not killing any goats. It said there was another way, so let's just go with that."

But the words from the Shadow Atlas bounced around in her head: *'The choice is yours to shut the gate. To sacrifice one more or wait. The future shows another way...'*

She couldn't dwell on it. They had to stop the gate from opening. The truth was, they had no idea what it meant, and it could just as easily be the book fucking with them, or the demon, or person, or whatever was behind the cursed tome.

"I suspect the book is trying to scare us," he said, but she felt the flicker of uncertainty roll off him.

Nice of him to say, but it had been right too many times. She glanced at Torin, and her pulse raced. He rose quickly and got out his phone.

Stop looking at him.

That dream had done a number on her, but right now, she had to stay focused; her weird feelings for Torin could wait.

The problem was she couldn't get him out of her head now that her eyes had been opened to a completely new side of him, a side she had to admit, she wanted to see more of.

"How long do we have till they get there, assuming they're going to the same place?" Azalea slipped the Shadow Atlas back into her bag.

Torin typed something into his phone. "If they know what they're doing, they'd open the gate at sunrise, when the veil lowers and the magic is strongest to connect between worlds. That's around 8 am, and it's 5 am here now. If we go now, we still have time to destroy it long before anyone finds it."

Azalea's heart raced. She felt like a real apprentice for the first time and knew for sure now that her hatred for Torin had washed away.

He stood there, frowning at his phone like an old man, and she couldn't help but want to forgive him for everything. Yes, he had done something terrible, but he had spent years making up for it, and he had never intentionally hurt her. All he had done was protect her and help her. She owed him, and he deserved forgiveness more than anyone. It was time she let him off the hook, and once this was all over and everyone was safe, she would make it up to him.

"Thanks for bringing me along." She smiled, knowing this might be the last time they went on a mission if this all went wrong.

He shoved his phone in his pocket but smiled back, and warmth trickled through her. "I couldn't exactly leave you behind."

"I mean it, Torin. We make a good team." She rose and put on her bag.

"We do." He nodded, and they stood there with their eyes locked. A low, pleasant hum of magic warmed her blood, and it felt like they were on the same page for once. Like everything would be alright.

He cut into the Hollow and held the doorway open.

"Let's smash some ancient monuments." Azalea tried to lighten the mood.

Torin cracked a slight smile. "Don't remind me. The historian in me is battling the idea of destroying one of the oldest examples of human settlement, but I'm sure I can forgive myself if we save the world," he said with a wistful look.

"If we save the world, how about we go on a proper holiday to see some non-magical ancient sites and not look for relics?" she suggested.

"Deal." He grinned, and a ripple of happiness filtered into her skin, setting her glowing inside.

She stepped into the darkness with a smile.

.

CHAPTER 39

The whole world felt off balance. Torin waited for the Hollow door to seal behind Azalea as the familiar darkness settled around them. He avoided looking at her. She knew how he felt about her, and now her emotions all felt slightly off like she didn't know what to feel, or she was hiding it from him somehow. It was disconcerting.

"I'll leave first. Check the coast is clear. Then you follow." He nodded with raised eyebrows until she nodded along. Her skin glowed with the eerie blue light of the Hollow. He refocused. He had to make sure she would follow instructions. It wasn't like she had the best track record.

She gritted her teeth, probably fighting herself not to argue. "Got it."

"Stay behind me at all times. You will not go off on your own or fight if we are attacked. If I tell you to, leave straight away. Cut into the Hollow, get out somewhere, and call your uncle."

She hugged her arms around herself. "I said I've got it."

He cut out of the Hollow. The air was still and fragrant with wild herbs as he stepped out into the dry grass. It was dark with no visible stars or a sliver of moon. Azalea stepped out after him, her breath misting in the air that must have been hovering around freezing.

They crouched low and Torin threw a shadow shield over them, keeping them hidden from anyone who might be looking.

"That's it up the hill." He nodded toward the bright white tent that looked like it might house a circus or sports field rather than an archaeological site. The spotlights around the outside made it stand out against the blackness of the night like it was the only thing that existed in the landscape.

Azalea crept behind a scrubby bush. "Do you think it's guarded?"

"Probably. Security, I can deal with. Hopefully, the Archmage or my father aren't here."

A jolt of panic shot through her and into him. "What if they are?"

"If they are, you leave straight away. I don't want my father to find you. I'll stay and try to get one relic off them so they can't open the gate." He hoped it wouldn't come to that.

Azalea remained silent. He doubted she would leave, but hopefully, she'd be sensible and stay hidden. Since she'd become his apprentice, she had become better at following instructions, at least.

"And how are we going to destroy the gate?" She rubbed her hands together and breathed into them.

Torin did the same. "We will use a combination spell by binding shadows with water magic to seep into the rock and freeze it, exploding it from the inside. Your water magic is your strongest element, right?"

"Yes, it is. You want to share magic with me?" Her voice was high with excitement.

It was becoming too natural for him to seek out her magic. He had no idea how it worked or what the limits were, and it was possible they could do things beyond the limits of other mages. They might as well try it.

"Let's not make a habit of it," he lied. All he wanted to do was share magic with her. He couldn't stop thinking about it. A thrill shot through him knowing she wanted to combine their magic. He had to admit he wanted to see what they could do.

They stayed low to the ground, creeping up the hill toward the giant white tent. To anyone who glanced their way, they would have appeared as a dark patch of shadows. As they got closer, he avoided the rough boardwalk that led up to the tent, opting for the rocky ground to the side. The walls of the tent were all open with a giant roof protecting the precious monolith structures inside and a large wooden deck surrounding the outside.

Torin's gut churned at the thought of destroying such an important part of history. It all felt so wrong, but there wasn't much of a choice at this point.

They crept under the deck, slogging their way as silently as possible through loose rock. At the edge was a gap between the deck and the stone wall below where flicking lights filtered through.

Torin's heart dropped as a voice rang out from below.

"What can you see?" Azalea whispered from behind him. There wasn't enough room for them both to look through the gap with the large poles on either side.

A chill shot down his spine, and he swallowed hard as he turned and crouched close to her.

"It's the Archmage. She's down there, and they have someone tied up. I can't make out what they're saying, though. I need to get closer. You stay here, and I'll go down."

☽ ☽ ☽ ● ☾ ☾ ☾

A sudden coldness shot right to Azalea's core. How could they be here already? This wasn't how it was supposed to go. She glanced at Torin. A wave of panic bounced back at her. He looked calm, but it was clear to her he was just as freaked out as she was.

No way she was letting him go down there alone.

"I'm coming. We can stay hidden; destroy the gate or steal a relic, then get the hell out. We need to do this together. You said it: our magic is stronger together." She wrapped her cold fingers around his arm, letting him feel the spark of magic between them.

She expected anger to roll off him, but she felt a ripple of concern and fear, and something that made her not want to let go.

"Even if we stop the gate opening, if anyone sees us using magic that way, they'll report us, and we'll never be safe. They'll take us down with them, and we could be locked up. The plan only works if no one is here to see."

Azalea swallowed. "I don't think it's about us anymore. We have to do something."

Torin had spent so much time locked up. She didn't want to be the one to put him back behind bars. Weeks ago, she would have loved the idea, but not now. Though if they failed, none of that would matter anyway. They had to try something.

Torin was silent and still.

She slid her hand down his arm, twining their fingers together. "Maybe that's what The Shadow Atlas and Jade meant by a sacrifice?"

"A sacrifice usually means death. But I'm not ready for either of us to be any sort of sacrifice." He squeezed her hand before pulling his away. "Just stay here, and I'll go down and get one of the relics. Be ready to leave if things go wrong."

"How will you get it?" She was no longer cold. Every inch of her body was hot and tense and felt like everything was wrong.

"By watching. So be patient. They still have hours until sunrise," he said calmly, but she could feel the same tension coming from him and bouncing back to her.

She nodded. Torin brushed past her in the narrow space, his magic screaming out to her. He paused for a second but kept moving.

"Be careful," she whispered.

"You too." He smiled, his eyes were solid black, and he looked every part the stealthy shadow mage. It was easy to forget when they spent so much time in the office that he was a highly trained assassin, not just the serious, archaeologist, book geek he appeared to be.

Azalea shuffled as quietly as she could into the gap below the deck where Torin had been. She conjured a shadow shield around herself to be extra safe, but she was well hidden in the dark. In the pit below, she sensed Torin as he dropped from the wall down onto the sandy floor.

The people were too far away to make out what was happening, but she could see the Archmage's bob of white hair shining as flashlights flickered around the tall stones in the pit. They must have already taken out any security present, and they had free rein in the area, not bothering to be quiet.

The monolithic standing stones were at the center of several circular pits surrounded by walls of stacked loose rock. There were at least four pits, and each had two T-shaped standing stones at the center. She could just make out the shadow that must be Torin, creeping toward the pit at the center where the Archmage was.

Be patient, Azalea. Although that seemed harder than getting down there and helping, she would do as she was told.

She bit her lip, watching as the shadow of Torin neared the central standing stones and froze. She was sure no one would notice them and had no idea how long he was planning on watching and waiting for the right moment.

If she had to sit here, she could do something useful. She eased herself onto the compacted earth and set her backpack on her lap. Everything was already covered in dust. The Shadow Atlas might know what to do. It was worth a shot.

Opening the book, she held the pencil to the page and admired the border that appeared. Beautiful gold edges of leaves and vines in unfamiliar designs, perhaps Turkish?

We are at the Echo Gate now. What did you mean by sacrifice?

Hello, brave mageling...

Within these stones a death takes place,

Take a close look, you know his face.

One death tonight, for an open door,

Another one, to shut once more.

Azalea: *Stop speaking in fucking riddles! Tell me straight.*

She didn't have time for this. But a sinking feeling hit the pit of her stomach after reading over it again. '*Take a close look, you know his face.*' She didn't want to look.

The death tonight will not be yours. This I promise. You will be the one to release me to my true form. It is known.

She stared at the words, unsure what to make of them. That wasn't even a riddle or a rhyme.

A blood-curdling scream of a man broke the night air, and Azalea shot up so fast she banged her head on the deck above. Wincing and rubbing her head, she shut the book and shoved it back into her bag. No way in hell she would release that book to its true form. She was certain she didn't want to find out what that was.

Slipping on her backpack, she crouched at the gap, her eyes straining to see what was going on in the center. The man who had screamed had his hands bound behind his back and was on his knees between the two colossal standing stones, bent over with his head down. He was pleading, but she couldn't hear what he was saying.

"Azalea," Torin hissed from behind her, and she nearly jumped out of her skin.

Her hands shot to her heart, feeling the rapid beats before she got over the shock of him appearing to speak again. He motioned for her to come out.

She crawled out from the hiding space, so they were in the open air just below the deck. The moment she saw Torin's face, she knew something was wrong.

"Did you get it?"

He shook his head. "We've got a bigger problem. She's got Erik down there."

Azalea's heart crashed into her chest, ten times faster than before. "You mean..."

"He's going to be the sacrifice." Torin moved into the space to look through the gap.

The words didn't quite sink in. Why would he be a sacrifice? He was one of her people. He'd grown up at the Tower of

London. He'd obviously failed her in getting information from Azalea, but this was extreme even for her.

"We have to help him." Azalea's hands were shaking, so she scrunched them into fists to ignore it.

"That's why I came back to get you." Torin's eyes darted around.

She took in a shaky breath, her mind whirling with insane ideas on how they could get Erik. "Let's get down there."

"Follow me." Torin pivoted around in the small space.

Her hands didn't stop shaking as she slunk after him, keeping low to the ground and close to the shadows that their shadow shields merged with as they went.

He stopped at a sizable gap between the wall and the deck and dropped about six feet into the pit. Reaching with two hands, he silently gestured that he would catch her. She could have easily jumped down herself, though perhaps not as silently as him. So she took up his offer and lowered herself over the edge. He gripped her hips, and warmth flooded through her. Resting her hands on his shoulders, she let him lower her carefully to the ground, his magic practically screaming to merge with hers. She ignored it, and so did he. Her feet hit the sand, and he stepped back.

"Please don't do this." Erik's voice echoed from somewhere across the pit.

Azalea froze at the sound, ears straining to hear. It had been easy to see where everything was from above. But not now that she was in the pit, it was impossible to know which way to go. The loose stone walls were far taller than Torin, and it appeared to be one giant maze.

"Which way?" she said, not bothering to hide the desperation in her voice.

"Come on." Torin took off at a jog, his footsteps silent in the sand.

Azalea followed. They wound through the maze of stone structures until Torin stopped as the path opened to a wide, circular room surrounded by stone. The T-shaped monoliths at the center were so much bigger than they looked from above, at least the height of a one-story building. Erik had gone silent.

"I'll distract the Archmage and try to get the relic. You untie Erik and run, then cut into the Hollow. Don't wait for me, okay?"

Azalea scanned the area. It wasn't just the Archmage Torin had to deal with. There were several Phoenix guards.

"Be careful," she said. There wasn't time for anything else.

"You too." Torin paused a second like he wanted to say something more. Instead, he turned and conjured a solid wall of shadows around him and stepped into the central space.

CHAPTER 40

Torin disappeared. She had no idea how he was planning on distracting the Archmage; all her focus was on Erik. He wasn't making noise anymore. He was tied between the two giant standing stones, his arms bound by rope, and his body slumped over with his head hanging forward, lolling to either side. He was still alive.

Azalea made herself small against an alcove in the wall of stacked rocks; her heart was drumming in her ears, making it hard to think. She watched for a second, assessing the best way to get over to him. The Archmage could have drugged or mind-scrambled him; hopefully, he'd be coherent enough to follow instructions and get himself up. There was no way Azalea could drag him as a deadweight.

An explosion sounded somewhere behind her, followed by the clatter of tumbling rocks. It must have been Torin. She glanced out to the open pit to see the Archmage and her guards running off.

Taking a deep breath, she tightened her grip on her elemer and ran straight at Erik. She skidded to her knees in front of him.

"Erik." She shook his shoulder, but he didn't look up. She went straight for the ropes that were cutting into his wrists. Her hands were slippery with sweat, and the knots were tight.

She tried to undo them, but they didn't budge. She began sawing with her elemer, but it was slow going, and the rope hardly frayed at all.

"Erik!" Azalea's voice cracked as she nudged his shoulder. He needed to get up now.

"Azalea?" Erik's voice was weak. He didn't look injured, but it was clear she'd done something to him.

A fireball shot past her head, too close. She raised her shield and rolled out of the way as several more shot past. One smashed into her barrier, sending her flying across the sand. She inched herself back until she felt the solid rock and angled herself behind the monolith. Up close, the giant T-shaped stone was covered in images of strange animals.

"I knew it wouldn't take much to get you to reveal yourselves," the Archmage said.

Azalea glanced around the edge of the stone. The Archmage was standing there, right in front of Erik.

Torin sprinted into the circular clearing, kicking up sand with two guards hot on his heels. Azalea felt his adrenaline and fearlessness as he blasted his way into this ancient arena. He twisted around and sent a shadow whip out at the same time that he raised a shield. Fireballs smashed into his barrier as his whip took out the two guards, sending them sprawling across the sand.

The Archmage walked to the center of the circular pit, stood over Erik, and placed a box next to him.

Torin's gaze went straight to Azalea, and she waved from behind the stones, though she was sure he could sense where she was.

He raced over and slid behind the stone next to her. He expanded the shield into a transparent lattice to cover them, but they could still see what the Archmage was up to.

"Leave Erik alone. He got you what you wanted. Why are you doing this?" Azalea yelled.

"There's nothing you can do for him now," the Archmage said calmly, not even looking up as she opened the box and took out one of the relics.

Azalea's breath hitched. This was it. She was really going to open the gate. Beside her, she could feel pure focus radiating from Torin. His eyes locked on the relics.

The two Phoenix guards struggled up, stumbled across to the Archmage, and stood on either side of her, though she didn't seem concerned if they were there or not.

"Those who are worthy will survive. I will make us stronger," the Archmage said aloud as if to a room.

"Let's just run at her and try to grab a relic?" Azalea suggested, knowing it was a shit plan, but she had no other ideas.

Torin's chest rose and fell with his heavy breath from running. "She'll just use that resonance spell on us. We'll never get close enough."

The Archmage chanted something under her breath and placed a relic into a slot in the stone. It clicked and began glowing deep green.

They were out of time.

"You go in front of the Archmage and keep her talking, and I'll run from behind and grab one of the relics. We have to try." Azalea's limbs were practically buzzing with magic, waiting to get out.

"Keep your shield up strong," Torin said with a nod, and he stepped out.

Azalea shot around the other side of the stone, but a wave of heat blasted her. She stumbled back as a ring of blue flames spread in a circle around the two standing stones, leaving Torin and Azalea just outside, pressing closer to the wall.

"Erik! Erik," she screamed. "Get up!"

They needed to get in there. If he could get up, they would have a better shot of escaping. For a second, Erik's head stopped swaying, and he seemed to try to lift it. His body listed to one side, and he didn't look up.

Azalea blasted shadows toward the Archmage, but the fire ate them up—it was too far. The Archmage was already placing the fifth relic into its notch in the rock. The four lined up below glowed deep red where they sat flush against the stone, perfectly locked into place.

Torin prowled the edge of the flames, blasting shadows in impressive solid lines like harpoons aimed straight at the Archmage. They smashed through the fire, but when they got to the center, the two guards blocked them with fire that spread out from their arms like petrol-covered shields. The shadows whipped around them and dissolved.

"Erik!" Azalea screamed and used Echo magic to extract small rocks from the walls and hurl them at Erik. "Wake the fuck up!" A few bounced off his back, but he didn't move.

"He can't hear you. Don't worry. He won't suffer," the Archmage said as she placed the sixth relic in the stone, and the ground rumbled. She gave a satisfied nod and moved to the second stone, stepping over Erik's ropes as if he wasn't even there.

Torin blasted shadows in all forms at the fire mages, but with the blue fire around them, nothing was strong enough. It seemed to suck the shadow magic right out of the air.

"It's not working," Torin said through gritted teeth. His magic was straining.

Panic threatened to crush Azalea's lungs. "I know."

"Give me your hand." Torin stopped his shadow barrage and held out his hand.

Azalea took it instantly. His power crashed into hers and grabbed her. It spiraled up her arms straight into her heart, and she closed her eyes, tilting her head back as it sunk into her very soul.

Her eyes flashed open, alert and full of sparkling energy.

Azalea summoned all the water symbols she could think of into a spell cloud in her mind and drew water from beneath the earth. It rose in tiny droplets all around her, summoned from distances she could never have imagined before. Torin's magic surged into her. She glanced at him, but he was focused on the gathering ball of water rising above them. He was pushing his magic to her, but they were controlling the water together.

The strain of the water had sweat streaming down her face and stinging her eyes. She forced the water into a silvery stream in the air and blasted it onto the blue fire with one great thrust.

A quarter of the circle spluttered and died down. It was just enough for her to run in. She headed straight for Erik as Torin blasted the shadows ahead of him, sprinting toward the guards.

The Archmage was still chanting, trapped in some sort of trance as she continued to place the relics into the stone.

Azalea skidded down in front of Erik as Torin ran straight at the guards. Mages weren't usually trained in hand-to-hand fighting, Torin had told her that, but he was skilled in all forms of combat, magic and physical. He slammed into the first one and swung around, low to the ground, and swept out the legs of the other.

Her gaze darted between Erik and the relics already set in the stones.

"I'm coming back, Erik," she promised as she ran to the monolith. Six relics were perfectly nestled into the stone like they'd always been there. They pulsed an ominous red as Azalea clawed at the fish relic, scraping her fingers on the rough rock. Wedging her elemer into the tiny gap, she tried to pry the fish out, but it wouldn't budge. Neither would the others. She tried to send magic into them. Water magic she turned into ice in an attempt to split the stone, but nothing worked.

A loud crack behind her sounded distinctly like bones breaking, followed by a gurgling or strangling sound. She felt a rush of satisfaction from Torin. She didn't want to look.

She darted back to Erik and cupped his chin, raising his head. His pupils were dilated and unfocused; his skin was clammy and hot.

"Erik, please wake up. We have to get you out of here."

"Get away from him!" the Archmage bellowed, and Azalea was flung across the ground like a doll being dragged by the hair by some invisible force.

"It isn't enough. My grandson is dead because of you. You have to ruin my plans as well," the Archmage said, her voice choked with emotion.

A blast of glacial water hit Azalea in the chest like a water cannon, pinning her against the stone on the far wall, threatening to puncture her skin with the force. It was like she was trapped in a wave, unable to surface. Water forced itself into her mouth and nose. Her lungs spasmed, coughing up water, only to have more go in.

She fell to the ground, her body racked with coughing. She vomited up a lake and collapsed on her side.

Her fingers wrapped around her elemer that she found in the clumping sand, and she forced herself up, eyes streaming.

Torin was face to face with the Archmage. The two guards were on the ground in unnaturally bent positions.

Azalea stumbled up. She had to get to Torin. They needed their shared power to get the relics and save Erik.

The Archmage's voice changed as Torin stepped toward her, filled with softness and lies. "Your father will be here soon to watch. Why not stay for the show? After all, I have you to thank for this. Join us, and I'll forget about this insubordination. We could use a powerful mage like you, and I can be very forgiving." She sent him a challenging stare.

"No thanks," Torin said bluntly, not taking his eyes off her.

"Such a shame," she said, almost to herself. She raised her elemer slowly and tilted her head. "I promised Korbyn I wouldn't touch you. So sit back and watch until he gets here." She blasted the invisible resonance spell right at Torin. Azalea slapped her hands over her ears and curled over as the waves of torture surged over her.

Torin bounced across the sand and slammed into the stone wall so hard the rocks collapsed onto him.

Azalea sprinted toward him, but a blast of water from the Archmage tripped her, and she smashed into the sand face first.

"You, we don't need. But I'll let you stay to watch so you know what it's like to have someone you care about die." She gave a humorless smile and tossed salt in a circle around Erik.

"You can't do this," Azalea cried. Her mouth was full of sand, and her body screamed in torment as she forced herself up. She didn't even know what hurt, but pain shot through her from every angle.

Torin groaned, but his crumpled form moved. Azalea pressed a palm to her heart. He was okay, but he was on the other side of the pit, and she couldn't get anywhere without being blasted by the Archmage again.

Azalea summoned Echo Magic and did the only thing she could think of. Picking up rocks with magic and pelting them in a barrage at the Archmage. She had to do something, but they all bounced off an invisible shield.

She stumbled across the floor as the Archmage placed the final relic into the stone. The ground groaned in response, and a flash blasted in every direction. Azalea shut her eyes to block out the searing light as she forced her body to crawl blindly toward the standing stones.

Azalea was screaming, her throat was raw. She had never felt so helpless in her life.

A deep chanting filled the space, and the air grew warm. Azalea couldn't open her eyes, but she recognized the Archmage's voice. Her chanting was passionate and in some ancient language.

Azalea pushed forward toward the light as the air grew hotter. She cracked open an eye and saw Erik's silhouette, dark against the blinding light. She could feel Torin was out there somewhere but couldn't see him.

She stumbled forward, willing herself to keep moving, to just make it to Erik. She wouldn't let another person die because of her.

Then the light was gone. Azalea reached into the air to meet the solid, though invisible, barrier.

She banged her hands on it, but it was too late.

The Archmage stood in the circle over Erik. Her eyes were all black, and a slow smile crawled across her face. The blade in her hand dripped red.

Erik slumped to the side, a dark line across his neck, and a stream of blood flowing out of him into the earth.

Azalea dropped to her knees and vomited into the sand. Erik was gone. He hadn't made a sound or fought. He probably hadn't even known it was happening.

The ground rumbled, and Torin was pulling her back. Her magic recognized him before she could see him.

Her legs wouldn't stand as the very earth came apart beneath their feet. The monolithic gateway stones stood strong as a net of green electricity pulsed between the standing stones like concentrated lightning. The Archmage stumbled out of the way.

Azalea was shaking all over. Her nostrils flared as she glared at the Archmage. Wiping her face with earth-covered hands, she spat out the dirt mixing with the sour bile in her mouth and clung to Torin until her feet were steady.

Azalea let go of him and, without warning, sprinted toward the circle and tackled the Archmage, throwing her against the giant stone. But she easily threw Azalea aside, pinning her to the stone with an invisible force.

"I knew from the start I couldn't trust you; of course, you sided with *him*." She spat. "But I am no murderer, this is for the good of our people. Sacrifices have to be made for the greater good. Erik knew that, and he will be remembered as a hero."

"I don't care if he's a hero! He's dead because of you. He's nothing now! Stop this all before it destroys us." Azalea had to yell over the rising wind rushing through the ancient temple. Her voice was hoarse and dry.

"This will make the world better, you will see, and I thank you for your part in gathering the relics. You have played an honorable role until now. I could make them remember you as a hero. It's up to you," she said calmly as if the earth wasn't coming apart under their feet.

Azalea remained pinned to the stone as the ground shuddered and heaved. Sections around them suddenly dropped into nothingness. She struggled against the force like the air was pressing her, squeezing her and sucking the liquids from her skin.

"I don't want to be a hero!" Azalea choked out. The air was being crushed from her lungs. Her gaze darted around wildly, but she couldn't see Torin. Her eyes fell on Erik, his head resting in his hand as if he had fallen asleep there. She choked back a sob, making it harder to get air. She squeezed her eyes shut. The light blasted straight up from the stones like a glowing tube that wavered between green and red. It could easily be mistaken for a tractor beam from an alien spaceship.

Torin's arms slid around her, and they tumbled onto the solid earth. She glanced around. They were back against the wall on the edge of the circle.

"Don't use any Echo Magic; it will kill you." Torin's eyes were black and filled with fear.

Azalea believed it. The air was vibrating with Echo Magic so thick she was surprised she couldn't see it as a fog.

Azalea's skin began buzzing as electrical energy crackled all around them. She squeezed her eyes shut. Torin's arms wrapped around her, pulling her to the ground. A violent roar grew louder. She imagined that was what a tornado would sound like, like the loudest train you had ever heard mixed with a wave, crushing you into the ocean floor.

The light simmered to a deep vermilion glow, and she dared to look up. The tent was gone, a flicker of white a thousand miles into the sky. The force of the beam must have sent it all the way to the stars. Torin's arms were still wrapped around her, and she could feel his rapid heartbeat and fear alongside her own.

This was it—the Echo Gateway was open.

Azalea's breath caught. Dark forms poured out from the light beam that had formed a bridge into the sky: creatures gliding, galloping, and slithering into the night from another world into their own. They were shapes of things she had read about in books: winged horses, great serpents, horrifying monsters she didn't recognize, and dragons. Creatures from the Echo Dimension.

"We have to close it before it spreads." Torin pulled Azalea up.

CHAPTER 41

"Where is the Archmage? I can't see her." Azalea glanced around, but every time her eyes fell back to Erik slumped between the two standing stones right below the gateway to the Echo Dimension. Magic from the portal blasted straight up to the sky in a stream of raw, red magic mixed with streaks of green. She forced her gaze away, waiting for the Archmage to appear.

"I don't know. I can't see her either." Torin's eyes narrowed, darting around as if expecting an attack.

Azalea crept toward the gateway, staying low to the ground. "I have to get Erik out of there."

"Keep an eye out for the Archmage. She must be here still." Torin followed without hesitation.

They crouched low against the wind that blasted from the gate. Sand and grit bombarded them, dying down a little as they made it to the center, right underneath it.

Azalea did her best not to look up at the horrific portal above them and focused on Erik. She felt like she'd held it together pretty well until now, but when she saw Erik's lifeless face, she nearly broke. Memories of Elam from less than a month ago piled on top of this fresh grief.

"You get his legs," Torin said kindly as if he knew she needed to be told what to do right now. Her brain was threatening a meltdown.

She picked up Erik's legs, and Torin lifted his top half and together shuffled from the gateway to the edge of the rocky wall.

Azalea slumped to the ground, cradled Erik's head in her lap, and Torin crouched next to her.

"The prophecies said another death could close the door. I could stop this." Torin didn't look at her, but she felt what he was about to do.

Torin darted for the place where Erik had been sacrificed. Azalea jumped to her feet and raced after him. She'd feel bad about Erik's head hitting the ground later. She couldn't think about it now. She needed to stop Torin from disappearing from her life when she finally wanted him in it.

"Don't do this, Torin," she screamed into the raging wind.

Azalea stopped in her tracks when the Archmage appeared, blocking her way to Torin and the gate.

The Archmage stood there with her thin lips pursed together, holding an enormous staff with a crystal on the end. A staff Azalea had seen before—at Erik's house. That was the project his dad had been working on. Had the bitch known she was going to kill his son when she commissioned him for that project? Had the Archmage killed his dad too? She didn't want to think about that or Erik's sister.

"You can still join us," the Archmage called to Torin. "I'll give you one more chance. Surrender to me now."

"Never. I can shut this gate down and destroy it. All it requires is a sacrifice, and one I'm more than happy to make." Torin didn't even look back, his focus all on the relics.

Azalea's heart plummeted to her feet. He couldn't do that. He couldn't just give up his life so easily.

The Archmage smirked. "I don't think you will. Nothing can shut the gate now, nothing but the gods. The relics were merely the key, and the door is now open."

"Torin, don't do this! It won't work." Azalea had never felt more helpless. There had to be a way past the Archmage.

"I have to." He let down his barrier, and his full emotions rushed across the space, straight into her.

Azalea doubled over like she'd been hit by a truck. She felt everything he felt; the overwhelming guilt and failure, regret, hopelessness, but deep down, there was also determination and love. Clearly, it wasn't enough.

Couldn't he see this wasn't his fault? He believed in some stupid prophecy that he would bring destruction to the world, but he was the good guy in all this. Azalea saw that now.

"What about Kira? Don't you want to see her?" Azalea was desperate. There had to be a way to stop him. She couldn't lose him as well—not an option.

Magic was roaring all around them. But she had to keep him talking. The Archmage didn't even look concerned. She probably wanted Torin to kill himself so he wouldn't be a problem anymore.

"Kira is alive. Your uncle is right. She won't want to see me." Torin looked up into the stream of light.

"What about me?" Azalea cried. It felt like her chest was being crushed, like she couldn't get enough air.

"I'm sorry. You know how I feel about you, Azalea. Everything I said in the dream was real. But you're much better off without me. Trust me." He didn't even look at her, but managed to pry out one of the relics. The stream of magic didn't get any weaker.

"Stop talking like that! You don't need to do this. It's open now and we can't close it." Azalea walked closer, testing the Archmage.

"Stay back," he warned.

The Archmage laughed as if she was enjoying the entertainment, her hands resting on her staff. She turned her face toward the light and smiled as if she were greeting the morning sun.

"It won't close the gate if you sacrifice yourself. You can't trust the bloody book! You're the one who keeps telling me that!" Azalea swallowed down the panic. She had to stay rational.

"Sacrifice magic is the strongest of all. If I do this voluntarily, it will cut power to the gate. I'm sure of it," Torin yelled. But made the mistake of looking at Azalea. Their eyes locked and she silently pleaded with him to stop.

The Archmage's expression flickered.

Azalea pulled her emotions in tight to her chest like a magnet. "If you think it will work, I trust you, Torin." Her voice was shaking, and tears stung the corners of her eyes.

The Archmage hadn't moved—she was observing them. Probably wanting to see both of them in pain.

"Just let me say goodbye," she pleaded, not letting him look away, so he was forced to see she meant it.

"No, stay away." His muscles tightened, and he froze in place.

Azalea walked toward him. She could feel his conflicted emotions; he wanted to do what was right, but he wanted her as well.

"Azalea," he growled and wedged another relic out of the stone.

She ran and threw herself onto him. She didn't give him time to think, and he was forced to drop the relic and open his arms. A moment of fear sparked through him, but their eyes met—his solid and black—and he pulled her into a desperate kiss.

The roar of the gateway dulled, and time stood still as their magic merged in a spectacular wave of power. It was the most natural thing in the world to kiss him. Her heart thundered in her chest; breaking open, unwarded and unguarded, making him feel every reason she couldn't let him go.

She melted into his arms, not wanting this to end as a new hum of magic grew around them.

He pulled away slowly as if he hated to do so, but their faces remained close. "You need to go," he breathed.

"No." She shook her head and wrapped her hands around his neck, pulling his mouth to hers once more. He kissed her back until she was breathless.

A new heat burned through her veins, but Torin pulled away.

"Our magic," he said as she stepped back in confusion.

Her breath hitched. The space between them was a delicate web of crisscrossed blue and purple light, the shared magic sparkling between them.

"I think we just strengthened the bond. You need to go now." Torin refused to look at her, despite everything they had just shared.

Anger rippled through her; he wasn't giving up that easily. "We can use it to destroy the gate." She took his hands in hers, pushing her magic into him.

"It will only make it open wider if we do that now." He dropped her hands and stepped away.

"Enough of this," the Archmage screamed.

But Azalea knew what to do. She could feel it building inside her, a new magic, a magic that didn't need a source from another dimension. It came from within.

She grabbed Torin's hand and raised her elemer to face the Archmage. "We won't let you hurt anyone else."

Azalea blasted a stream of solid silver light right at the Archmage. It was like liquid mercury, iridescent and mesmerizing, but light as air. The blast of power hit the old woman straight in the chest and sent her flying across the sand.

Torin hadn't pulled away. Rather, he entwined his fingers with Azalea's and pulled her out of the circle toward the Archmage, as if realizing what they could do.

He raised his elemer and sent the same blast of light toward the Archmage. Azalea closed her eyes as a surge of magic pulled away from her, but it felt right, like the balance between them could always be reset and recharged.

"That was amazing," he breathed.

"Tell me about it. Now let's get out of here. In case she gets up," Azalea said.

"I'm not leaving until I shut the gate down."

Azalea's heart dropped to her feet. He still wanted to do it. "There's another way, another path. The book said." She swallowed, gripping his hand tight. "It said that was the harder path, but we can face it together."

He dropped her hand, and the power of the new magic trickled away. She held in a whimper and tried to mask her desperation.

"I don't want you to do this." Her voice shook. She was going to have to resort to drastic measures to stop him—to save him.

"I'm sorry. It has to be this way." He shook his head slowly and tucked a loose strand of hair behind her ear. She sank into the warmth of his palm against her cheek.

"Me too." She leaned in and brushed her lips against his, soft as a feather. This wouldn't be such a bad way to spend your last minutes alive. Too bad she wasn't giving him that option.

Her hand slid to his neck, deepening the kiss as salty tears crept between their lips. She pushed hard on the pressure point in the exact spot he had shown her on his neck and sent her magic into it, still melded with his, and he slumped to the ground.

"I'm sorry, Torin," she whispered. Did he really think she would give up on him that easily? There was another way to save the world, and she was going to find it.

She let out a sob, suddenly feeling very alone. She hadn't been able to save Erik, but she could save Torin from his ridiculous savior complex. There was no way they could shut the gate now; it was too late.

She brought a shaky finger to his neck to check he wasn't dead, and his magic sparked to meet hers. Good.

The gate continued to rage behind her like wildfire blasting into the sky. It wasn't just magic coming out; it was also all those creatures being released into their world.

Azalea gathered up all the relics and tossed them in her bag. Somehow she had to cut into the Hollow and drag Torin in, then find the way back out.

"Well, well, well, what do we have here?" a voice appeared behind her. A figure crouched over the Archmage.

Azalea twisted around in shock, darted in front of Torin, and threw up a grid-like shadow shield. A trickle of icy fear spiked down her spine. It was Korbyn Dumont.

CHAPTER 42

A zalea stood protectively in front of Torin and nearly tripped over her backpack she must have dropped at some point. She carefully slipped on the bag and held her elemer facing Korbyn Dumont.

Torin's father moved closer with a look that made her want to crawl under a rock and hide. He didn't look much like Torin. He was short and wiry with light skin and graying hair and a goatee, though he had the same scowl as Torin which sent a shiver down her neck. Torin obviously took after his mother, which was a good thing.

"Aren't you just full of mysteries, Azalea Blackbourne?" Korbyn looked her up and down. He held a large staff, similar to the Archmage's, but his was ebony and carved with runes. A clear, jagged crystal was set on the top.

"That isn't my name." Her hand shook. She had to get them into the Hollow now. A whip of darkness slashed at her hand, and her elemer dropped. She kicked her elemer toward the wall, well away from Korbyn, and grabbed Torin's hands, using all her strength to pull him to the wall near Erik. She was running on pure adrenaline.

She grabbed her elemer and slid it into her belt, not taking her eyes off Torin's dad. But he wasn't looking at her. He stared up at the beam of light shooting above them and slowly turned around.

"How rude of her to not wait for me to open the gateway." He sighed. "Is my son alive? I told Esther to leave him out of this."

He was on a first-name basis with the Archmage. That couldn't be good.

"He's alive. Just leave us alone. Neither of us will join you," Azalea spat. Trying to see a way to get them into the Hollow. She needed a distraction. Korbyn was too close and would stop her if she made a move.

"I wasn't asking *you*," he responded. "Though I am curious as to why you are protecting the man who murdered your father. Surely after the last time we met, you found out the truth? Did he tell you how easy it was? How he slipped into the House of Snakes' party and how your father hardly put up a fight."

She ignored his baiting. "You killed his mother. How can you expect him to come back to you?"

His eyes narrowed, and his hands wrung around the staff as if he wanted to strangle someone. Good, she was getting to him. Not the best plan, but it might buy time until she came up with a better one.

"Because he is my son, and it is where he belongs. Is it so hard to believe I want him at my side as the reign of Shadow Magic begins?"

"You've sentenced the world to destruction." She held Korbyn's glare as her hand wrapped around Torin's wrist, silently pushing magic into him to make him wake up. She regretted knocking him out, but at least he was still alive.

"I've set the world free. And I have a feeling I have you two to thank for bringing this about. You stopped him from making the sacrifice to close the gate, didn't you? I can see it in your eyes. It was the only loophole, but it's too late now. He always was a soft, pathetic boy. You chose for him." He chuckled.

"You don't know what you're talking about." Azalea set her jaw. Torin's magic flickered in her hand.

"He's going to hate you for this. Maybe I'll let you live, just so you know what that feels like." Korbyn glanced down at the Archmage and nudged her with the end of his cane. A weak moan slipped from her lips, and he nodded, as if mildly satisfied she wasn't dead.

"You're sick," Azalea spat.

She pulled Torin's hand into her lap and closed her eyes. His magic flowed freely into her, faster than before, like it was waking up. The Echo Magic in the air was growing so thick it would be easy to draw on it by accident. It was screaming at her to use it; she had to be careful.

Focusing all her attention on the new magic, it blended both their powers seamlessly; it wasn't cold like Shadow Magic, it was warm like her own blood, natural, but fizzing and sparking at the same time. It felt right.

"On the other hand, maybe I'll just kill you both," Korbyn growled.

Azalea's eyes flicked open to see his wild and angry. He had seen their magic. It glowed around her hands, silvery like moonlight.

She remained close to Torin but uncoiled from the ground into a crouch, still holding his hand. The magic built up in her palm, and she raised her arm, locking eyes with Korbyn.

"You're not taking either of us." Silver light burst from her palm, blasting at Korbyn like a solar flare. She didn't know what it was; all she knew was it didn't come from any dimension and that she wanted to hurt him. He raised a shield, but the barrage of magic shredded his shadows.

Tension vibrated through her body, every muscle fiber focused on channeling the light.

She didn't look at Korbyn. Her cells were buzzing close to the edge of burnout. Taking a breath, she relaxed her shoulders and let the magic drop. No time to think. She grabbed Torin's elemer from the ground, and tucked it in his belt, then used her elemer to cut into the Hollow. She wasn't sticking around for a fight.

Korbyn was sprawled on the ground near the Archmage. *Good job. You piece of shit.* She didn't think he was dead. Somehow she knew she would have felt it through the new magic.

She called to the new magic to help her make Torin lighter. It didn't work. Leaning over him, she took his hands, pleading with their shared magic for him to wake up. What if she'd screwed up the pressure point thing? What if he didn't wake up? Had she used too much of his sleep magic with it?

She shook him, maybe a little too hard, wishing she could use Echo Magic to summon some water. "I'm sorry for everything. Please wake up now." She stroked his short hair and ran her fingers across his cheek.

She glanced back. Korbyn still hadn't moved, and neither had the Archmage. Guilt clawed at her chest at the sight of Erik. There was no way she could pull both of them into the Hollow, but she trusted the Archmage would get him back to his family.

"I forgive you for my father. I forgive you for everything. Please just wake up!"

She cut into the Hollow and tried to haul him onto her shoulder. She couldn't get him up.

"What the fuck?" A groan broke through Torin's lips. "You knocked me out?"

Azalea nearly dropped him but lowered him back to the ground and pressed her forehead to his. "Thank the gods you're okay. I'm so sorry."

He glanced around, confused, and his face fell. She felt the realization hit him as he remembered what had happened as he looked up at the gateway blasting above them.

He frowned and shuffled to sit up. "Is that my father? Is he dead?"

Azalea sank back on her heels in the sand. "Yes, it's him, but I don't think he's dead." She nibbled her lip, waiting for him to lose it.

"You did that?"

She nodded, her heart beating faster every second. Nothing seemed so bad now that he was awake. "I took some of your magic, sorry. We need to get into the Hollow now. Can you get up? Shit." The Hollow had closed again.

He seemed to be in a trance-like state, glancing between the gateway and the mix of dead and unconscious bodies around them.

"You should have let me shut the gate." His hands curled into fists.

"You know why I couldn't, and it's too late now." She swallowed hard. They had as good as admitted their feelings to each other now.

"I'm so tired." His eyes closed, and he lulled back down.

"Wake up." She shuffled over to him and shook his shoulder.

His eyes blinked open.

"Get into the Hollow now, or we're going to die. Neither of us has enough magic to fight anymore, and we can't close the gate."

"But—"

"There is another path; the book said. Just get up!" she ordered.

She cut into the Hollow again, and he used the wall to pull himself up, then draped his arm over her shoulder. She unceremoniously dumped him into the Hollow and swiveled his legs to stuff them in. She clambered over him on hands and knees, the freezing air a welcome relief from the heat of the Echo gateway.

Please shut. Please shut. She stared at the seam of the Hollow, willing the darkness to seal faster.

They had made it. She let her shoulders slump. Everything was so quiet, impossibly still after the roar of magic they left behind. All she could hear was her own heartbeat.

Torin hauled himself up and looked at her. "Did you say those things and kiss me just you could knock me out?"

"No, of course not. I meant what I said, and I wanted to kiss you. You must have felt it." The guilt came up in a wave. His father had been right. She had decided for him, and now he would hate her.

"Gods, I'm stupid." He rubbed his hand over his face.

"It's not like that, Torin." Her limbs were getting heavy. She didn't have the energy left for anything, let alone fighting with him.

"I can feel your emotions. You feel guilty, you can't hide it."

"You're interpreting my emotions wrong. I feel guilty about Erik, and the world, and all the people we let down. Not about you." She threw her hands up in frustration.

His guilt flooded back to her as she reminded him that they had failed.

"You can hate me all you want later. But right now, we need to get out of here. Can you cut out to Blackbourne Manor?" There was no time for this now.

He closed his eyes and shook his head as if he didn't want to believe any of this was true. It was clear he was going to take the full burden of their failure on his shoulders. "Fine."

He glanced down at his hands and fell back. "I don't have enough magic. I'm near burnout." He looked around, confused.

"Sorry, that was me. I took it when I was fending off your crazy dad. Here, take some back." She linked her hand with his, pushing her magic into him, the opposite of before and much easier this time. But she could also feel his consciousness flickering in and out. He needed help. He stumbled as her magic went into him, and he dropped to the soft blue floor. She shook him hard.

"Torin, wake up. We need to get out of here, and I don't know where his house is."

"Wow," he said in a daze.

Wow was the right term for their mysterious magic, but now they were both running on low batteries.

He cut out of the Hollow, and they stumbled out into a black-and-white winter wonderland where the sun hadn't yet risen. Snow glowed bright white in the lamplight of the black iron gate they appeared at. He only made it a few feet, then collapsed.

"Please stay awake." Azalea was close to tears. Torin's eyes slipped shut again as she fumbled for her phone in her bag.

She called her mum.

"Mum, it's me," she said in a rush.

"It's so good to hear your voice, Petal. We were worried sick."

"I'm outside. Come to the gate quick. I need help."

CHAPTER 43

Torin was unconscious again, spread out on the ground, his nice coat getting all wet in the damp snow. Azalea pulled him against her, so he wasn't lying in a snow pile as headlights from inside the gates neared, beaming at her like lasers trying to burn out her eyes. She shielded her face as the car stopped; the gate groaned open, and she saw her mum's face.

She closed her eyes briefly and took a deep breath, letting relief wash over her.

"Are you okay?" Her mum rushed over, her blonde hair frizzed up, escaping its scrunchie and looking wild, but Azalea had never been so glad to see her.

"I'm fine. But he needs help. The gate to the Echo Dimension is open. We couldn't close it," she blurted out. "He needs to wake up. The Echo Magic will be here soon." Her gaze darted to the sky, half expecting the red glow to have followed her there.

A man Azalea didn't recognize trudged up behind Leda. He had a slight limp but moved fast for an old man. He was wearing overalls covered in oil stains with the sleeves rolled up, and offered no greeting, just hauled Torin up under his armpits and dragged him in the gate to the truck.

"Be careful," Azalea squeaked out.

"What's wrong with him? Is he injured?" Leda's eyes filled with concern.

Azalea swallowed. She knew Torin wouldn't want to go inside, but he had little choice in the matter now. "He's—um. I think it's a sleeping spell. He keeps falling back asleep, and I need him awake."

"Right, let's get him inside, then. RoRo will have a cure of some sort, I imagine."

"Everyone knows not to use Echo Magic, right?" Azalea said.

"Yes, we've warned as many people as we can. What happened?" Leda asked.

Azalea bit her lip. "I'll explain when we're inside. But it was the Archmage and Korbyn Dumont. They're working together. Where's Uncle Fabian?"

"I see. He dropped off your friends and left again with some woman. He's not back yet," her mum said.

The old man frowned but didn't comment as he flung open the doors to an old truck that looked like it might have come straight from WWII.

"Grab his legs, would ya?" he said, and Azalea and Leda helped maneuver Torin into the back on the floor. He'd clearly done this before.

Once Torin was in, Leda threw her arms around Azalea in a tight hug. "Gosh, I'm so glad you're okay. We've been worried sick."

"It's okay. I'm fine, Mum," Azalea said, barely keeping it together. The warm arms around her made her want to melt into the safety of her mother's embrace and block out whatever was coming next. She might be alive, but everything was *not* fine.

Leda pulled away and smiled as she brushed Azalea's hair off her face and tucked it behind her ear like she used to when Azalea was a kid. Azalea forced a strained smile her mum would see right through.

They both clambered in the back of the truck with Torin, and Azalea found a scratchy wool blanket to put under his head, and she nestled into an uncomfortable spot by the wheel hump and took Torin's hand. His magic buzzed into her, the subtle glow hidden by her bag. At least that seemed to be dimming down now. Her shoulders slumped, finally able to relax.

She ignored Leda's sideways glances from where she sat near the door. But to her credit, she didn't ask any more questions. Just as well, because Azalea wasn't prepared to explain whatever the hell had happened that night.

It was a short trip up the driveway, and suddenly, they were in front of the gigantic house. The door creaked open, and Azalea tapped Torin, trying to get him to wake up. He wouldn't budge.

"I think we'll need some help to get him inside." Azalea's gaze darted around, half expecting Fabian to pop up.

She jumped out and wrung her hands in front of her. It seemed they had done this before. A woman came out with an old-fashioned basic stretcher, and in no time, they whisked Azalea through a maze of rooms; a grand reception hall, a floral wallpaper-lined hallway, a billiards room, and finally they were in the library, though it seemed to be a makeshift war room by the looks of plans on the walls and tables strewn with papers, computers, and empty coffee mugs.

There were several giant couches and a massive stone fireplace. A wave of heat threatened to knock her over; Azalea hadn't realized how cold she was and ordered her body to stop shaking.

They eased Torin onto a deep red sofa that was long enough to even fit his feet. The old couple dashed off somewhere, and it was just her, her mum, and Torin in the big room.

A mumbling came from Torin, and Azalea perched next to him, tapping his face lightly.

"Hey, Torin. Wake up. We need to find another way to close the gate." Her hand rested on his chest, and her eyes darted to her bag on the ground, knowing the Shadow Atlas was probably the answer.

"What's wrong with him?" RoRo marched in. Her warm presence filled the room with vibrant energy as Azalea jumped up and threw herself at her grandmother.

"RoRo! It's so good to see you. It was some sort of sleeping spell and a pressure point thing," Azalea blurted out, her arms curled around RoRo's neck. She smelled of home, like rosemary and candles and earth.

"It's lovely to see you too, dear." RoRo pulled away with a relieved smile that spread across her cheeks. "If that's the case, I've got something to fix him up. When he wakes next, he can take it."

RoRo flitted off, her long dress covered in orange and red roses whooshing around her as she went.

Azalea perched on the edge of the couch next to Torin. Unsure what else to do to try to wake him. She didn't want to freak him out and get cursed or stabbed if he was shocked awake.

"That's Torin, isn't it?" her mum said softly.

A spike of realization shot through Azalea. Her mum might not be okay with him being there. Azalea had been so worried about Fabian; she didn't even consider her mum's feelings. This was the man who had murdered the father of her child, Azalea's father.

"I'm sorry, Mum. I should have asked you first. I didn't think." Azalea grasped her hands in her lap.

"Nonsense. If he needs help, you did the right thing. You're a good person, Azalea." Leda smiled, and a weight lifted from Azalea's chest.

"Are you two getting on better now?" Leda raised her eyebrows as if hinting at something.

Azalea's eyes threatened to mist up. "We were... until now. He might not be happy when he wakes up," Azalea warned. "But he's a good person, Mum. He's more than made up for everything he's done. He tortures himself more than any prison could." That was the truth.

"It takes great strength to forgive. I'm so proud of you, Azalea." Leda's voice wavered.

Azalea glanced up to see her mum wiping her eyes but smiling to herself. Turning quickly back to Torin, Azalea squeezed his hand, hoping he would feel it, feel her magic. She would probably have to tell him she had forgiven him face-to-face at some point. In the meantime, he really needed to wake up so they could start finding solutions that didn't involve him dying. Where was RoRo?

He shifted his weight suddenly and sat bolt upright. His eyes were wild and all black. Azalea held her breath. But he pulled her into an unexpected hug.

"Thank the gods you're okay. I had a horrible dream that the spirits got you." Torin's breath was warm on her neck.

Azalea froze, unable to react. She breathed in the scent of him, sweat mixed with smoke and the lingering summeriness of the Echo Dimension, and she relaxed in his arms, just for a second.

He pulled back and pressed his forehead to hers, smiling. She closed her eyes, her hands resting on his chest. There was no more visible sparking of their magic, but she felt the warm fizz of it where their foreheads touched.

"I'm sorry," she whispered so only he could hear.

He would remember any second, and this moment would be over. He pulled back, their eyes meeting—and there it was. She let her hands fall, and he pulled away.

"You knocked me out again, didn't you?" Torin accused, rubbing his eyes and blinking. He seemed determined to stay awake this time.

"Again?" RoRo marched back in.

"I only did it once," she whispered to him and shuffled along the couch to give him some room.

Torin swiveled around, his feet hit the floor, and he was bolt upright on the edge of the couch next to Azalea. RoRo had a steaming mug in her hand. Azalea felt horrible as his eyes grew wide as he looked around, and he realized where they were.

"Um—Torin, this is my mum, Leda, and Grandmother, RoRo," Azalea said. *Please don't flip out.*

He took in a sharp breath.

"It's very nice to meet you both. Azalea has told me a lot about you. I'm sorry if my presence is disturbing. I will be leaving as soon as possible," he said, gentlemanly, but with a strong undertone of anger aimed at Azalea.

"You are very welcome here, Torin. We can all turn over a new leaf." Leda folded her hands on her lap and nodded to him, seeking agreement.

Torin swallowed and looked down. "Thank you."

Azalea felt the pain roll off him. He didn't think he deserved forgiveness.

"I did not expect Azalea to bring me here. Fabian is going to kill me," he growled and glared at Azalea.

"I won't let him. Did you want me to leave you at the gate in the cold?" she said, scared he would take off at any moment.

"I wanted you to leave me at the *other* gate so the world wouldn't be destroyed," he muttered under his breath. His hands curled into fists, and he took a deep breath with closed eyes, then put up his mask of non-emotions.

"We didn't raise Azalea to leave people behind. Here, have this. It should stop that sleeping spell loop you seem to be in." RoRo handed Torin the cup.

He took it and sniffed the contents.

"What's in it?" Azalea asked as RoRo put a wool blanket over her shoulders, and she wrapped it tight around her. She was freezing, and everywhere was starting to hurt, but she didn't think she had any major injuries, and she had to stay awake.

"Coffee. Best thing for a sleeping spell. Knocks it right off course," RoRo said, matter-of-factly.

"Thank you." Torin took a polite sip. "I'm sorry again. I'll leave as soon as I can. I need to get back out there."

"Nonsense. We can come up with a solution together here," RoRo said as if they were planning Christmas dinner rather than how to close an inter-dimensional gate.

"Azalea told you what happened?" Torin blinked; he seemed to be focusing hard on staying awake. The coffee was working.

"Not yet. We understand the Echo Dimension gate was opened. The others should be down shortly to listen in. I'm sure you don't want to repeat it more than you need to," RoRo said.

Leda sat calmly on an armchair across the coffee table, and RoRo sank into the other.

"Who made it back here?" Azalea asked, wrapping the blanket tighter around her to try to stop the shivering. She glanced at the clock; it was 4:50 am.

Her question was answered when Faraday burst into the room full tilt and clambered up Azalea's leg and into her arms. "Faraday! I'm so glad you're okay." She kissed the cat on the head and let his purrs rumble into the crook of her neck where he head-butted her chin. Danni and the others must be here, too.

Sure enough, Danni rushed in next, closely followed by Van and Jade, all looking very sleepy but relieved. After hugs all around and Torin trying to keep his coffee upright, they pulled up more chairs. Azalea sat next to Torin on the sofa, not close enough to touch, and they finally got down to explanations while Mrs. Yates poured everyone tea.

Azalea explained everything that happened while Torin glared into his cup and added the occasional detail, his foot tapping annoyingly on the ground. When she got to the part about Erik, she froze up.

"They needed a sacrifice to open the gate." Azalea swallowed hard unable to get the words out. As much as Erik had been a jerk lately, she hadn't wanted anything like this to happen to him. Just a week ago, she'd been lying in his arms happily. Blissfully unaware of the nightmare of a turn this would take.

"You've gone pale, dear. Do you need another cup of tea?" RoRo stood up.

Azalea shook her head, her eyes stung with unshed tears.

"It was Erik," she choked the words out.

Van's hands shot to her mouth with a gasp. "Erik was—No..." Van shot across the room and sat on the other side of Azalea, wrapping her arms around Azalea's shoulders. Azalea gripped her arm tightly, fighting the urge to break down.

"What happened?" Danni said as if she didn't believe it, her question directed toward Torin.

"We tried to get to him, but the Archmage was playing a game with us. She chose him on purpose to hurt Azalea, or to punish Erik, or to punish his father for something. Though she seemed to think it was an honor for him. We couldn't save him in the end and she killed him." Torin tensed, and his anger rolled onto Azalea and broke her out of her spiraling.

Danni swallowed, her eyes wide with disbelief. "So that's how she opened the gate?"

"Yes, and then Torin tried to kill himself to close the gate. So I stopped him." Azalea crossed her arms. Feeding on Torin's anger with new motivation. She knew the others would be on her side, even if Torin didn't agree.

Danni threw a cushion at Torin. "After everything I've done for you? You go and try to kill yourself?" She rushed over and hugged him.

"I got the relics together. This is all my fault," he said through gritted teeth as he peeled Danni off him.

"It's not your fault the Archmage and your father are psychopaths, and you weren't given a choice in taking on the job. None of this is your fault," Danni said, basically yelling it at him.

Azalea rested her head on Van's shoulder. At least she had someone agreeing with her. She was worried she'd done the wrong thing. She'd done it for selfish reasons, so maybe it wasn't right. But she was glad Torin was alive, and that was all that mattered while she knew there was another way.

"There will be another way to close the gate. It was closed once before." RoRo took a biscuit and dunked it in her tea.

"Yes. By the gods." Leda nodded.

"Well, if we have to go get the gods themselves, then we shall," RoRo said.

"There *is* another way. The prophecy said there were two paths." Azalea's eyes darted purposefully to Jade, aware they would ask where the prophecy came from.

"What did it say? Where did you hear it?" Danni asked.

"*The choice is yours to shut the gate; To sacrifice one more or wait. The future shows another way; A harder path for those who stay,*'" Azalea answered. The words drilled into her brain, repeating over and over.

The room was silent. "It came from Jade." Azalea nodded at her, feeling guilty for throwing her under the bus, but she wasn't ready to reveal the Shadow Atlas.

Jade raised her hands to her temples, looking just as shocked as everyone else.

"So I picked the harder path. It's not the end of the world. Or hopefully won't be. Though I did see some dragons fly out," Azalea said nervously.

"Dragons?" Van squeezed her arms and went rigid.

Jade paled and moved from her perch on the arm of a chair onto the ground, leaning against the sofa.

Change of subject: She explained how the Archmage was working with Korbyn Dumont and how she had some sort of staff that still allowed her to use Echo Magic, despite the air being filled with enough magic to blast her apart.

After all the explanations, Torin looked like he wanted to kill someone. The coffee obviously made him jittery. Perhaps he needed a real drink? No. That wouldn't help anyone.

"Can I talk to you alone, Azalea?" Torin said coldly.

She nodded, and her mum gave her a look that said, 'are you okay?' She nodded with a forced smile and followed Torin out the doors at the end of the study.

The room they stepped into was humid and smelled strongly of chlorine. A huge swimming pool took up the bulk of the space with all kinds of plants around the edges, like a tropical conservatory. The roof and walls were glass and outside she could see snow piled up on the edges of the windows.

"I can't believe you did that to me. I could have fixed everything. The bloody curse is true, after all. I've officially caused the destruction of the world." He paced the edge of the pool, hands fisted at his sides.

Azalea remained still and pulled the blanket closer around her. "It's not your fault, Torin. It's the Archmage and your father's. You can't blame yourself."

"No, I can blame you as well," he snapped.

It stung. "The book said there is another way. I know there is, we just need to find it—together." She took a step toward him but stopped when she saw his face. He was like a sun radiating anger.

"That book is dangerous. We should get rid of it before something worse happens."

"No, it can help us." No need to mention the fact that it expected her to free it, whatever *it* really was.

"Was everything you said a lie?" he asked.

Tears of frustration stung the corners of her eyes, but she wouldn't let them fall. "No. How can you even say that when you can feel what I feel? Is it so hard to believe I care about you and didn't want you to die? That I couldn't face living in a world without you?"

His face fell as if he felt sorry for her. She could feel it on him. Pity. Was he so far gone that he didn't believe anyone could love him? She wasn't saying it was love, but it was something.

The double doors from the study flung open, and Fabian stormed in. Azalea moved to Torin's side and raised her elemer. Fabian didn't stop, his elemer was streaming shadows behind him.

"You! I told you not to come here," Fabian growled. His eyes were dark, a disturbing smirk on his face like he finally had an excuse to take a shot at Torin.

CHAPTER 44

Azalea didn't take her eyes off Fabian as he stalked toward Torin like a wolf with prey in its sights. Footsteps of others entering the room sounded behind her, but she remained at Torin's side. Danni moved around him, ready to jump in, though she wouldn't be able to use any Echo Magic.

Kat, dressed in her black House of Ravens combat outfit, followed Fabian in and stood with her arms folded as if waiting to see how this would unfold.

RoRo, Leda, Jade, and Van hovered near the door.

"I'm more than happy to leave," Torin said sharply, baiting Fabian and standing with his arms crossed.

Fabian cracked his knuckles and stopped in front of Azalea and Torin. "Oh, you're not leaving."

"Let's not do this again." Azalea raised her elemer, letting the shadows stream silently in front of her.

"Can't even fight his own battle," Fabian scoffed.

"Of course, he can. But this isn't the time to be fighting battles. We have much larger problems. Like that." Azalea pointed to the sky through the glass roof panels.

A deep red seeped across the night air like blood being absorbed into the clouds; tints of green streaked alongside as dark forms moved against the deadly glow.

This wasn't the sunrise.

"What did you two do?" Fabian stared up at the sky, the same as the others.

Gasps and mumbling came from everyone gathered at the door.

"We did everything we could." Azalea's voice cracked. Tension from Torin skyrocketed behind her, but he said nothing. She wanted to take his hand, to tell him it would be okay. But she wouldn't risk doing that in front of people, especially Fabian. Torin thought she had kissed him so she could get close and trick him, but he couldn't be further from the truth. That kiss meant everything to her, and she didn't want to go back to the way things were.

Fabian inched forward. Azalea stood her ground, unsure what to do.

"Fabian, back down. We've got bigger things to worry about right now." Danni stepped up next to Azalea.

"I will not accept this! You all let this man into my home knowing what he has done. He has brainwashed Azalea, and none of you seem to care. Will none of you stand up to him?" Fabian spat, waving his elemer in front of him wildly as shadows streamed from the blade.

Danni looked between the parties, probably unsure what to do without her fire magic, though she looked ready to fight. "Fabian, I'm warning you. Stop this."

Azalea glanced back at Torin. He had his arms crossed and was staring at Fabian, not reacting at all to the challenge.

Azalea conjured a lattice of shadows in front of them, unsure how far Fabian would actually go. Kat, the terrifying woman who looked every bit the part of a deadly assassin, stepped closer to Fabian. It wasn't clear which side she was on.

"This ends now." Fabian stomped his foot. "He wields the hand of death, for gods' sake! Every child knows what that means!" Fabian lashed out with a shadow whip, striking Azalea's barrier. But it held strong, though she didn't have enough magic to keep up this charade for long.

"Fabian!" Azalea's mum shouted.

"I won't let you hurt him," Azalea said, as calmly as she could manage. She didn't want to hurt her uncle, but if he was serious about wanting to kill Torin, she wouldn't hesitate in using their new magic to take him down. She didn't know what it was capable of and didn't want to give away the secret about their bond, but she wasn't about to let Torin get hurt, and he didn't seem to have any wish to defend himself right now.

Fabian shook his head slowly. "Move Azalea."

He raised his elemer, but Leda shot forward and grabbed his hand, yanking it behind his back.

"You will not hurt my daughter!" Leda yelled.

Danni and Kat had her back and narrowed in. Kat took his legs out, and his elemer went flying off to the side. Kat had him flat on the ground in seconds, sitting on his back, straddling him, and Danni had him handcuffed in a split second.

"I wasn't trying to hurt Azalea," Fabian mumbled into the ground.

Azalea let down her shield with a long exhale.

"We are all in this together now," RoRo said. "If you're going to continue to act like children, I guess I'm going to have to take charge. This is your family house, Fabian, but it's Azalea's too. She has invited this man here as her guest, and this is no time for fighting."

Fabian's face pressed into the tiles, and Kat didn't look like she was going to move. She appeared to be enjoying it.

"We need Torin. He knows more about the relics, the Archmage, and his father than any of us put together. So you will act civil. Do you understand?"

Fabian raised his head as far as he could and glared at RoRo. "Fine. But these two are hiding something, and I'm going to find out what it is." He glared at Torin, then his eyes fell on Azalea. He'd seen the spirit go through her when they were at the Tower. He knew something was up with them.

"We all need to work together because we could be stuck here for a while. You will not shed more blood in this house. Does everyone agree?" RoRo looked around the faces in the room. Azalea nodded furiously as everyone mumbled or nodded in agreement.

Azalea moved closer to Torin, and he crossed his arms with a nod of acknowledgment. RoRo seemed satisfied and nodded to Kat, who didn't move straight away.

"Remind me why I rescued the lot of you and brought you here," Fabian mumbled. But he appeared to have calmed down. Kat got off him in one swift motion, and he scrambled up. Danni tossed Kat the keys with a wink, and Kat took her sweet time unlocking the handcuffs. Fabian let out a huff and brushed himself off, not looking toward Azalea and Torin.

"You alright?" Azalea turned to Torin.

His gaze went to the sky. "I'm fine."

"Holy shitballs," Van exclaimed as an explosion of green light hit something in the sky overhead, and they all ducked. But nothing hit them. It just fizzled out far above. The air filled with the hum of magic, and the hairs on Azalea's arms raised as if static electricity was all around her.

"'Holy shitballs' alright," Danni repeated and dashed away, presumably to check on the twins.

Torin marched toward the French doors that led outside and swung them open as the sky burst with the roar from the Echo Dimension light spreading above them.

Everyone filtered out onto the lawn, crisp with a layer of ice. The sky glowed brilliant red, split by streaks of green. Dark shapes peeled off, and smaller streaks of green shot down to the earth like meteors. Azalea instinctively ducked as one of the things crashed into something overhead and exploded like an emerald firework.

Down on the lawn, families were gathered outside their tents and gers, all staring up at the sky in terror.

"The barrier wards seem to be holding," Fabian mumbled as he squinted up at the sky.

"They should keep the worst of the magic surge out," RoRo said. "We'll be safe in here."

"What about outside?" Azalea asked.

"As long as people don't use Echo Magic, they should be fine if they stay inside and their houses don't get hit by the explosions. The magic won't hurt them, though that might be another problem." RoRo nodded to a point low on the horizon, and everyone looked.

Azalea instantly thought of Isaac. She should go get him.

"Is that a—" Jade stared wide-eyed.

"Dragon," Kat said as the silhouette of a dragon cut across the red sky, its massive wings slicing through the air, banking in a tight turn as if it were an owl silently hunting prey.

This can't be good.

"Shit, I better get back to the Tower before Korbyn gets back there," Kat said.

"Um, he might be a while. I knocked him out and left him at the Echo Gate with the Archmage," Azalea admitted.

All eyes were on her. "Torin knocked out the Archmage," she added to take the attention off herself.

"It's a long story." Torin deflected the attention and turned to Kat. "You'll come back?"

"Yes. But I'm going to maintain my cover as long as possible," she said.

"What about Kira?" Torin asked.

"I'll bring her here when I can," Kat said, but she gave Torin a look of pity. "The House of Ravens needs you, Torin. Don't do anything stupid."

Azalea watched Torin closely, and her stomach flipped on his behalf. It was clear he desperately wanted to see Kira but was terrified. And so was Azalea. Would he go back to the House of Ravens if they managed to take down his father?

"We can't stand around here gawking at the sky all morning," RoRo said. "We need to make a plan, then you lot can get some sleep."

Azalea spun around. "We can't sleep. We need to fix this now!" Her eyes were wide, taking in the concern on everyone's face.

"You're no good to us without sleep. Same as you, Torin." RoRo gave the orders. Around them, the roar of the Echo Dimension light was building.

"And I suppose you have a solution?" Fabian sneered. Still looking sour from being ganged up on.

"Like Leda said before, the gate was closed by the gods once. They can do it again." RoRo said.

"Which gods?" Van wrapped her arm around Jade as they flinched with every explosion that hit the barrier. Azalea inched closer to Torin, just enough so she could feel his warmth but not touch him.

"It was Enki of the House of Owls and Enlil of the House of Eagles, the only gods powerful enough to build such a gate and close it." Leda stuffed her hands in her overall pockets.

"Can we talk to them in the Desert of Dreams?" Azalea nibbled her lip. She'd had enough of gods and dreams, but if it was the only way, it seemed like an easy enough solution.

Fabian glared at her as if she said something horrible. "Why would you suggest that?"

"Because when I took the elixir of the gods, I met Ninhursag and Ereshkigal there. They are gods, aren't they?" she said, hopefully, covering their backs.

"Goddesses, yes, dear. But Enki and Enlil are not like the others. They are the most powerful and have had nothing to do with human affairs since they left this realm. They only sent representatives." RoRo's hand went to her chin as if in thought.

"But we could ask some of the other gods. They might have useful information," Azalea said.

"I can go there. It doesn't hurt to ask," Torin said.

We can go there, Azalea thought to herself.

Overhead, the dragon glided off in the distance. Silhouettes of other creatures dotted the sky yellow and green mixed with red to create a beautiful tropical-looking sky. Or what would have been beautiful if it wasn't so horrific. Azalea swallowed, hoping the barrier would hold.

A shiver coursed down Azalea's spine. Her whole body was still shaking; it was either shock or cold, or maybe both, but her energy was on low battery, and this was all becoming a bit much to cope with on no sleep.

A weight fell on her shoulder, and she nearly jerked away but saw it was Torin's coat. He draped it over her and let his hand rest there for a long moment, along with the warmth of his magic. She let out a slow breath and risked looking up at him with a smile. He gave her a brief nod, and she pulled the coat around her over the blanket. Gods, she was so glad he was alive.

"I can go to the Echo Dimension and talk to the gods to find a way to shut the gate," Torin said. Dead serious.

Azalea nearly jumped at the unexpectedness of his voice.

"You'll what?" she said. Awestruck that he would even think that was an option.

"Didn't your prophecy say *'The future shows another way; A harder path for those who stay?'* Is this not harder?" he said, almost teasing her. Goading her to take on a challenge that might get them killed. He had a death wish, that much was clear.

Fabian put up his hand lazily. "I'll go too."

"Me too." Kat gave a sharp nod.

"I'm coming too," Azalea added. No way they were all going without her, and Fabian and Torin going together did not sound like the best idea.

"No," RoRo, Leda, and Torin all said at once. All looking at her.

"Why not?" She wanted to stamp her foot and call them out for treating her like a child. That would not help her, though.

"No one with Echo Magic can go. It's too dangerous. You'll risk getting burned out if you so much as use a drop of magic by accident," RoRo said.

"I'll get one of those staffs like the Archmage had. The ones Erik's dad made." A sick feeling crept into her stomach, remembering Erik.

"I can go alone," Torin said.

"Mate, you're not exactly the friendliest bloke. You think you can talk an all-powerful god into doing a favor for you? No way," Fabian said.

"And you think you can?" Kat put her hands on her hips. "I'll go wherever Torin goes."

Fabian glared at Kat.

"We can talk about this later." RoRo clapped her hands, gesturing for everyone to go back inside. "You all need some sleep and to cool off. I will talk to the shamans here, and we will hold a council meeting later this morning once we see what the damage is during the day and once we make sure everyone is safe. Agreed?"

Everyone agreed.

"And I think I might know someone who can help." RoRo's voice trailed off in thought as she turned to head inside.

"I'll be back, Torin." Kat hugged him goodbye. "It was nice to meet you, Azalea." She waved and marched off across the courtyard, dragging Fabian with her.

"Get some sleep, you lot. If you want food, see Mary in the family kitchen. Otherwise, Jade and Van can show you up to your rooms. They've been a great help with organizing," Leda said as she put an arm around Azalea's shoulder and squeezed her in close.

Azalea couldn't face eating. Both she and Torin followed the others inside in a daze, back through the maze of rooms. Azalea fell into her mum's arms in a big hug at the base of a grand staircase and said goodnight. Leda and RoRo wandered off somewhere, and they were left with Jade and Van.

They trudged upstairs and followed a long hallway of doors. Van directed Azalea into a room near the end on the left and pointed Torin to the staircase on the right, straight across. There were two attic rooms up there. Jade and Van had one on the left at the top. Torin had the other on the right.

Fabian must have been feeling generous to give them all rooms inside the house rather than outside in the camp. More likely it was RoRo. Danni and the girls were across the hall from her, and her mum and RoRo were the two doors before hers.

Azalea shut the door and fell onto the bed. How had everything gone so wrong? Erik was dead. The gate was open. Torin was mad. But she couldn't help feeling happy—happy that Torin wasn't the one who had died. Did that make her a horrible person? She was terribly selfish to think like that, she knew. But she couldn't face this world if he wasn't in it.

She lay on the bed for an hour, fully clothed and wrapped in a soft wool blanket with Faraday on her and Torin's coat next to her. She hadn't stopped shaking since she'd gotten back and knew she needed some sleep to replenish her magic.

There was an en-suite bathroom, but she didn't have the energy to shower. She managed to take off her shoes and change into a t-shirt and clean underwear; she was glad she'd packed them.

She couldn't lie there, not knowing what Torin was thinking. She couldn't face the idea that he hated her. It made her stomach turn, and she wouldn't get any sleep until they sorted this out.

She had a feeling that Torin was also awake. She wanted to talk to him before they had the council meeting to get their story straight and consult the Shadow Atlas in case there was another way.

More than that, she needed to make sure he was okay. Butterflies jumped in her stomach at the thought of going up to his room.

Fabian certainly wouldn't approve of her being there, but she didn't care. She put on jeans and warm socks and crept toward the door. Hoping the floorboards of the old house were more reliable than the ones in their cottage.

She slipped down the hall and treaded lightly up the steep stairs that lead to the two attic rooms, pausing with each squeak of the floorboards. She lightly tapped on Torin's door and held her breath. Hopefully, Van and Jade didn't hear.

CHAPTER 45

Torin swung the door open and gestured for her to come in. He didn't seem surprised to see her. He shut the door silently and went straight to the bed and sat down, not making eye contact.

Azalea took a deep breath and wandered into the room where eerie red and green light from the window merged into the warm yellow of the industrial-style copper lamp on the bedside table. It was like a hotel room with a fresh white bedspread and a variety of green and white patterned cushions that took up half the bed.

"Nice room." She avoided the window, not wanting to see what was out there.

Torin looked down at his hands. "You shouldn't be here." Waves of mixed emotions glided over her. He was so conflicted she couldn't separate one emotion from another.

"I know, but I wanted to make sure you were okay." She stopped by the small desk and picked up a pen. She needed something in her hands.

"I'm fine," he said.

Azalea clicked the pen in and out. "I know you're not. But we need to talk."

"You don't need to explain it. I know why you kissed me. If you want me to forgive you, then fine. I forgive you." He waved a hand as if it meant nothing.

She straightened her shirt with long, nervous strokes, marched toward the bed, and sat down. Right next to him. She forced her hands onto her lap, still gripping the pen, unsure where else to put them. "I don't know how many times I'll have to say this, but I meant what I said before. I care about you, and I couldn't let you die. I know it seems selfish, and you'll never understand. But I didn't want to live in a world without you. Okay." She stood up and stared at the window, ready to run out of the room so he couldn't reject her further. At least she had said it now.

Scarlet light glowed through the sheer curtain as if the world outside was ablaze. And it might as well be. She swallowed back the guilt, imagining all the potential destruction spreading across the world. She told herself to be brave and turned to face him.

"You were confused. You didn't have a choice." His Adam's apple bobbed, and he looked down at his hands.

"Is that what you really think? Is it so hard to get into your head that I like you? It might have taken me a while to realize it, but it's there, and it's real." She frowned down at him. How could he think that?

"It isn't real, Azalea."

"I'm going to slap you soon," she warned.

He squared his jaw and looked at her, his deep brown eyes locked on hers. "The bond is stronger."

"I know." She bit her lip and nodded in agreement. It was pretty obvious at this point.

"We can't let it get stronger, or we won't be able to break it."

"It doesn't matter anymore, Torin. There are more important things than our bond. If we can use it, I think we should." She slid onto the bed next to him. "We use it, and we can keep looking for a way to break it. If Enki and Enlil are so powerful, maybe they'll be more help than Damu and his stupid deals." She wasn't even sure if she wanted to break it anymore.

Torin remained silent.

"That could be a solution. Am I right?" She studied Torin's face for clues. His expression remained unchanged, frowny and serious. But she felt a glimmer of hope spark from him to her. She didn't react but knew she was onto something.

"We shall see. Your grandmother was right. We need sleep before we make any big decisions."

Her heart sank. He was kicking her out. "Okay, but you're not going anywhere without me. And we should ask the Shadow Atlas what to do as well, before the meeting." She twisted away from him, and her feet met the fluffy white rug beneath the bed.

"We will. But you should leave before your uncle finds you here." Torin kept any emotion from his voice, but she knew he felt the opposite. He didn't want her to leave. But she wasn't going to push it.

"Fine. But remember the dream. It was real, Torin. When I kissed you, it was real. You felt it; just remember what it felt like." She refused to look at him and rubbed her eyes. "I'll go now."

She stood up, but a hand wrapped around her wrist.

"Wait." Torin pulled her toward him.

"What, Torin? Just be honest with me so we can stop going around in circles." She stood in front of him as frustrated tears threatened the corners of her eyes.

"I don't want you to go." He glanced up at her, and she saw—she felt he meant it.

Azalea sank back onto the bed next to him, and her hand slipped into his, her pulse racing at his sudden change in heart. His magic sang all around her.

"This is confusing, Torin." She studied his face. They were in uncharted territory now.

"I know, and I'm sorry. Maybe it's from the bond, maybe it's real. I don't know." He took her hand with both of his, stroking the top of it, keeping his eyes down. His raw feelings were out there for her to see, and they barreled over her like a wave that took her breath away.

He looked up, and she slid him a curious glance. "Say it," she whispered.

"I want you, Azalea." His gaze lowered to her mouth, and suddenly his lips were on hers. He pulled her in closer, his fingers sliding up her back, sparking magic where they trailed across her spine.

The kiss shattered her. *This* was coming home. This was what had been missing and what she needed all along.

The world exploded in stars around her. Or maybe it was in her head. Her whole body was electric and filled with this new magic. She felt the rapid beat of his heart, and the magic in his blood burning and calling out to hers. His lips were soft and hot against hers, and she didn't want it to end.

He pulled away, and she took a breath, smiling as their lips parted.

"Is this normal for you?" Torin glanced around.

She opened her eyes to see the stars were real. All around them, a fog of shimmering silver magic swirled lazily like a drifting ocean current. They shuffled back on the bed, and Torin's arm slipped around her, exhaustion finally catching up with her as she lay on her back resting against him and staring up at the strange magic.

He was actually smiling.

"This is better than a dream." Azalea's eyes began to close. She knew she shouldn't stay here, but there was nowhere else in the world she wanted to be.

"About this bond," Torin started.

Azalea's eyes shot open. "We can be careful. No one else needs to know." Torin was back in panic mode. She could feel it.

"Let's not do anything like this in public." He waved his hand across the magic as it began fading.

"Agreed. Our hands aren't glowing when we touch now." She held up her fingers intertwined with his. They still buzzed with energy, but there was no more glowing.

She glanced at Torin. His eyes were closed, and she smiled.

"Maybe we just needed to get it out of our systems, and now the magic will be more balanced," she suggested. Their shared magic could hold a solution. It seemed like too good of a thing to not use.

It felt so right, so natural to be lying there beside him. She tried to block out all the horrible things from the past day, but they were right there beneath her skin. She squeezed her eyes tightly to shut out the image of Erik.

"You could be right. It could draw more spirits in though," he said sleepily.

She swallowed and concentrated on the present moment. "Or we could have a new power to fight them off."

"Not if Damu had anything to do with this. Let's just keep this a secret until we either master the powers and seal the bond or find a way to break it."

"You would want to seal it?" Azalea raised up on her elbow, shocked he'd even suggest it.

"If we carry on like this, we will. Maybe we should tone it down and not get too close." His words did not match his actions as his arm pulled her in closer to him, and he kissed her neck.

"You mean not have sex?" she said bluntly.

He smiled and lay back, his eyes slowly closing. "Just an idea."

"I'm sure we can control ourselves until we fix everything and find out more about the bond." She stared up at the ceiling, wondering if that was something they could do. This door was now wide open, and they'd stepped all the way through. Was there any going back from here?

"Let's get a few hours of sleep and hope your uncle doesn't come looking for you. Then we can meet with the council. Okay?"

He made it sound simple. But there was so much more to it than just the Echo Dimension gateway. There was still his friend Kira to deal with, plus his father, the spirits, and now keeping whatever was going on between them a secret. Plus, there were dragons flying around the world. That couldn't be good.

She squeezed her eyes shut and let the exhaustion stop her from caring. "Tomorrow we will fix everything."

"If you say so," Torin said as if he didn't believe it. But he pulled her in close, and she felt like everything might just be okay.

Also By Jenny Sandiford

Read The Shadow Atlas Prequel for Free!
Go to jennysandiford.com

The Shadow Atlas Series

Acknowledgments

A huge shoutout to all the lovely readers who have been patiently waiting for this book to hit the shelves. My spontaneous move from the United States to Australia set the book back a wee bit. But we got there in the end and I hope you enjoyed it!

I want to extend a big thank you to all the book reviewers, bookstagrammers, and early readers who have shown tremendous support for this book. Your reviews, posts, shares, and kind words have been incredible.

The biggest thanks to my husband Michael. I wouldn't be able to do any of this without you. Also, this is an advanced warning that I'm slowly turning our house into a library—we're going to need more bookshelves...

Beth, Liz, Nicole, and my mum, Maggie, kindly beta read the rushed draft of this book when it was riddled with terrible grammar. Thank you, your feedback was incredibly helpful!

I couldn't do any of this without my editor, Mandi Oyster. Thanks for making the publishing process less daunting with your expert editing and support. Your suggestions are always spot-on and have made all the difference.

I would also like to thank Amy McKenna for her fantastic proofreading skills and comments throughout the book that always make me smile!

A big shoutout to Bethany Arliss, my fellow fantasy author and critique partner, for your motivation, troubleshooting, brainstorming, beta reading, and blurb swapping. It's fun to be publishing books in the same month!

Finally, I'd like to thank my cats, Chinggis and Shimo. Though they were no help in writing this book, they were always there to provide cuddles, stare at me, knock things off my desk, or walk across my computer while I typed. This book is dedicated to my two crazy kitties.

About The Author

Jenny Sandiford

Jenny grew up in small town New Zealand on a steady diet of fairytales and fantasy books. She lived in Mongolia for nine years with her husband where they spent the unfrozen months of the year living on the edge of the Gobi Desert mining gold. When she isn't writing, Jenny enjoys hiking, meeting new animals, and loves to curl up in a sunny corner with a cup of tea, a cat, and a book. She lives in Darwin, Australia, with her husband and their two street cats from Mongolia.

CONNECT WITH JENNY ON:

Website: jennysandiford.com
Instagram: instagram.com/JennySandifordAuthor
Facebook: facebook.com/JennySandifordAuthor
Goodreads: Jenny Sandiford

WANT THE LATEST BOOK RELEASE NEWS?
Sign up for monthly updates!

jennysandiford.com/subscribe